THE
PROBLEM
WITH
MIRACLES

A NOVEL BY
S K JANSKY

ELECTIO PUBLISHING
first century principles.
a twenty-first century approach.

The Problem With Miracles

By S K Jansky

Copyright 2018 by S. K. Jansky. All rights reserved.

Cover Design by eLectio Publishing

ISBN-13: 978-1-63213-468-4

Published by eLectio Publishing, LLC

Little Elm, Texas

http://www.eLectioPublishing.com

5 4 3 2 1 eLP 22 21 20 19 18

Printed in the United States of America.

The eLectio Publishing creative team is comprised of: Kaitlyn Campbell, Emily Certain, Lori Draft, Court Dudek, Jim Eccles, Sheldon James, and Christine LePorte.

Without limiting the rights under copyright reserved above, no part of this publication may be reproduced, stored in or introduced into a retrieval system, or transmitted, in any form, or by any means (electronic, mechanical, photocopying, recording, or otherwise), without the prior written permission of both the copyright owner and the above publisher of this book.

The scanning, uploading, and distribution of this book via the Internet or via any other means without the permission of the publisher is illegal and punishable by law. Please purchase only authorized electronic editions, and do not participate in or encourage electronic piracy of copyrighted materials. Your support of the author's rights is appreciated.

Publisher's Note

The publisher does not have any control over and does not assume any responsibility for author or third-party websites or their content.

To: Kay
Hope you always
believe in miracles!
S.K. Yonosty

This book is dedicated to my Pa.
Over a drink poured from a mason jar,
he once told me that if there was
something I wanted to accomplish
in my days here on Earth,
to make sure I got it done.

And to my mom, my sister Judy,
and niece Anna who remind me daily
that you never know when
those days on Earth will end.

May it not have been the end
but just the beginning.

"Extraordinary claims require extraordinary evidence."

—Carl Sagan

The basic test for scientific theories comes from observation.

Something tested over and over again with the same outcome becomes evidence—proof, as it were.

The problem with miracles is they are singular events.

Miracles can't be tested. They only happen once.

CHAPTER 1

On August 20, 1977, the Voyager 2 was launched by NASA from Cape Canaveral, Florida. Voyager 1 had launched in September of that same year. A team headed by astronomer and astrophysicist Carl Sagan spent almost a full year compiling the contents for what became known as the Golden Record—a twelve-inch, gold-plated copper disc containing a message from Earth. Two were made, one attached to each spacecraft. The record contained 115 images, sounds of Earth, a wide variety of music, and a message from then-president Jimmy Carter which said, "We are attempting to survive our time so we may live into yours."

I turned seventeen in July of 1977. Later that August, I started my senior year in high school. The Voyagers 1 and 2 were the topic of my astronomy and space science class that first day. I wanted to write romance novels and had only taken the class because someone told me it would be an easy A. I wasn't at all interested in science. Luckily, among all the black and white pictures and equations which made no sense to me—I didn't really care for math either—I found something I thought utterly romantic, perhaps even cosmically romantic. Ann Druyan, the creative director on the team, had worked closely with Carl Sagan developing the Golden Record. Carl was fifteen years Ann's senior—the older man. That was always romantic.

Ann had been searching and searching for a selection of Chinese music to include on the disc. When she finally found a song called "Flowing Stream," she was so excited she called Carl at his hotel and left him a message.

He called back an hour later, and by the end of their conversation, they were engaged, and that's not even the best part. After the phone call, Ann had another idea for the record. She proposed taking an EEG, which would measure the electrical impulses of the brain, turning it into sound, and putting it on the disc. Let me tell you, this was high tech stuff in 1977. Carl loved the idea. While the sounds of her brain and nervous system were recorded, Ann meditated. She said what she was thinking while meditating was "the wonder of love, of being in love." The hour-long recording was then compressed into a single minute. When played, it sounded like a string of exploding firecrackers. How romantic is that!

In 1977, I also lost both my parents. Just before Thanksgiving, while on their way home from seeing a movie, they were killed by a drunk driver. Before they left that night, they had made a deal. Dad was dragging Mom out to see *Close Encounters of the Third Kind*, and in turn, he agreed to see *Oh, God!* on their next movie night. I have never been able to watch either film.

Shortly after the funeral, I started having nightmares about the accident. I could have been with them that night. Dad had wanted me to go along and see the movie, but Mom said I had to spend the evening working on my unfinished science project. It was a pretty rough year. My alter egos crept into my subconscious sometime around then. I'm not really sure why, but the three of us have been constant companions ever since. You know, the little voices in your head that argue back and forth. Doesn't everyone have those?

Grandma Fae, my mom's mom, moved into my parents' house. She said I'd feel more comfortable there. Honestly, I wasn't comfortable anywhere. I was lost and really felt alone in the universe. I was an only child. Both my mother and father were only children as well, which made my extended family pretty much nonexistent. On top of that, my only living relative—my grandmother—was adopted. So even though I had a great uncle and two great aunts somewhere, they weren't truly related at all.

The fact that Grandma Fae was a very religious person made my life easier or more difficult, depending on how you looked at it. We were in church a lot those first few months after my folks died. We went on a daily basis—every weekday morning, Saturday, and of course Sunday—sometimes twice on Sunday. Church was okay, though it was quiet. I could think in church. Think about God. Think about Heaven. Is there really a Heaven? I just wasn't sure anymore. I know Grandma believed there was. After the accident, I cried for days. I couldn't stop. Grandma came up to me, looked me straight in the eye, and said, "You have to stop thinking of death as the end. It just might well be the beginning."

Grandma Fae tried to make things normal for me. She let me have friends over and was a bit overprotective at times but was, for the most part, pretty cool. I guess she knew better than I what it was like to be alone. One night, she even opened up to me about growing up in an orphanage run by nuns. It sounded awful, but Grandma said the 1930s and early 1940s were hard times in comparison to the present. That's the night she gave me her locket. She always wore it around her neck. It held a picture of a young man. She said she had no idea who the man in the picture was, yet she held it dear—the only thing she owned that she truly valued. Grandma and I got quite close over the next few years. She kept up the house all the while I was in college. She said I needed a home to come to on weekends and holidays. Grandma passed away the year after I graduated college. It made me feel all alone again and made me believe love was just a painful thing.

Within three months, I sold the house and was off to New York. I had convinced myself I would be an overnight success. My degree in journalism was my ticket. I would write the world's greatest romance novel. It would sell a gazillion copies, and I'd be rich, meet a handsome guy, and live happily ever after. I was so naive!

A year and a half later, I was still in New York but had downsized to an apartment in Queens and was looking for a waitressing job. Still working on my first novel, I had yet to meet that handsome guy—or any guy for that matter. I still felt alone in the universe. One evening when I felt especially alone, I sat on the floor in the middle of my tiny apartment listening to some oldies station—songs from the sixties. Those tunes took me back to my childhood. Wearing an old boho cardigan that had been my mother's, I could still smell her perfume lingering in the threads. I pulled my knees to my chest and wrapped my arms around my legs, the easy guitar strumming numbed my mind. I closed my eyes and let the music take me to a happy place.

CHAPTER 2

July 1997

I was on my way to see John. I had finished the final chapter of my latest novel. It was ready for editing. I was thinking about taking a few weeks off when a notion crept its way into my brain. I should take a trip! I never took trips, unless of course it was a book signing tour. Good Pat and Bad Pat took up sides immediately. It was hard to believe they had been around for more than half my life. John—my editor and "the guy" or "a guy" or *my* guy, I guess—found my alter egos very entertaining and had named them Good Pat and Bad Pat. Actually, they were neither good nor bad, just always on opposite sides of the fence. Yes, I had finally met a guy. We'd been dating for over five years, but now he was proposing marriage, and that thought scared the heck out of me. As far as my other goals, I had yet to sell a gazillion books but had made the best seller list. For the most part, I was happy.

That is, up until this last weekend. John and I had gone to see a new movie that had just opened. *Contact* with Jodie Foster and Mathew McConaughey. It made me sad, made me miss my dad. That, along with all the talk about the twenty-year anniversary of the city's blackouts of '77, just reminded me it had been twenty years since the accident. There were times I felt so alone, and now this proposal thing . . . I wasn't at all sure about that. G-Pat and B-Pat hadn't even begun to debate that issue.

Perhaps my little alter egos were simply a way of coping with life. Yet, this trip thing . . . they just wouldn't let it go. They were overly enthusiastic. *A trip? Are you kidding me? You're only asking for trouble.* and *A trip! Of course you need to take a trip — get away — see the sights!* If that wasn't enough, those darn little voices also wanted me to be spontaneous! Which should have been a dead giveaway that something or someone else was controlling my thoughts, because I never did anything spontaneously. Well, since up and moving to New York anyway. Everything I did was well planned and thoroughly thought out. I was no longer naive about anything. I stopped at the first gas station I saw and bought a map. Perhaps I needed a change.

I burst into John's office without even knocking.

He was a bit startled but recovered quickly as he stood up from his desk, straightening his suit vest by tugging at the hem. "Pat! What's up?"

I opened the large paper map and spread it out, paying little attention to the manuscript he had scattered across the highly polished Burmese Blackwood desk. John smirked. Then, with the palm of his hand, he rubbed the back of his neck. His brow furrowed as he raised his eyebrows and asked, "Looking for something?"

"No," I assured him, "I'm going on a trip." His lips turned slowly to a snicker, and his eyes laughed at me. He did have a way about him, I had to admit. He had the classic look of a born and raised New Yorker — the all-knowing attitude even when he hadn't a clue.

"Oh, I see." He nodded then playfully added, "And you need directions?"

"No, you're going to pick the spot."

"Pick the spot?" he echoed.

"Yes, close your eyes, point your finger, and pick my vacation spot."

His pointed finger hovered over the map for a while then suddenly and almost involuntarily pointed to the tiny dot of Bay View.

He talked me into staying until the book edits were done, but two weeks later, I started out for the small city.

After driving a little more than 200 miles, I began to wonder why on earth I was doing such a crazy thing. I had never even heard of Bay View. It was just a dot on a map, and not a very big dot at that. Moreover, it would take me the entire day to get there.

By late in the afternoon, driving became monotonous. I found a small diner just off the highway and pulled off the road. I scanned the flip-open menu while the waitress, who couldn't have been more than twelve—okay, maybe fifteen—snapped her gum and twirled a curl of her blonde hair with the end of her pencil.

"Just a burger," I said flippantly while rolling my eyes, hoping she knew I was less than impressed with her lackluster attitude.

"Do you want fries with that?" she whined, oblivious to what I thought of her.

As I ate the overcooked hamburger and French fries, I contemplated scrapping the whole idea and just driving back home. Unconsciously, I rubbed the locket that hung around my throat. I never played with my jewelry, never twirled a necklace, fidgeted with a bracelet, nor even twisted the rings on my fingers. Yet there I was, finding comfort in its familiarity. Unclasping the chain, I cradled the heart-shaped locket in my palm for a moment before opening the cover to reveal the picture of a striking young man. The black and white picture was small, and it had yellowed with age. I often wondered who the Adonis-like stranger was but was sure that simply speculating about him was more fascinating and would most likely prove to be far more romantic than the truth. Until that summer, I thought stories were always more romantic than real life.

At the time, I suppose some might have found my and John's relationship romantic, yet to me, it was more matter-of-fact. Surely, it was not the head-over-heels, swept-off-your-feet, take-your-breath-away romances I'd always written about. I thought love like that didn't really exist, and yet I was sure the hope of it was what made me reluctant to accept John's proposal.

I snapped the locket shut and fastened it back around my neck as I closed my eyes and weighed the current debate. ~ *Let's just forget this whole crazy idea, turn around, and head on home.* ~ *Are you kidding me? We're over halfway there. Where's your sense of adventure?*

I picked up my purse and sweater and paid the bill. I was sure the voice I had sided with was right, as suddenly Bay View sounded like a wonderful place to visit. And, for the first time, in earnest, I tried to determine if that were Bad Pat or Good Pat.

By nightfall, though, I once again began to doubt my decision. I hadn't seen any form of civilization in hours—only winding roads and trees. When I was just about to pull off to retrieve the map, I saw the little green sign that read Bay View, five miles. I coasted into the small town and searched for anything that resembled a hotel, as I wanted a warm bath, a soft bed, and the comfortable pajamas I had packed. The highway ambled through the outskirts of the city, and just as I thought I might have to stop and ask someone where I could find accommodations, a grand old house surrounded by wrought iron fencing came into view. The rusty old gates were swung permanently open. The large, black-lettered sign that hung by wire on the fence just to the left of the drive read:

BOARDING HOUSE;
ROOMS RENTED BY THE DAY,
WEEK, OR MONTH

Almost instinctively, I drove up the shrub-lined drive, parked, and got out of my car. The mansion loomed in front of me like something out of a late-night scary movie. The building stone had turned green from the ivy shrubbery that crawled up the entire front of the facade like a creature stretching out its tentacles. It reminded me of that movie about the kid in the jungle with the overzealous plant on steroids that swallowed up whole cop cars. Yet the grandeur of the building's once-magnificent presence lingered. There was something intriguing about the old place. The mahogany entry doors, once beautiful, looked worn, scratched, and perhaps even a little warped, yet something was beckoning me to come inside. I grabbed my bag out of the trunk, walked up the few steps, and turned the knob. When I stepped through the front door, I felt like I had just come home.

The manager said his name was Ted or Todd or whatever it was he mumbled. Once I shelled out the deposit, he led me to a room. Without so much as giving me a chance to get a good look at the stately old manor, he raced up the grand old staircase, taking the steps two at a time. Clean linens were bundled under his arm like a cowboy's bedroll, and my suitcase was swinging from his hand. I scurried behind him like an obedient child. When we reached the top of the stairs, I followed him down a long, narrow hallway. B-Pat and G-Pat took the opportunity to weigh in on the matter: *We're only staying one night. ~ Are you kidding, I love this old place!*

Reaching the end of the corridor, he inserted a key into the last door and swung it open. Hastily, he pointed out the shared bathroom at the end of the hall and explained that there was no cooking in the rooms, along with the fact that I could get clean linens daily for an extra fee. He then deposited the bedroll on the bare mattress and shut the door behind him. I rolled my eyes as he left the room, thinking I had perhaps made a poor choice. I swore I'd never be spontaneous again, and was convinced it was Bad Pat who was voting to stay in the dimly lit room with the drab, dirty-beige walls that pleaded for a coat of fresh paint. I picked up my small suitcase from just inside the door where the manager had dropped it. I crossed the floor to place it on the only other piece of furniture in the room–a small chair, which stood just under a small window. I wondered how I found myself in such a place. However, by the time I had made up the bed with the linens, taken a leisurely bath in the deep clawfoot tub in the shared bathroom, donned my comfy-fuzzy favorite pair of pajamas, and crawled into bed, I felt quite content. The cot of a bed looked lumpy and bumpy but proved not to be, and I felt undeniably comfortable once snuggled in.

Sometime after that, I had fallen asleep and dreamed of Mary. A young girl, whose name was Mary Watson, was boarding a train. I instinctively knew the era she was in by the old train station surroundings and the manner in which she was dressed. I was sure it was the mid-1920s. It was a small rural station with a wooden platform, not crowded, but lively. It was fall, early fall. The trees were bursting with an array of color—crimson red, vibrant gold, and even those that had yet to turn offered a dramatic green. The colors were crisp from the cool night's breeze, yet with the rising sun, the summer's heat had returned and was almost stifling. It was a stale, breezeless, tension-charged kind of day that usually came before a storm. Mary stood next to her father. She was young, sixteen perhaps. She was innocent. I could see it in her eyes. She was also very pretty. Her hair was the color of wheat, but more than that. If you've ever driven through the countryside and come up over a hill to a field of wheat with the sun shining upon it and a gentle breeze making it dance like it was alive—that was the only way to describe the color of Mary's hair. Her perfect complexion would have been the envy of any woman. Her features were soft and delicate, yet distinct and classic. The type of young woman you just knew would mature into a timeless beauty. Not unlike most of the heroines I wrote about. My head was always full of characters—beautiful brave young women and dashingly suave heroes that filled all the pages of my novels—but this one was different. Mary was neither brave nor daring. She was more like me—a little forlorn mixed with a tinge of self-doubt—though I was sure Mary was more afraid than I ever remembered being. I could feel it. She was saying goodbye to her father.

"Oh, Papa," her voice quivered. She was trying to be brave, but her tears wouldn't stop. She buried her face in her father's shirtsleeve and wondered why she had to leave on the train and go to meet her Aunt Matilda and get a job in the city working for the Coltons. She didn't even know them!

Her father cradled the back of her head in his palm and hugged her tightly to his chest, deeply inhaling the sweetness of her golden hair. He kissed her forehead softly. "Goodbye, pumpkin."

My heart ached for him as I watched him force his lips into a smile while he begged his arms, as well as his heart, to let her go. Mary reluctantly pulled herself from his embrace and somehow forced herself to move toward the train. I could feel the weight in her legs as she reluctantly climbed each step. She repeated softly to herself, "Don't look back. Don't look back." Reaching the top step, she ran her hands through her thick blonde hair then wound it tightly at the back of her head. She pulled hairpins from her pocket and secured them into place. She felt just as trapped as those strands of hair, but there wasn't much she could do about it.

As she settled herself into the velour cushion, I found myself snuggling my head into the feather pillow. Then the rest of the story came to me. I felt sorrow learning that Mary's mother had died when she was only eight. Learned, not dreamed. Not imagined, but learned. It wasn't ideas weaving thoughts in and out of my mind as a storyline developed, but more like facts of which I had just become aware. Mary had a brother—Johnny—who had died in the First World War. She was going to the city because her aunt had found her a job.

It was very clever how he had made it all look like my idea, made me think it was my next novel coming to life. I threw back the covers and jumped from the little cot. I needed to get to a phone, needed to call John. I needed a computer, a desk, a couple reams of paper, and some coffee. I had work to do.

CHAPTER 3

August 1926

The smell of coffee tickled Mary's nose and meandered through her thoughts as though it were part of her dream. She was in between sleeping and being awake. She liked that place. Slowly, she noticed the train was still, and she opened her eyes. Next was the sound of the porter making his way down the aisle, offering steaming hot coffee. Before she knew it, she was fully awake, and the porter was standing next to her.

"Coffee, miss?" he asked.

She refused politely. The porter, noticing her disheveled appearance from her unpleasant sleep, offered, "There are sleeping berths you could retire to, miss." He knew she had stayed in the riding car the entire night but hadn't been able to bring himself to wake her. Mary blushed. She knew she should have moved to the berth when most of the other passengers had done so, but the storm they had encountered just after sunset had worried her too much for her to crawl into the little cubby. She simply thanked the porter, and he went on his way.

She looked out the window toward the train platform. Last night, the glass had been covered with a smeary mess from soot and rain, but it was now reasonably clean. She was sure she must look a fright and strained to see her reflection in the pane as she wet her fingertips with her tongue and smoothed down her hair.

"Good morning, Miss . . .?"

Mary turned to look at the bold little man for an instant before she realized he was inquiring of her name, yet before the thought registered enough for her to respond, he continued in his nasally voice.

"So the conductor tells me you all ran into a little bad weather last night."

Mary nodded her head silently in response. She found him quite unnerving, even though he wasn't horrible looking, she supposed. He had a roundish face, with small eyes. She thought they were blue, or perhaps brown. It was hard to see them behind the wire spectacles he wore. His hair, a sandy brown, was slightly receding at the top.

"You've been riding long?" he asked, settling himself into a comfortable position in the seat directly across from her. She noticed he was stout, to the point that when he sat, his folded hands rested on his belly and not on his lap.

"Since yesterday morning," she replied shyly.

"Well, it sure didn't break up the heat any," he chortled as he reached into his pocket for a kerchief. He removed his wire spectacles and wiped the tiny drops of perspiration from his brow.

Mary's puzzled look made him clarify his statement.

"The storm, I mean. It's still hotter than blazes. And it made the train an hour off schedule to boot." He returned the kerchief to his pocket, as he reached for his watch, which hung on a long gold chain.

Mary wondered what time it was but didn't bother to ask as he had already snapped the cover shut and returned the watch to a small vest pocket.

"Bellows. Ezra J. Bellows is the name, but my friends call me Izzy." He extended his hand, and Mary shook it timidly.

"I've been on a buying trip. Have to get the new fashions in the store before fall. You wouldn't believe how many waistcoats I've looked at this week."

Mary sat quietly as she smoothed first her dress and then her hair, then suddenly realized that Mr. Bellows was asking her another question.

"Pardon me?"

"I was inquiring of your destination?" he clarified.

"Bay View," she stuttered slightly.

Ezra Bellows laughed. It was a deep throaty gurgle. "Well, my goodness, what a coincidence. Did I mention I own a clothing store?"

He didn't wait for a response, just marched his dialogue right over the top of Mary's head. Her raised eyebrows had done nothing to stop him. "Yes, we can dress 'em from top to bottom, inside and out," he boasted. "Did I tell you I have a son?"

Mary said nothing, nor did her expression acknowledge his question. It didn't take her long to realize that he was going to continue the conversation whether she responded or ignored.

"Probably about the same age as you," he prodded. "He's sixteen. A strapping young lad, he is. How old do you think I am?" he insisted. "Just guess, take a guess."

"Forty!"

The number came out of nowhere and spurted from her lips before her mind even registered the thought. Then she waited. She waited for the look of shock if the number was too high, or a kind smile if the number were less than his actual years. Neither emotion crossed his face. Instead, he fell silent immediately after he mumbled, "Thirty-two." Mary couldn't help the feeling of embarrassment that rose within her chest. She kept telling herself she hadn't meant to hurt the man's feelings. She lowered her eyes, but it wasn't helping the uncomfortable way she felt. Finding some kind of inner strength, she moved closer to the window, turned her head to look at the countryside, and tried to pretend he wasn't there.

After a short while, Ezra lifted his chin and, without turning his head, let his eyes absorb her loveliness. How breathtakingly beautiful she was. He thought to himself how lucky he had been to find a vacant seat across from her when he boarded the train. Perhaps a little weary looking, but still a choice bit of calico. He had offered his reason for travel in hopes she would do the same. He thought how strange it was that suddenly the new fashions in men's apparel, which he had deliberated over for weeks, had somehow become unimportant in her company. Forty, had she said forty? The number echoed in his head as he slowly moved his eyes over the young thing. Yes, she was young, so young. How could he have imagined she would think of him as anything other than an old man? He wondered why he had stated his age so apologetically. After all, thirty-two wasn't old. It just felt old. *He* felt old. Forty, she had said. Yes, he thought, he felt forty.

She was young, sixteen perhaps. She was dressed neatly in a simple cotton dress, thin with wear. Ezra watched shamelessly the rise and fall of her breast as she breathed in a slow and steady rhythm. Her innocence made her seem like a child, but her body was surely that of a young woman. Ezra dragged his gaze slowly over the length of her. Her hands lay neatly folded in her lap. He was convinced the flowery print covered shapely thighs and calves. He noticed the worn shoes, which were missing a few buttons here and there, and only because of his fashion sense, knew they were extremely outdated. A farm girl, he supposed. Probably her first time away from home, he presumed. Her name was Mary, he did know that much, and she was going to Bay View. Perhaps they would meet again. He toyed with the thought for a moment, but Bay View was a large city. He wished she had been more talkative.

Her sun-streaked hair was pulled back from her face and pinned haphazardly at the nape of her neck. Ezra noticed the way she constantly smoothed it and rechecked the pins, leading him to believe it usually hung free around her shoulders. Her eyes, though he could not see them with her head turned toward the window, were vivid green. Never had he seen such green eyes. They were like emerald forests. What mysterious wonders they must hold. Watching her so intently, he began to imagine her hair floating down from its confines to float freely around her, her emerald eyes shining with the brilliance of hidden jewels in a mysteriously tangled forest. Her soft skin, how silky it would feel to his touch. Slowly he dragged his eyes down the length of her, letting his mind linger over each inch of unmolested virgin skin, imagining how tantalizing it would feel under the tips of his fingers. Suddenly something began to stir within him. At first, it had been almost unrecognizable. Had it truly been so long since he had felt that way? Had hatred and shame not only turned his heart to stone but his body as well? Yet there was no denying the feeling slowly building up inside him. He closed his eyes, almost afraid of the creature who dared to break down the wall he had built around himself. He hung his head. It was those eyes, those mesmerizing green eyes.

CHAPTER 4

Matilda Bryer waited at the Bay View train station for her niece's arrival. She paced back and forth impatiently, waiting. The noonday sun beat down upon her, and she waved her lace handkerchief insistently at her face, trying to circulate the stifling air. She straightened the hair combs that held her mousey brown hair off her neck, then attempted to flatten a persistent curl near her temple that refused to stay in place. It was of no use—the humidity always caused her hair to curl and wave. She pushed at the nosepiece of her wire-rimmed glasses, inching them back up her nose and over her lackluster hazel eyes, though the sweat slid them right back down again. She furrowed her brow and pinched her nose in defeat. She scolded herself silently for not phoning the station to inquire if the train was expected to be on time before closing the library to hurry there only to find it was delayed an entire hour.

Now, at the age of forty-three, Matilda was quite set in her ways. She had never married, and if she were to admit to the truth, she had never had the opportunity. Her one true love was Mary's father, Julius Watson, but that was a love filled with bitterness and sorrow. Now, after so many years had passed, she still cursed the day she first met him, and yet she knew she also cherished it.

She found it quite befitting that she would now be responsible for the welfare of Julius's only daughter. She wondered why she had even suggested such an undertaking to her dead sister's husband. She would not allow herself to admit it was out of spite, for deep in her heart, she felt Mary should have been *her* daughter. Hers and Julius's. She had tried to get the girl after Jolene died, and again after Mary's brother had been killed, but now that Julius would no longer be able to care for the child, Mary would be hers. Julius would be left without anyone, the same way she had been left after he and Jolene had snuck away in the night to be married.

As all the old memories seeped back into her mind, her muscles tightened, and her back stiffened, which only accentuated her tall, thin frame. Oh why, she wondered, had life been so unfair? Was it fair that Jolene had been blessed with beauty and she had not? Was it fair that Julius had courted her only to be closer to Jolene, who was too young to have a beau? Was it fair that she believed all the sweet things Julius had told her, only to realize later he had been thinking of Jolene as he had spoken them? Oh, but as hard as she might try, she could not hate Julius, for she could still remember his gentle touch, his soft caresses, the way her skin would tingle when his hand gently brushed her cheek, the burning flame that would rise within her when she dared to let him kiss her lips. No, she could never hate Julius. He was the only man who had ever paid her any mind. She had convinced herself, after years of practice, that it was Jolene who was to blame. Jolene had stolen her one true love, her only hope for happiness.

The distant sound of a train whistle broke her concentration, and she turned to see the billowing smoke filling the air in the distance. She stopped her pacing and replaced the nervous energy by tapping the toe of her shoe against the wooden platform. The train at last chugged slowly to a stop in front of her, and the station became a frenzy of porters pushing baggage carts and placing steps. Passengers weary and impatient to get to their destinations or embark on their journeys filled the small platform. Matilda, her impatience building, stretched her neck and strained her eyes up and down the length of it, peering into every face as the many people began to bustle around her. Julius had told her she would be sure to recognize Mary, as she was the spitting image of Jolene at that age. "At that age," he had written, and Matilda couldn't help but believe he had written it on purpose, to remind her that Mary was the same age now as Jolene had been when she and Julius ran off together.

Where is that girl? she silently insisted. People rushed past her as she stood firmly against their nudges and jolts.

"Excuse me." The man tipped his hat slightly to apologize for bumping into her.

Matilda, recognizing the voice, turned immediately.

"Well, what a surprise!" she practically squealed. Her shrill voice grated on the man's nerves much like a cat's claws sliding down a tin roof.

"Well, well, Miss Bryer." His tone was cold and definitely irritated. "How nice to see you."

Matilda ignored his sarcasm.

"I'm so glad I bumped into you," she shrieked. "I was wondering if you would be free tomorrow?" Not waiting for a reply, she hurried her words, wanting to get them all out before he had a chance to refuse her invitation. "I thought you might be able to join us on a picnic. My niece is coming in on the train, and I thought you would like to meet her."

Matilda was unaware that her piercing tone was keeping her from hearing the poor man's decline of her invitation.

"No, I'm sorry," he was almost pleading now.

"Mary, oh Mary!" Matilda shouted as she waved her hand in the air to get her niece's attention as soon as she saw her peeking out from the train. She scurried across the platform, grabbed a startled Mary by the hand, and practically dragged her back to where she had been standing.

"Mary," Matilda puffed, slightly winded. "I want you to meet a very good friend of mine. He lives just across the hall from me."

Mary, staring at the woman who had just grabbed her and still trying to make sure it was indeed her Aunt Matilda, turned to accept the man's extended hand. She placed her delicate hand in his before lifting her eyes to greet the beaming face of Mr. Ezra Bellows.

"Well, my my. This is a coincidence," Ezra Bellows said and nearly drooled as he placed his free hand over Mary's and enclosed her trembling fingers between his anxious ones. "So this is your niece?" he inquired of Matilda, though he had not removed his eyes from Mary's face. Not waiting for a reply, he continued, still staring at Mary, though he was addressing her aunt. "What was it you were saying about a picnic, Miss Bryer?"

Mary sat quietly on the seat next to her aunt as they drove away from the station. She had convinced herself she would never have to see Mr. Bellows again once she arrived in Bay View and had remained seated when the train had stopped, giving him time to exit. Only after he had disappeared into the crowd had she moved to the exit. She had even peeked out onto the platform to make sure there was no sign of him. Now, as her luck would have it, she would spend yet another day with him, on a picnic no less.

"So, Mary, how was your trip? You must be exhausted!" Matilda asked, not taking her eyes off the road.

"Not really," she answered over the noise of the auto. "My trip was fine."

"So tell me, dear, what do you think of Mr. Bellows?"

Mary contemplated her answer carefully. From her aunt's display in front of Mr. Bellows, it was plain to see she thought quite highly of him. Finally, she answered. "He seems very nice. Is he a widower?"

"Why do you ask?" Matilda asked defensively.

"Well," Mary fidgeted with her hands, "he mentioned that he had a son."

"Oh." Matilda smiled, shaking her head in acknowledgment. "Tom ... you'll meet him tomorrow. I'm sure he'll join us on the picnic. Though I should tell you," her voice lowered, as if someone else were around to hear what she was about to say, "he's a bit of a strange boy. Well, not strange," she paused momentarily, then whispered, "I think he's a bit simple-minded."

"He must have been quite young when Tom was born?" Mary questioned, not so much out of curiosity, but simply trying to make conversation with the aunt she hardly knew.

Matilda's head tilted slightly, but her eyes stayed affixed to the road ahead of her. "Why would you say that, dear?"

"When he and I were talking on the train, he told me he was thirty-two, and he mentioned that his son was about my age."

Matilda peeled her eyes from the road for a split second to confront her niece. Then she quickly turned her attention back to her driving. Her eyes squinted through her spectacles, and the wrinkle lines increased on her forehead. "You and he spoke on the train?"

"Well, yes," Mary answered, wondering why her aunt seemed so agitated. "He happened to be seated across from me. We didn't speak all that much, though."

"Well, Tom is at least your age. You must be mistaken, dear. Perhaps he said forty-two."

"Perhaps," Mary agreed, though she knew she was not mistaken.

Mary pretended to be interested as her aunt chatted gleefully about Mr. Bellows. He was not only a friend, but they lived across the hall from one another. Mr. Bellows Men's Apparel, simply called Bellows, was a large clothier, which had previously been Goldman's Mercantile. Erected decades earlier, Goldman's Mercantile was on street level and the second story was his family's home. When Mr. Bellows purchased the building, he had the second story renovated into four separate apartments. He and his son lived in one, and he rented out the other three, one of course to Matilda Bryer.

Finally, Matilda fell silent, and Mary was glad for that. She kept her head turned in hopes she would not ask her any more questions. As they passed field after field, small signs came into view, and Mary read them silently:

EVERY SHAVER—NOW CAN SNORE

SIX MORE MINUTES THAN BEFORE

BY USING BURMA SHAVE.

That night, Mary tossed and turned on the sofa bed Aunt Tildy had made up for her. The tiny apartment was very hot, and though an occasional breeze drifted through the open window, so did the noise from the street below. She tried to keep her mind focused on something other than the noise or the heat, but all that came to mind was the annoying Mr. Bellows and his son Tom. She had met Tom when they got back to her aunt's apartment. Instantly, she found him more repulsive than his father. He was short and stout, like his father, but his hair was darker and had a slight curl. When he smiled, it was the same ridiculous grin as that of Ezra Bellows, a smirk that attempted to mask the fiendish glimmer the eyes held. Unlike his father, Tom's eyes were dark, almost black. Mary didn't like to look at him. She feared those empty dark eyes would swallow her up. Sleep eluded her. Each time she closed her lids, those dark eyes paraded through her head. When she finally managed to dismiss thoughts of Tom Bellows, she couldn't help but recall the question Mr. Bellows had asked of her aunt earlier in the evening, inquiring if there had been any more attacks in the city while he was away. To think that someone was attacking young women in a city she was now to call home was terribly frightening. It was almost dawn before exhaustion overtook her and she had finally fallen asleep.

He had played the beast's game for a long time before he finally lost to his cunning nature. Now, there was no stopping him. The beast had tasted the reward of victory, the enjoyment of the spoils. His satisfaction came from the prize awarded for winning the game. He now demanded attention. It didn't matter whether his opponent agreed to the challenge. He was no longer a contender, but the victor, and his host only a pawn.

CHAPTER 5

Mary stood in front of the small mirror that hung over her aunt's bureau in the single bedroom apartment. She stretched her arms over her head and yawned. Her aunt had awoken her early so she could take her to the Coltons' before she went off to work at the library. Mary hadn't slept well. It was her second night of tossing and turning on the sofa bed.

"Hurry along, dear," Matilda's squeaky voice drifted in from the kitchen.

Mary dressed quickly in her freshened-up cotton dress, her other belongings having been sent to the Coltons' directly from the train. Now she wished she had kept out one of her better dresses. Still sleepy, she walked into the kitchen, brushing her long golden hair.

"Oh dear," Aunt Matilda scolded, "that will never do. You need to pin up your hair. Mrs. Colton is a very proper woman. I'm sure she will provide you with a uniform, and I'm sure she will expect you to keep your hair in proper order."

Not uttering a word, Mary dragged herself back to her aunt's bedroom and reluctantly dug through the bottom of her satchel for the Kirby grips she had so eagerly deposited there the day before, then pinned her hair to resemble her aunt's. She had seen a picture of the latest haircut fashion on the cover of a *McClure's Magazine* at the train station and debated momentarily how she would look in a bob.

The entire half-hour drive to the Coltons', Mary sat silently, listening to her aunt's seemingly unending last-minute instructions.

"Don't ever talk back to Mrs. Colton, or anyone in the house for that matter. Always mind your place. Remember, the Coltons are your employers. Don't complain about anything. You know, there are probably a hundred young girls that would love the chance to have this position."

Mary wasn't sure she understood the whole arrangement, why Papa had sent her away to live with her aunt when she'd actually be living and working for the Coltons, but she had learned not to question Papa once his mind was made up. Perhaps she should tell him about the hundred other girls, yet she somehow knew it wouldn't make a difference. She worried about him, though. He seemed to be visiting old Doc Gate much too often of late, even though he said it was nothing she should concern herself with. Her aunt was still lecturing when the Coltons' home came into view. Matilda stopped her auto machine outside the heavy iron gates, and Mary stared at the enormous structure and couldn't imagine someone actually lived there. It was bigger than the hospital in Spring City where they had taken her mother when she got the influenza. She watched her aunt push a button on a small box encased in the brick cornerstone that hinged the iron gates. A strange sounding voice came through in sequence with the static.

"May I help you?"

Mary sat dumbfounded, her eyes wide and mouth agape. After her aunt had answered back to the voice in the box, the tall iron gates swung slowly open as if by magic.

She stared in awe at the massively imposing brick mansion. The main part of the house stood three stories high and twice as wide. A four-story turret loomed just to the right of the main entry doors, which were of a highly polished dark mahogany and intricately carved. Two-story wings jetted out in either direction from the main house. The house was bigger than anything Mary had ever seen. Aunt Matilda had told her the Coltons were well-off, but that seemed like an understatement, for she was sure this was not a house but a castle. She had seen one in a magazine once, and this was pretty close.

"Well," Matilda's voice was impatient, "come on, dear."

Mary was still sitting in the auto. Her eyes wandered over the entire facade, and she hadn't realized her aunt had exited the car. Matilda was already knocking when Mary reached her side. After a short time, the door opened, and a pale man dressed in dark pants, a white shirt, and a brocade vest ushered them in.

Mary's eyes darted around the large entryway, trying to see everything at once. She quickly surmised her whole house would most likely fit into the one room. She immediately wondered what on earth the Coltons did with all the other rooms in the house.

She stood quietly next to her aunt while taking in the entire expanse of the room, from the marble floor to the enormous crystal chandelier that sparkled from the high ceiling. Several small chairs and tables lined the walls. A large polished wood and marble table stood in the middle of the room and on top an enormous vase filled with beautiful flowers. Two marble cherub statutes, nearly Mary's height, stood stately at the entrance to a hallway that seemed to go on forever. The man with the brocade vest said they could sit if they liked and that Mrs. Colton would be with them momentarily before he disappeared through one of several doors which lined the hallway.

A grand sweeping staircase rose from the center of the room, and Mary's head raised as her eyes raced up each step and then suddenly halted on the figure of the woman who stood near the top. Mary watched the woman as she slowly descended the stairs. She supposed she was about the same age as her aunt, possibly a bit older, but that was the only thing this woman and her Aunt Matilda had in common. She had broad shoulders and an ample bosom and was neither thin nor fat, but more solidly built. Her hair, dark brown, curled back from her stern face that held no real expression. Even her eyes, which were coldly blue, seemed void of emotion.

"Good morning, Miss Bryer," she said, and her firm voice filled the entire entryway. She had reached the bottom step.

"Good morning, Mrs. Colton," Aunt Matilda responded. Mary stood silently by her side.

"This must be your niece?" Mrs. Colton inquired as she crossed the marble floor, her heels clicking on the polished surface.

When she stood directly across from them, Matilda answered, "Yes, this is Mary."

Matilda gently nudged her niece.

"How do you do, ma'am?" he said, her voice barely audible.

"I hope you had a nice trip, dear."

By the woman's tone, Mary wondered if she was really interested in what kind of a trip she had. "It was fine," Mary responded. Then with a subtle glare from her aunt, she quickly added, "Thank you, ma'am."

"Well, I can see we are going to get along just fine." Mrs. Colton sneered, and her steel blue eyes suddenly glittered with an expression Mary couldn't quite comprehend.

"Well, then," Matilda said abruptly, "I must be getting off to the library."

"Of course," Mrs. Colton agreed. "You go right ahead. Mary will be just fine. And as I told you before, Miss Bryer, you are welcome to visit Mary any time you like." Then she added for clarification, "On her day off, of course."

Matilda hugged Mary halfheartedly, and then with a brisk turn, she was gone.

"Well, now." Mrs. Colton, crossing back toward the staircase, stopped suddenly, realizing Mary still stood silently near the door, clutching her satchel. "Come along," she ordered. "I'll show you to your room."

Mary followed obediently behind her up the grand staircase, listening carefully as Mrs. Colton dispensed information.

"I've had your trunk put in your room—it arrived yesterday. Once you're unpacked, I'll have Charles carry it up to the attic for storage. This is the main stairway," she waved her hand as if introducing Mary to the steps. "You will not use it unless instructed to. Later, I will have Margaret show you around the house and introduce you to the others. Bea will tell you what is expected of you, what your duties will be, and what you can and cannot do." She briefly looked at Mary to emphasize her point.

The stairway wound around as it rose, so that now, at the very top, they faced the front of the house, where they paused for a moment. A large window overlooked the front entrance, and Mary watched as Aunt Matilda's auto machine passed through the front gates, which then magically closed behind her. In some strange way, she suddenly felt she might miss her aunt.

Then Mrs. Colton's arm was waving again. "Christina's room. Christina, my daughter," Mrs. Colton huffed, indignantly noticing Mary's confused look and taking it to mean she had no idea to whom she was referring. "She's still asleep. I will call for you when she is ready to meet you. Her room is down the hall, as are mine, Mr. Colton's, and James's. No one is permitted down that corridor unless instructed to be there."

Mary's expression had again questioned as she wondered who James was, but Mrs. Colton had already turned and was waving her arm toward a new corridor.

"Down this wing are the guest rooms. Charles, the butler—I'm sure he greeted you and your aunt at the door—also has a room in this wing." She turned and proceeded down a long and narrower corridor in the opposite direction. They passed several closed doors before stopping in front of the last door on the right.

"This will be your room," she said, opening the door and practically pushing Mary into the small room.

"I'll let you settle in. You may use the facilities at the end of the hall to freshen up," she said coldly. "If you need anything, you may ask Bea. She can be found in the kitchen, directly down these stairs." She pointed to the narrow stairway directly across the hall from Mary's room then closed the door. Mary listened to the sound of her heels clicking on the floor until they faded away then stood silently in the middle of the small room, unsure of what to do until she turned and spied her trunk. Kneeling in front of it, she dug out the key from her satchel and opened the lock. She lifted the cover and dug through her belongings until she found what she was looking for—a silver-framed photograph. She stared hard at the faces of her mother and father. The picture had been taken just before Mama had gotten sick.

A man had come through town offering to take peoples' pictures. Papa, knowing Mama wanted one, dressed up in his Sunday clothes and paid the man the ninety-five cents to have it taken. The photo had a place of honor in the parlor on a little round table next to the Bible.

As tears gently began to trickle down her cheek, she hugged the silver frame to her chest. There was a soft knock on the door. She quickly rubbed away her tears and set the frame gently back into the trunk.

"Come in," she said shyly.

The door opened, and a round-faced girl with curly, brownish-red hair bounced into the room.

"Aye, Mary?" she questioned. Mary nodded stiffly. The girl walked over to the edge of the bed and plopped on it, as would a mischievous child ready to bounce up and down.

"Me name's Margaret Fitzpatrick, but ya can call me Maggie, everybody does. Bea sent me up here to see if you be needin' anythin' and ta welcome ya to the Colton Castle." She giggled as she threw her arms in the air to present the house to Mary. "That's what I be callin' it, as Mrs. Colton thinks she's the queen, don't ya know."

Mary sat quietly marveling at Maggie.

"Ahh, but you'll be learnin' to like it here. Though I hear ya be watchin' over Ms. Christina. That one's a handful, she is."

"You work here?" Mary questioned shyly as she raised herself off the floor and moved across the room to sit on the bed next to Maggie.

Maggie nodded her head. "Be doin' most of the cleanin', don't ya know. I dust, I scrub floors, I wash windows, I sweeps the carpets, and by the time I'm all finished, 'tis time to start over again."

"You clean this whole place by yourself?" Mary asked, in total amazement.

"Well, most of it," Maggie replied. "'Ceptin' when the Coltons be havin' a party, then Mrs. Colton hires others to be helpin'."

"Can I ask you something?" Mary asked cautiously.

"Whatever be your likin'," Maggie responded with a toss of her curly hair.

"Where is it that you're from? I do so like the way you talk."

Maggie giggled insatiably. It was an infectious chuckle, and soon Mary was cackling right along with her. After both girls had finally caught their breath, Maggie told Mary she was from Ireland, and many of the servants in the house were from different countries. Bea, the cook, had been there for many, many years. She was from Germany, and though she had come to America almost thirty years ago, her German accent still heavily tarnished her English. Charles, the butler, was from England—a pretty stuffed shirt was how Maggie described him.

"If you think I be talkin' strange, wait till you get a load of Jeannette," Maggie giggled. "Most of the time she's talkin' in French. Mrs. Colton brought her back from France on her last trip there. She's been here a few months now, but I still can't be understandin' most of what she's sayin'."

"How old is Miss Christina?" Mary asked, suddenly curious about the child that she was to be looking after.

"Ya hasn't met her yet then?" Maggie asked, her tone becoming somewhat peculiar.

"No, Mrs. Colton said she was still asleep. Is she a small child?"

Maggie's laughter filled the room and bounced off the walls. "Small?" she snickered, "'Tis not a word ya can be usin' when talkin' about Miss Christina."

Mary stared at Maggie, and though her face held a slight grin, simply because it was hard not to be caught up in Maggie's laughter, she was sincerely worried about caring for a young child. After all, she had no experience caring for children. What if she were to do something inappropriate? She didn't want to upset her aunt, who had made it quite clear she had done Mary an enormous favor in securing this position for her, and after meeting Mrs. Colton, she certainly didn't want to make her mad either. Her superior demeanor made it apparent she was not a tolerant woman. The smile faded from Mary's face as she started to worry about her new position. All Aunt Matilda had told her was that she would be caring for the Coltons' daughter.

"So how old is she?" Mary almost demanded.

Suddenly realizing that Mary was truly concerned, Maggie stifled her laughter.

"'Tis not a child at all," she finally answered. "Though she be actin' like one most of the time. She's fourteen, she is!"

"Fourteen!" Mary's shrill voice echoed in the sparsely furnished room. "Why do they need me to watch her? Is there something wrong with her?"

Maggie started giggling again. "Nothin' a stiff strap wouldn't fix. She's a spoiled one, she is. She's been through three nannies in the last year. Bea says that's why Mrs. Colton hired you. Guess she thinks someone more Christina's age can occupy her time. She hasn't any friends, ya know. No one can stand her. 'Tween me and you, I'd rather be scrubbin' the floors than havin' to spend time with Miss Christina."

Maggie stood up then, and as she moved to the door, she added, "When you're done unpackin', come down to the kitchen, and I'll shows ya around."

Mary unpacked her trunk as quickly as she could. She was anxious to meet Bea, and Jeanette, and strangely enough, even Miss Christina. She placed the silver frame with her Mama and Papa's picture on the small table that stood next to her bed. She desperately missed her Papa, but perhaps this place wouldn't be as dreadful as she had imagined.

He tried to tell himself that he wouldn't let it happen again, but he knew he had little control over it. The beast had a way of making him believe he needed what only the beast could acquire for him. It was not he that stalked the prey; it was not he that lusted in the dark of night. No, its need was greater than his. Yet he knew that he too would pleasure in its actions. Yes, it was hungry, and it needed to feast. He knew he would not be able to stop it from taking what it needed.

CHAPTER 6

Mary stood silently, unnoticed, at the bottom of the narrow stairway, surveying the large kitchen. Double-high cabinets lined two entire walls, and she considered the many odd-looking contraptions that sat on the counter. An enormous cook stove with eight burners, a large and small oven, and side warming ovens stood prominently on another wall. Mary wondered how they kept it so white and shiny. A double copper-lined sink encased in its own cabinet rested against another wall. A good-sized wooden table, surrounded by a dozen wooden chairs, stood in the middle of the room. Mary observed the sizable woman who stood with her back to her, pinching a piecrust into a pan on the counter. She was dressed in a light-blue cotton uniform and sturdy black shoes, and she wore her gray braided hair wound at the back of her head. As she turned, Mary saw she had a kind face, with plump rosy red cheeks and smiling eyes.

"Ahh," she sighed as she wiped her floured hands on her well-used apron and crossed the room. "Dis mus' be Mary!"

She hugged Mary as if she were a close relative or good friend.

"Sit down, sit down," she said and ushered Mary to a chair. "Let me git you somet'ing to eat."

She opened a tin on the cupboard.

"Bea likes to be feedin' ya all the time," Maggie said as she came bounding into the room and spied Bea filling up a plate with cookies. Bea shot her a cross look which instantly turned into a broad smile as she set the plate of cookies on the table in front of Mary. Maggie reached for one and Bea smiled.

"Ah, but you like my cookies," she scolded as she pinched Maggie's cheek.

From another cupboard, she retrieved a glass and then ambled to the other side of the room to a metal cabinet that stood by itself. Mary watched curiously as she opened one of the two large doors and produced a pitcher of milk. Mary studied the cabinet, which took up as much room as did the large eight-burner stove. It had two doors and was sparkling white with shiny silver latches and handles. On top sat a large, round box, patchworked with holes.

"What's that?" she questioned Maggie in a whisper.

Maggie raised her eyebrows and turned her head in the direction of Mary's pointed finger. "'Tis the refrigerator," she said and shrugged.

"The what?" Mary asked again.

"Ya know, an ice box. It don't be needin' any ice, though. It runs by electricity."

Mary sat wide-eyed and stared at the odd-looking icebox, wondering how electricity could keep things cold. Oh, they had electricity in their house, but it just gave off light. A few years back, men had come and strung wire to big poles, and they ran some of the wire to their house. Papa had to put in a lot of other wires and gadgets, and he had gone to Mr. Hanson's store to buy bulbs to screw into the things they called a socket where the electricity came out. Papa had told her Mr. Fletcher, their neighbor, hadn't bought himself any of the bulbs, so he had to put a bucket under the hole where the socket was, else when they turned on the juice, as the men had called it, the electricity would leak all over the floor. Mary found out later Papa had just been teasing her, but Papa never told her about any iceboxes that used electricity. Mr. Hanson had a recording machine at the general store that ran on electricity, but she really didn't understand how that worked.

Staring at the icebox, Mary just couldn't fathom how electricity could keep things cold. She knew all too well, by experience, that light bulbs got very hot.

Bea set the glass of milk down in front of her. Mary poked it cautiously. At that exact moment, a loud buzzer rang. She jumped.

The glass tipped, and the entire contents spilled out onto the table. Maggie rose from the stool she had perched herself on, grabbed a dishtowel from the rack, and tossed it through the air toward Mary.

"Her highness be callin'," she said, and then, with a toss of her head, she left the room. Mary looked to Bea questioningly as she sopped up the spilled milk from the table.

"In every main vroom of da house, dare is a buzzer button," Bea explained, pointing to the large silver plate high on the far wall, which held more than a dozen tiny light bulbs. The one marked parlor was lit. "Da Coltons can ring from any part of da house to da kitchen. Din somevone in da kitchen knows to go to that vroom, whichever light is blinking." Bea smiled and nodded her head as though her explanation should have cleared it all up for Mary. "It has to be extra loud, so's I can hear it at night from my vroom," Bea added.

It all puzzled Mary, yet she supposed if electricity could make milk cold, almost anything was possible.

Just then, Maggie came bouncing back into the kitchen through a swinging door on the opposite side from which she left.

"Miss Christina be ready to meet ya," she said in the most dignified voice she could muster as she somewhat gracefully extended herself into a not quite illustrious but somewhat hilarious bow. Bea swatted her from behind, and she nearly fell into Mary's lap. They all laughed while Maggie rubbed her backside.

Mary stood, straightened out her dress, and smoothed down her hair. With wobbly knees and sweaty palms, she followed Maggie out the kitchen door, down the hall through the front entryway, and into the parlor. Mrs. Colton and Christina sat precisely on either end of the low-backed, red velvet upholstered divan. Mary noticed how they both sat so straight, right legs crossed over left, hands folded over the knees. They reminded her of the bookends that stood on a shelf at Mr. Hanson's store. Maggie deposited Mary directly in front of the two Colton women, and with a simple curtsey scurried out of sight. Mary stood quietly, trying to steady her shaking legs, wondering if they too could hear the pounding of her heartbeat that seemed to be echoing in her ears. Through half-lowered lids, she surveyed Christina. She was pudgy, but not in the same way as Maggie, who was taller and more evenly proportioned. Mary assumed Christina was shorter as she sat scooted up on the edge of the divan so that her feet could rest on the floor. She had golden-brown hair that somewhat resembled Mrs. Colton's in color but fell in waves to her shoulders. She wore a pink satin dress covered with fine white lace, and Mary couldn't help but notice how the seams appeared to be straining as they attempted to hold in her bulk. She wasn't a very pretty girl, nor was she homely. Her face replicated her mother's and held little expression.

"Mary, this is my daughter, Christina." Mrs. Colton made the introduction as if she were introducing Mary to someone of great importance.

"How do you do, miss?" Mary curtsied, imitating Maggie. Christina sat silently as though she were someone to be admired.

"Christina is going to have her breakfast now. If she wishes, you can join her so you two may chat and get acquainted." Mrs. Colton rose from the divan. Right on cue, Christina rose from her pedestal. They passed through the grand entryway on their way to the dining room like an odd sort of train, Mrs. Colton followed by Christina, followed by Mary who couldn't help but notice the way Christina's overabundant caboose swayed as she walked. Her recent train travel so fresh in her mind, she was quite tempted to raise her arm, pull an imaginary cord, and yell "Woo woo!" However, just thinking about it was entertainment enough, and she followed behind them silently. As they entered the dining room, Christina seated herself at the table, while Mary positioned herself silently in the corner, marveling at all the beautiful fine dishes encased in glass-faced cabinets. A crystal chandelier hung from the ceiling and danced its shadows over the enormous highly polished dining table, which Mary estimated to be at least twenty feet long. High-backed chairs covered in a beautiful tapestry cloth lined both sides of the table, and sideboards filled with shiny silver bowls lined one entire wall. The swinging door, which Mary assumed led back into the kitchen, swayed back and forth as Mrs. Colton disappeared through it.

As soon as she was sure her mother was out of earshot, Christina said softly, but in a sharp tone, "Well, come sit down across from me so I can get a better look at you." Mary did as she ordered but kept her eyes lowered. "Don't think we're going to be friends or anything." Christina's voice was threatening. "I'm just going along with this silly idea to please Mother. I'm fourteen, and I don't need a nanny or a companion. And I certainly don't need a common farm girl hanging around me all the time either!"

The swinging door pushed into the room, and Christina fell silent as Bea entered and served her a large plate filled with two eggs, several pieces of crispy fried side pork, some delicious-looking corn muffins, and a large glass of orange juice.

"Where's my milk?" Christina bellowed. Mary wanted to yell back at her, "I spilled it, you spoiled little girl," but she sat quietly.

"I'll bring it in directly, dear," Bea said calmly as she turned to Mary, and out of view of Christina, rolled her eyes in Christina's direction. Mary watched in silence as Christina gobbled her plate clean and emptied her glass of juice and the milk, which Bea had hurried back to her.

Then, at the suggestion of Mrs. Colton, Christina led Mary up to her room so they could get to know each other. As they neared the grand staircase, Mary paused, remembering Mrs. Colton's orders about not using the main stairs unless instructed to do so. Halfway up the steps, Christina stopped and turned to Mary, who was waiting at the bottom.

"Are you coming or not?" she roared. Mary, considering that to be permission enough, followed Christina up the stairs and down the large corridor. Christina opened the door to her room, and Mary timidly followed her. Once inside, she stared in fascination at all the beautiful things in the spacious room. A large four-poster bed, over which hung a canopy of white draped lace, stood prominently against the far wall. The bed itself was adorned with a white satin and lace coverlet. Two large windows were decorated with lace as well. Mary marveled at the pretty things that seemed to be everywhere she looked.

One wall lined with white shelves held an array of dolls, toys, and elegant music boxes. She noticed one doll in particular that was poised on the middle shelf and dressed in emerald green satin, its glass eyes of the same color shining brilliantly. The doll's golden hair looked almost real, certainly not made of yarn as her childhood dolls had been. She had the most beautifully painted face, with rose-colored cheeks and red lips. Her face looked so perfect and delicate. Christina noticed Mary was staring at it and said the head was made of porcelain and very expensive. Mary crossed the room simply to get a better view of the beautiful doll. She thought of her mother and imagined the doll could have been fashioned in her likeness. She softly smiled as she imagined her mother, at that very moment, was just as beautiful floating as an angel in God's heaven.

"Don't touch it!" Christina shouted as she leaped across the room and grabbed for the doll. Their bodies collided, pushing Mary off balance. She stumbled over a small footstool and tumbled over it backward, falling down to the floor. Christina's pudgy little hand grabbed for the doll but caught only the edge of the satin dress. As she turned to see Mary falling to the floor, she accidentally pulled the doll from the shelf, and it slipped from her hand. Time and motion seemed suspended as both girls watched helplessly as the doll with the green satin dress floated and billowed as if it wore a parachute carrying its passenger to safety. Christina tried again to grab for the doll but only managed to upset its descent. It turned upside down, and the beautiful head hit against the lower shelf, shattering into a dozen pieces, all falling to the floor. Both girls stared in silence at the headless doll and her once beautiful face, which now lay scattered on the rug.

"You broke it!" Christina bellowed. Her face bunched up, and her eyes narrowed into mere slits. Mary picked herself up, apologizing repeatedly, offering to buy Christina a new doll.

"Just get out of my room! I don't want to see you anymore today!" she screamed. Mary hurried to the door, opened it, and stepped into the hall. As she turned to pull the door shut behind her, she watched as Christina purposely poised the toe of her shoe over a piece of the red painted cheek that lay jagged-edged, astray from the many other pieces. Then slowly, she lowered her foot onto the small piece of delicate porcelain and crushed it into the rug.

CHAPTER 7

James couldn't take the stuffiness of the office building anymore. It was a beautiful day in New York, and he had been cooped up all week with the "good ol' boys" as his father referred to them. He wasn't at all sure how they slept at night. Not eighteen months earlier, they had forced the workers to add four hours to their already fifty-hour workweek. Now they sat on the twenty-second floor of the Woolworth Building in their oversized boardroom at a polished rosewood table which prominently stood atop a William Morris tapestry. They were surrounded by gilded trim and brocade drapery discussing whether they should decrease the wages by twenty percent. They were sure to turn a tidy profit now that the Federal Trade Commission was allowing them to use the name "rayon" instead of having to label it "artificial or imitation silk," but of course the employees didn't need to know the long and short of it. It always seemed to James the more the good ol' boys got, the more they wanted.

"So, have you heard Walter is scouting out land for a new building?" one of the ol' boys asked him. James knew he was referring to Walter Chrysler—he had heard the rumors too. The difference was right at that moment, he really didn't care. He had to get out of there. He needed some air. The tie he wore felt as though it was strangling him, and the stiff collar was starting to dig into his skin. He made a quick excuse to his father and hurried out of the room without so much as a goodbye to his colleagues. He would hear about that later.

He headed to the men's room at the end of the hall, his tie and collar removed by the time he reached the door. Tucking them into his jacket pocket, he removed his coat and laid it over the chair that stood in the corner of the room. He crossed the tiled floor to the row of sinks, his footsteps echoing in the large, empty room with the high ceilings and tiled walls. He glanced at his reflection in the mirror and turned on the faucet. He splashed the cool water over his face several times before reaching for one of the neatly folded towels on the little cart that stood against the wall. Looking himself over in the mirror, he admired his new suit. He had picked it up earlier in the week. The light gray pinstriped material was perfect for this time of year. The crisp white shirt and form-fitted vest, even without the jacket and bright purple and yellow tropical flowered tie Langsdorf had paired it with, looked good. He ran his fingers through his dark hair, picked up his jacket, walked out the door, and headed back down the hallway. Taking the elevator to the lobby, he quickly made his way across the expanse to the revolving door he knew would empty him out onto Broadway. From the street, he could grab a Checker cab, or maybe he'd just walk. The sun was shining, and he couldn't get out fast enough. The light breeze hit his face even before he stepped out the door.

He breathed in a long, deep breath and exhaled slowly. *Now, where to go*? He thought about The Landmark Tavern but decided having to hide away on the second floor, just to have a drink, was no better than sitting in the stuffy boardroom. He lifted his eyes as he turned around and scanned the buildings that all seemed to grow taller and taller with each year that passed. He wanted to get out of the city. The twinkle in his eye appeared just before the smile came across his face. He strategically placed his thumb and first finger on either side of his tongue and produced the perfect hailing cab whistle, then his arm flew in the air. "Hey, cabbie!"

He literally jumped into the back seat with the enthusiasm of a boy playing hooky. "Coney Island," he called out to the driver as he pulled the door shut.

They crossed over the Brooklyn Bridge then headed south toward Ocean Parkway. The closer they got, the more he could smell the salt air coming in on the breeze. Then, there it was. The Thunderbolt loomed in front of him. He leaned his head out the back door of the cab to marvel at the sight of it—the steep drops, twists, and turns. He loved the roller coaster and was already feeling around in his pocket for a quarter.

As he waited in line, ticket in hand, he looked around at the variety of people milling around the park. Since they had finished the subway line in 1920, the place had really filled up. James remembered coming to the park with his dad and mom when he was a kid, at least once every summer. It was not nearly as crowded as it was now. It was nice they had gotten rid of all the bathhouses and opened up the beach, put in the boardwalk, and most of all, brought in Thunderbolt. He felt like a kid on Christmas Eve. He was next in line.

After three times around, he opted for a nice stroll down the boardwalk. His left hand shoved into his pants pocket and his suit jacket, suspended by two fingers, slung over his right shoulder, he strolled the wooden deck, people watching. *Well,* he thought, *more like girl watching.* He softly smiled at a blond cutie as she passed by him. There was another just to his left—brunette this time. *Two and a half miles of boardwalk, hundreds of pretty women, and all afternoon. What more could a fella want?* he thought. A brown-eyed brunette caught his eye. Once she passed, he turned and glanced over his shoulder to see if she looked as nice going as she had coming.

The straight-faced, dark-haired, five-foot-two young woman behind him looked up at him with fire in her eyes.

"You could give a girl a little warning, you big palooka," she barked as she grabbed his shoulder to steady herself while removing the toe of her red-heeled shoe from under his foot.

"I'm sorry, so sorry," he said. Yet not so sorry that he wasn't also looking her over while offering his apology. She was stylishly dressed, almost flashy. Her dark hair and dark eyes were accentuated by the white and red day suit and matching wide-brimmed hat she wore. She wasn't beautiful, but something about her attracted him. He had a feeling about her, not so much a physical attraction, but definitely something. He cupped her elbow, steadying her, while she slipped the shoe, which had come off as she tried to release it from under his, back onto her foot. She looked up at him and at the same time rolled her eyes and planted an "I'm holding my temper" tight-lipped grin on her face.

"Thank you," she said through gritted teeth. Not letting go of her elbow, James steered her out of the foot traffic on the overcrowded boardwalk and over to a safer position near the railing. She hadn't objected, and he took that as a good sign. He looked out over the crowds of sunbathers to the gentle waves rolling onto the shore. School was not back in session yet, and the beach was crowded with families and children. He was waiting for her to make the next move.

"So what's your name, or should I just continue to call you palooka?" she asked with a New York accent, but James also noticed a hint of something more, and he was intrigued. She was a slight girl, but not shapely. Not high fashion, but tastefully dressed. She was fiery in a refined sort of way. She was, to say the least, absorbing.

"James, my name is James. And yours?"

She hesitated slightly, looking him up and down then straight in the eye before she answered, "Rachel."

She said it loud and clear and proud. He silently admitted to himself he found her a bit intimidating, which fascinated him even more.

He convinced her to allow him to buy her lunch. Though she had refused several times, he somehow knew she would ultimately accept. He had to agree to eat at a particular stand where she could watch them make the food. She was convinced there were those who would spit in your food if you weren't looking. They sipped sodas and talked at length about nothing—about everything. By late in the afternoon, they were still talking as they strolled to Doumar's for an ice cream cone.

"You just can't get a waffle cone like this back in Bay View," he said, not realizing that Rachel's gentle nudges were steering him toward the beach. She was bold, brassy, and magnetic. She was twenty, James had found out. He had guessed her to be a bit older. Technically, she lived with her father and stepmother, but she had more or less been on her own for a while. James had silently obliged her, and suddenly they were standing on the edge of the sand. It was late in the afternoon, and the full sun bounced off the water and filled the air with a humid breeze. Rachel seemed deep in thought as she absentmindedly removed her high-heeled shoes and began to drag her feet through the warm grains. Suddenly, she halted in her tracks and turned to James.

"*Bashert!*" she shouted.

Catching him quite off guard, he stared at her, unsure of what she had said, or what he thought she'd said. After shaking his head and scratching his cheek, he tilted his head a bit.

"Excuse me?"

"*Bashert,*" she repeated.

James leaned a bit closer, knowing full well he had now heard what she said but still had no idea what she said.

"*Bashert,*" she repeated a third time. "It's a Yiddish word. It means . . ." she hesitated for a moment, tilting her head back and forth and pursing her lips from side to side as if mulling it over in her mind. "It means *meant to be,*" she finally said.

"Okay," James acknowledged. "What is bashert? What is meant to be?"

She eyed him up and down as an exasperated mother might look at a willful child. That fiery look was back in her dark eyes as she scoffed at him. She was talking with her hands now

"You . . . me . . . why we met today. This. That. *Bashert!* It is *bashert.*"

"Okay?" James responded slowly.

She shook her head back and forth as she resumed her path to the water, all the while scolding James for his inability to understand the concept. "*Bashert*" she repeated. "It . . . it means many things. It can be like a coincidence, but not, you know?"

James was shaking his head, first up and down, then side to side. "No, no," he said. "I don't know."

She stopped suddenly, indicating the little patch of sand they were standing on was where she wanted to sit. He did so obediently, though he wasn't quite sure why. Laying his suit jacket across his lap and stretching his legs out in front of him, he crossed first his arms and then his ankles. She folded her legs underneath herself and was sitting effortlessly beside him. She removed her wide-brimmed hat and laid it between them. She looked him straight in the eye and repeated the word a final time.

"*Bashert* is why you turned around and bumped into me. It's why we have spent an entire afternoon together even though there is no . . . no . . ." she paused ". . . spark between us."

James found himself nodding his head as she spoke. He agreed with her, about the no spark anyway. There was no romantic intrigue at all, at least not on his part, and yet, in her own way, she was a very alluring young woman.

She continued, still waving her hands in front of him for emphasis. "But it's more than that. It's like something unexplainable happens so that something else doesn't happen, or sometimes does happen."

"Okay," he finally agreed, "it's *bashert*. So now what?"

"So now what, what?" she asked, throwing her hands in the air. "So now, nothing. We have to wait and see. Only He," she pointed to the heavens, "only He knows why."

James chuckled. "Oh, this is about destiny? That's this b*ashert* you speak of? Fate? Everything happens for a reason kind of stuff?"

Rachel looked at him with sad eyes. "I hope for you a happy life, James. I hope you make the right choices."

With that, she stood up and began to remove her skirt and then her blouse. James was both disappointed and relieved to see that underneath she wore her bathing attire. She was thinner than he had been led to believe. The blousy swim outfit looked completely harmless though possibly a tad short. James watched as she went skipping off to the water. He watched her for a while, and then his mind turned to thinking about what she had said and wondering why he found her so captivating. Then suddenly there was some kind of ruckus down by the water. He looked up to see her being led away by two policemen. He picked up his jacket and her hat and clothes she had discarded in the sand and hurried across the beach in her direction. Within shouting distance, he called out to her, "Rachel, Rachel! What's going on?"

Paying little attention to the two burly officers who were practically dragging her from the beach, she shouted back in a defiant tone, "They say my skirt is shorter than the allowed length. I tried to explain to them that it's proportionately correct." As the two flatfoots passed James, with Rachel in tow, she turned and winked at him. He managed to hand the cop nearest to him her clothes and hat, which the man bundled up under his arm as he struggled to keep a grip on her arm. Rachel was small, but she was feisty. Then she was gone, disappeared to the other side of the beach. James just stood there among the crowd, all who had gone on with what they had been doing before the commotion. He would be catching the train with his father first thing in the morning. He'd probably never see her again.

"Bashert," he whispered, shaking his head.

CHAPTER 8

Mary yawned and patted her hand over her mouth. Maggie was making most of the conversation, as was usual, but Mary loved to listen to Maggie almost as much as Maggie liked to talk. The two of them often spent long hours into the night talking and giggling in one or the other's room. Tonight, they sat in Mary's room, both clad in their cotton nightgowns. Mary sat propped by pillows, legs crossed, and covered to the waist, while Maggie lay belly down, sprawled across the foot of Mary's bed. Legs bent at the knees, she twirled her feet in the air. They had been kept very busy the last few days preparing for the Colton men's homecoming. Mr. Colton and his son, James, had been in New York on business. Maggie had informed Mary that they had left just two days prior to her arrival and were expected home on Saturday. A big party was planned for the evening, as they had been gone an extended amount of time.

"What kind of business is Mr. Colton in?" Mary questioned as she tried to fight off sleep, her eyelids heavy and her head nodding every now and then.

"He makes money," Maggie said flippantly and then giggled.

Mary raised her eyebrows, and a skeptical smirk came to her lips. She really was starting to wonder if Maggie thought her totally naive and laughably gullible.

"No, really," Maggie insisted. "'Tis what he does. Just how he be doin' it, I don't know. He owns some kind of factory, he does. I think maybe they make material or clothing. Mr. James and him are always goin' down to the plant. I think he owns other stuff too. I always be hearin' Mrs. Colton talkin' about collectin' the rent from people."

"What's James like?" Mary asked as she adjusted her pillows and repositioned herself.

Maggie fell silent for a moment, her eyes in a glassy stare.

"Well?" Mary prodded.

"Oh, Mr. James," Maggie swooned. "He's a real sheik, he is."

Mary's puzzled expression prompted Maggie to explain further.

"He's a sheik, ya know, a real cake-eater, a ladies' man."

"But what's he look like?" Mary insisted.

Maggie swooned again. Mary giggled.

Maggie began to describe James as she had last seen him, the night before he had left on his latest business trip. Her words seemed to drip from her mouth as she described him to Mary.

"He's tall with black hair that waves perfectly. His skin is smooth, and his eyes are like blue pools that reflect light and sparkle with thousands of tiny stars. His lips are full, and when he's smiling, it's a broad, wonderful smile. His voice is deep and melancholy. He stands straight and tall, he does, and his arms, when they wrap around ya, are strong and powerful, but gentle and invitin'."

Mary stopped giggling and stared at Maggie, her eyes wide as her mouth hung open in disbelief at the words Maggie spoke.

"Oh, stop your gawkin'," Maggie snapped. "Ya asked me what he be like."

"Is he your beau?" Mary asked shyly. Maggie laughed as she rose to her knees, crossed her legs underneath herself, and plopped herself back down at the end of the bed while Mary quietly stared at her, annoyed by her reaction to what she thought to be a logical question.

"Mr. James could be havin' any girl he be wantin'. All he'd have to do 'tis ask. Why would he be wantin' me?"

"He sounds like a cad to me," Mary declared.

Maggie sighed. "Ah, we come from opposite ends of the earth, me and Mr. James."

———————◦◦———————

Maggie fell silent as her thoughts turned to James. She wondered why she spoke so highly of him when the truth was she was still mad at him for what he had said the night before he left on his business trip. There had been a small dinner party at the Coltons' and, of course, James's latest interest, Diane Beaumont, was in attendance. By late evening, James, quite inebriated, had bumped into Maggie in the entryway and had teasingly slapped her on the behind. He had then embraced her and given her an innocent peck on the cheek. It hadn't been the first time he outwardly displayed affection toward her, but it was the first time anyone had witnessed it. Diane had just been coming out of the library and had gasped in disbelief. James had simply laughed at her concern as he left Maggie and crossed the entryway, apologizing by saying, "Oh come on, Diane, it's just the maid."

———————◦◦———————

"How is it you came to work here?" Mary asked, thinking it best they change the subject. At first, when Maggie told her Mrs. Colton had paid her passage to America, Mary had thought how wonderful the Coltons were. That is, until Maggie told her, in the strictest of confidence, for she knew what she had agreed to was illegal, that in repayment of her passage, she had to work for them free of charge for ten years. Maggie said she thought ten years was a long time, but she had agreed to it just the same, as coming to America was worth any price. She had come to America when she was thirteen. She was now seventeen.

"Only six more years," she chimed, making it somehow sound like a very short time. "And it'll go faster now that you be here."

Mary was very glad to have found a friend like Maggie.

Saturday morning came all too early for Mary, but she rose from her bed and readied herself for what she had been told was to be a busy day. Mr. Colton and James were due home that morning, coming in on the ten o'clock train. There were scores of preparations to be done before the party that evening. Mrs. Colton told her she would be helping Bea in the kitchen. She had so wanted to help Maggie and the rest of the help serving large silver trays of food. Maggie had told her all about what the parties at the house were like. The hired help would arrive early and dress in the uniforms Mrs. Colton provided them. They would replenish the food trays and help serve. The guests would start arriving around eight o'clock—a great variety of people according to Maggie. The first to come would be the Coltons' friends. There would be bankers and lawyers and businessmen, and Maggie said even the mayor might be there. They would be dressed up in "soup and fish"—real fancy black suits, Maggie had clarified for her. Their wives would be wearing long silk gowns with glittering diamond necklaces or shiny white pearls and furs wrapped around their shoulders. There would be people all around the house. Maggie's job would be to walk around through all the rooms offering glasses of cold champagne or carrying big silver trays filled with tiny little sandwiches to all the guests. Then, later in the evening, more people would come. There would be musicians in the grand room, and everyone would eat, drink, and dance until late into the evening. It all sounded so wonderful to Mary. The only problem was she would be stuck in the kitchen with Bea and, most assuredly, miss it all.

For most of the morning, she helped Bea in the kitchen. She peeled carrots and cleaned a variety of vegetables. She mixed bowls and bowls of wonderful, tasty concoctions Bea had put together. She stuffed little pastry shells Bea had made the day before with the most delicious fruit mixture. And she washed lots and lots of dishes. She didn't mind, though. She liked working in the kitchen with Bea. It reminded her of when she was a little girl with her mother.

As she scrubbed vigorously at a stubborn scorch at the bottom of a pot, she glanced at the clock that stood on the side counter. It was nearly ten o'clock. Soon the Colton men would be arriving home. Charles, the butler, had left earlier to pick them up from the train station. She would finally get to meet James Colton. She wasn't quite sure what to expect after all the stories she had heard about him. According to Maggie, he was the "cat's pajamas." Mary wasn't sure exactly what that meant, but she knew Maggie adored him. Jeanette, to whom Mary seldom spoke, said, "Eh ess mush too 'andsome for 'is own goud." Bea said he was a dear boy. Mary knew he certainly wasn't a boy. Christina told her James was ten years older than she was. She wasn't sure how things were in the city, but where she came from, when a man was twenty-four, he was a man, not a boy by any means.

Mary jumped as the intercom buzzed. She would never get used to that thing. As Bea walked toward the buzzing contraption, Mary hoped she hadn't noticed she had just been standing there daydreaming. Bea flipped the buzzer switch up and down twice to indicate to the sender that the message had been received.

"Vell, dear," Bea said, smiling as always. "Miss Christina is going to save you from vrinkled fingers. She probably vants you to go to her vroom and fix her hair before James and Mr. Colton arrive."

Mary dried her hands on the dishcloth that hung on a hook near the sink and knew she would probably have preferred the wrinkled fingers.

She was pleased, however, to find Christina was actually in pleasant temperament, as pleasant as pleasant could be for Christina. In the few weeks that had passed since her arrival, Christina had at least become tolerant of Mary after she realized Mary would be at her every beck and call. Mary really dreaded fixing her hair, as she knew it could take nearly an hour to comb through. She couldn't understand what Christina did while she slept that managed to turn her hair into such a tangled mess. She was sure the thick, sticky lacquer she insisted be sprayed on after perfect marcel waves were formed had something to do with it.

"Hurry up," Christina pestered as Mary tried to hasten the process, which only caused the comb to get tangled and pull at the knotted hair. "You're doing that on purpose!" Christina whined, slapping at Mary's hands.

After a full hour and a half, hair finally done to perfection, and Miss Christina properly stuffed into a white and pink lace and taffeta dress, she was ready to greet the returning travelers. Mary wished she had time to tidy herself up a bit and hastily checked her own reflection in the mirror. Then she walked to the door, opened it, and waited for Miss Christina.

"Where do you think you're going?" Christina snapped at her. Mary stood silently as Christina tossed her head, depositing her freshly waved hair behind her, and walked toward the door. "I want you to tidy up my room, press the blue dress with the puffy sleeves, find the matching shoes, and see Bea about a yard's length of blue satin ribbon for my hair. I want a bath ready at six, and because Mother said you would be busy helping Bea in the kitchen this evening, lay out my nightclothes and turn down my bed before reporting back to her."

Mary stood staring at the door Christina had just slammed in her face. She had just assumed she too would meet the Colton men upon their return. She silently scolded herself. She had to remember she wasn't a member of the family, just part of the hired help.

He didn't know why he let those green eyes haunt him, but they did. He tried to go about his day-to-day business, but they were always waiting for him when night fell. There, alone in his bed, they pursued him. They tormented him. They were unforgettable, those green eyes that shimmered with tears. And they always awakened the beast.

CHAPTER 9

The afternoon flew by as Mary busied herself attending to all Miss Christina's requests and helping Bea with last-minute details. By six o'clock, the Colton family had all retreated to their respective rooms to prepare for the evening. The extra help had arrived, and Bea was instructing them on their duties. The dining room was set for a banquet. Mary had never seen such a spectacular sight.

"'Tis more food than you ever seen, eh?" Maggie asked as she entered the room and spread her arms wide as if to gather in everything in one sweep.

"It certainly is!" Mary said, truly amazed.

Maggie crossed the room, swinging her hips and head back and forth until she stood beside Mary and then holding her head high and chin extended. Mary, a perplexed look on her face, was trying to determine why Maggie was acting so peculiar.

"Don't ya be noticin' anythin'?" Maggie finally questioned, lifting her chin even farther into the air and raising her chest so that Mary couldn't help but notice the fine silver necklace decorating her neck. Mary stepped closer to examine the new piece of jewelry Maggie was undoubtedly trying to get her to notice—a small teardrop-shaped diamond suspended by a delicate silver chain.

"It's beautiful," Mary whispered as she carefully cradled the jewel in her fingertips and watched how it glimmered in the light from the chandelier. "Where'd you get it?" she asked, gently letting the necklace fall back to Maggie's throat.

Maggie smiled a devilish grin and rolled her eyes as if to give Mary the impression she wasn't going to tell her. Then her bubbling excitement got the best of her, and she blurted, "'Tis from James."

"Really? He bought it for you?"

"Yes." Maggie gleamed with delight. "From New York!"

Maggie wanted so much to tell Mary what James had said when he gave her the gift, how he was sorry about his words the night of the party, that he had been so upset about the whole thing while he was in New York, and how he had never wanted to hurt her. Moreover, the gift of the tear-shaped diamond was to ask for forgiveness for any hurt he might have caused her. That he hoped she understood they were very good friends, and he was sorry if he had spoiled that by his inconsiderate words. He had begged her forgiveness, not knowing she would have forgiven him anything just for the asking.

Both girls stood face-to-face, eye-to-eye, in unprecedented silence. Maggie could tell by the look on Mary's face she was struggling to ask why James would buy her such a gift. Knowing she hadn't told Mary about the incident that led to this present of apology, she waited to see what Mary's response would be. Finally, to Maggie's relief, Mary broke the silence by simply saying, "It's a very nice present."

"Thank you," Maggie replied, for more than just the compliment, and tucked the necklace inside her blouse and out of sight. Perhaps she'd tell her all about it someday.

"Come on, I want to show you something else!" Maggie squealed as she pulled Mary by the hand and then dragged her through room after room, weaving their way through the house until they stood before the large wooden doors near the end of the west wing. Mary had never ventured this far into the west wing, and she felt uncomfortable just being there. It was the same feeling she'd had when Betty Sue talked her into going down to Miller's pond last summer. Betty Sue had told her there were the most interestingly beautiful flowers that grew down on the edge of the pond, and Mary just had to see them, knowing all along that a few of the boys had planned to go swimming there that afternoon. Mary's curiosity had gotten the best of her, and she had watched right along with Betty Sue as the boys swam and horsed around in nothing more than their underclothes. She felt quite guilty about the whole thing for a long time, and she hoped Maggie wasn't up to something that she was going to have to feel guilty about.

"I don't think we should be here," she whispered.

Maggie laughed as boldly as she always did. Mary waved her hand furiously to quiet her before they got into real trouble.

"Oh, you're nothin' but a fraidy cat, Mary," Maggie scolded. "Come on."

Maggie turned the large brass knob on one of the big wooden doors, and before it had completely swung open, she pushed Mary inside. Mary stood, her body statue-like as her neck craned from side to side, trying to see the entire room at once.

"This," Maggie stated, once again spreading her arms wide and then swirling around, "'tis the grand room."

"And grand it is!" Mary echoed.

The room was bigger than any she had ever seen. Sparkling chandeliers, even larger than the one in the dining room, hung at intervals across the ceiling. Brocade-backed chairs stood along the walls, and small tables surrounded by chairs were positioned in clusters all around the room. Along the end of the entire back wall was a wooden bar with a shiny brass footrail, and the wall behind it was covered with mirrors. Gleaming wooden shelves held crystal glasses of all different shapes and sizes. In the center of the room was an open area, and Maggie explained the guests would dance there. The music was provided by a ten-piece orchestra that would arrive around eight o'clock and play into the wee hours of the morning. Maggie said at first they would play music strictly for the high hats, but later on in the evening, they would really let it fly for those who wanted to cut a rug. And if they played "Sweet Georgia Brown," Maggie said someone might have to be there to hold her down, or she might just be overcome by the music and cut a rug right along with the rest of them. Mary cautiously crossed the room and stood in the middle of the dance floor. Wrapping her arms around herself, she floated across the floor. She didn't know much about cutting a rug, but she did love to dance. She closed her eyes as she swayed around, imagining what it would be like to dance to a ten-piece orchestra in this very grand room.

"Vhat's going on here?" Bea demanded sternly. Mary's eyes flew open and watched the broad smile she had silently wished there cover Bea's face. As Bea entered the room, the extra help tagging behind her, Maggie and Mary scooted past them out the door. They quickly wove their way back through the house and into the kitchen where they both giggled with delight.

Not long after the party had started, Mary was envious of Maggie, who had been coming in and out of the kitchen, each time leaving with a big silver tray full of tiny sandwiches, only to return in short order with a tray of crumbs. On each return to the kitchen, she would bring new details from the party to Mary's waiting ears. Mrs. Hammerstead, the mayor's wife, was wearing an awful dress that was bright pink. By 9:30, Mr. Harper, the town clerk, was already intoxicated. Mary didn't find it as humorous as Bea until Maggie explained to her about Prohibition. Mary had heard the word before but hadn't been exactly sure what it meant. Now that she knew, she was going to be sure to write to her father about it. She knew Mr. Fletcher and Papa drank the corn squeezin' Mr. Fletcher made. Papa kept some in a mason jar on a high shelf in the kitchen, and that was certainly alcohol. She remembered her brother Johnny telling her so. She wondered if Papa knew it was against the law.

By 10:30, Mary could hardly stand the suspense. She just had to see what was going on all around the house while she was stuck in the kitchen. She pleaded her case to Bea how she had never even been to a party.

"Unless you count Betty Sue's birthday party, and that didn't really count because I only got to stay a short time, because by the time I got to Betty Sue's house, everyone was already inside, and it took me almost half an hour to run past the big black dog and up to the porch, and by then all the children were done playing games and ready to eat cake, and the cake wasn't even very good because Mrs. Fletcher wasn't a good cook, and, and . . ." She was out of breath. Bea had finally given in, knowing Mary just had to get a glimpse of the party or she would certainly come apart.

So there she stood in the doorway between the kitchen and the dining room. The heavy door that swung on big hinges was open ever so slightly as she held it with her foot, peering through the tiny crack, being very quiet like Bea had instructed. She wasn't quite sure why, though. There was really nothing going on in the dining area. Most of the guests, by that time, were in the grand room dancing to the wonderful music that faintly made its way through the big house. Mary sighed as she leaned more heavily on the door frame, observing the few guests that popped in and out of the dining room. It was at least a glimpse. There were three young women who seemed to be permanently seated with Christina on some of the many chairs that were lined up against the wall. Mary listened as Christina told her faithful eating companions about the wonderful present James had brought her from New York. Mary knew, from Bea's report, that Christina and the other three had been sitting there most of the evening, trying at least one of everything from the feast spread before them. Christina held her arm up to show them the gold bracelet adorning her pudgy little wrist.

"And it's *real* gold," she mumbled through a mouthful of strawberry tart. Each girl oohed and ahhed through their own full mouths. Mary closed her eyes and leaned her head against the doorjamb. She wondered if she should continue her eavesdropping or return to the kitchen. After all, she mused, Maggie's tidbits of what was going on in the grand room were much more interesting than watching Miss Christina and company stuff themselves.

"So here's where you've been hiding." A deep male voice filled the dining room. Mary's eyes popped open and strained to peer through the tiny slit. The tall, dark-haired man stood facing Christina, allowing Mary only a view of his back. She silently cursed herself for missing his entrance. Christina diligently wiped strawberry tart from her lips and whined back at him. "I have not been hiding. I've been here all evening."

The tall, gangly girl sitting closest to Christina sniveled, "Where have you been all evening?"

"Well, Miss Chourchaine, I've actually been tied up speaking to some colleagues about very dry and boring business matters."

Mary's mind was reeling. Could this possibly be James Colton?

"We were all just admiring Christina's bracelet." Miss Chourchaine's voice was as thick as syrup as she batted her eyelids in an attempt to be sultry. Mary wondered if she were going to have a spell or had some type of ailment.

The man nodded his head in her direction and then, once again turning to Christina, he teased, "This afternoon you made me promise to save you a dance, and now you've forgotten." Christina's companions all seemed to be in some type of trance as they just stared at the tall man in a strange display of adoration. Mary's eyes burned into the back of his head, waiting, hoping he might feel he was being watched and instinctively look over his shoulder. But her plan didn't seem to be working.

"No, I haven't!" Christina retorted as she handed off her plate to Miss Chourchaine and rose to take the gentleman's extended hand.

"Excuse us, ladies. My sister and I have the next dance."

It *was* James Colton! As they exited to the entry hall, Mary dared to lean a little more heavily on the door, widening her viewing crack, only to be caught off balance. The door flung open, and she practically tumbled into the dining room. Luckily, by that time, her only audience were the three young ladies, all aghast at her display. She recovered, quickly straightening herself and acting as if she had tripped over something. She moved quickly across the room, hoping to still get a glimpse of James Colton. Coming to the entryway that led to the long hall, she watched disappointedly as he and Christina disappeared down the corridor that led to the grand room.

The beast was relentless by nature. He never tired of the game. It was becoming a constant battle to try and suppress his want for amusement. Though he would only surface under cover of darkness to perform his deeds, to reap his reward, he was always present, badgering the host day after day. The game had to be played, even though his victory was now inevitable. His need was greater than the host's will. He knew it was just a matter of time. The beast would win again.

CHAPTER 10

Mary had gotten her first pay from Mrs. Colton, who had made it quite clear that the doll she had broken was very expensive. Rather than deduct for it all at once, she said she was doing Mary the favor of deducting only a portion at a time. Mary, just excited about getting her first pay, could hardly wait to be excused from the room.

She sat on her small bed and carefully opened the envelope, peeking inside. Then, opening it wide, she turned it upside down and watched the bills float, one by one, onto the beige counterpane that covered her cot. When the small cascade had finished, she carefully checked the manila envelope before depositing it on the small table. Picking up the bills one at a time, she examined each of them. Eighteen dollars! It was the most money she had ever had at one time. She counted it three times, just to make sure her first two inventories were correct.

After lying around her room the entire morning until she thought she would go quite mad, she decided to take a walk to the library where Aunt Matilda would be working. Perhaps she could find an interesting book to read, or at least pass the time.

She left the house through the kitchen door, as the servants were not allowed to use the front entrance. Bea bid her farewell with "Be careful, dear."

As she strolled in the sunshine of the beautiful fall afternoon, she absently reached her hand into her jacket pocket to make sure the two dollars she had carefully deposited there before leaving were still in place. Running her fingers across the smooth, crisp bills set her mind at ease, and she continued her steady pace down the walk. She wasn't at all sure what she planned on doing with the two dollars, but she had decided to put sixteen dollars of her earnings away. She would save it. For what. she wasn't certain.

A beaming smile crossed her face. It was a good day. Bea had apparently been wrong about the early snowfall she had predicted that morning. Both Mary and Maggie had chimed in that it was too early for snow. Bea had insisted that because her knees ached, it was most certainly going to turn cold and snow before the day was done.

As Mary walked, she noticed how many of the leaves had fallen from the trees, but those that remained seemed to be shouting the last hurrah of fall. Red, gold, and bright orange all shone above her as the breeze danced them in the sunlight.

At last, she reached the mountain of steps leading to the doors of the library. Once inside, she marveled at the rows and rows of shelves that held countless books of various colors and sizes. What a wonderful place it must be to work, she thought to herself, and for an instant, she almost envied Aunt Matilda. She carefully walked toward the massive front desk, being certain not to shuffle her feet or let her heels click on the floor. She knew from her first visit two weeks earlier that any noise in the library annoyed her aunt immensely.

Her painstaking attempt to enter silently was rewarded as she now stood directly in front of her aunt, only the counter between them. Matilda, scanning number after number as she flipped through rows of small white cards, had not even noticed her.

Mary stood motionless. Not even her steady breathing was audible. She pursed her lips slightly, and her brow furrowed, contemplating the best way to get her aunt's attention without startling her. Finally, she cleared her throat ever so slightly. "Mm-mm."

Aunt Matilda immediately lifted her head, her squinty eyes peering over the top of her wire-rimmed glasses.

"Yes," she whispered before she even realized it was Mary. "Oh," her voice softened from its business-like tone, "it's you. What on earth are you doing here, dear?"

Mary couldn't decide if her aunt sounded annoyed or just surprised.

"I had the—"

"Shhh," Aunt Matilda scolded, instantly silencing her. She came out from behind the counter, grabbed Mary's hand, and led her to the back of the library, where they entered through a large door into a small storage room. Matilda left the door open slightly, allowing her to keep her vast domain in view.

"Now," Aunt Matilda's voice was still a whisper, though Mary had noticed on the journey to the small room only a few people were actually in the library, "what were you going to say, dear?"

Mary took a deep breath as if she were going to speak in a loud voice, and then she whispered, "I have the day off, and I just thought I'd come over to say hello, and maybe, perhaps, get a book to read."

She had to wait for her aunt's response, as once again Matilda was peering through the open door, surveying the nearly empty library.

"Well," she finally stated, not scolding, as Mary had feared, but just matter-of-fact, "I'm glad you did. I have something for you. I received a letter from your father. Apparently, he didn't know how to post it to you at the Coltons', so he sent it to me."

Mary could hardly hide her excitement as she tried to rip the envelope from her aunt's hands after Matilda produced it from her skirt pocket.

"Now ..." her aunt was almost lecturing as she dangled the envelope in front of Mary's face, unaware she was doing so, as her head was again turned toward the open door, "if you like," she continued, waving the envelope with each word, "you could stay here at the library until I close at five o'clock, and then we could have time to talk before you return to the Coltons'."

"Yes, yes!" Mary impatiently agreed, silently vowing to endure anything as long as her aunt would hand her the letter.

Her waiting fingers snatched the envelope the very second Matilda released her grip. She tore it open, unconcerned by the noise the ripping paper made, nor the shushing noise Aunt Matilda made as she left the room. Quickly finding the first chair she could, and sincerely trying to be quiet, she sat down and unfolded the one-page letter. She read from *Dear Mary* to *Love Papa* so many times that by five o'clock, when her aunt was getting ready to close the library for the evening, she had committed the letter to memory.

Outside the entrance, Mary waited as her aunt turned the key to lock the large doors and then checked each one twice.

"What did your father have to say, dear?" Aunt Matilda inquired.

"Oh," Mary sighed, "just that he missed me and that the weather was turning cold and things like that." She hoped her aunt would be satisfied with her measly answer. Although the letter really hadn't contained much more, it was her letter, not Matilda's.

Aunt Matilda could not upset her, even if she tried. She was as happy at that moment as she had been in weeks. She had the day to herself, she had finally received a letter from Papa, and she had two dollars in her pocket. Instantly, she shoved her hand in her pocket to verify the contents. Aunt Matilda was rambling on about how she really hadn't expected anyone for dinner, and she wasn't sure what she could prepare on such short notice, but . . .

"Let me treat you to dinner at the diner," Mary blurted out the invitation just as quickly as the thought had popped into her head.

Aunt Matilda stopped short, turned, and bumped into her. But before she could protest, as Mary was sure she would, it was Mary's turn to ramble on.

"I got my first pay from the Coltons, and I'm really not sure what I'd do with the money otherwise. I'm so happy. I'd like to treat you for the trouble I'm sure I've been to you." Matilda accepted the invitation more readily than Mary would have ever imagined. And so, as if now on a mission, the two set off, walking briskly toward the diner, which was only a few blocks from the library.

They both ordered the special, a chicken dinner. Aunt Matilda, didn't want Mary to spend her hard-earned money foolishly, and Mary, very unsure of what a diner charged, was suddenly concerned that what had earlier seemed a tidy sum of money would now not be enough to cover whatever the charge might be.

The two women engaged in small talk about how things were going with the Coltons and, of course, Matilda's unending infatuation, to Mary's dismay, with Mr. Bellows. Mary noticed the waitress strolling toward their table with a small white piece of paper. She set a thin smile on her face as the waitress put the ticket in her extended hand, still worried the figure on the ticket would be greater than the amount in her pocket. One dollar and ninety-eight cents. She beamed. Her aunt, noticing her relief, offered to leave the waitress a tip, which she explained to Mary was customary, and she would be more than happy to cover it as Mary had so generously provided her dinner.

As they left the diner, Mary realized for the first time that she almost felt as though her aunt was really a part of her family and not just an old spinster lady she happened to know.

Evening had started to set in, and the wind had picked up as they left the diner.

"I guess I hadn't realized it was so late," Aunt Matilda fretted. "I really don't like the idea of you walking all the way back to the Coltons' alone. By the time you get back there, it will be dark, and with that man loose somewhere in the city, well, I just don't like it," she huffed.

Before Mary could object, Aunt Matilda whined that she was sure Tom would be home and perhaps he could walk her back to the Coltons. She was certain he wouldn't mind, and she would just feel so much better about it. She had also half-heartedly offered to drive Mary there in her auto machine, but she did only use it for long distances and would rather not waste the gasoline.

"It has gone up to twenty cents a gallon," she complained.

On the short walk to her aunt's apartment, Mary prayed feverishly Tom would not be home or would just refuse her aunt the favor.

As they stood in front of the door to the Bellows' apartment, Aunt Matilda knocked softly. She presented Mary and then asked the favor in such a manner that anyone would have thought by the acceptance of the deed they were practically saving her life. She gave Mary a quick hug and said a hasty goodbye.

Once outside, Mary and Tom walked silently at a steady pace, which Mary set. She kept her head straight forward and tried to imagine he was just a stranger who happened to be walking next to her. She noticed how the night air had now turned cold. Sporadic bursts of wind caused the fallen leaves to circle around their feet as they walked. Tom was being completely silent, and Mary was indeed thankful. She certainly didn't want to make conversation, at least not with Tom. She didn't like him at all. For all her aunt knew, he could be the one committing those awful acts Ezra Bellows had spoken about. Either the thought of that or the wind, she wasn't sure which, sent a chill down her spine, and she hugged her arms about her. Instantly, Tom lifted his arm and wrapped it around her back. She jumped away, and a small scream escaped her lips.

"What are you doing?" she demanded.

"I, I . . ." he stuttered, shocked at her display. "I thought you were cold. I was just going to warm you up," he snapped. The words held more a tone of anger than apology.

"Well," Mary scoffed, trying to look intimidating, "don't ever touch me again."

Tom shoved his hands into his pants pockets, and his eyes grew darker as he said, "Maybe I should just let you walk the rest of the way by yourself."

"That would be just fine with me," Mary huffed back at him then watched him turn on his heel and march back the way they had come. Mary tossed her head, and with chin held high, turned and resumed her pace into the night air.

She was glad to be rid of him but then suddenly realized she didn't like being alone either. She tried to convince herself she was just being silly. *After all*, she mused, *back home I'd walk by myself from Betty Sue's house after dark, and I wasn't afraid then. Oh, but this city was a much different place than home.* She found herself checking over her shoulder and realized it was the odd noise the wind made as it swept past her. The tree limbs creaked in the strengthening wind, and off in the distance, there was the insistent howling of an agitated dog. It had grown quite dark now, and the moon, only a sliver in the night sky, added little comfort. She stiffened as she noticed the lamps of an automobile approaching from behind her, but she kept her gaze straight forward, not wanting to be noticed by anyone. The whine of the engine slowed as it neared her, and she could tell the driver was veering over closer to where she walked. She quickened her pace slightly, hoping it would just go away, but to her distress, it appeared to be following her. Then it jolted to a stop, and she heard the door open.

"Ma'am," the voice was deep and masculine, yet soft, and almost inviting. "Could I offer a ride?" he questioned. "It's turning quite cold, and snowfall is expected."

Mary's brain was urging, *run, run,* but something else urged her to stop and turn toward the gentleman standing next to the motorcar. Dark shadows from the tree-lined street allowed her only the silhouette of a tall ,slender man—no more, and no less.

"Do you have a distance to go?" he inquired.

Something in his voice—she couldn't pinpoint it—sounded familiar and truly concerned for her welfare.

"A few miles," she offered shyly.

The man jogged around the auto, opened the door, and with a sweep of his hand, motioned her into the vehicle. "Your carriage awaits."

Her brain, screaming now, said, *no, no,* while her feet moved slowly toward the auto and the inviting voice. She settled herself into the seat, and he shut the door. As he got in next to her, she wished that the street lamps provided better lighting with which to view him.

"Where to, miss?" he asked, putting the car into gear.

Mary suddenly realized she didn't know the name of the street that the Coltons lived on.

"The Coltons'," she finally stated, matter-of-fact.

"Oh," was his response.

Her mind rebuked. *He knows you don't live there. Why would a Colton be walking out by herself? He probably realizes you're just a servant, and now he's disappointed he bothered to stop.*

As they drew closer to the Coltons', Mary suddenly remembered the big iron gates would be locked, and entrance only allowed by informing the house of your presence. Her conscience told her to just ask him to drop her off by the servants' entrance gate. *No,* she silently quarreled, *then he'll know you're just one of the servants.* Maybe he knows the Coltons, and with your cotton dress and worn cloth coat, he already knows you're not one of them, she contended mutely, until the big gates stood in front of them. She was silent as he reached out the auto's window and pushed the button. She predicted the coming events in her head. Charles would answer the buzzer with his usual "May I help you?" and she would have to endure total embarrassment or, worse yet, be reprimanded by Mrs. Colton. She closed her eyes, wringing her hands in her lap.

"May I help you?" Charles's starched voice came scratchily through the little box.

"The gate, please," was all the man next to her said.

She slowly opened her eyes as she noticed the auto was moving again and watched dumbfounded as they proceeded through the opening gates. Rounding the big circle drive, the motorcar came to a stop in front of the main entrance. As the man helped her from the auto, she kept her head lowered. *If I ever meet him again,* she thought, *perhaps he won't recognize me.* She knew she could never identify him, as she still hadn't really seen his features. The large door swung open.

"Good evening," was Charles's only statement, monotone as ever.

Depositing her on the steps, the man said a hurried goodbye as she shuffled through the open doorway, not even thanking him for his time. She and Charles stood alone in the grand entry hall. She picked up her head, looked Charles straight in the eye, stood on her tiptoes, and gave him a kiss on his pale white cheek.

"Thank you," she gleefully chimed.

"Whatever for?" he asked.

It was only after she had scurried down the hall toward the kitchen that Charles chuckled as he placed his palm over his freshly kissed cheek.

CHAPTER 11

Lying on his back, James Colton stared blankly at the ceiling above his massive carved cherry wood bed, contemplating the events of the evening. He knew Charles had not let on to his little caper. Charles was a good old fella. Hell, he was probably more of a father figure to him than his own father. Indeed, he mulled, wasn't it Charles who had taken him to the clothier for his first real suit? A low chuckle escaped his lips as he recalled the old man's words when he had asked how the girl had reacted.

"She kissed me!" he had declared, and James could see the poor man's embarrassment but had noticed it had brought some color to the chap's pale complexion.

James repositioned himself among the feather pillows, closed his eyes, and recalled the first time he had seen Miss Mary Watson. It was the day he returned home with his father from the New York business trip. It was late afternoon before any guests had arrived. He had been in the library with the elder Colton, discussing business. As always, he was trying to get his father to see things his way, which of course was the wrong way, according to William Colton. He had listened to a half hour of his father beating his gums as to why modernization was not only costly but foolish, and then the subject of—in his father's words—that confounded Henry Ford, who was talking about instituting a forty-hour workweek, was brought up. James, who had paced the room from one side to the other, wasn't really listening by then and had let the voices from the next room wander into his head. They were muffled but definitely female. He nonchalantly positioned himself near the slightly opened library door, in hopes of overhearing their conversation. One voice had been Maggie's—James knew it well—but he hadn't recognized the other voice. They had been discussing Christina. Maggie had spoken next, referencing Christina as the little Dumb Dora, which James sadly knew was a more suitable description of his sister. He had leaned his tall frame against the heavy door so that it would appear he hung on every word his father uttered, nodding his head every so often just for appearance, while he had let his eyes focus through the opening, perhaps to catch a glimpse of the two young women. Maggie appeared to have been dusting as she moved around the room waving a cloth to and fro. Mary, whom he didn't know at the time, followed her around, repositioning knickknacks and doodads that Maggie was leaving out of place. James had caught just a glimpse of the young girl with the golden hair pinned tightly to the nape of her neck. Finally, they had both stood in front of the tall shelf that held the many music boxes his mother collected. In perfect view, James had hoped the shelves' contents would keep them there long enough for him to get a good look at her. When he had, he instantly knew she was the most enchanting creature he had ever seen. Even from that distance, he could almost feel the smoothness of her creamy skin. She had a perfect little nose and cherry red lips, and he doubted she had applied any lip rouge, which all the dolls were doing these days. Her neck was thin and long and lovely, and the smooth curve of her hips was accentuated by the little white apron tied tightly around her waist. For the first time, he agreed with his mother's decision to have the help wear those silly outfits.

He threw back the overpowering feather quilt, which suddenly seemed to be smothering him.

"Why is it so hot in here?" he muttered to himself.

Swinging his feet to the floor, he stood up and crossed the room to the French doors. He pulled open the flocked brocade drapery and peered out the glass windowpanes. He could hear the wind howling through the trees, and the cold draft that blew through the small crack between the doors felt good on his bare chest. Fallen leaves that had landed on the small balcony outside his room were being swirled into a small pile in one corner. The sliver of moon in the cloud-covered sky shed little light on the dark night, but enough to notice the fluffy white flakes that had started to fall and swirl in the night air. James chuckled, thinking to himself that Bea had been right as usual. She had told him earlier that evening, when he had inquired of Mary's whereabouts, that it was going to snow that evening. James knew by now you didn't doubt Bea's weather predictions. She was just never wrong. He remembered when he was a little boy and would sit for hours with Bea in the kitchen watching her cook, never tiring of her stories. She would tell him when it was going to snow and when it was going to rain, and he couldn't recall one of her predictions ever being incorrect. She would tell him all about her life in Germany, and how she came over to "dis country" on a big boat, with her mutter and vatter, and her husband. There had been a bad sickness on the boat, and her mother and father had died, never making it to America. So she and her husband found a place to live, and her husband went to work. They were going to have a big house someday and fill it with lots of children. But they waited a very long time, and they never had any children, and that had made her husband very sad. James remembered the story exactly as Bea had told it to him when he was a child. *Then, von day, I kissed my Hans goodbye.* She always looked so sad when she came to that part. *He left for vork, but he never came back home to me. I tink he could not be happy with no little vons. So din I vas all alone, and I had to get a job, and your Mama, she hired me to take care ov you and dis big house.* James remembered how Bea's story had made him feel sad for her, but he was very glad Bea lived in his house. By the time he was ten, it was Bea he sought out to discuss his childhood problems. He ran to her when he got hurt. He looked to her for advice, attention, and affection. His parents, especially his mother, resented his relationship with Bea. When his sister Christina was born, his mother decided she would not hire a nurse to care for the baby but would do it herself. James chuckled now as he muttered to himself, "What a wise decision."

He suddenly remembered Bea's comparison earlier that evening of Mary and his sister Christina. James was certain the closeness in their ages was their only likeness. *She's very young, Mr. James,* Bea had scolded. *Just a couple years older dan your sister. Dis is her first time avay from home. You be nice to her.* She had waved a big wooden spoon at him teasingly.

As he continued to stare out into the darkness, he recalled the second time he had seen Mary. It was the very next day after overhearing the conversation in the parlor between her and Maggie. He had slept in that morning, as the party had gone quite late the night before. When he had finally awakened, the sun was invading his room with waves of golden light, as he had not thought to pull the draperies on the French doors the night before. He had arisen cautiously, his head pounding and body aching from the liquor he had filled it with. He had crossed the room with the intention of yanking shut the drapery to stop the insistent rays of sun from burning his eyes. His hand clenched full of red brocade, he had quickly glanced out the window and noticed movement in the gardens. It was Bea and Mary. Bea was busy cutting and snipping away at the last blooms of autumn flowers. Mary stood next to her, holding a basket in which Bea was placing her treasures. A light breeze blew against the young girl's frame, pulling her light cotton dress taut against her body. James observed her silhouette. Even in his state of discomfort, he was urged to look on, watching until the two women left the garden.

That afternoon, he had interrogated Christina about Mary. In short order, it was plain to see Christina detested her. Most likely, James supposed, because Mary possessed everything Christina did not.

"She's mean, and she thinks I'm ugly, and she tells me I should do this, and I should do that. I think she should just mind her own beeswax!" Christina had shouted at him. Then, because James offered her no sympathy, she had told him Mary had broken her favorite doll. James had responded by saying he thought another doll was her favorite, after which she had retorted, "Oh, go chase yourself."

He had finally appeased her by offering to replace the doll, and not to his surprise, she had said she would rather he buy her something else, which he also agreed to, but she had refused to offer any more information about Mary.

He had continued his investigation with Bea, who was really no help at all and would provide only basic information, being her name and position at the Coltons'. He had joked that he was not inquiring about a soldier, and Bea could disclose more than name, rank, and serial number. But the only additional tidbit he received was the fact that Maggie and Mary had become quite good friends.

He had instantly sought out Maggie and had made plans to meet with her the next afternoon at the ice cream parlor. He knew it was one of her favorite places, and plying Maggie with ice cream was the equivalent of using liquor to do the same with most other people. He hoped he could disguise his interest in Mary enough that Maggie did not become suspicious. He knew Maggie was no longer mad at him. His gift of the little tear-shaped pendant and his apology had made things right between them. He had certainly never intended to hurt her. He thought she now realized they were just friends—well, perhaps a bit more than friends. His reputation of being a ladies' man certainly preceded him. His father said he was sowing his wild oats. James believed he was just playing the part. After all, he was the most eligible bachelor in town. He was young, and apparently the women found him attractive, and probably more important to them was the fact that he stood to inherit a sizable fortune. It wasn't that he didn't work for it. After all, trying to contend with his father in the business world was a very difficult proposition. Not that his father was a bad businessman, but given the opportunity, he knew he could certainly increase profits substantially, and probably more securely. He certainly didn't like the way his father invested so heavily in the stock market. But, he presumed, the time would come for his turn with the family fortune. He supposed he couldn't do any worse with his mother's money than his father had. For if the truth be known, his mother had come to the marriage with what was now the Colton Empire. Not that his father hadn't contributed to it over the years, but had William Colton not married Cordella Shell, he would not have been a wealthy man. James did know for certain he never wanted to marry for the sake of marriage. Now, at the age of twenty-four, his mother had been prodding him for months that it was time to consider the bonds of matrimony. James knew if Cordella Colton had her way, Miss Diane Beaumont would certainly be the next Mrs. Colton. After all, the Beaumont money would coexist handsomely with the Coltons'. The problem was James didn't love Diane. He knew such a foolish little thing like love didn't matter to his mother, or apparently Diane for that matter, but it mattered to him. He wasn't at all sure what true love would feel like, but he knew he would recognize it when, and if, it came. He didn't want a business arrangement like that of his parents, and he didn't want just a physical attraction—as did most of his friends. He wanted a forever and ever kind of love, one you didn't walk away from just because things didn't work out the way you planned. The kind of love you never walked away from, because it was stronger than any other force on Earth. He dearly believed, in all the world, each person was allowed one true love. He also believed most people never found it, some never looked for it, some never knew what they were looking for, and some just settled for less. But for him, it would be the once in a lifetime or nothing at all.

Maggie had given him all the information she knew about Miss Mary Watson. He had grilled her for an entire afternoon, but she was unaware he was doing so as he also filled the conversation with dazzling descriptions of his latest trip to New York. Maggie had been mesmerized by his account of the moving picture he had seen, *The Gold Rush* with Charlie Chaplin. She was most interested in the story line of the prospector who had fallen in love with the saloon girl. Maggie, in turn, had answered all of his questions, including sharing with him the fact that Mary now had Thursdays off.

After returning home from the plant on Thursday, he had inquired of Bea as to Mary's whereabouts and was told she had gone to the library. After a quick change from his stiff collar shirt and jacket to a pair of khakis and large collared sweater, he had grabbed his polo jacket and left the house. By the time he reached the library, it had already closed for the evening. He had been circling the tree-lined street when he happened to notice the small diner and the two women seated at a booth close to the front window. He presumed the lady seated across from Mary was the aunt Maggie had spoken of. But there was no mistaking the enchanting girl he had yet to meet, but who intrigued him like no other. It was most definitely Mary.

He had parked the roadster down an adjoining street, concealed, yet giving him an ideal view of the front door of the diner. By the time the two women emerged, the sun was almost set, creating sweeping violet rays over the city. Letting them get far enough ahead so as not to arouse suspicion, he had pulled out and followed them. After a short distance, they had ducked into a door next to Bellows Men's Apparel, and he found another inconspicuous place to park the roadster. Only a few moments had passed when the door reopened, and Mary and a young man had emerged back out onto the walk. By then, the sun had faded, and James could not get a good look at the young man by her side. He had followed them from a good distance for a number of blocks, then edged a little closer as it appeared the young man was putting his arm around her. He had sped up the auto and drove past them as the two appeared to be arguing, certain he had gone by unnoticed. He then swung around the block and waited patiently at the cross road before edging his way back out onto the street. He had driven past the man, walking in the opposite direction, and was delighted by the opportunity to stop and ask if she needed a ride.

How close she had been, seated next to him in the roadster. His hand, as he had reached for the shift lever only inches away from her knee, could have brushed it with his fingertips. Even though he had not done so, he had felt something in the closeness, something he had never felt before, something he wasn't able to describe. It was just a feeling, a very wonderful feeling. She had been silent in the car sitting next to him, only answering his one question of where to drive her. He knew Charles would recognize his voice and open the gate without question, and he was sure Mary had not seen the wink he had given Charles when he opened the door to them. Charles had understood and hadn't balled things up. He hurried off, deciding it best she not get too close a look at him. And according to Charles, she was none the wiser.

The howl of the wind outside the French doors suddenly made him shiver, and he returned to his bed. Re-fluffing the pillows, he closed his eyes, but he couldn't sleep. He knew she was in the house, his house. Breath suspended, he listened. The house was quiet but for the wind outside and the steady beat of his heart pounding in his chest.

The demon was becoming impatient. The game had been played, and he was once again the victor. He wanted his due reward for convincing his host that he too would share in the prize. When the demon won, so did the host. The belief in that was the demon's secret to winning the game.

CHAPTER 12

Mary examined her image in the mirror, turning her head from side to side. Maggie had somehow managed to take all her long golden hair, wrap it, pin it, and tuck it in, leaving only the very ends to curl out, making it look as though her hair had been bobbed in the latest style. She noticed Maggie's reflection in the mirror, eyebrows raised into a worried position, waiting for her approval.

"I love it!" she squealed, restoring Maggie's delightful smile.

There was a soft knock. The door opened, and Bea stuck her head past the half-opened door.

"You two lollygaggers better get a move on," she scolded. "Da extra help is already arrived, and dare's vork to be done. Oh, and Mary, your hair's da cat's paws," she added merrily before disappearing behind the closing door.

Both girls giggled at Bea's attempt to be chic, and even Mary, whose speech was being renovated by Maggie, chimed in, "Cat's meow!"

"I'll be goin' down," Maggie said as she handed the comb to Mary. "Ya get dressed, and I'll be tellin' Bea you be right along."

Mary checked her new hair one last time in the small mirror before seizing her freshly starched dress and apron. She dressed as quickly as possible while still using extra care not to disturb her new bob. She couldn't believe her luck. She was going to get to serve in the grand room. By the time she got down to the kitchen, the order of things was almost chaotic. But Bea was, as usual, seeing to it that it was at least an organized chaos. Mary had learned quickly that Bea could be undeniably firm when the situation called for it, as was evident by the orders she was shouting out to the temporarily hired help.

"Take dese to the grand room," she said as she thrust a large box full of tiny pumpkins and gourds at Mary. "Dey just arrived, and Mrs. Colton vants dem added to da decorations the groundskeeper is displaying."

Mary obeyed eagerly and hurried off to the grand room. She loved the grand room. It was the corridor she had to pass through to get there that troubled her. She entered the small passageway from the main entryway. She wasn't sure what it was that bothered her so—it was just a feeling she had each time she passed through it. The corridor followed the same curve of the turret, the wood on each side of the passageway curved to match its outside counterpart, from the main foyer through to the west wing of the house. There were no windows, of course, and Mary wondered if that was the reason it seemed to encase her, giving her an eerie impression. Normally, she would have gone through the library to enter the west wing of the house, thus avoiding the creepy passageway, but thanks to Bea, she knew Mr. Colton and James were in conference in the library. She still hadn't met the younger Mr. Colton, and she was beginning to wonder if she ever would. It seemed she was always just one step behind him. She would come into the kitchen, and Bea would tell her she had just talked to him. In fact, just that morning, he had apparently just left Christina's room before Mary had arrived there to help her with her attire for the costume ball. Emerging from the corridor, she scurried into the large entryway of the west wing and stood facing the large double doors of the west entrance, where within an hour or so, more than a hundred guests would drive up and be ushered from their autos, have their hats and coats taken from them, and be led into the grand room for the evening's festivities. The west wing was certainly the larger part of the house, encasing the library, the grand room, and several smaller rooms where coats were hung and entertaining supplies were stored. Bea had been a wealth of information about the house and had explained that Mr. and Mrs. Colton had added the west wing shortly after they had married and took up residence in the stately mansion. The west wing also housed separate facilities for both men and women. Mary giggled, remembering how speechless she had been when Maggie had given her a tour. There was a whole room filled with velvet-covered chairs and settees and small tables. When the Coltons were entertaining, Maggie explained, there would be ladies' maids stationed in the room to help the guests touch up their lip rouge or apply cold compresses for those who felt overcome by the festivities.

Down a short hallway, there was a staircase leading to the second floor, where there were rooms for overnight guests or couples who needed a secluded room for a quiet getaway or simply to rest. Mary hadn't a clue what Maggie had meant until she had noticed her lifted eyebrows and the sinful smirk that had crossed her lips. Mary had gasped then, and Maggie had, of course, giggled at her naivety.

Indeed, Maggie proved to be quite informed when it came to matters between men and women. She found herself thinking about Maggie's enlightenments often and would shyly question her about kissing and the petting she spoke of. Late at night, when the house was quiet and she lay in her bed staring blankly at the ceiling, she would recall the ride with the stranger and how the closeness of his hand to her knee had made her leg quiver and her body tingle. She wondered if the activities Maggie spoke of could be more exciting. Her thoughts, as they frequently did of late, quickly returned to that evening in the car with the intriguing man. She wondered if he would be at the party that evening. After all, he had known where the Coltons lived, and Charles had apparently recognized his voice and allowed him entry through the gate. He could be a friend of the family and would certainly be invited to the magnificent Halloween costume ball. Anxiousness managed to suppress the mounting fervor as she suddenly imagined that he indeed would be at the Colton home that very evening and perhaps recognize her. Surely, any chance of seeing him again under similar false pretenses as their first meeting would be impossible. And all the fantasies she'd had the pleasure of having in the last few weeks would be only that.

Suddenly, all the worrisome thoughts left her as she peered through the open doors into the grand room. Mr. Olson, the groundskeeper, and Freddie, his son, had somehow transformed the room—with its elegant high-hung chandeliers and shiny marble floors—into a mysteriously alluring, almost mystical forest clearing. Mr. Olson had brought in large tree stumps and small saplings and numerous potted bushes and shrubs. He had laid down heavy tarpaulins over a good portion of the floor and covered them with bushels of brightly colored leaves, representing a path that wound its way through the pretend forest. Large sheets of cloth, the color of midnight, had been draped from the ceiling and billowed around the chandeliers. The iridescent glow from behind the cloth created an imaginary night sky spotted with hazy stars. The only evidence left of the grand room was the stately bar that lined the back wall. The many tables and chairs had been scattered into small areas, and only a portion of the marble floor had been left uncovered for dancing.

Like Bea, Mr. Olson was bellowing orders out to anyone in sight. As Mary carefully wound her way around the room toward him, there was talk among the many hired help bustling around that a great magician by the name of Harry Houdini was apt to be at the party. He was back in the States, and perhaps the guests would be entertained with one of his amazing feats of magic. She would certainly like to see something as unique as that, Mary thought to herself. She wasn't certain, but she thought the man's name sounded familiar to her, and she decided he must indeed be famous if even she had heard of him. The night was sure to hold more excitement than Mary could imagine, and she could hardly wait for it to start.

He knew by late afternoon that he would have to go out that night. He knew he could not hold off the beast through another day. Those green eyes had been feeding the monster for weeks now.

CHAPTER 13

Cordella Colton sat at her dressing table that was scattered with jars and tins of powders and creams. She stared past them all into the large mirror that revealed every line and wrinkle of her aging face. She slapped the sagging skin that hung under her chin in an attempt to make it go away, then pushed at her baggy cheeks and tugged at the wrinkles around her eyes. Her cold blue eyes pierced into those of her own reflection, trying to comprehend that the pudgy and red-blotched face was her own. Determined not to believe it was her likeness, she invited the idea that the image in the mirror was that of her mother, coming back from the dead to scold her aging offspring.

"So, Mother," she spat at the mirror, "what naive advice do you have for me now?"

The mirrored image, unblinkingly silent, stared back at her. She picked up the silver-handled brush that lay on the silver tray, perfectly positioned between the matching comb and hand mirror. Shaking it at the image, she cursed. "I should have known you'd have nothing to say to me, Mother. Are you shocked by what I have become?"

She taunted the image in the mirror as she rose from her cushioned seat and began pacing around the room, brush still in hand, waving it through the air. "This is what I've become, Mother!" She opened her arms wide and spun around then chided the mirror, not grasping the reality that the image had vanished when she had stood. "The complete opposite of you. Were you so naive you didn't realize that you could have taken charge instead of weeping into your pillow every night? You thought love was the key, but I guess he showed you it didn't matter. Didn't matter!" she repeated as if her mother had contested the statement. "You taught me well, Mother. Your love for that man got you nowhere. You had no way out. The key wasn't love, Mother. It was money! And I am in charge of mine . . ." She hesitated, glancing over her shoulder at the mirror as if to make sure she still had her mother's attention, oblivious to the fact the image was no longer there. "A small fortune, Mother, and it's all mine—well, mostly," she scoffed.

"It's all about choices, Mother. Unlike you, I made the right ones."

Her pacing had brought her back to stand in front of the dressing table.

"Money can buy happiness, Mother!" She replaced the brush to its position on the silver tray as she sat down on the velour seat and reached with her other hand for an engraved cigarette case. She flipped the latch and removed one perfectly slim rolled cigarette, placing it precisely between the first and second fingers of her left hand. The reflection in the mirror caught her eye, and she squared herself to it. She laughed then, a deep, cynical laugh. "Truly a disgusting habit," she sneered at the reflection. "But it is the chic thing to do these days, so I simply must." She lit the cigarette and inhaled deeply, then slowly allowed the smoke to escape through her nostrils.

"Were you really so innocent, Mother, you didn't fathom manipulating father with anything other than your love? Your love for him that left you sobbing into your pillow night after night. What did all that love you had for him get you?"

Something resembling sympathy floated momentarily on her face but just as quickly disappeared as she scoffed at the image in the mirror and crushed out the burning end of the cigarette into a crystal dish. She laughed again, this time a revengeful snicker that floated past her lips, now deep red with lip rouge. "Yes, Mother, perhaps money cannot buy love, but neither does love always bring happiness."

William understood, unlike her father, what could be done about adulterous husbands. He knew all too well who really controlled the Colton fortune. She had seen to that right from the start. She had made certain that every document was prepared to her exact specification, and though, from all outward signs, it would appear her husband ran the business matters, she and her attorney knew the truth. As it was, if she were to die tomorrow, William would be left with a mere pittance of her great fortune, now that James was old enough. She sighed deeply as she once again picked up the brush from its resting place on the silver tray. She toyed with a few loose hairs and contemplated having Maggie sent up to tighten the pins, although the silly little twit would probably only worsen its condition. She so preferred the way Jeannette fashioned her hair, but she supposed the girl was resting as the doctor had instructed. She had certainly picked a fine time to be indisposed. After all, the costume ball was one of the grandiose events of the season. Some of the most elite guests were not from Bay View but came from New York or Chicago simply to attend the festivities. In fact, this very evening they were to have the privilege of the company of Mr. and Mrs. Harry Houdini.

She and William had had the magnificent opportunity to have met them in Paris earlier that year. She found Mr. Houdini to be very chic and quite a handsome fellow, and William had been totally enamored by his performance. William had extended a dinner invitation to the performer and his wife, and they had so graciously accepted. The four of them had chatted late into the evening at a quaint French restaurant, and to William's dismay, Ehrie—as he had asked to be called—would not reveal a single bit of insight into his great escapes. His wife, Bess, was equally as charming, and Mrs. Colton was immediately taken with them both. She had been so delighted to receive their affirmative reply, indicating they would be in the States as they were touring with a newly opened, full-evening show that cast the entertainer in three roles—magician, escapologist, and debunker of mediums. Usually she dreaded the ordeal of hosting such extravagant affairs and only endured them as it was her responsibility as the most prominent family in the area.

She relished the fact that at least this evening's affair would be enjoyable with the attendance of their special guests. She was sure Mr. Houdini would not refuse a small performance for their entertainment. After all, from what his wife said, Ehrie was completely enveloped in his work and loved nothing better than to amaze people with his talents.

Cordella rose from her padded seat and crossed the room to the gold-plated frame with the small buzzer positioned on the wall next to the door. She needed someone to come up to draw her bath. She pushed the buzzer several times, knowing that once was sufficient. She moved toward the bed and sat down on the edge, removing her shoes and rubbing her feet when she had done so. She had been inconvenienced enough with the fact that Jeannette was unable to style her hair. She was certainly not going to draw her own bath.

CHAPTER 14

Mary, humming softly to herself, made her way through the house toward the west wing with a large tray of appetizers. It was the third time Bea had filled the tray, and Mary had become quite comfortable offering selections to the exotically dressed guests that filled the grand room. She never could have imagined such a gay party. All the guests wore such fantastic costumes. There were knights, pirates, and even monsters dripping with realistic-looking blood. There were princesses, witches, and fairy tale characters. Everyone was talking about the most interesting subjects, and Mary found herself lingering long after a guest had selected one of the tiny sandwiches she was offering so she could listen to the conclusion of their discussions. Mr. and Mrs. Houdini had graced everyone with their presence and were truly the most sought-after guests of the evening. Mrs. Colton, costumed as Queen Elizabeth I, was busying herself with making sure every one of her other guests was aware that the Houdinis had most graciously accepted her invitation as they were such good friends now after dining with them in Europe. At one point, Mary had to stifle herself from almost giggling aloud as she overheard Mrs. Colton for the third time telling of her friendship with the Houdinis to yet another guest. Each time Mary overheard a conversation, the Houdinis and the Coltons became better friends. By the time Mrs. Colton was relating the story to Mrs. Hammerstead, the mayor's wife, the Houdinis were such good friends they had traveled extensively throughout Europe together.

As Mary emerged into the entry hall, she noticed Charles standing in front of the double-doored entrance to the grand room. The doors shut tightly behind him, he stood tall and stern as if a guard at the queen's palace. Mary gave him an inquisitive smile as she neared him.

"I'm sorry, miss," he offered apologetically. "Mr. Houdini has agreed to perform a bit of entertainment and has asked that no one leaves or enters during his performance."

From the look on his face, Mary's disappointment must have crushed the old man. Suddenly a twinkle of excitement sparked in his old gray eyes as he practically knocked Mary over and grabbed the tray from her hands. He set the tray, full of finger sandwiches, down on one of the several tables that stood in the entryway. Taking her hand and checking up and down the length of the entryway, he led her across the marble floor toward the coatroom, where all the guests' wraps were hanging neatly. It was surely better stocked than the most expensive furrier in town. Still tightly clasping her hand, he led her to the very back of the small room to a short and narrow door that went almost unnoticed, as it blended perfectly with the wood panels of cedar that covered the four walls. He reached into his pocket and produced a ring, which held several keys. Fingering through them until he gripped one small key, he inserted it into the tiny keyhole in the door placed precisely in a knothole of the wood. Using the key as a handle, he pulled the door open to reveal a small passageway, approximately three feet wide and five feet tall. Mary peered past him into the dark entrance and for a brief moment was convinced that Charles had gone daft, and now, with no one around to save her, she was sure he was going to lock her in a forgotten tunnel under the house. Then, ever so faintly, she could hear the laughter drifting its way through the tunnel, and looked to Charles for an explanation.

"It's a heating tunnel that surrounds the west side of the entire house," he explained. "It was built to encase the large furnace and supply heat to this wing. It's just a tunnel that gives access to all the heating ducts. Go ahead!" he urged, pushing her toward the entrance. "It's dark for a short distance, then you'll see a light. Just follow it, but be very quiet. Mrs. Colton will have my hide if she finds out. Don't stay too long."

He placed his hand on the top of her head and gently pushed her down while steering her through the opening. Once she was inside, he shut the door behind her.

The darkness surrounded her, and for an instant, she stood completely still, petrified, but then she heard the faint voices again coming from the passageway and mustered the courage to move forward. Not being able to see where it was she was going through the darkness, and having to crouch, she took small steps. To help guide her way, she placed her hands gently on the walls to either side of her—they were warm and made of stone. After about twenty feet, the tunnel turned sharply to the right, and a faint light appeared ahead of her. She quickly and quietly made her way toward the light. As she drew closer, she could hear the murmur of voices once again. Finally, she reached the large grate, through which the light immersed into the dark tunnel. She bent down to peer into the grand room. She could see several of the guests seated at the small tables, and several standing guests, all attentive to the performer. A hush had fallen over the room, and only small whispers filtered into the passageway. Unfortunately, her view of Mr. Houdini was blocked by a gentleman's leg, standing immediately in front of the iron grate through which she peered. She recognized the costume as the man who was dressed as a civil war general. She recalled the royal blue uniform and long sword that hung from his belt. She had only seen him from the back but remembered his dark black curly hair and his prominent stature. She could hear the performer, though, as he spoke in his accented voice, explaining to the audience that his wife was locking the chains around his ankles and wrists.

"Please, please, someone come forward and examine the chains," he invited anyone to make sure they were indeed secure. Everyone laughed when the chief of police finally volunteered. He then explained that his wife would open the trunk, and he again invited anyone in the audience to examine it. Mary, in haste, trying to reposition herself to attain a better view of whatever it was the gentleman's leg concealed, had forgotten the tunnel was only five feet in height. Her stature being five foot five, she soundly cracked her head on the stone ceiling, and she uttered a small gasp of pain. Instantly, her eyes closed, and her hands flew in the air, one to hold her hurting head, and the other to cover her imprudent mouth. She rubbed her head, and even through all the hair Maggie had piled and pinned there, she could feel a bump beginning to swell. She opened her eyes reluctantly, praying silently there would not be a crowd of people staring back at her. To her relief, no one in the room seemed to have noticed her intrusion, and mysteriously, the civil war general had disappeared, leaving her a direct view to Mr. Houdini, who by then had been securely locked in the big wooden trunk. She crouched silently, her hand still perched atop her head. Mrs. Houdini stood next to the trunk, while inside, her husband struggled to free himself and amaze the captive crowd. Mary wondered if it was hard to breathe in the trunk.

Suddenly, a rush of warm air began to filter through the tunnel, and Mary began to feel lightheaded. She pulled her hand from the iron grate on which she had placed it to steady herself in her new crouched position, and she rubbed the back of her neck. The coolness of her fingertips felt good on her warm skin, but soon she felt the unmistakable feeling of dizziness building inside her. She steadied herself as best she could, and thought it best to get out of the tunnel as quickly as possible. She stood carefully, not wanting to again bang her head, which was suddenly throbbing. The sound seemed to echo off the tunnel walls and rang loudly in her ears. *No*, she silently persuaded her mind, *the sound was that of footsteps. Someone was coming down the tunnel from the other direction.* She started down the narrow tunnel and shot a quick glance over her shoulder. *Was there a shadow? Was it her own shadow?* She wasn't sure. She turned back into the darkness, her own footsteps quickening. The turn was just ahead of her, but it was so black now. *Do I turn to the left?* she silently questioned herself. *Why am I so confused?* The footsteps were coming closer. *No*, she thought, *it's my own heart beating that's echoing in my ears. The turn, is it to the left? It's so dark and so very warm. Just a few more steps*, she thought. *Did Charles lock the door after he pushed me into the tunnel?* It was dark, so dark, and it was so warm, so very, very warm. It was summer. It was a lazy day. They were swimming, she and her father. But where was her brother Johnny? He had been flying through the air, but he wasn't laughing—he was calling her name. Then someone came up from behind her, from under the water, and pushed her, pushed her out of the water onto his shoulders. Then she was flying through the air and plunging down into the water. Fear enveloped her. She couldn't find her way out. She was pulling,

pulling through the water with her arms and kicking with her legs but she couldn't get out. She couldn't get air. She opened her mouth. She needed air, but she knew there was only water surrounding her. Her mind begged her not to, but her lungs pleaded that she must. She inhaled deeply and descended into the depths of darkness.

Mary tried to open her eyes. Someone was calling her, softly repeating her name.

"Mary, Mary," they were calling, but she couldn't find them. Everything was blurry, white and blurry. Then another voice. They were saying something. What were they saying? *A nasty bump, someone fainted, few days, good as new.* She was in a cloud of smoke, and suddenly contemplated her own breathing. Was the room filled with smoke? Could she take another breath? She cautiously inhaled. No, it wasn't smoke that surrounded her. It was fog, a cloud, a fluffy white cloud. Where was she? The voice was softly beckoning, again calling her name. It sounded familiar.

"Mary, Mary."

She forced her eyelids open. Blue, shining blue, pierced through the white cloud. Was it the clear blue sky shining through the cloud that encased her? No, they were eyes—crystal blue eyes. Eyes she had never seen before. They were blue, but an iridescent blue. They sparkled and shimmered and drew her in. Tiny specks of blue, dancing in crystal pools.

"Mary," the voice whispered.

A deep male voice, but only a whisper, and the sweetness of the tone lingered in her ears and lulled her back to sleep.

As she forced her eyelids open once again, she tried to focus on the face of the person calling her name. It was a perfect face, to match those entrancing eyes. He had high cheekbones and a chiseled jaw, and skin that was surely as smooth as silk. His wavy dark hair framed his face, and those eyes, those piercing blue eyes. Mary convinced herself she was staring at the face of an angel, for no man she had ever seen, or could have even imagined, was as celestial as this man who was whispering her name. The cloud once again enveloped her, and as her eyelids slowly closed, she convinced herself she must have died and gone to heaven, for where else could there be downy white clouds and beautifully captivating angel blue eyes?

Mary's eyes fluttered open, she knew, for the third or fourth time, though this time she felt as though she had control of them and they would not systematically close before she could comprehend where she was. The room was dark, the only light cast from the moonbeams that filtered through the balcony door's glass panes. Her eyes, becoming accustomed to the dim light, darted around the room, trying to fathom where she was and what she was doing there. She focused on the cherry wood bed frame that loomed above her, and instantly her memory jolted into place. She was in James's room. She had been there only once before, with Maggie, to change the linens on the bed, but she had never seen such a massive bed frame. Now, she recalled it instantly. She gasped silently. *Oh my! I'm in James's bed! Why am I in James Colton's bed?* Her mind began to race. *If this is real, and I'm not dreaming, why am I here?* Slowly, the events of the evening replayed in her head. She reached to feel the bump on her head, which would be there if her memory were serving her correctly. Satisfied she had not gone crazy—she recalled the tunnel and hitting her head—she still had no explanation as to why she was in this room and in this bed.

The rhythm of steady breathing drifted into her thoughts, and her head moved toward the sound, followed slowly by her eyes, almost afraid as to who might be producing the noise. There, in the shadowy room, slumped in an overstuffed chair, was the angel she recalled dreaming about. It was the man dressed in the civil war uniform. He was fast asleep. She examined his face, so incredibly handsome he was.

Suddenly, a thought popped into her head. *Could this be James Colton?* Then, envisioning the faces of Christina and Mrs. Colton, she contemplated. Certainly, there could not be such a momentous difference of appearance in the members of one family. *Yet,* she debated to herself, *who else could this be? After all, this was his room. And,* she supposed, *the elder Mr. Colton was quite handsome, for an older man.* James shifted in the chair, and Mary held her breath as he rolled his head from its resting place on the wing of the chair to rest on the opposite side. She watched his arms, which were folded across his chest, as they steadily moved up and down in unison with his breathing. Assuring herself he was not going to awaken, she dragged her eyes back toward his face. In this new position, the light from the moon, as if a dim spotlight, shone on his face. Mary let her eyes rest there. He was so pleasing to look at, and she presumed she could watch him for hours without tiring of it. She inspected carefully every curve and every line—his straight jaw, his full lips, his perfectly proportioned nose, his silken lids and long dark lashes. As her lingering eyes moved across his face, she noticed a small scratch above his left eye. It appeared to be a recent abrasion, as the small droplets of blood that had been drawn had yet to be cleaned away. She sincerely hoped it would not leave a scar to blemish his perfect complexion. Her eyes continued their journey toward the top of his head and noticed the small droplets of perspiration that hung on his brow. A small ringlet of wavy hair had fallen to his forehead and clung there. She thought about what it would be like to run her fingers through his thick, wavy hair and wipe his moistened brow, or to brush the back of her hand over his cheek, or to softly let her fingertips caress his full lips. She lifted her fingers to her own mouth and ran them smoothly across her parted lips, and then softly, the back of her hand across her own cheek. She wondered what his touch would be like on her skin. Grabbing a handful of quilt, she pulled aside the coverings that had been tucked up under her chin. She knew the warmth in the room that induced James's perspiration was not the cause of her sudden fervor. Her hand floated softly around her neck, and she let her fingertips dance lightly on the soft skin in the little hollow at the base of her throat. She shivered slightly and wondered whether her body was evoking her thoughts, or rather, her thoughts had provoked her body's response. She couldn't help but wonder if his touch would feel different from her own. Quickly, she grabbed for the quilt, tucked it back up under her chin, and silently demanded her mind and her body both to suppress this newly discovered sensation. She closed her eyes and let the rhythm of his steady breathing lull her back to sleep.

CHAPTER 15

I yawned and stretched my arms over my head as I glanced over my shoulder to the small window, wondering if it was day or night. I had lost track of time, which was the norm when I was writing. What wasn't normal was the story I was writing. I still had no real plot in mind. Well, other than of course the obvious boy meets girl-boy loses girl and then, by the end, everyone lives happily ever after scenario I always wrote about. Yet I wasn't even sure who the guy and girl were. I mean, I was pretty sure James was the hero, but I wasn't positive who the heroine was. Was it Mary? I stood up and paced the small room for a moment before collapsing onto the cot. Perhaps it was Rachel—and *bashert*! I don't know Yiddish and had no idea where that term had come from. It had just appeared on the screen in front of me, like I was a stenographer or something. I checked it out after I had finished that chapter—it really was a word. I had been writing nonstop since the PC arrived earlier that morning. To my astonishment, John hadn't even argued with me about my continued habit of printing to paper as I wrote. He had been so accommodating as of late.

What bothered me more than not having a plot or knowing for sure who the heroine was were the references to the beast. *Where on earth is that coming from?* How could I be referencing a character when I had no clue who or what he was? He was definitely obsessed or perhaps even possessed. I was sure of that. I could feel it. Even G-Pat and B-Pat were in agreement on that one. I hadn't liked writing those entries and wondered momentarily if I even had. Those words weren't mine—they had just seemed to flow onto the page. *Kinda like the whole bashert thing,* I thought. And of course, the fact that it was already well into the story and there was hardly any mention of intimacy. *What will my readers think about that?* What would John have to say? I knew every bit as well as he did it was the erotic scenes that sold romance novels. I stood up and hugged my arms around myself. I was chilled.

CHAPTER 16

The sound of running footsteps echoed through the length of the dark alley that ran between the river and the back of the tall row of buildings that lined the street. Then suddenly, only silence as the man slumped against the wall of a tall brownstone. He could feel the warmth of the bricks, which had retained the heat from the day's sun now long into the cool night. He was breathing heavily, and puffs of his warm breath swirled in the cool night air. He removed the dark cap he was wearing and ran the back of his hand over his sweaty brow, pushing his matted hair to the side. He turned his hand over and ran his palm over the length of his face, suddenly realizing his cheekbone seemed swollen. It stung as he moved his finger slowly back and forth over it. When he rubbed his finger against his thumb, he knew instinctively the warm, sticky substance was blood. He brought his hand to his lips and licked the tip of his finger. He knew the taste of blood. The little trollop must have scratched me, he thought, as he spat the taste from his mouth. He retrieved a neatly folded white handkerchief from his pocket and dabbed it gently to his swollen cheek. A smirk appeared on his lips, as from somewhere deep within him, an evil howl boiled to eruption from his mouth. The insistent sound of a wailing siren silenced him for an instant and then appeared to have intensified his wicked splendor as his guttural chuckle continued.

"I had to hit her." He spoke only to himself in the deserted alley. Silently, he argued with himself, trying to persuade the host that the blow to her jaw had been necessary to stop her screams for help. He rolled the handkerchief into a ball and crushed it into the palm of his hand. Then, tightening his fingers around it, he formed a fist. He rubbed the back of his fist with his other hand as he crossed the alley to look out over the river. The

moonlight sparkled and danced on the water, and it reminded him of her eyes. He closed his own eyes, trying to recall her lovely face before he had altered it with the back of his hand. The image of her quickly bruising swollen jaw—now etched on his brain—upset the host. He extended his arm and opened his fist, letting the bloodstained linen float from his fingertips down toward the water. He didn't notice that it fell short and landed among the rocks and debris scattered at the river's bank. Previously oblivious to the fact that he might not be alone in the alley, he now scanned up and down the length of it to make sure no one was around. Satisfied, he turned and walked slowly down the alley. After only a short distance, he crossed back toward one of the many brick buildings. There, under a wooden stoop, he deposited his dark jacket and cap into one of several empty and long forgotten wooden crates stored there. He shoved his hands into his pants pockets and continued on his stroll. There was a spring in his step that had not been there before. His lips now formed into a soft smile, and a look of contentment blanketed his face.

CHAPTER 17

Mary pulled at the woolen scarf that covered her head and tried to tuck the ends down inside her collar. The wind howled through the trees, and the limbs, mostly bare now, creaked with resistance. It was a cold, gray day, and the threat of snow loomed in the clouds. Days had become noticeably shorter in the last two weeks. Now, with only having Thursday afternoons off, there simply wasn't time for her to walk anywhere and be back before dusk. Nevertheless, she had felt the need to get out of the house, if only for a little while, to get some fresh air. Mrs. Colton had informed her that because she had missed three days of work while she stayed in bed with the bump on her head, she would need to make up the time by taking only a half-day off for the next six weeks. She had found out both Bea and Maggie had informed Mrs. Colton she had received the bump when she was helping Bea in the kitchen on the night of the costume ball. Maggie said they both recited in synchronized unison how she had been getting something out of a cupboard when she dropped a dishtowel and had bent down to retrieve it. Then, standing upright, she had hit her head on the open cupboard door. Mrs. Colton was none the wiser. It had been Monday morning before Mary became fully aware of the entire account of that evening when Maggie had come to her room to check on her.

Maggie, finding her fully awake for the first time since her mishap, was quick to share all the details with her. Mary had sat up in bed and propped herself with pillows, settling herself, while Maggie recounted the whole event. Apparently, that night, James had been in the grand room, watching Mr. Houdini's performance, and thought he heard someone in the heating tunnel. He had entered the tunnel from a second entrance, behind the bar. He said he had recognized Mary and had called out to her, but she had only hurried her steps. Mary was shocked. How had he recognized her if she had never even met him? Maggie hadn't answered Mary's question and had instead simply continued her story. James had reached Mary just a few feet before the entrance to the coatroom. When he had come up behind her, she had started swinging her arms at him. She had struck him right in the forehead. Mary had gasped when Maggie told her that she was the one that had given him the scratch on the forehead. It had been difficult in the cramped tunnel, but James had managed to scoop her up into his arms just as she was fainting. He then had Charles procure the doctor, who was attending the ball, as he carried her up the back stairway, through the west wing, and down the corridor into his room. Maggie said James had stayed with her through the night. He himself had moved her to her own room early the next morning, cradling her in his arms. Maggie said Mary had only moaned slightly but had never woken up. James was also the one who had fabricated the story Bea and Maggie had offered to Mrs. Colton. Maggie recited for Mary James's exact words.

"What my mother doesn't know certainly won't hurt her, but it will make life simpler for all of us, I'm sure."

Mary had been totally astonished by Maggie's account, not remembering any of it for herself. When Maggie had finished, Mary thought she should really go and thank James for all he had done for her. However, Maggie informed her he was gone, on another business trip. Mary had made a promise to talk to him the minute he returned.

By the next day, Mary was up and back to normal—except for the fact that James Colton now filled her thoughts and she could not dismiss his face from her mind. She was thinking of him now, as she again tugged on her scarf, which the wind insisted on trying to pull from her head. Her cheeks stung from the cold, and several times she had turned and walked backward to shield herself from the blustery wind. She wished she had taken Bea's warning to dress warm a bit more seriously. She remembered Bea's other advice about being home before dark and decided it best she start back toward the Coltons'. There had been another attack in the city. It had happened the same night as the costume ball. Maggie had told her the chief of police, who was at the Coltons' party that night, had been summoned about midnight. He had been ushered out of the grand room by Charles to the two men in uniform waiting for him in the entryway. Maggie said Charles had stayed close by to listen in and find out what all the commotion was about.

It seemed another young woman had been attacked in the park that very evening. Charles hadn't heard any of the details, as the police chief had quickly ushered the officers outside.

Now, as she neared the estate, the tall turret came into view, and she quickened her pace almost to a run, knowing warmth would be found once she was inside. A gust of wind momentarily took her breath away, and she again tugged at her scarf. Crossing the street, she slowed her pace so as not to trip over the mounds of dirt. The ruts in the road caused by motorcars had frozen into place.

She looked up at the house, peering between the wrought iron fence toward the second story, then lowered her eyes down the height of the bricks to the front entrance, where she noticed the black police car with its big emblem parked on the drive. She finally turned the last corner and headed toward the side gate. Tiny flakes had started to fall, and she chuckled at Bea's correctness once again at predicting the weather. Once she passed through the side gate, she ran across the small stepping stones, up the few steps of the post-lined porch, and then burst into the kitchen, where she knew she would at last find warmth and be rescued from the bitter wind.

Bea was seated at the sideboard, a cup of tea untouched in front of her. She was rubbing her hands together as if they ached. Maggie stood at the door that led to the front entry. She held it slightly ajar with her head stuck into the small opening. Both women turned as Mary bolted into the house. They simultaneously shushed her.

"What's going on?" she whispered as she quietly closed the door behind her and removed her coat and scarf.

Maggie stuck her head back into the crack, while Bea provided an explanation.

"Da police come to da house, just after you left," Bea said, still massaging her hands. "He asked for Mr. James. Din vhen Charles tell him he not here, he vanted to talk to da Missus."

Maggie stepped away from the door suddenly, and Charles entered the kitchen. Maggie, Bea, and Mary all stared at him, awaiting his report. Mary noticed how straight he stood, his face set with a blank expression as usual. He looked directly at her then, and she noticed a subtle change as his eyes seemed to soften, and his lips formed into a slight smile.

"Miss Mary," he said, "I wanted to tell you how sorry I was about your misfortune. I should have never let you go in that old tunnel."

Maggie, growing impatient, huffed at Charles. "What did the police want?"

Charles readjusted his position and removed the wry smile from his face. "Well, from what I could overhear, Mr. Egan had some piece of evidence that was found in conjunction with those attacks in the city. He said he was hoping to talk to Mr. James about it."

"What was it?" Maggie demanded.

"I don't know, I couldn't see what it was he showed Mrs. Colton."

"Well, what else did ya hear?" Maggie snapped. Charles, knowing Maggie's sharpness was just out of concern, continued without haste.

"Mrs. Colton told Mr. Egan that James had left the ball early and was with Miss Beaumont that evening, and currently, he was away on business."

"I thought you said he had stayed in his room with me?" Mary contested, suddenly confused.

"He did!" Maggie snapped.

"You see, dear," Bea provided in a soft voice, "Mr. James had Charles tell Mrs. Colton dat he vent to see Diane dat night. He didn't vant his mother to know dat he vas vith you upstairs. No vone other dan Mr. James, da doctor, and da four ov us knows da truth. Luckily Diane vasn't here dat night, she vasn't able to attend the party, as she vas ill."

"Do you think we should tell them the truth now?" Mary asked shyly.

"No, no, I tink we should just leave vhat's done, done for now. Ve'll vait and see vhat come ov it first."

They all agreed.

CHAPTER 18

Police Chief Jud Egan sat in his small office, staring at the only piece of evidence he had, a white linen handkerchief stained with blood. Yet he wasn't at all sure it had anything to do with the case. The only witness, other than the four women who had been attacked, was the man who had found the latest victim. He hadn't really been of any help. His name was Leroy Stacks. He claimed he had been out walking around eleven thirty. He said he often walked late at night when he couldn't sleep. He had seen the figure of a man running between two buildings down by the waterfront. He hadn't thought much of it at the time until he had crossed the street to stroll through the park, where he found the poor girl. She had been left there sobbing, her cries of help, by then, faint. A thorough search of the alleyway and riverfront had turned up only the bloodstained handkerchief.

The mayor was leaning hard on Jud to catch the monster that was molesting the young women of *his* city, but as Jud pondered over the facts, he wondered what he had to go on. There were a few insignificant similarities among the four women. They were all approximately the same age and about the same stature but appeared to have nothing else in common, except for the fact they all had green eyes. He originally suspected that was just coincidental, but now he wasn't so sure. The first victim was a young girl who lived alone and worked as a nurse at the hospital. The second happened to be the mayor's wife's second cousin. The third was a dancer at one of the known speakeasies that lined the waterfront. Of course, they served only tea, and the establishments were passed off as just social gathering places. Jud shook his head in silence. That was a whole other case, he thought to himself, but as the mayor consumed as much bootleg liquor as anyone else in town, it was a matter Jud didn't need to deal with.

The latest victim came from a poor family and lived down on the east side of town in the tenements. She cleaned homes during the day and relied on a service to find her other odd jobs for the evenings and weekends. On the night she had been attacked, she had been assigned by the service to a job on the far end of town. She was supposed to have worked very late, but she had left the assignment early—around ten o'clock—as she hadn't felt well. She had originally arranged for a ride with another girl, but as she left early, she had had no alternative but to walk the five miles home. She had only been about halfway there when she was assaulted as she passed through the park that stood in the center of town.

Jud grabbed the handkerchief and looked at the tiny, inconspicuous insignia that was hand-stitched on one corner. The owner of the men's apparel shop had recognized it immediately. He said it was imported Irish linen and very expensive. Then, almost as a sales pitch, he had added he was the only apparel store in the state that carried such an item. He also offered the only reason he stocked them at all was by request of one of his very best customers, Mr. William Colton. Mr. Colton had inquired about their availability about five years earlier. He had a friend who purchased them in Boston and found the quality unparalleled. Mr. Colton guaranteed that every Christmas he would purchase a dozen handkerchiefs as a present for his son James if the owner would stock them for him. The shop owner also stated that this particular handkerchief could not belong to James Colton because his father always had the ones he purchased sent over to Mrs. Pitts who hand embroidered them with James's monogram.

"At least that's what he told me his intentions were," the man had dubiously added. He did suppose he had other customers buy the handkerchiefs over the years, but very few, he assured Jud, because they were *very* expensive.

On a hunch, Jud had gone out to the Coltons'. He thought that perhaps James might know of someone else who carried a similar handkerchief. Perhaps he had recommended them to a friend or noticed someone who had purchased the apparently unique item. Mrs. Colton completely misinterpreted the reason for his visit and thought Jud was in some way indicating James was a suspect. Jud had apologized profusely and assured her that in no way was that his intent. In her apparent agitated haste, she had quickly offered an alibi for James's whereabouts the night of the costume ball, when the last attack had taken place. Jud had no real intention of checking it out. He knew James was at the costume ball earlier in the evening, as he himself had talked to him there. Mrs. Colton claimed he had left the party around ten o'clock and would have been found in the company of Miss Diane Beaumont. It all made sense. James had told Jud in their conversation that Diane wasn't feeling well, thus her absence at the party. Jud concluded James might have left the party to comfort her if she were ill.

Jud had been summoned from the party about midnight. He knew the incident had happened at about half past ten or so, from the girl's recollection. She, like the others, wasn't much help with any real identification. They all described the man as between five-ten and six-foot-two. Two of the women referred to him as stocky, one said he was heavyset, the other said only of medium build. All four said he wore some type of black or dark mask over his head, into which holes had been cut for his eyes, nose, and mouth. One reported that she thought she had noticed a lock of wavy dark hair. One said his eyes were blue, two said brown, and the fourth couldn't remember. The latest victim said she had managed to scratch his face, but she wasn't exactly sure where. She recalled that as she tried to tear at his mask, her finger had poked through one of the holes. She was sure she had scratched hard enough to draw blood.

The small, bloodstained cloth lay on top of the open files of the victims, in the middle of Jud's desk, where he had tossed it. As he moved it back and forth with the end of his letter opener, he couldn't help but recall Miss Beaumont's words as they seemed to echo through his head. *He had quite a nasty scratch above his left eye.*

He hadn't planned to contact Miss Beaumont to check out the alibi Mrs. Colton had given. After all, James Colton as a suspect was a ridiculous idea—at least he had thought it was. Now he just wasn't sure. One thing he was sure of was he certainly wasn't going to be making any accusations where the Coltons were concerned without some hard evidence. He wasn't about to open any old wounds. He recalled too vividly the whole mess seven years earlier with the suicide of Genny Mueller. He had been too quick to make accusations then, and the press had had a field day. Yet Diane's words seemed to haunt his thoughts. He had happened to run into her the day after his visit to the Coltons. They had engaged in small talk, and he had politely stated he was sorry to hear she hadn't been feeling well. Puzzled by his concern, she had asked him what gave him the impression she had been ill. He had responded that he must be confusing her with someone else he had heard about, dismissing the subject by accusing his bad memory. He had resumed the dialogue by inquiring of her absence at the Coltons' costume party. She told him she had declined the invitation. Though she hadn't gone into detail, he surmised she and James had had a quarrel. She did, however, offer the fact that she had not talked to James in quite a while. She said he had telephoned her several times over the last few weeks, but she had made herself unavailable and had no intention of returning his many messages. Then she had added, as almost an afterthought, that she had bumped into him the day after the party, at the train station. They hadn't spoken, but she had noticed that he had quite a nasty scratch above his left eye.

Jud had gone back to his office after that conversation to retrieve the files of the victims. Files in hand, he had set out once again to question the young women. His intent was to prove none of them knew James Colton, and he was hoping most, if not all, hadn't even heard of him. Thus, he could dismiss the nagging feeling that James had something to do with the case. All he really had on him was a handkerchief that the store owner had said probably didn't belong to him and a small scratch on his forehead.

Now, he sat and stared at the victims' open files, again using his letter opener to move the handkerchief from side to side so he could read over his notes from the day before. He had read and reread them countless times. The only thing he had managed to prove was that James Colton did know all the victims, and they knew him. The speakeasy the dancer worked at was, of course, James's favorite one to frequent. The woman said James had even bought her a drink once. Jud smiled as he recalled the way the woman had stuttered when she had said "drink . . . I mean cup of tea."

The mayor's wife's second cousin had actually dated James for a short period of time a few years back. The nurse happened to be the one who cared for James when he had broken his arm last February. Jud had assured himself the last victim he talked to would squash the whole—he was convinced—coincidence. After all, he had surmised, how could James know this poor girl that lived down in the tenements? It was her words he had scribbled down on the paper inside the file, which now stared him in the face. As it turned out, she had worked as temporary help for the Coltons at several of their large parties over the past year and a half, including the costume ball on the very night of her attack.

She had told Jud, through bruised and swollen lips, she was sure James wouldn't remember her, even though he had spoken to her.

"I served him a glass of champagne that night," she said, stumbling over the reference to alcohol, just as the waitress had done. "He thanked me, and then he told me," she had hesitated, casting her eyes down to Jud's shoes, "that I had the loveliest green eyes."

CHAPTER 19

James pulled his favorite sweater over his head and then sat down on the edge of his bed to pull on a fresh pair of socks. It was good to be home. He could hardly wait to see Mary. The day's business meetings had been nothing but a waste of time. He hadn't proved a thing to his father, though he had to admit, he hadn't really tried. He usually relished a good argument with his father and colleagues, especially on the subject of production, but his heart just hadn't been in it. James knew that trying to get the stubborn old money-hungry fools to realize treating their employees better would actually make them more money was like trying to keep the state dry with Prohibition laws.

James wiped his brow with the back of his hand. The whole thing made him mad, but he was sure times were changing. Men like Henry Ford knew it. He was sure that soon the rest of the country would have to follow.

He scoffed at his wrinkled brow as he stood in front of the large mirror that hung over his bureau. "Enough about business," he said to his reflection. He had other things to think of now.

He brushed through his hair, all the natural waves springing back to their original position once the brush passed through them. He knew, thanks to Maggie, that even though it was Mary's afternoon off, she was in her room. Setting the hand brush down on his bureau, he leaned closer to the mirror to assess the line of pinkish skin on his forehead.

"A few more weeks and it should be gone," he said and shrugged his shoulders.

He left his room and walked toward the east wing. As he entered the narrower hallway, memories of his childhood came rushing to greet him. The doors of the many servants' rooms, where he and Bea had played hide and go seek, were all closed. He had spent most of his childhood in the kitchen, or the servants' part of the house, so as not to disturb his mother, who was always entertaining and being the perfect hostess at her many parties. He had loved running up and down the hall and ducking in and out of the servants' rooms.

As an adolescent, he recalled many different young girls his mother had hired. When he was about fifteen, he realized that each new maid would be prettier than the last. Sometimes there would be as many as three or four of them at one time. He had tried to make friends with a few of the girls, but his mother always made sure to put a stop to it.

James stopped in front of the door to Mary's room and stood silently. He was not sure what he was going to say to her. He only knew he could think of nothing else, no one else. He thought about her beautiful face and enchanting green eyes. He thought about her sweetness. He thought he had to get to know her better. He knocked softly and waited in silence. After a short moment with no response, he again rapped softly at the door.

Her voice floated to his ears. "Come in."

He turned the knob and slowly pushed the door open. Mary, sitting on her bed, reading a letter, didn't look up, so he stood quietly just inside the doorway, filling his eyes with her beauty. She turned her head, slowly dragging her eyes from the page, and then, startled, jumped from the bed.

"Oh!" she gasped. She quickly folded the page and stuffed it into the pocket of her dress. "I, I," she stuttered, "I thought it was Maggie."

James smiled a broad smile as he chuckled and came to stand across from her. "I'm sorry. I didn't mean to startle you."

Mary felt her knees weaken, and she pleaded silently for them to support her steadily.

Both stood in silence, their eyes captured in a magnetic embrace. She could feel her face beginning to flush with the heat that rose in her body and finally pulled her eyes from his. James responded by breaking the silence between them.

"I just wanted to see how you were. Fully recovered from that nasty bump on the head, I hope?"

"Fully recovered," Mary confirmed shyly, nodding her head. Then, as almost an afterthought, she added, "Sir."

James looked wounded. "Please don't call me sir."

Mary noticed the way his eyebrows narrowed together as he frowned. She could see the tiny scar above his eye she knew she had produced. Her heart urged her to lift her fingers, to softly touch the now healed injury she had caused. But her head cautioned her to mind her place, and her wobbling knees forbade her any movement at all. She could hear the sound of her own heart beating as silence once again stood between them. She wondered if James could hear it too, for it seemed to be pounding loudly against her chest. She cast her eyes to the floor, for she didn't know what else to do. James, searching for something more to say to her, was silent. He, James Colton, who was never at a loss for words. He, who had been schooled under the very best private tutors and could debate with the best of them. He, who Bea said had a golden tongue and could speak more sweetly than the honeybee, was at a loss for words. His mind offered his voice suggestions, but none he could actually speak. A soft smile touched his lips. She had called him sir, which meant she thought of him as some sort of superior—an employer, her boss. He hadn't expected that response. Then, as their eyes met again, James knew he better say something before his arms took it upon themselves to embrace her and pull her close to him. He longed to caress her soft skin and silky hair, to breathe in the sweetness of her, to tell her how he felt about her. The silence reaching the point of intolerance, James said, "Well . . ."

At the same time, Mary uttered "I . . ."

Mary spoke only after James insisted that she go first.

"I just wanted to thank you for, for . . ." she stuttered again. "for helping me the other night," she finally said.

"Well, it was certainly my pleasure." He once again smiled the broad smile that enriched his already flawless face and made Mary's cheeks turn a deeper shade of crimson.

Before the silence could overtake them again, Mary asked, "What was it you wanted to say?"

"Well, I was just going to mention that I was taking Christina to a moving picture show tonight, and I was wondering if you would accompany me?" Then he hastily added, "I mean us, accompany us, Christina and me." The words seemed to stumble off his tongue.

"I would love to," Mary instantly responded, then hoped she hadn't sounded too eager.

"Fine, fine, until later then."

Back in the hallway, he set his pace as though on a mission. He had to find Christina and inform her he was taking her to the showhouse, whether she wanted to go or not. He hadn't planned on taking Christina anywhere, but he felt he needed her as an excuse to get Mary to accept his offer. And probably, even more important, to make it appear to his mother Mary was accompanying them as Christina's companion. Things were not exactly copacetic between his mother and him because he had made up the little story about Diane being ill the night of the costume ball, when the truth was she had refused to attend because of the little escapade between he and Maggie in the entryway weeks earlier. Not that he cared what his mother thought, but he knew she could make things rough for Mary if she wanted to. He knew if his mother were to think for one minute he and Mary were in any way having a relationship, it would definitely make things difficult. He remembered clearly the speech he had been given over and over when he was just eleven or twelve and had wanted to be friends with some of the servants.

"They are not like us, James," his mother would say. "Why can't you understand that?" And then, of course, there was Genny, poor Genny. Genny was one of his mother's many maids. She was an orphan girl his mother had hired years ago. The orphanage over in Jefferson County had been one of Mrs. Colton's favorite places to find servants. She had hired many girls from the orphanage, until the incident with Genny.

The director of the place praised her for the invaluable service she was doing for the community and apparently relished the fact that Mrs. Colton would take some of the older girls off his hands. Older boys were much easier to adopt out, as they made good farm hands, and of course, most people wanted the younger children.

Genny came to work at the Coltons' house when she was fifteen. The agreement with the orphanage was that Mrs. Colton hire the girls. James always thought that hire was the wrong word, as the girls received no actual pay—simply their room and board. He found out years later his mother had coerced the director into bending the rules a bit, letting her hire the girls rather than taking custody of them, the latter of which would have made her responsible for their actions as well as for their well-being. The girls would stay in the Coltons' employ until age eighteen, at which point they were free to leave or become an actual employee, which would require they be paid. Whether they were hired or not was entirely up to Mrs. Colton, of course. It was apparent after the first few girls had come and gone that once they turned eighteen, even though some would have chosen to stay, Mrs. Colton always found some excuse not to hire them. After their dismissal, she would simply make another trip out to the orphanage and pick out a new younger girl. The poor girls were simply turned out into the street with minimal warning, and usually no place to go. The orphanage would no longer take them in because of their age.

After a while, the girls caught on, and word spread among them quickly that they would only be at the Coltons' until their eighteenth birthday. If they chose to go with Mrs. Colton, they should keep in mind they were going to be turned out into the street, most likely the day after they turned eighteen. Not many girls refused the opportunity, however, as they found living at the Coltons', the better of two evils. For most, it was the first time in their lives they had their own room, home-cooked meals, and new clothes—if only a uniform—

to wear. Most would go out and find employment prior to their imminent dismissal. Unfortunately, Genny Mueller hadn't been privy to this bit of information. She had arrived at the orphanage only days before one of Mrs. Colton's trips there. She, along with her parents and younger brother, were immigrants from Germany. They had just settled into a small farming community when the influenza epidemic ravaged most of their town. Both Genny's parents and younger brother had died. Genny ended up at the orphanage.

James recalled with great fondness the day Genny had come to the estate. It happened to be her birthday. She had just turned fifteen. James was sixteen. Instantly, the two had become friends. They would spend every free minute Genny had together. They would talk and laugh and listen to the phonograph or read books and magazines James would provide. Bea had also instantly liked Genny, and the two of them also became very close. Genny said Bea reminded her of her 'oma' in Germany, who she longed to return to. But she knew her parents had saved long and hard for their passage to America, and she'd never have that kind of money. So she would pretend Bea was her grandmother. Bea teased that she hoped she was younger than Genny's grandmother, but she felt honored just the same. James had wanted to give her the money. He didn't know how much it would take, but he was sure there was plenty in the trust fund his grandfather had set up for him. The only problem was he couldn't touch the money until he turned twenty-five. He dreaded the thought of Genny going back to Germany and never seeing her again, but sometimes he would find her alone, crying in her room, and it would make him feel very sad for her. Genny had only been there a short time when Bea and James had conspired a plan for her to return to Germany. In the many months that followed, Bea had saved all she could from her earnings for the "send Genny home fund." She had told James, "I can do vithout dat new vinter coat von more year." James, of course, contributed every penny of his weekly allowance.

Then, about three months before Genny's eighteenth birthday, Mrs. Colton had taken a trip to the orphanage and had returned with not one, but two new girls—Laura, age thirteen, and Ruth, who was fourteen. The very first night the new girls had come, they, along with

Genny, had stayed up late into the evening in Genny's room, talking about the orphanage and the Coltons. At one point, Ruth had asked Genny where she would be going to work when she left the Coltons'. Genny, totally unaware of her imminent dismissal, had been shocked to hear Ruth's stories of past girls. By the time they went to bed that night, Genny had clutched in her hand the name and address of a possible employer. Ruth had told her that her older sister worked for the Coltons the year before Genny, and when she got thrown out on the street, a Mr. Phillips had given her a job. She had the address for Mr. Phillips, as it was where she wrote to her sister. Ruth wasn't sure what kind of job it was, as her sister would never actually say, but her sister had visited her twice at the orphanage, and she had been wearing very nice clothes and had even given Ruth a whole five dollars. Ruth was sure she must have made very good money.

The very next day was Sunday, and Genny had left the Coltons' as she always did to attend church. Although she usually returned around lunchtime, no one thought it too odd when she hadn't. It had been a beautiful summer day, and everyone, including James, assumed she was out enjoying herself, just strolling around the city. That afternoon, James, along with his sister and parents, had left the house to attend a social gathering. When Genny hadn't returned by dinnertime, Bea had begun to worry. Mr. Colton returned to the house long before the rest of the family. He had told Bea he hadn't felt well and had left the party to come home and lie down. Bea had immediately informed him of Genny's absence. He had told her if Genny hadn't returned by dark to wake him. Genny had returned very shortly after that, and though she had gone straight to her room, Bea assumed everything was fine.

Months passed, and as Genny's eighteenth birthday neared, James and Bea had counted out their collective contributions and were sure they had ample money to send Genny back to Germany. Bea had made plans to bake a big cake for her, and she would let James tell Genny about their surprise. In afterthought, James supposed the preoccupation with the surprise had kept them from noticing how Genny had been so different—so distant—after that Sunday afternoon. To this day, he could hardly stand to think of what had happened on that day, what Genny must have gone through, and what it had caused her to do. In some ways, he blamed himself for never sharing his plans of the fund with her. He often wondered why she had never questioned him regarding the information Ruth had shared with her. Why she had never questioned him as to why he, himself, had never told her about the imminent dismissal that would come on her eighteenth birthday. He wondered if she had thought he hadn't been friend enough to tell her. If she had only asked, he could have told her the truth, that it had simply never occurred to him she had never been told.

The whole ordeal sent the entire town into a frenzy. James still vividly recalled the headline in the paper his mother had tried so desperately to keep him from seeing—"SERVANT GIRL COMMITS SUICIDE"—and the article that followed that blatantly stated the girl had been with child and subtly implied that Mr. William Colton was the father. The investigation had gone on for months before the truth in the matter was confirmed and his father's name had been cleared. But it had left many scars on everyone involved, scars that kept James from becoming too close to anyone. Deep wounds that made him use caution in matters of the heart.

But now there was Mary. This sweet girl had awakened something deep within him. She had somehow reached inside him and set his mind awhirl and his whole being on fire. He didn't completely understand this new emotion, but whatever it was, it made him feel more alive than he ever had before, and he hoped it would never end.

He knocked soundly on Christina's door.

"Go away!" she bellowed.

He burst into her room and informed her boldly, "We're going to the picture show. Be ready by seven!"

CHAPTER 20

Mary examined her reflection in the small, smoky mirror that hung in her room. She smoothed her hair, which Maggie had pinned for her. Not in a bob, as she had fashioned it before, but this time, she had pulled it back and curled the long tresses. It had been Maggie's idea to style her hair when she had informed her she was going to the moving picture with Miss Christina and Mr. James. Mary hadn't told Maggie it was James who had personally invited her. She had found out days after the tunnel incident that Maggie had been slightly jealous of the attention James had displayed toward her, and she certainly didn't want to compound the problem. Yet she found it disappointing not to share with Maggie how she felt about James.

She scoffed at her reflection, suddenly sure she was making too much of the invitation. Maggie had mentioned she had gone to the moving pictures with James and Christina before, and James had even taken them for ice cream after. Maggie said Mr. James was just nice that way. Mary was certain she had just been invited to accompany Miss Christina—nothing more, nothing less. Yet a small voice inside her head insisted there was something more. Was the wonderful feeling that had completely overtaken her by his closeness as he stood in her room to invite her only been felt by her? Was the sweetness in his voice just his voice? Did he not feel the same sensation she had experienced? Was the sparkle in his eye always there, sparkling for everyone to see?

"You've gone daft!" she sputtered to her own reflection, then argued with herself silently as she turned from the mirror. *I'm just going to see a moving picture. I should be happy for the opportunity. James is just a very nice man who's invited me to accompany him and his sister. That's all there is to it!*

She looked down at the dress she wore and decided it was a very pretty dress. The muslin fitted itself to her small frame. The large white collar, edged with blue trim, outlined the smooth skin of her neck, and the soft blue silk band, wrapped just below her hips and extending to one side, was tied in a neatly pressed bow. The bottom of the dress fell in pleats, and she loved the way it swayed when she walked. Maggie had gotten a few strands of matching blue ribbon from Bea and had intertwined it through the curls she had fashioned in Mary's upswept hair.

"I look fine," she declared as she picked up the shawl Maggie had loaned her. Just then, there was a soft knock at the door. She crossed the room and opened it apprehensively. Instantly, all her worrisome thoughts melted away as she looked at James. He was dressed casually in pants and sweater, and the scent of his cologne teased her nostrils. Their eyes met almost immediately.

"You look very lovely," he said as he extended his arm to her. Mary instinctively placed her arm through his extended one. Following him into the hallway, she pulled the door shut behind her. Neither spoke as they walked arm in arm toward the main hall. Their steps moved in unison, and each was aware of their closeness. They paused briefly at the top of the grand staircase. James's original plan was to continue to Christina's room so the three of them could proceed to meet Charles, who was waiting out front with the car. Then, at the last minute, he decided it would be better to take Mary down and then come back for his sister, and besides, he just didn't want to let her go. Mary had not noticed his slight hesitation as they proceeded down the grand staircase. She was too worried about what Mrs. Colton might say if she were to see her using the main staircase, on the arm of her son, no less. Something about the moment seemed magical to James. As they took the first step, he unthinkingly slid his free hand over her fingers that rested lightly across his arm. As he did, she looked up at him with a soft smile. Her eyes, bright with anticipation, sparkled in the light from the crystal chandelier, and his heart leaped in his chest. As they reached the landing, where the stairway turned down into the entryway, he paused momentarily, his arms wanting to encircle her, to pull her close to him. His lips longing to gently cover hers. He wanted to embrace her. He wanted to tell her how he felt when he was near her, how he felt when he simply thought of her. But they simply proceeded down the staircase. He left Mary seated in the entry hall as he bounded back up the steps to fetch Christina, who he had nearly forgotten. In an instant, he reappeared on the landing, and Mary watched, stifling a giggle, as James seemed to be dragging Christina down the stairs as she hopped along, still trying to slip on her shoe.

They were all silent in the auto, only because Christina had managed to position herself between Mary and him. Charles dropped them in front of the showhouse, and Christina waited with Mary in silence near the ticket window while James purchased their tickets. He then extended both arms, which Christina and Mary each accepted. They walked to the front entrance, where a man, in what Mary thought a funny suit, opened the door for them. They entered the lobby of the movie house, and Mary was instantly mesmerized by the drapery, chairs, and settees, which were decorated with heavy brocade upholstery of deep red. Her eyes darted around the lobby, trying to take inventory of everything she saw.

"Haven't you ever been to a showhouse before?" Christina snapped, quite disturbed because she thought Mary's naivety was drawing attention. James was trying to usher both girls along, but Christina insisted on stopping by the candy vendor. She wanted raspberry vines, as it was the only reason she had agreed to come along. Once James purchased her a bag of the flavored licorice, they settled themselves into the perfect seats. James lavished both girls with his description of several different theaters in places such as New York, Detroit, and Los Angeles. He described the imperial staircases, gilded ornaments, elaborate rugs, marble statuary, massive crystal chandeliers, epic murals, and ceilings painted with fleecy white clouds. He told them a ticket could cost as much as a dollar. Christina was jealous that she had never been to any such movie theater—which made her no better than Mary—and promised herself she would talk to her mother about the situation. As the lights lowered, they all settled comfortably into their seats to watch the film, *The Hunchback of Notre Dame* starring Lon Chaney. James explained to them just before the music started that it was an older movie and had actually premiered two years earlier. Mary didn't care in the least, and her eyes were glued to the image appearing on the screen. James, who had chosen to sit between the two of them, leaned over several times during the picture to comment to Mary about one thing or another. Christina, feeling somewhat neglected, huffed a rebuttal each time while chomping on her candy. By the time the show ended, Christina was whining loudly at James that she really hadn't liked the movie, while Mary kept her eyes glued to the credits as they appeared on the screen, not wanting the film to end. She simply couldn't dismiss the disfigured image of Quasimodo from her mind. How could people be so cruel, she wondered? With James's prompting, she finally stood and realized that Christina was already in the aisle.

"Hurry up, you two!" Christina bellowed. "I need to get home and speak to Mother!"

Mary smiled in Christina's direction. Up until a few months earlier, she hadn't known people could be so rude either. She obliged Christina's request begrudgingly, and she followed James out of the row, still attempting to catch every last glimpse of the plush seats and ornately woven floor coverings. James waited while she stepped out into the aisle, allowing her to walk ahead of him. By then, Christina was several feet in front of them, and James took the opportunity to casually place his hand on Mary's back, guiding her gently up the aisle. The sensation of his hand placed in the small of her back instantly sent a tingle through her entire being. A smile covered her face as she straightened her back and slowly proceeded up the aisle of the theater.

Charles was waiting for them right out front, as expected. They rode home in silence, Christina glaring at Mary the entire way. As Charles pulled the auto to a stop in front of the entry steps, Christina, still upset by the entire evening, huffed, "She can't get out here! She should be using the servants' entrance."

As James was opening the door and climbing out of the auto on the opposite side, she added boldly, trying to sound like her mother, "Charles, you can leave Mary off at the servants' entrance before putting the auto away."

Paying no attention to Christina and her ambling exodus from the vehicle, James darted around the auto, opened the driver's door, and whispered briefly to Charles. To Mary's surprise, Charles pulled himself from the seat, and James slid in behind the wheel. Charles scurried to Christina's waiting hand as she was still trying to pull herself from the seat, blindly searching for what she assumed would be James's offering of a courteous helping hand. Before Christina had a chance to realize whose hand she had taken, the auto was slowly proceeding down the drive toward the side of the house and the servants' entrance. Mary, at first quite amused by the whole thing, suddenly speculated what Ms. Christina might force her to endure to compensate for James's actions, but right at that moment, she didn't care.

James turned the auto down the side drive, usually only used for deliveries. He slowed to a stop just outside the servants' entrance. He shut down the motor and got out of the car without speaking a word. He opened Mary's door and offered her his hand. Accepting graciously, she placed her hand delicately in his and stepped out of the auto. They stood silently, facing each other. The glow from the full moon cast a broad light through the barren trees onto the crisp leaves that were scattered on the ground. James fought off the desire to pull her close to him and instead delighted in the glorious sensation of simply holding her hand in his. Mary, becoming uncomfortably aware of the silence between them, offered conversation on the only subject that came to mind.

"It certainly is warm for this time of year."

"Yes, it is," James responded as he gently pulled her aside and closed the door of the auto. Still holding her hand, they walked toward the porch at the side entrance of the house.

"My father calls this time of year Indian summer," Mary said. "He says after it turns cold, you can always expect a few more nice days before winter sets in."

James was silent. He was still holding her hand when she reached the top step of the porch, and he turned her gently to face him. Standing one step below her, they now stood face-to-face. The covered porch partially secluded them from the moonlight, and James admired her face shadowed by his own silhouette. Mary had not resisted the gentle tug on her hand to turn her toward him, but he could now feel the slight trembling of her fingers, and he gently squeezed her hand within his own.

She stood silently, unable to speak. Her heart was racing in her chest. Her knees that had supported her steadily the entire evening now began to wobble, and she tried to muster all her strength to steady them. She had never kissed a man before. Never had she known any man well enough for one to attempt to kiss her, and yet somehow, she knew it was about to happen. Standing there in the shadows, her brain was screaming it loud and clear. James Colton was about to kiss her. The realization of it set her mind to reeling as her thoughts buffeted one another. *Maggie!* her conscience screamed. *Maggie loves James. You mean nothing to him.* Yet despite the barrage of sensible arguments her mind offered, her body persisted. Her heart now pounded frantically with the anticipation of his lips touching hers. Her body, foreseeing his inevitable advance, began to send a shiver through her, encouraging her to seek his certain warmth. Her breath quickened, and even though the unfamiliar heat of passion was starting to build from somewhere within her, her body quivered, as if she were chilled.

James dropped her hand, which he had gently held, and reached for the shawl that hung loosely over her shoulders. He delicately pulled at the ends, snuggling it around her and tucking it just under her chin. His fingers lightly brushed the smooth skin at the base of her throat and ached to linger there. A fragile whimper escaped her lips, her body's response to inescapable submission, as every nerve melted to the sensation of his touch. James, well-accustomed to reading the signs clearly, also sensed Mary's hesitance. He reluctantly stepped down a step, then gently lifted her hand and delicately brushed it with a kiss.

"Thank you," he whispered. "It was a wonderful evening." He stood silently then as he watched her quickly disappear through the door and into the house.

CHAPTER 21

By six thirty in the morning, the big old house was already filled with the glorious scent of freshly baked bread. The wonderful aroma teased Mary's nose and awoke her from her sleep. Suddenly remembering what day it was, she jumped from her bed and dressed hurriedly. She was eager to spend the day with her friends, and without Miss Christina. As she descended the servants' stairs to the kitchen, a rich bouquet of varied smells invaded her nostrils. Bea was standing at the kitchen table sewing up the wonderfully large turkey she had just stuffed with bread, seasoning, sausage, and nuts. Two large loaves of freshly baked bread lay neatly on a white cloth on the side cupboard. Pumpkin was simmering on the stove, to which Bea had added spices of nutmeg and cloves, and two perfectly shaped crusts awaited in pie tins that rested on another side cupboard.

"What can I do to help?" Mary questioned, eager to help with the Thanksgiving dinner.

"Vell," Bea replied, wiping her reddened cheek with the back of her hand, "vhy don't you get a bit of breakfast first?"

"Oh, no," Mary replied. "I'm saving all the room I can for dinner."

"Very goud din. You can fetch da table linens from da butler's closet. Day vill need to be pressed. And din prepare da dining vroom table. Set places for five!" she shouted as Mary raced out the kitchen door following her instructions.

Mary quickly found the white linens in the butler's pantry, though she dreaded using the device Bea used to iron. The A-Best-O electric iron was a nuisance as far as she was concerned. She would rather have heated the iron on the stove, as she did at home, than deal with the cord of this new contraption. And though Mrs. Colton said the iron had something called a thermostat to prevent scorching, Bea confirmed that wasn't actually the case. In spite of the obnoxious cord that dangled from the light socket, Mary spent hours pressing the linens to perfection before taking them to the dining room. Bea had already chosen the dishes, crystal, and silver and had them standing on the sideboard. Mary set the table with great care, paying special attention to the placement of the silverware, just as Bea had taught her. As she placed the crystal water goblets just above the etched china plates, she hoped she could be careful enough at dinner not to chip or break anything. This would be the most elegant table she had ever dined at.

The entire Colton family had whisked off to Mrs. Colton's sisters for the Thanksgiving holiday. According to Maggie, it was a long-honored tradition. Just as long-lived was Bea's tradition of preparing a huge Thanksgiving feast for the servants who were left behind. According to Maggie, all the best china, silver, and crystal were used, and though Maggie didn't know if Mrs. Colton knew about it or not, she had added that she really didn't care. Bea spared no labor in preparing everyone's requested favorites as well as the traditional dishes like turkey, yams, and cranberries. When Mary questioned Bea as to why she went through all the work when the Coltons weren't even there, she had responded that it was the one dinner she prepared because she wanted to, not because she had to. It was done with love for friends—friends she considered her family—and that made it not a chore but a pleasure, something she enjoyed.

Mary couldn't help but think of her father. She was sure he wouldn't be having a Thanksgiving feast, but she at least hoped he was eating right without her there to prepare his meals.

The table was set to perfection, but still Mary stepped back and checked it over one last time. As she moved her eyes from one place setting to the next, checking that everything was placed exactly, she counted off the settings, indiscriminately assigning a place to each guest.

"Bea, Maggie, Maggie's friend Joseph, and me." Silently she wondered who the fifth place was for. Charles and Jeannette had both had the misfortune of accompanying the Coltons. She was sure Bea had said to set the table for five, and she had set out five place settings for her. She crossed the room and pushed with her shoulder at the heavy door that led to the kitchen.

"Bea," she hollered, without looking up as she entered the room, "why am I setting the table for ..." She stopped suddenly as she looked up to see where Bea was and stared into the eyes of James Colton.

"Happy Thanksgiving," he said, smiling broadly. A smile that melted Mary's knees and caused her to forget whatever it was she was saying.

"I was just telling Bea how much I was looking forward to that turkey she's roasting in the oven," he said as he looked fondly in Bea's direction. Just then, Maggie came stumbling down the stairs.

"What are you doin' here?" she questioned James before even acknowledging Bea or Mary.

"Well!" James replied, trying to sound offended. "How about 'good morning,' or 'Happy Thanksgiving,' or at least a little more enthusiasm, instead of 'what are you doin' here?'" he mocked in the same forlorn tone Maggie had used.

Maggie straightened herself, plastered an exaggerated smile on her lips, and batted her eyelids excessively. Then, throwing her hands into the air, she brayed, "Good morning, James. Happy Thanksgiving to ya! And whatever gives us the pleasure of your company on this fine day?" Then, as her smile melted from her lips, and her shoulders slumped, she added, "'Tis that better?"

James laughed a hearty laugh. "Much better, my dear." He crossed the room to give Maggie a hug. "So how's this new gentleman friend I've been hearing so much about? A real sheik, is he? Bea tells me he's coming for dinner."

"Yes, he is, and ya be nice to him," Maggie scolded James as one would a mischievous brother.

Mary watched quietly as the two of them joked together. Maggie seemed different to her. She had noticed over the last few weeks quite a change in her dear friend. Meeting this man, Joseph O'Dooley, had seemed to make her older, more grown up somehow. He was all Maggie ever talked about anymore. They had met quite by accident at a market when Joseph was having trouble making a purchase, and Maggie had come to his aid. She told Mary he was a steady man, a man of character and conviction. She said he had goals, and the determination to attain them, and she wanted to be part of his plans. He was a hard worker and eager to make a good life in America. Just like Maggie, he had no family here. He had come to America from Ireland only two years earlier. He worked hard and was saving his money to buy himself a piece of land. Mary watched Maggie now as she ate one of Bea's banana muffins smothered in butter and told James between bites all about Joseph. It was plain to see Maggie no longer thought of James the way she once had. They seemed to be more like good friends, and very comfortable together, which made Mary quite happy and, in an odd way, a little jealous.

The clock that sat high on the shelf above the side cupboard began to chime. It was ten o'clock. Suddenly Maggie jumped from her seat.

"Oh, my," she wailed. "He'll be here soon, I have to get ready." She dashed for the stairs and managed to stumble up them, just as she had come down earlier. James laughed, while Mary and Bea both stifled their snickers.

James stood and looked at Bea, who was pouring the cooked pumpkin into the pie shells. "She's really got it bad, huh?"

"I just hope he's a nice boy," Bea replied as she scraped the pumpkin from the side of the pan.

The buzzer in the entry hall rang loudly, indicating someone was at the front gate. Both James and Mary began to cross the room, saying in unison, "I'll get it."

Bea, wiping her hands on her apron, said. "Never mind, da boat of you. I'll get da first look at dis Mr. Joseph O'Dooley. You two can start peelin' da yams." Then with a teasing smile, she left the room, pushing at the pins that held the braided bun on the back of her head.

"Well, I guess we get to peel the yams," James said as he crossed the room to the sink, where Bea had earlier laid a small pile of yams. Mary retrieved two paring knives from the drawer and a pot from the cupboard. As she neared where he stood, she could feel the tautness begin in her stomach, the feeling that crept up inside her when he was near, a feeling she was learning to welcome. A feeling that no longer frightened her but urged her to move forward. They stood silently, next to each other, alarmingly close. So close Mary began to wonder if she should shift her weight from her left foot to her right, might they touch? Might their arms brush? Would he think it forward of her, or would he think nothing of it and move away? She wondered if he was looking at her but didn't look up to confirm. She kept her eyes fixed on the peelings that dropped aimlessly into the corner of the sink. She pondered whether she should say something, but nothing came to mind. She unthinkingly peeled at the yam as her thoughts turned to the night they had stood on the porch at the back of the house. How he had held her hand in his. The way he had wrapped the shawl around her. She remembered his touch when his fingers brushed her neck, and how she thought he was sure to kiss her. Since then, she had tried to imagine what his kiss would be like. How his lips would feel on hers. How it would feel to be held in his strong arms.

"I think that one's probably done." James's deep voice caused Mary to jump. She looked at him as though she had forgotten he was there, so deep in thought she had been. As what he said registered, she looked down at the yam she absently held in her hand and realized she had shaved it down to half its original size. Slipping the well-peeled yam into the pot, she quickly reached to seize another, only to realize that James had finished peeling the entire pile while she had whittled away at the one.

Suddenly, Bea burst into the room with the strapping Mr. Joseph O'Dooley following closely behind her. Joseph was, as Maggie had described him, a brawny man with reddish-brown hair and a kind face with smiling eyes. Bea introduced him to both James and Mary and then sent Mary off to see what was keeping Maggie.

When Mary and Maggie returned to the kitchen, James and Joseph were engaged in meaningless conversation regarding the weather. Both men stood as they entered the room. Mary waited by the stairs as Maggie eagerly greeted Joseph with a lengthy hug. Bea was back at work mixing something in a large bowl, seemingly oblivious to the others.

James cleared his throat as if to disengage himself from their embrace and said, "Well, Bea, what else do you need help with?"

"I tell you vhat," she said, stopping her rhythmic stirring of whatever it was she was concocting. "Vhy don't you young folk go find someting to do and let me finish up here. Perhaps a nice valk before dinner? Enjoy da veather vhile it's nice," she added. "Dare's a snowstorm brewing, ya know."

"A snowstorm?" Joseph scoffed. "'Tis fifty degrees out."

"If Bea says it's going to snow, believe me, it's going to snow," James replied, backing Bea's statement. He knew it was a sure bet where Bea and weather were concerned. "Although a walk does sound like a splendid idea. Why don't you girls get your wraps, and we'll meet you outside."

James crossed the room and put a loose arm around Joseph's shoulder. "Come, Joseph, let me tell you all about Maggie," he said with a silly grin as he led Joseph toward the side door. Maggie shot a quick glance in his direction.

When the girls joined them, Joseph was rolling a cigarette and offered one to James, who declined. Licking the edge, he rolled it neatly and placed it between his lips. Maggie quickly leaped to his side and linked her arm through his.

"Quite ta place you got here," Joseph said with his heavy Irish accent.

"It's my mother's family's estate," James replied casually.

Maggie and Joseph walked toward the back of the house. Mary watched them as she came to stand next to James. Joseph dropped his arm from Maggie's and swung it behind her, encircling her waist, causing Maggie to move closer to his side. Reaching the back of the house, Joseph stopped and looked around. He nodded his head to the west, as he shouted back to James without turning to address him, "'Tis that the barns?"

Mary followed James as he strolled over to Joseph and Maggie.

"The smaller building is the old carriage house. We use it for the autos now. The other larger building was the stable. It was quite extravagant in its day. My grandfather Shell owned quite an impressive stock of finely bred horses. Unfortunately, they're all long gone now. It's a shame the place isn't used for much more than storage these days."

"It don't be lookin' in disrepair," Joseph surmised as he changed direction and set out toward the stables.

"Oh, no. Grandfather spared no expense in building that one. It will most likely stand another hundred years. Would you like to see it?" James offered, assuming Joseph was going to take a look whether or not he was invited to do so.

Mary quickened her step to match the others and couldn't help but feel as if she were tagging along. Maggie was silently content, snuggled at Joseph's side, and James had seemed to gain interest in showing the stables to Joseph as he lengthened his stride to catch up to him. As they neared the stable, Mary realized what a large building it truly was. She had never been up close to it before and had only viewed it from the distance of Miss Christina's second-story window. As they walked around to the front of the stable, James quickly moved ahead to open one of the large double entryway doors. He stepped aside to usher them all in. Mary quickly scanned the area. James was certainly right about his grandfather sparing no expense in its building. She had never imagined anyone would have had such an elaborate housing for horses. Unlike the dirt floor of her father's barn, the stable floor was laid with brick. Large wooden and iron stalls lined the side walls. Mary counted silently. There were eight on each side, sixteen in all. An area at the back had tiled walls with long, dark wooden benches. A cleared area, also tiled, had been used as a grooming area, James said. Mary thought the stable quite impressive until James explained what they viewed was only part of the full stable. The first room, he explained, had been used for the Shells' personal horses. The second and third extensions, both equally impressive, were used for guests' horses. Back in its day, it was often the case that numerous overnight guests visited the estate, and it was necessary to have proper lodging for their steeds. The second floor, directly above, held sleeping quarters for the drivers and grooms.

"Does ya mind if we have a look around?" Joseph inquired, the excitement in his voice evidence that he was in awe of the grandeur of it all.

"Be my guest," James said and waved his hand, inviting Joseph's curiosity. Joseph scurried off into the next room, Maggie still clinging to his side.

"He seems like a nice fella, don't you think?" James asked of Mary.

"Yes, I suppose so," Mary replied, still admiring the iron and wood stalls. "You know," she said, more thinking out loud than speaking to James, "my father would truly admire this place."

"Tell me about your father, Mary," James asked, turning to her.

"I beg your pardon?" Mary questioned, not sure she had heard him correctly.

"Your father . . . what kind of man is he?"

"Oh," Mary replied as she turned and leaned against a heavy stall door, "he's a very special man."

"Indeed, he must be," James said, moving closer to her. He raised his arm and grasped the cold iron rod of the stall door above her. "Only a special man could have such a special daughter."

As the words left his mouth, he regretted them. They sounded insincere, even to his own ears, the kind of cheap lines he used on the dolls down at the waterfront. He released his grip on the stall rod and let his hand fall to his side.

"I mean, I think you're very special. From the first time I saw you, there was something about you. I would really like to get to know you. I mean ..." He seemed to be stumbling over the words, not letting them take form in his thoughts before they came tumbling out of his mouth. "I would like, oh, I don't know what I mean!"

He moved away from her.

"There's something about you that scares me, Mary Watson, something I can't explain." He turned back to look at her, and her expression was such that he stepped back and tried to explain himself. "Perhaps 'scare' is the wrong word," he said, trying to make her understand. "You don't scare me. What I meant to say was you amaze me, you inspire me, you make me not understand things I thought I was so sure of."

Mary stood silently, only half hearing James's nonsensical utterings, still trying to fathom how it was he knew her last name.

He just stood there then, staring into her eyes, just wanting to embrace her, to whisper softly in her ear that he thought he loved her. Yes! He loved her. He wanted everyone to know. He wanted to shout it out. In that very instant, that momentary pause as he looked into her eyes and she into his, he knew he had chanced to stumble onto that once in a lifetime love that he thought he might never find. He hadn't known what it would be like, what he would feel, or how he would know. Yet there it was, running through every vein and nerve within him, pounding on the door to his heart. His heart had opened, and the rush poured through him and sent out the message to every fraction of his being until he knew he would explode unless he acknowledged the existence of it.

"I love you," he said.

He was silent then, waiting for her reaction. Waiting for, what seemed to James Colton, an eternity. Mary waited too. Waited for whatever was supposed to happen after James Colton spoke those words. She simply stared into his eyes. A single ray of sunlight found its way through the stable window and danced in his eyes just for her. Then, with seemingly no movement at all, he embraced her. Their bodies pressed softly against one another and melded into a new and exciting yet very familiar oneness. With just inches between their lips, their eyes locked, their breath nearly suspended while they connected somewhere on a deeper level than the physical one. Her eyes fluttered to a close as he kissed her. The touch of his lips gently upon hers lit a fuse somewhere deep within her. As his tongue tenderly parted her lips, the fuse burned quickly until it ignited into a great fireball that exploded through her entire body. The room spun, and the floor fell out from under her feet, and no one, other than she and James, existed at all.

Suddenly, Maggie's resounding laughter echoed through the empty stables. As James hesitantly pulled from Mary's embrace, her eyes fluttered open just as Maggie and Joseph emerged through the doorway.

"Oh, James," Maggie squealed, "you have ta hear what Joseph just told me." She was completely unaware of what she had just interrupted.

Mary leaned heavily against the stall door, trying to steady herself.

"What's that?" James questioned as he backed away from Mary, and though his voice was steady, he was sure they could hear the pounding of his heart and notice the smile that refused to leave his face.

"Tell them," Maggie urged, placing her hand on Joseph's chest, still suppressing a giggle.

"Well," Joseph obliged, "I have this mucker, a friend," he clarified for James and Mary's benefit. "He was getting' what he thought ta be a questionable supply of hooch, so he sent a small vial of it ta be tested."

Maggie began to giggle again, anticipating the balance of the story she had already heard.

"About a week later," Joseph continued, raising his voice a little over Maggie's snickers, "he gets back this report in the mail, and it says, 'Dear Mr. O'Malley, we have analyzed the sample ya sent us, and we have bad news. Your horse has the diabetes.'"

Mary laughed with the rest of them, though she hadn't even heard a word Joseph had said.

Everyone was silent on the walk back to the house, other than a giggle or two from Maggie each time Joseph would whisper something in her ear. James and Mary walked just behind them, side by side, and no one knew that he held her hand in his.

"So," Maggie asked of James as they were all seated around the large dining table, feasting on the wonderful dinner Bea had prepared, "you never did explain why it 'tis you're here with us today?"

"Well," James replied as he finished up a bite of turkey, "I truly hated the thought of missing the celebration of this wonderful holiday with my aunt and her family. However, I thought I might be coming down with a cold." He coughed, an exaggerated phony sound. "So I stayed behind."

Everyone laughed.

CHAPTER 22

Mary stood at the small window in her room, watching the snowflakes as they swirled in the outside air. Bea had certainly been right in her prediction. The temperature had dropped and it had started to snow just after midnight. Mary had looked out the window periodically throughout the night as she paced her small room, unable to sleep. Now, at half past eight in the morning, the ground was covered with at least eight inches of fluffy whiteness. She supposed she should go down to the kitchen to see if Bea needed her help. She had been up and dressed since half past seven, but she just hadn't found the courage to go down to the kitchen. She was positive she could not act as though nothing was different about her, as it certainly was. She was different. James Colton had changed her, and she was certain everyone would notice the difference. She hadn't slept but a wink the entire night, too afraid she would wake up and realize it had all been just a dream. But it wasn't a dream. James Colton had said he loved her.

She tore herself away from the mesmerizing flakes she had long stared at, left her room, and proceeded down the stairs. She hadn't bothered to pin her hair, though she knew the Coltons were expected back by the noon hour.

"Good morning," Bea said, and her cheery face greeted her.

"Good morning," she returned absentmindedly as she concentrated on putting a frown on her face, which was nearly impossible because her thoughts of James seemed to automatically cause the corners of her mouth to lift until she grinned from ear to ear.

"I bet I have some news dat vill put a smile on dat face of yours," Bea said as she pulled out a kitchen chair and offered it to Mary. "Mrs. Colton just phoned. Da storm is hittin' dim even vorse dan here. Dey von't be back until da veather lets up. Perhaps not until Saturday or even Sunday. Looks like ve get a few more days to ourselves."

The smile that leaped to Mary's formerly sullen face assured Bea her news was taken well. She didn't want to ruin it with Mrs. Colton's other message. "Mrs. Colton vants all da bed linens changed today, da guest vrooms, too." Bea sighed. "You and Maggie can start vright after breakfast, pullin' the sheets, and send down the soiled linens for me to launder." Her eyebrows raised at the word soiled, knowing, as did Mary, the linens in the guest rooms had all been changed after the costume ball, and there was really no need for the ordeal as they had not been slept in since—other than Mrs. Colton's need to see to it the staff was kept busy in her absence. But certainly Bea was taking on the bulk of the work, so Mary wasn't about to complain.

She roused Maggie from her bed, using the enticement of her being able to spend more time with Joseph if she would get going. Maggie obliged, dressed quickly, and was halfway down the stairs before realizing it wouldn't matter how quickly she finished her chores, as Joseph had to work until six o'clock. Just the same, but less enthusiastic, she ate breakfast and then followed Mary back to the second floor and plodded behind her down the narrow servants' hall and then down the long corridor.

"I'll fetch what clean linens 'tis in the cabinet," Maggie stated as she veered off toward the large wooden cabinets at the end of the west wing. "You start to strippin' Miss Christina's bed."

Mary stripped the beds in both Christina's and Mrs. Colton's rooms before Maggie returned. "I was about to come looking for you," Mary teased. Maggie stuffed a handful of bed linens into Mary's arms and said, "Here, why don'tcha go do James's room, and I'll starts in here."

"Isn't he still asleep?"

"Oh no," Maggie replied as she snapped a clean white sheet open across Mrs. Colton's bed. "He left the house hours ago."

"Oh, but wouldn't it go faster if we worked together?"

"Would ya just go do James's room?" Maggie implored.

Mary turned and left the room, quite confused by Maggie's brashness. She walked the length of the west wing until she came to the last door. James's door stood slightly ajar, and she pushed it open with her forearm, still hugging the bundle of clean linens. The door swung open, and she walked into the darkened room. After laying her bundle down on the dresser, she crossed the room and opened the heavy brocade draperies. She noticed there were at least two, perhaps three, more inches of snow than her last observance. As she turned to get started on the bed, James spoke to her.

"Good morning, Mary." His voice was soft, yet it resounded through the quiet.

"Oh," Mary squealed, more than a little startled by his presence as she looked up to see him standing in the small alcove in the corner of the room.

"Maggie said you had left. I, I . . ." she stuttered slightly. "I was coming to change the linens on your bed."

"I know," James replied. "I had her send you in here." He crossed the room to stand directly in front of her. "I wanted to speak to you. I wanted to tell you I was sorry." He paused. "About yesterday."

Questions immediately popped into her head, yet they all came too suddenly. *He's going to tell me it was a mistake. He didn't mean to tell me he loved me. He didn't mean to kiss me. It was a cruel joke.*

"You seemed upset last evening. I hope I wasn't the cause. I wanted to tell you I was sorry to have been so bold as to kiss you so passionately, or at all, without your permission. I hope you'll forgive me. I wanted to speak to you last night, but I . . ." he hesitated, "didn't have the opportunity." The truth was, he had been afraid to speak to her. He could have gone to her room after everyone had retired. He had even contemplated doing so, but he was sure it would only make matters worse. Either he would frighten her, coming to her room in the dark of night, or he wouldn't be able to tell her how he felt. Like his attempt to talk to her in the stables, his words might get jumbled as they left his mouth, and he wouldn't be able to make her understand what it was he so wanted her to know.

Mary steadied her knees and inhaled deeply, silently promising herself not to weaken because of his closeness and tell him truthfully the thoughts that filled her mind. Tell him she was not upset he had kissed her. Tell him how she felt when they were near. Tell him she couldn't get him out of her thoughts. Tell him she had never been kissed by a man before. Tell him she had never been in love and had no idea what it felt like, but the way she felt about him was something she had never felt before either, and it was unexplainably wonderful. Tell him she had been quiet at dinner and while everyone talked afterward because she couldn't stop thinking about their kiss. She opened her mouth to speak, but the words got stuck somewhere in her throat. As she dared to look into his eyes, her legs turned to jelly, and her knees wobbled.

With no doubt in his mind, he read her silent response and moved a step closer. He reached out to her and let his fingertips delicately brush her cheek. Her skin tingled from his touch. He lingered there momentarily then moved half a step closer. His fingers moved slowly from her cheek toward the back of her head, through the golden strands of hair she had not pinned. Mary raised her head as he took another step forward. Now, just inches apart, their eyes searched deeply into each other's. A soft sigh escaped her, and from some unknown depth of her existence, her mind persuaded her arm to reach for him. Her hand slipped behind his head, and her fingertips stroked the soft curls on the back of his neck, their eyes still locked in each other's gaze, each remembering their lips' first meeting the day before. James lowered his head slightly. Mary's eyes closed as his arm encircled her, pulling her closer. Their lips met, and fireworks filled her head and cascaded through her entire body. His kiss was tender as it moved from her lips to her cheek. Nearing her ear, he softly whispered, "I love you, Mary."

He waited only a short time for an echoed response. When none came, he said, "Spend the day with me."

She pulled gently away from his embrace to look at him.

He said, "I want you to spend the day with me, to talk, to tell you my dreams. I want you to get to know me the way I believe I know you." Her expression caused him to continue. "I do know you, Mary. I feel like I've known you all my life. I know that sounds crazy, but it's the way I feel. I've watched you since you first came here. I've begged Maggie time and time again to tell me all that you share with her. I know all about your family, your mother, your brother, Johnny. I've even prodded Christina for information. I know all about you, Mary Watson, and I know now that I love you. Say you will spend the day with me?" he pleaded.

She searched his face, not knowing how to refuse him, not wanting to refuse him. She spoke softly. "I have to finish up some chores with Maggie first."

"I know," he chuckled. "Maggie told me. She also offered to complete the task on her own."

"Oh, I couldn't—" Mary started to say, but James's laughter stopped her.

"She also said you would refuse to let her do so," he said, smiling the broad smile she was becoming quite accustomed to seeing. "So first, I'll spend the morning assisting you and Maggie with my mother's ridiculous orders. If," he smiled once again, a smile that melted Mary's heart, "you agree to spend the remainder of the day with me."

She replied simply with a nod of her head.

The entire morning, and part of the afternoon, the three of them spent together, stripping and remaking bed after bed. James made several trips to the dumbwaiter, sending Bea pile after pile of linens to be laundered. They joked and laughed and appeared to be all good friends appreciating each other's company. When they finally finished, they enjoyed several of Bea's warmed up leftovers for a late lunch. Maggie phoned the boarding house where Joseph lived to leave a message for him that they could go to the moving pictures that evening, and he should call her when he got home. James had provided Maggie the money, stating that it was a tip for her services in getting Mary to come to his room that morning. Maggie knew full well it was simply an attempt to get her out of the house so he could be alone with Mary for the evening. Maggie found it quite humorous how smitten James was with Mary but had promised him she would keep quiet about it. After lunch, Maggie scurried off to ready herself for Joseph, informing everyone she would first be taking a leisurely bath and might just borrow a little of Jeannette's eau de toilette to fragrance the water. Mary had offered to help Bea with her seemingly endless pile of linens, which needed to be laundered, but Bea refused her help. However, she accepted Mary's offer to clean up the lunch dishes before she scurried off to the waiting piles of sheets.

Placing the last dish into the drip pan, Mary dried her hands as she walked over to the side door and looked out to watch the diminishing snowflakes fall gently to the ground. The storm was winding down but had left a foot and a half of snow to cover the barren and frozen ground.

"Isn't the snow beautiful?" she asked of James as he came up behind her.

"Yes," he replied, "it is. Let's go try it out," he snickered, turning her around to face him.

"What?"

"Let's go outside."

Bundled in warm winter wear of coats, mittens, scarves, and boots, they made their way out into the freshly made winter wonderland, where snow clung to the bare branches and softly fell and melted on their warm faces. It had been a joint decision to build a giant snowman. James had circled and circled the base around the grounds until, even together, they could no longer roll it. When they finished, the man of snow stood over eight feet tall, and James had to retrieve a ladder from the carriage house to adorn its face with coal eyes and a carrot nose. As a final touch, he had removed his own scarf and stretched it around the snowman's neck, tying it loosely at the ends. As they stood back, admiring their work, James lifted his gloved hand with the intention of placing it to Mary's cheek. A clump of snow that clung on the edge of his glove slid silently off and dropped at the base of Mary's neck, where it quickly melted and trickled inside her coat and blouse.

She jumped, and a look of surprise covered her face.

James laughed. "I'm sorry," he chuckled.

She bent down and grabbed a handful of the fluffy white snow and playfully threw it at him. He snickered at what he thought a poor attempt at making and throwing a snowball.

"Oh," he said and laughed as he, in turn, bent and grabbed a handful of snow, "so it's war, is it?"

"Yes!" she cried enthusiastically when his lightly packed snowball hit her in the back, and she turned to grab her own weaponry. Snow flew through the air as they each, in turn, tossed handfuls of fluffy white balls in each other's direction. They placed themselves strategically, using the snowman as the front line between them. After several missed attempts to hit James, Mary took the time to tightly pack a well-rounded handful of snow and then sailed the ball through the air, as if pitching to Babe Ruth himself. This time Mary's throw was as perfectly aimed as if it came from the arm of a disgruntled pitcher, and the ball hit James squarely in the head. He flinched and turned, appearing to Mary to be in true pain. She ran to his side.

"Oh, James!" she cried. Just as she reached him, his arms swung through the air and encircled her waist, pulling her down into the snow on top of him. They rolled together through the fluffy white drifts until they resembled miniatures of the snowman they had just built. Then, purposely stopping their motion, James pinned her softly on the blanket of snow, his body half covering hers. He kissed her softly, and then with more passion as his body urged him on. She responded eagerly, wrapping her arms around his neck. Her body, warmed by him, melted into the soft whiteness that surrounded them.

It was growing dark as he hesitantly pulled himself away from her, stood, and helped her from the ground. They walked arm in arm to the house. The house was quiet as they shed their layers of wet clothing. Maggie had already left to meet Joseph, and Bea was out of sight. James built a fire in the library fireplace while Mary changed and prepared them both turkey sandwiches, which she carried to the library on a silver tray. James had procured a bottle of wine from his father's private collection and had filled glasses for both himself and Mary. Mary accepted the glass hesitantly, worried she might be breaking the law by drinking alcohol. She brought the crystal glass to her lips and sipped a small amount. To her surprise, it tasted fruity, and she drank it eagerly. James refilled her glass without hesitation but silently noted he probably shouldn't give her any more than that. He took a seat in the corner of the overstuffed leather couch and invited her to sit next to him. Still a bit overwhelmed by their closeness, she sat comfortably nearer the other end. He smiled with a mixture of amusement and admiration at her actions. They both eagerly finished the sandwiches she had made, and she offered to make James another, but he declined.

Mary finished her second glass of wine and moved closer to James, where they talked for hours. By the time the third—and James had insisted, last—glass of wine had been finished, Mary's head lay on his chest as his fingertips swirled through her hair, and he recited poetry by Thomas Moore.

> The day had sunk in dim showers,
> But midnight now, with lustre meet,
> Illumined all the pale flowers,
> Like hope upon a mourner's cheek.
> I said (while The moon's smile
> Play'd o'er a stream, in dimpling bliss,)
> "The moon looks On many brooks,
> The brook can see no moon but this;"
> And thus, I thought, our fortunes run,
> For many a lover looks to thee,
> While oh! I feel there is but one,
> One Mary in the world for me.

CHAPTER 23

James descended the steps of the grand staircase on his way to the parlor, where, according to Maggie, his mother was waiting for him. Maggie had advised him that what she perhaps wanted to see him about had something to do with the Christmas party, which was to be held Saturday evening. Maggie said his mother had been going over the guest list when she sent her to get him. James was dreading the party. He knew he would be forced to attend and would undoubtedly have to entertain the attentions of several of his mother's friend's daughters while he watched the woman he loved serving champagne and finger sandwiches to his mother's stuffy friends. He thought it would at least, perhaps, be a change from having to entertain Diane Beaumont, who apparently was still mad at him. She hadn't returned any of his phone calls, and as an afterthought, he assumed it was probably best she had not. He had only tried to get in touch with her to apologize, but he was sure she would have taken it for more than that, which would leave him once again strapped with her. Although, with her out of the picture, he was sure his mother would be quick to try and replace her with a new prospective daughter-in-law, and he wasn't really up to that either. He could only concentrate on Mary. It was so hard to have her live in his house and not be able to openly profess his love for her. His mother, of course, would never allow it. So James had to be careful, and so did Mary. As for now, Maggie was the only person who knew of their secret relationship. And though she had vowed herself to secrecy, both James and Mary knew Maggie's nature didn't lean well to keeping secrets. Charles most likely knew there was something between James and Mary, but surely nothing he'd speak of. James hoped by telling Mary the awful truth about Genny Mueller, he had convinced her his mother would go to great lengths to see to it things went the way she wanted them to go. He knew how she thought. In her mind, she could overlook a physical relationship with a servant, but certainly not a romantic one. She would stop at nothing to destroy Mary, should she have even the slightest knowledge about his love for her. They had to be careful until the time was right.

As he entered the room, his mother, without looking up from the papers she had scattered on the small bureau, said, "Sit down, James."

She stated it as would a teacher to a schoolboy. James obliged her, though he noted her tone and added it to the infinite list he kept in the back of his mind, labeled "why I ran away from home."

As he took a seat, he silently noted that he should change the name of the list he had started when he was about ten.

Once he was seated, Cordella Colton looked up at him. "I wanted to talk to you about the Christmas party this Saturday. Now, I know you and Diane had a . . ." she hesitated slightly, "should we say, a misunderstanding. I really think you need to be a little more discreet in your liaisons with the hired help."

James's mind raced. How could she have found out about Mary and him so quickly? Who could have said anything? Though his mind shifted into full gear as his thoughts paraded through his head, his demeanor held steady and true. The only explanation for his mother's inquiry kept leading him back to Maggie, but why would Maggie tell his mother? Maggie . . . Maggie—his mind shouted her name over and over. Finally, his brain's constant pounding of her name made him realize his mother must be referring to the night Diane saw him kissing Maggie in the entryway, so many weeks ago. A wry smile crossed his lips as he calmly responded, "Yes, mother."

"Well," she said stiffening her back, "I've taken the liberty to discuss this incident with Diane, and I think she now understands." She hesitated again. "Well, let's just say I explained things to her. Anyway, she will be attending the party on Saturday evening as your guest. Agreed?" She did not wait for a reply from James but simply dismissed him by returning to her papers.

James left the room still smiling. His mother's meddling in his life was going to provide the perfect camouflage for Mary and him. After all, he at least knew where he stood with Diane. He knew what type of girl she really was. He was sure, once unneeded, she would be able to bounce right into another relationship with someone else, the marigold that she was, and in the meantime, it would seem as if they were simply dating again. As he bounded up the staircase, he chuckled to himself. Yes, Diane was the definition of the word marigold. She was certainly out to marry gold, and he was quite certain it didn't matter whose.

Cordella Colton had nonchalantly watched her son as he left the room. He and Diane would make such a lovely couple, she thought. Diane would eventually understand she would simply have to overlook his masculine transgressions. As long as he kept them discreet so as not to embarrass her, what truly was the difference? She had certainly learned to not let these matters interfere with her marriage, unlike her mother who had let her father's unfaithfulness completely destroy her. She had hoped James might have grown up not following in the footsteps of the men before him. She had left his rearing to Bea, for that purpose. Bea was a sturdy, motherly type, though she had no children of her own. She came from a peasant background, which in Cordella's experience seemed to produce men more capable of being faithful to their wives. Now, it was clear to see that it was simply a product of breeding and not the rearing.

She had assured Diane this incident was of no real concern. It was a trivial thing, really, considering what she herself had had to endure. She hadn't related to Diane the incident with Genny, that silly little orphan girl, but it had certainly come to mind. It had been then she suspected that Bea's rearing of her son hadn't turned out as she had hoped. When all was said and done, it turned out it wasn't James's child that Genny carried, nor was it her husband's, as she had also suspected—but she supposed it very well could have been either.

Cordella Colton assured herself that she claimed no responsibility in the girl's death, though even after all these years, when the incident came to mind, she felt the need to silently discuss the matter with her conscience. No, it just wasn't her fault, she once again assured herself. After all, who knew the foolish girl was going to go and hang herself?

She had simply offered a solution to the girl's problem when Doctor Meyer had informed her of the girl's condition. Genny had apparently gone to Doctor Meyer, not knowing any other doctor than the one who had been to the Coltons' on several occasions. He, of course, telephoned Cordella immediately following Genny's visit. He apparently thought Cordella, being the girl's employer, should know she was twelve weeks along. Who else was she to assume was the father but James? They were constantly together. When she confronted Genny, the girl insisted she had not been with James in that way, and the baby she carried had been conceived out of a violent act, which of course led her to assume it was William's doing. She knew he found the young thing attractive. She had caught him ogling her more than once. William, of course, was not a violent man, but a little too much alcohol could have explained his actions. She supposed she could have questioned the girl further for information, but all the silly little thing could do was cry and wail nonsensically. In any case, it all fit together. When she worked the weeks backward, she arrived at the weekend the family had attended the summer social, and William had come home earlier than the rest of them, saying he hadn't felt well. When she asked Genny if that was when it happened, the girl shook her head affirmatively. It was certainly plain to see what had to be done. She had torn the page from her husband's personal register that bore the name of Doctor Garrigan, although he was not deserving of the title—his medical license had been revoked years earlier for performing questionable procedures, and it was common knowledge he still performed them discreetly for a sizable fee. She had given the girl the page listing the doctor's name and address and told her the appointment had been set. All she needed to do was to go there. She thought the girl understood. She had taken the precaution of paying the doctor in advance. She certainly wasn't going to hand over five hundred dollars to Genny with no guarantee the girl wouldn't just run off, and then, when the money ran out, be back for more with blackmail threats.

She was just as shocked as anyone when they discovered the girl's body hanging from the staircase of the turret, and the page from her husband's register left lying on the floor with a scribbled note written in German on the reverse side. Bea had translated the note once for them, and then several times for the investigators. It said, "I cannot live with what I have done. Believe me, I did not know what the doctor was doing until it was too late. Please forgive me."

Cordella would have just swept the whole matter under the rug, so to speak, but of course, the police had to be called in. An autopsy indicated the girl had forcibly miscarried. Then, of course, the press had gotten wind of the whole thing. The autopsy results, along with the page from her husband's register listing the name of Doctor Garrigan, led them to make accusations that William Colton was the father of the girl's child, and he had forced her to go to Doctor Garrigan for an abortion—allegations Cordella believed at the time to be mostly true. Of course, Doctor Garrigan was brought in for questioning but denied everything, never divulging the payment he had received from Cordella. Eventually, the police had somehow stumbled onto the truth of the matter, finding the name and address of the man Genny had gone to see about a job on the same day as the summer social. After lengthy questioning, he, to the relief of everyone involved, finally admitted to raping the girl. Although it was never confirmed, it was believed the police had made a deal with him, overlooking several other offenses, including running a prostitution ring, providing he admitted to the assault. William said it was because of the pressure he was putting on them to clear his name and stop the press from the field day they were having. He had, of course, threatened a lawsuit against the paper, but he dropped it quickly when Cordella had confided in him that she had torn the doctor's address from his book to give to Genny and had paid Doctor Garrigan. Eventually, the Coltons were able to dismiss the whole matter with a clean slate.

Cordella sighed deeply, staring unseeingly at the guest list she held in her hand. *Clean slate,* she thought to herself. *Well, clean to the public anyway.* The whole matter had caused a terrible rift between James and her. He, of course, blamed her totally for the girl's death. William said he understood her intentions completely, and yet the matter had caused them to drift further apart as well. And, of course, Bea had never forgiven her either. She hadn't asked for, nor did she need their forgiveness. After all, she certainly was not to blame.

CHAPTER 24

James dressed quickly in the tuxedo Charles had laid out for him. Guests had already been arriving by the time he made it home from the plant. There had been quite an accident that afternoon, and of course, he was left to smooth things over, as his father knew he would.

"You're so much better at dealing with those people." His father's words echoed in his head. "Those people." Just who did he think those people were? And why was it the social class he apparently belonged to felt a need to tag the word "those" in front of people? Why couldn't his father simply have said he was better at dealing with people? An idealistic smile touched his lips as he wondered if the workers down at the plant referred to his father and the like as "those people."

Fumbling with his tie, he left his room and headed toward the servants' wing. He had to see Mary before he proceeded to the grand room. He hadn't had the chance to see her alone all week, and he needed to make sure she understood why he would be with Diane at the party that evening. He was sure Mary would be serving, as Jeannette was once again plagued with an ailment of some sort. He certainly didn't want Mary getting upset if she were to see Diane draped on his arm, as he was sure by evening's end she undoubtedly would be.

He waited only momentarily after a soft knock at her door went unanswered. She was most likely already downstairs busy helping Bea with things. Other than the costume ball his mother held every

October, the Christmas cotillion was certainly the biggest event of the year in Bay View. The house would be full for days with out-of-town guests, family, and friends.

James bounded down the servants' stairway to the kitchen. The room was a maze of hired help, being commanded by a red-faced Bea shouting orders. Trays of hors d'oeuvres lined every available counter space as well as the large wooden table. James nonchalantly reached for a small, triangular-cut finger sandwich, only to be slapped by Bea's waiting hand.

"You not changed since you ver five, Master James," she scolded, flashing him a quick smile. Then she returned to the business at hand. Half of the extra help Mrs. Colton had hired spoke only Irish. Bea was finding herself having to issue all orders through Maggie for translation. James put a friendly arm around her shoulders.

"Don't get the screamin' meemies on me now, Bea. Just tell Maggie to pretend they're me. She'll have no problem then because she sure has no problem hollering at me. Right, Mag?" Maggie shot him a cross glance, affirming she had overheard his statement. He then picked up the sandwich Bea had earlier slapped his hand for and whirled around to stand behind Maggie.

"Where's Mary?" he whispered in her ear.

"She be out servin' already," Maggie grumbled back at him. Then with a bit of desperation, she asked, "Can ya explain grand room ta this one here," she pointed to the little man who stood smiling in front of her. "He's ta be helpin' at the bar, not in the kitchen."

"I'll do better than that," James replied as he popped the sandwich into his mouth. Steering the man by the shoulders toward the door, he yelled back at Maggie, "I'll deliver him there myself."

James made his way toward the grand room with the small man, who apparently spoke no English and was dressed in a black suit twice his size, belted tightly around his waist to keep his pants from falling down. The exquisite sound of an excellent quartet performing Christmas selections drifted to James's ear as they neared the grand room. He hummed along, unaware he was doing so. Stepping into the large west wing entryway, he scanned the many faces, looking for Mary, and chanced to lock eyes with Diane Beaumont as she was being helped with the removal of her coat.

"James!" Her high-pitched shriek cut through James like a knife, and the feigned giggle that followed twisted the imaginary weapon. She was actually a beautiful woman, if James were to stop and think about it—her high cheekbones, dusted lightly with just the perfect amount of rouge, and her dark hair, done in upswept curls that framed her delicate face. She was quite shapely, and even at first glance held an air of refinement. Yes, he thought to himself, if one didn't know Diane, she would appear to be quite the catch, but he did know her, and that was enough said. He forged an imaginary smile and crossed the room to greet her.

"I'm happy you came, Diane," he said and kissed her extended hand. Diane fluttered her eyes in a gesture of pure and—James was fully convinced—simulated delight.

"Do we now have a chaperone, or have you the need for a bodyguard?" Diane asked, raising her eyebrows in the direction of the small man who had followed James across the entryway. James had nearly forgotten about his charge as he stepped backward to see to whom Diane was referring, and he nearly knocked the poor fellow over.

"Oh," James said, startled, "I almost forgot. I need to see to it he gets to the bar if you'll excuse me a minute."

"Oh no, you don't. I won't be letting you out of my sight this time, Mr. James Colton." She smiled heavily, as though she were scolding a mischievous pet, then locked her arm through his. "You can procure me a glass of champagne while you deliver your charge."

James, with Diane clinging to his side, entered the room cautiously, his eyes darting from table to table in search of Mary. The room was crowded with far too many guests for James's taste. He more enjoyed intimate dinner parties, where one could have a good conversation rather than shouting over the din of the crowd while trying to have a chat with the person sitting right next to you. As he crossed the room, with Diane clutching his arm and the small man in the too big black suit trotting closely behind him, he finally spotted Mary. She was offering a silver tray filled with assorted pastries to the mayor's wife. He hastened his step across the floor, wanting to quickly deliver the little man where he belonged and then, hopefully, deposit Diane into a conversation with someone so he could make an excuse to slip away and talk to Mary. Luckily, one of the other bar waiters spoke English as well as Irish, and the little man was quickly put to work washing glasses at the back bar. James was quick to spot a mutual acquaintance of his and Diane's and briskly steered Diane across the room. As they veered close to the dancing area, Diane seized the opportunity and stopped James dead in his tracks. As he turned to question her sudden halt, she quickly wrapped her arm around his neck and waited patiently for him to lead her into the waltz.

James, though annoyed, chuckled slightly at her subtle request. "Would you like to dance, Diane?"

"I thought you'd never ask." She smiled as innocently as she could muster.

As he led her into the first step and turned slightly, he stared directly into Mary's green eyes as she turned from the table she was serving. James hesitated for a moment, not wanting to let go of the spell those eyes held him in. His momentary pause seemed to Diane mere politeness, allowing the servant to pass with her tray, but when she didn't move, Diane became annoyed. Tossing her head, she snipped, "Do you mind?"

Instantly, Mary responded to the command. "Excuse me. I'm so sorry," she whispered as she swiftly passed by them.

"Your mother's right. It's impossible to find good help these days." She instantly fell back into step with James, who had only circled her around the floor to watch Mary's exit. He absentmindedly continued the motion, wanting only to run after Mary, to pull her into his arms and whisper into her ear that he was sorry for Diane's behavior, sorry that anyone would talk to her that way, and promise her he would see to it that no one would ever again treat her like that, like one of "those people." But instead, he continued through the motions of waltzing with Diane, pulling her close to him, only for the fact he then did not have to look at her, nor she at him. They didn't have to speak, and he could think, think of Mary.

The evening crawled on, at least for James, who couldn't seem to pry Diane from his side, though he had tried time and time again. The one time she allowed him out of her sight was to fetch her another glass of champagne from the bar, as her glass, in her opinion, had been empty much too long, and the man making the rounds was much too slow. Of course, as James made his way to the back bar and then waited there while the glass was being refilled, Mary had been nowhere in sight. He did, however, spot Maggie and managed a brief conversation with her. She had assured him Mary, though upset, understood he was with Diane just for appearances' sake.

Luckily, James had found seating at a table with a few of Diane's acquaintances, allowing them to take part of the burden of conversation. James would nod his head now and again, pretending to be interested in their idle chitchat as he kept a watchful eye on the entrance.

Mary had again entered the room, and he watched her as she moved from table to table with her tray full of offerings. The softly lit room lent an aura of enchantment to her as she floated from table to table. He watched intently as she bent from the waist to offer an older gentleman a selection. A soft beam of light silently bounced from the silver tray and illuminated her face. Her eyes sparkled with tiny shimmering lights, and James became instantly mesmerized by their beauty.

"Don't you think so, James? James, James!" Diane's voice pushed its way into his head and invaded his thoughts.

Somehow he managed to pull his eyes from Mary and turn to her. "I'm sorry, what?"

"Oh, never mind." She decided that perhaps they should dance again as it appeared to be the only way to keep his attention.

As she led him toward the dance floor, he couldn't help but notice Mary had moved on to another table. The quartet was playing something slow and melancholy. James didn't listen closely enough to recognize the melody as Diane wrapped her arm around his shoulder. He led her deftly through the motions, turning as he needed, to keep an eye on Mary's whereabouts.

"Is there something wrong, James?" Diane asked in a voice just above a whisper. James had to ask her to repeat her question.

"You seem so distant tonight," she said as he turned to look at her.

"I'm sorry. I guess my mind is elsewhere." He then quickly added, "You know, there was an accident at the plant today." An offered excuse as to what subject his mind might be preoccupied with. Placing her right palm to his cheek, she moved closer to him and whispered, "Perhaps this will take your mind off your worries."

He watched speechlessly as her eyes closed, and he felt her hand move from his cheek to the back of his neck, pulling his head toward her. As her lips pressed firmly into his, he closed his eyes, mostly out of habit, and let her uninvited tongue intertwine with his.

Mary had noticed Diane leading James toward the dance floor. She had watched as they floated across the floor. She knew James was with Diane for appearances' sake, just as Maggie had said, and yet, when she had first seen them together earlier in the evening, the pangs of jealousy had leaped from her stomach to her throat, and tears had stung her eyes.

Now she stood inconspicuously watching them dance until Diane placed her fingers to James's cheek, then she fell back into the shadows along the sidewall. She placed her now empty serving tray on a service cart and stood quietly watching as Diane whispered something to him and then wrapped her fingers around the back of his neck. An enormous empty yet heavily weighted feeling lodged itself in the pit of her stomach. Her heart raced and pounded against her chest, somehow knowing what was about to happen, and yet silently pleading that it would not. Then, when Diane's lips pressed against his, whatever it was that had lodged itself in her stomach instantly pushed up into her throat. Her every emotion seemed to explode in unison as she watched James's eyes close and his lips press against Diane's. Her heart began to beat too loudly in her chest, and her chest, heavily burdened, seemed to labor with each breath. Finally the realization of what she was witnessing pounded like a hammer in her head. She somehow persuaded her legs to move her across the floor, weaving through the tables of seated guests until she was out of the grand room. The entryway was crowded with guests as she pushed through them blindly, not knowing where she was headed, only that she needed to get away. She needed to be somewhere where she could let the sobs, which were building inside, escape. Somewhere where the tears that had already begun to stream down her cheeks could rush forth. Somewhere where she could wrap her arms around herself and stop the hurt that throbbed within her. She found her way to the back staircase that led to the second floor of the west wing. She climbed the steps hurriedly until she reached the upper landing. Without a care as to whether anyone was in the west wing or not, she entered the hall and proceeded down the long corridor toward the servants' wing. Her tears fell silently down her face, and she wiped them away with the back of her hand. As she finally reached the sitting area at the top of the main staircase, there he was, suddenly standing directly in front of her. Appearing slightly winded, he moved slowly toward her. Her arms hung at her sides, and her fingers clenched themselves into fists. As he neared her, his arms reached out. She knew he would try to embrace her, and when he did, her clenched fists would be ready to pound against his chest, and the words would spill from her lips. Words of hate, for she hated him. She hated him with every inch of her very being. Hated him for kissing Diane, hated him for even being with Diane. She hated him for pretending to love her, hated him for making her fall in love with him. Then, as he reached her, and his arms began to encircle her waist, the realization of her thoughts collided with his touch, and she collapsed in his arms, burying her face against his chest. His arms encircled her trembling body, and her now un-fisted hands encircled his shoulders, pulling herself into the warm embrace of the man she loved. In one swift motion, James bent slightly and scooped her into his arms. She tightened her grasp around his neck, her face still buried in his chest as she sobbed. James walked down the long corridor to his bedroom, turned the knob, and pushed open the door. He walked into the dimly lit room, attempted to swing the door closed with his foot, then crossed the room and gently lay Mary down on his bed. He lay next to her, his arm bent and his hand propping up his head. He gently wiped the tears from her cheeks with his fingertips.

"I'm sorry," she sobbed. "It's," she sniffled, "just that . . ."

"Shhh," James whispered softly. "I'm the one who's sorry."

"You kissed her."

James smiled softly. "She kissed me. There's a difference."

He bent his head and placed gentle kisses on her tear-stained cheeks. "I love you, Mary. Nothing will ever change that."

A soft but firm knock on the half-opened door startled Mary. James, still lavishing her with tender kisses, didn't move, but questioned, "Yes?"

From the hall came Charles's familiar voice. "It is I, sir, Charles. Miss Beaumont sent me. She said you were feeling ill? Can I be of service?"

James, still staring into Mary's eyes, didn't turn his head as he responded to the unseen Charles. "I'm fine now. Tell Diane I'll be down shortly."

"Very good, sir."

As Mary listened to Charles's echoing footsteps, she attempted to raise herself up from the bed. "I better get back," she said. "Bea will wonder where I've gone."

James pulled her gently back to the bed with his free arm. "No, let me go down and excuse myself from the party and arrange for Charles to take Diane home. The party's almost over, and she already thinks I'm not feeling well."

Mary knew very well the parties lasted long past midnight, sometimes even to three or four o'clock in the morning, but when she started to object, James touched his finger to her lips.

"Please stay here and wait for me. After I see to Diane, I'll find Bea and tell her you're not feeling well. Maggie will cover for you. Please promise me you'll wait here for me?"

She nodded, not being able to refuse him anything.

It didn't take much for James to convince Diane that he wasn't feeling well, as he had pretended he was going to be ill when he had run from her arms to get to Mary. After informing her that he would have Charles see to it she got home, he once again, and very convincingly, placed one hand on his stomach while covering his mouth with the other. Diane was eager to bid him farewell with a "hope you feel better soon" as she encouraged him to take his leave. Once out of her sight, he quickly sought out Maggie, who was just coming from the kitchen on her way to the grand room. He, in as little detail as possible, explained the situation to her. Then he hugged her for her promised cooperation in seeing to it that Bea, as well as anyone else questioning Mary's whereabouts, would be informed that she had taken ill and had gone to her room. Jeanette was already confined to her bed with some ailment, so perhaps whatever she had was contagious, or so Maggie should offer if anyone became suspicious about both James and Mary becoming ill at the same time.

The sound of approaching footsteps caused Mary to sit up and move to the edge of the bed. She instantly began to wonder what she would do if the person, fast approaching the room, was not James. She fretted. *What if it was Charles again, or Diane, or Mrs. Colton?* Instantly, she leaped from the bed and scurried to the alcove, trying to assure herself if someone other than James should come into the room, she would at least be out of sight. Her breath quickened as she heard the doorknob turn and then the slight squeak as the door began to open. The dim light from the hall cast a long shadow into the room as she huddled closer to the wall of the alcove. When James softly whispered her name, she breathed a sigh of relief and stepped out from the shadows.

James turned on the small lamp that sat on the nightstand, which immediately cast soft shadows into the room. Mary stood silently, waiting for him to come to her. When he did, he cradled her face in the palms of his hands.

He looked into her vivid green eyes, still moist from the tears she had shed. The soft glow from the lamp created dancing sparkles in the emerald green. The shimmering twinkle mesmerized him, calling him to look deeper until he was sure he was looking into her very being, and it captured him—his breath, his heart, his everything. He let his lids close then, the vision of her seared into his memory, and he kissed her softly.

Mary trembled with his touch. The realization that she loved this man had heightened her every sense. Everything about him electrified her—the thought of him, the sight of him, the soft words he spoke, the smell of his cologne, his touch, the taste of his lips on hers.

The soft kiss ended, and as he looked back into her eyes, Mary suddenly noticed something in his face that had not been there before—a look of uncertainty.

He softly whispered, "I love you, Mary." Then, with an unusual urgency in his voice, he said, "Please, tell me you love me too."

She smiled sweetly at him. "I do, James," she whispered softly. "I do love you."

CHAPTER 25

Mary strolled silently through the quiet house. She paused momentarily in the parlor to watch the fire Charles had started earlier. It flickered and snapped its flame, trying to mesmerize the observer. The fragrant smell of the enormous cedar tree that stood in the corner of the room tickled her nose, and she crossed the room once again to marvel at the beautiful ornaments that hung from its sturdy branches. The Coltons had decorated the tree together, an apparent time-honored tradition Mary thought odd for them. She and Maggie had been summoned to unwrap the fragile ornaments for the family to hang from the tree. While Mrs. Colton's continual warnings to be careful with them made her nervous, she had managed to unwrap all the crystal teardrops and hand-painted glass bulbs without mishap. The tree sparkled with brilliance as the fire's glow bounced light from ornament to ornament, and the crystal teardrops danced with the illumination. Though the entire house had been gaily decorated for the season and the Christmas cotillion, the decorating of the family's tree meant the holiday was upon them.

The Colton family had been invited to the mayor's house for dinner. James had told Mary he had tried to beg out of the invitation, but his father had insisted he attend, and as his father didn't insist on much of anything, he felt obligated to accommodate him. James told her Diane Beaumont would unfortunately also be in attendance, but he assured her he would not so much as offer her a goodnight kiss.

"I'll tell her I feel a cold coming on, and surely she would not want to risk catching it so close to the holidays." He had produced a fake sneeze to show Mary just how convincing he could be. She had giggled at his fabricated illness and told him soon Diane would think he was truly plagued, with all the recent ailments he was inventing. She assured him she would busy herself by wrapping the presents she had purchased for Bea and Maggie.

"And me?" he had asked, almost childlike.

"Oh really, James, what could I give you that you don't already have?" she had answered teasingly.

He had smiled softly and pulled her close to him.

"Nothing," he answered. "As long as I have you, I want for nothing."

She passed through the parlor toward the main staircase and wondered if the present she had bought for him was truly appropriate. As she ascended the main stairs, which she only dared to do when the Coltons were not home, she wondered if he would like the monogrammed silver flask she had purchased. She had used an entire month's pay to buy it. Maggie said it was a very handsome present and James was sure to think it was the bee's knees. Of course, when she had purchased it, she told the store owner it was for a friend who liked to carry tonic for medicinal purposes. Maggie told her it was silly to make up such a story as the store owner knew very well what it was to be used for. After all, everyone that was anyone carried a hip flask around with them, even women. Mary knew James carried a flask. He had even offered her a drink once. She had declined, though he said it was very smooth Canadian whiskey. She had noticed, however, that his flask was plain brown, sort of a leather-covered bottle, while others she had seen carried by some of the men at the Colton parties, were quite decorative. The store owner had shown her some very handsome gold and silver flasks, ornately decorated, but when he showed her the shiny silver one that he said could be engraved with a gentleman's initials, she had instantly made her decision. She hoped James didn't think she was condoning his breaking the law by giving him a means to carry around alcohol. It was just that she had no idea what else she would buy for him.

She entered her room and found the brightly colored scraps of material and lengths of unneeded ribbon Bea had given her to use as wrappings. She would have so preferred the beautifully colored paper Christina was using for her gifts, but of course she couldn't part with any of it.

Mary knelt on the floor to reach under her bed to retrieve the gifts she had hidden there and noticed the corner of a piece of paper sticking out from beneath her pillow. She reached across her bed and plucked it from its hiding place eagerly, knowing it was another note from James. He had left her many notes over the last couple of weeks. Some were just simple little messages saying he loved her. Some were two or three sentences, telling her she was beautiful and he could not wait to be with her, while others were full-page sonnets bequeathing his undying love. All were signed F.A.E. She looked at the sheet of paper on which James had written:

"If you dare to catch my cold (ha-ha), meet me in my room at midnight. Love, F.A.E."

She folded the little piece of paper and again tried to fathom just what F.A.E. stood for. James had refused to tell her, at her every request. He simply said, "You'll see."

She had tried several silly guesses—funny as elephants, fat and entertaining, and even more serious attempts such as fondly and effectionately, but James had just laughed, again saying, "You'll see," adding, "besides, affectionately is spelled with an a," though he knew very well she knew that too.

Tucking the little piece of paper into her pocket, she pulled the gifts out from under her bed. There was a hair comb for Bea and an autographed picture of Rudolph Valentino for Maggie. Mary had been disappointed after showing the picture to Christina—simply looking for approval—when Christina informed her it wasn't really Mr. Valentino's signature, but just a copy of an original.

"Like a picture in a newspaper," she said. "They are just mass produced."

Mary hoped Maggie would like it anyway.

She scolded herself once again for taking anything Christina said to heart. Christina was just a cruel person, and it was little wonder she had no friends. Mary had learned for the most part to simply tolerate her for who she was.

The Coltons arrived home around eleven o'clock. Mary had immediately been summoned by Christina to help her prepare for bed, even though she had already turned down the quilts earlier in the evening. Christina was simply exhausted from the evening's festivities and could not find the energy to undress herself. As Mary tucked her under the coverings, Christina had to recap for her the wide array of food they had had for dinner.

James lay awake staring at his ceiling in his softly lit room. He had just heard the clock that stood at the far end of the west wing chime the half hour. It was eleven thirty, and he doubted he could wait another half hour for Mary. He rolled over and opened the drawer on the small nightstand next to his bed and pulled out the small velvet box he had put there earlier. He opened the box slowly and sat upright to once again admire its contents. Two small identical heart-shaped lockets, both engraved with the letters F.A.E. He gently lifted one out of the case and flipped it open. As he had done several times before, he admired the tiny picture it held.

He had found the lockets at Mason's. They were certainly not as nice as Tiffany & Company in New York could have offered, but then he wasn't headed to New York again before the holiday. He had been out shopping and had already purchased presents for the family, but he had wandered through shop after shop trying to decide on the perfect gift for Mary. When the jeweler showed him the delicate heart-shaped pendant, he knew it to be the perfect gift. The jeweler thought it a bit odd that he wanted two of them exactly alike, except one to hang on a delicate chain and the other to be placed on a heavier chain. Although it was not uncommon for men of distinction to wear jewelry, they were usually not adorned with trinkets, and certainly not heart-shaped lockets, but James knew it was the perfect gift.

Identical heart-shaped pendants. His pendant would hold a picture of her, and hers a picture of him. Both would be engraved with his undying vow of love, F.A.E.—Forever, Always, Eternally. James knew he was driving Mary mad by not telling her what the letters stood for, but she would soon learn their meaning when he showed her the lockets and presented one to her for Christmas.

After he had purchased the lockets and instructed the jeweler on how to engrave them, he hurried off to Mary's aunt's apartment to see about obtaining a small picture of Mary suitable for the locket. James recalled how Mary's Aunt Matilda had been quite surprised by his visit but was quick to allow him entrance to her small dwelling. She had thought his request rather odd when he asked if perhaps she had a picture of Mary. Not wanting to tell her about the lockets, he had only offered it had something to do with a Christmas present. She had produced a small album of photos. Each picture was neatly pasted on heavy paper, using small, black triangular corner holders, and had been meticulously labeled with date and content. She had offered him a seat on her small divan, while she sat directly across from him on a wooden-backed chair. As she carefully flipped through the pages, she had again tried to procure James's intentions for the photo. Again, he stated it was for a present and had then added he bought presents for all his mother's employees, so as not to pique her interest. As she flipped backward and then forward through the album, not offering James more than a glimpse of its contents, she said, "Well, I'm afraid the only picture I have of Mary is surely most unsuitable for your needs. Whatever they may be," she had added coyly.

"May I see it?" James asked, sounding a bit agitated. After all, he thought to himself, she doesn't even know what my needs are.

She turned the album around for him to view. "I'm afraid it's the picture of her class graduation from school last year. She sent it to me herself."

James reached for the album to get a closer look. Matilda surrendered it a bit unwillingly. He had quickly scanned the photo of four boys and half a dozen girls. Instantly, he spotted Mary. A bit younger looking, perhaps, because of the large childish bow adorning her hair, but still his beautiful Mary. The picture would be perfect to fit into the locket. The problem at hand was how to get Miss Bryer to part with it. He certainly couldn't tell her he would be cutting up the photo, as he only wanted the small piece that contained Mary's face. Furthermore, she had said it was her only picture of Mary.

"I'd like to make you an offer, Miss Bryer," he had said in the most persuasive voice he could, without sounding too bushwa.

He had procured the photograph with nothing more than a promise to have Mary's picture, as well as Miss Bryer's, professionally taken to adorn the photo album—after Christmas, of course.

He tucked the locket back into its velvet nest and placed it back into the drawer, then lay back to once again stare at the ceiling, awaiting Mary's arrival.

CHAPTER 26

It was late, around four o'clock. I smirked, recalling John's views on proper reference. That even though I had been up all night, if it was after midnight, I was to say it was very early, not late.

I had been calling John every evening, at his request. He wanted to know how the book was coming. I had been writing nonstop for days now. If I kept up this pace, I would be done in no time.

I stood up from the desk, deciding I might lie down for a few hours before getting back to work. John had teased me earlier that night on the phone, that if this were the kind of vacation I was taking, I might as well have stayed at home. He had also said he missed me. I, however, was not so quick to offer a like response.

As I lay down on the small bed and closed my eyes, I thought about John. I supposed I missed him too, but I didn't want to relay that to him and give him any false hopes of how I was going to answer his proposal. I suddenly realized G-Pat and B-Pat had never debated the proposal issue. I thought that rather odd.

It had been weeks since he had asked me to marry him. He had been sincere when he told me I should take as long as I needed before I answered, but I knew I couldn't make him wait forever. I did love John, but not in the forever and ever sort of way. I just didn't think he was the right man for me. We had nothing in common. He, of course, argued that we had everything in common. I was a writer, and he was an editor—the perfect relationship, in his opinion. He was energized by the fast-paced New York lifestyle. He loved to attend the opera or a Broadway show. He lived in a loft, right in Manhattan, and he wore Armani suits and John Lobb shoes. He loved all the hustle and bustle, and it suited him. I had my apartment in Manhattan too, but I was rarely there. I couldn't live that way all the time, not day after day, year after year. I sure thought that was what I wanted when I moved there so many years ago, but I much preferred my small cottage farm in RUNY (Rural Upstate New York). I could be myself there, dress in blue jeans and an oversized sweatshirt. Let my hair down, so to speak. I couldn't write in Manhattan, as it turned out. My thoughts there were as jumbled as the city's traffic. John, of course, couldn't stand being in the country for more than a few hours. It bored him, and the quiet drove him quite mad.

Just before I drifted off to sleep, I was positively sure I still had no idea which way I was going to answer his proposal.

CHAPTER 27

Christmas morning, Mary awoke very early. She and Maggie had made plans to attend worship service together. It was the one luxury they were allowed by the Coltons, as long as they were back in time to help Bea with the meals and tidying up. Though the Coltons had opened gifts on Christmas Eve, there would be plenty more to open Christmas morning, and Mary and Maggie would certainly be needed to clear away the wrappings. Of course, she wouldn't be able to be with James until much later that evening, when they would exchange presents in the privacy of James's room. She was getting quite used to meeting James late in the evening. After everyone else had long retired, she would sneak to his room through the darkened house. They had decided should the need arise, it would be much easier for her to hide in his room, should someone interrupt them, than for him to hide in hers. Though they had never encountered the need to hide from anyone, she often thought of having to duck into his wardrobe closet or slither under his bed to conceal herself. When she cleaned his room, she always made sure to dust extra carefully under the bed.

She had bumped into Maggie the last few evenings in the corridor, as Maggie herself had been sneaking up the back staircase after a late night with Joseph. Maggie spoke of nothing but Joseph these days. How big and strong he was and what a wonderful husband he would make, and sometimes, to Mary's embarrassment, how intimate they were. Although Maggie knew Mary and James had a relationship, Mary refrained from discussing it, even with Maggie. James was so concerned about what his mother might do should she discover the truth. Just a few more months, he would say to her. She wasn't sure what difference a few months was going to make, but it didn't matter. She was happy, and having her and James's relationship a secret somehow made it feel even more special. She wished she could confide in someone, though. She wanted to share with Maggie how she felt about James. To tell her how they would talk for hours in the darkness of his room, and how she would constantly have to shush him when he would speak or laugh too loudly.

She spent Christmas Eve afternoon with her aunt, and they had exchanged gifts. Her aunt had given her a book—*A Christmas Carol* by Charles Dickens. She had purchased a lace vestee and collar set for Matilda. Her aunt had said she greatly admired it. She had told her aunt of her concerns that she hadn't heard from her father in almost a month, but as usual, Matilda told her she fretted too much, and she should put a smile on her face before the other guests arrived. Mary had thought she would be spending the afternoon with just her aunt, but to her dismay, Matilda had invited Ezra and Tom Bellows over for the afternoon's festivities. Mr. Bellows was very jovial, though he complained of the snow and cold, and Tom hadn't said much of anything between mouthfuls of the exquisitely decorated cookies her aunt had prepared. She had in earnest tried to be cordial to him, but every time she looked his way, he was staring at her. There was truly something evil she saw in his eyes, and though her aunt had encouraged her to befriend him, she simply could not. Mary supposed, however, all in all, it had been an enjoyable afternoon.

By two in the afternoon on Christmas Day, the entire Colton family, all stuffed with Bea's baked ham and candied sweet potatoes, were off to deliver Christmas gifts to some of their closer friends, apparently another family tradition. Once the dishes were cleared and washed, Maggie, Bea, Jeannette, and Mary sat around the big kitchen table exchanging the presents they had bought for one another. Maggie was thrilled with the picture of Rudolph Valentino that Mary had bought her, even after Mary told her Christina had said it was just a copy. Maggie had swooned over it just the same. Jeanette had given each of them a small bottle of perfume that each of them, in turn, wrinkled their noses at—when she wasn't looking of course. Mary was slowly opening the gift Bea had given her and soon discovered a small beaded purse. Maggie squealed, "How chic!" as she ripped open her present from Bea, hoping it would be the exact same thing. When it was, she squealed all the more.

As Mary started to open her present from Maggie, the phone rang, and Bea rose to answer it. Maggie stopped her squealing but still danced around the kitchen, swinging her new bag. She was delighted by the noise the draped beads at the bottom of the purse made as they clicked against one another. Bea was saying "ya" for about the third time before she said, "Mary, it's for you."

Then she shushed Maggie.

"For me?" Mary questioned, a little surprised. As she crossed the room to take the phone, she whispered to Bea. "My aunt?"

Bea covered the mouthpiece with her hand saying, "No, 'tis a man."

"Papa?" Mary shrieked as she nearly dropped the earpiece in her rush to take it from Bea.

"Papa?" she squealed into the phone.

CHAPTER 28

Doctor Gate, "Doc" as folks called him, waited patiently on the small train platform at the edge of town. In the distance, he could see the billowing smoke in the clear, cold sky, always the first indication the train would be arriving in due time. He rubbed his old hands together vigorously then smoothed them over his wrinkled face. He once again doubted his decision about contacting Mary. He knew it went against everyone's wishes. He was sure Matilda would scream her complaint first chance she got. Matilda didn't much concern him, though. She had been screaming the first time he laid eyes on her, some forty odd years ago now, when he brought her into this world. A crooked smile touched his lips as he thought to himself what a young man he had been then. *Where did all the years go?* he wondered before his thoughts turned to Julius. His condition had worsened each day over the past few weeks. Yet each time he had asked Julius about notifying Mary, he had said no. Doc remembered Julius's words clearly. "Don't you go calling Mary. I sent her away so she wouldn't have to see me the way I am now." His words had been labored as he fought for each breath he took. Doc had tried to explain to Julius it wasn't fair that Mary not be able to say goodbye, but he wouldn't listen. From somewhere, he had scraped up enough energy to raise his voice to Doc when he said, "We said our goodbyes four months ago. All she could do here is weep over me. Now leave it alone."

He had collapsed onto the pillow then and closed his tired eyes. Doc had sat there beside him for hours, listening to his faint breathing and wondering if Mary could even get there in time. He had finally decided she at least had the right to know about her father's condition and had gone downstairs to phone her. He had gotten the name and address of the family Mary was staying with from one of her recent letters to her father. As he was waiting for someone to come on the line, he thought several times about hanging up. It had been Christmas Day, after all. As the train came into sight, the old doctor took a deep breath and fixed a rehearsed smile on his wrinkled face.

In the short ride from the train station back to his house, Doc tried to prepare Mary for the visit with her father. He had deteriorated so quickly in the past four months, Doc felt he couldn't prepare her enough for the shock that awaited her. Even in the two days it had taken her to get there, Julius's condition had worsened considerably. Doc knew it was just a matter of time now, days, perhaps only hours.

When they reached the house, he told Mary to use his office to freshen herself up a bit, and he'd go check on her father. As he reached the top of the stairs, Miss Emma, his housekeeper and nurse, was tiptoeing out of Julius's room. She spoke in a whisper. "I heard you pull up. Is Mary with you?"

Doc nodded, then asked, "How's he doing?"

Emma knew Doc Gate only too well. She had been his nurse for nearly thirty years and his housekeeper for the last fifteen since his wife passed on. She knew what he was really asking was, "Is he still among the living?"

"He's asleep," she whispered.

Mary freshened up as Doc had told her to do. Doc had a way about him that people just automatically did what he told them to do without question. She then tiptoed up the stairs and into the room where Doc said her father was. Doc had told her that her father was asleep, and it was probably best not to wake him. He said she could sit quietly by his bed until he awoke. She crossed the room with some apprehension, awaiting the first glimpse of her father's face. Even though Doc had forewarned her that her father's appearance had changed as he had lost a considerable amount of weight and would appear pale, she stopped and stared at the man who lay motionless in the bed. He looked so frail. His cheeks had sunken in, and there were dark circles under his eyes. Mary nearly collapsed in the chair next to his bed and stared blankly across the room. Bright sunlight, filtered by the lace curtains that hung on the window behind her father's bed, cast ornate silhouettes on the wall. She stared at the shapes, at first wondering why they were there, and then realizing where they came from. For a moment, she thought it odd she should concern herself with such a trivial thing at that moment, but then she realized it was much easier to worry about the shadowy shapes on the wall than to think of anything else. She stared at the patterns as her mind went blank and her body went numb.

Julius peered through half-open eyelids at the figure sitting next to his bed. He had heard the angels singing again. They had been coming to him in his dreams more often of late. Their song was sweet and inviting. The light was bright in the room. *Am I still in the room at Doc's house?* he wondered. His eyes, still trying to focus, realized it wasn't Doc sitting in the chair, and he thought perhaps it was Emma. *That's funny,* he thought to himself. *I can still hear the angels' sweet tune.* He tried to concentrate, but the bright light kept his eyes from focusing. He became aware of his hand lying across his chest and tried to feel the *thump-thump* of his heart. Not feeling the rhythmic pounding, he thought to himself with little concern, *I must have died.* Then, trying to reason with his thoughts, he silently contemplated that if he had died, he couldn't still be lying here in Doc's house. *And who is that sitting next to me?* He forced his eyelids to open a fraction more. *It's Jolene! My sweet Jolene. I died and have gone to meet her!* She was as beautiful as the day he had married her. Her golden hair glistened in the bright light, and her face was young and sweet and innocent. He wondered then if he were to speak her name, if she could hear him, now that he had passed on too.

"Jolene?" Not hearing his own voice, he wondered if he could no longer speak, or if he could just no longer hear. "Jolene?" he whispered again.

Mary pulled from her unseeing gaze at the shapes on the wall and turned to look at her father. Again, he whispered her mother's name. "Jolene?"

"No, Papa," she whispered back. "It's Mary, Papa."

She watched his eyes close as he drifted back to sleep. Mary fell to her knees next to his bed and wept quietly. She prayed silently through her tears that he would get well. He had to get well. She stayed there beside him through the night, against Doc's wishes that she should retire to the room down the hall. She wasn't about to leave her father, not again.

The touch of a hand, softly stroking her hair, caused Mary's eyes to flutter open. Then, instantly remembering where she was, she raised her head and stared into her father's eyes.

"Papa," she choked. Her father smiled at her and nodded.

"So that old coot went and called you . . ." Julius's words were ragged but not labored.

"Oh, Papa," Mary sobbed.

He placed his calloused palm against her soft, tear-stained cheek.

"Don't cry, Pumpkin. Everything's going to be all right."

Just then the door opened, and Doc stepped into the room. Julius looked at him, an angry yet understanding gleam in his eye.

"How's a body get something to eat around here?" Julius growled.

Doc smiled back at his friend. "You're looking much better today, Julius."

Doc crossed the room and helped Mary to her feet.

"And you, young lady," he said in a mock scolding tone, "didn't listen to me, did you? You look as though you haven't gotten a wink of sleep. Now, why don't I see if I can get Emma to get you both some breakfast?"

As the old doctor left the room, his smile left his face. Julius did look better, but that worried him more than anything. He had seen it many times in the fifty years since he became a doctor. It seemed to happen most with those that had a lingering illness. Just when they seemed to have about reached the end, suddenly, if almost miraculously, they seemed to get well—the rise before the fall, so to speak. Doc knew from years of experience Julius had reached that point. He contemplated on sharing this information with Mary. Would he also tell her how the bank took over her father's farm shortly after she had left town, how it had been sold at auction with all the household items? Should he tell her how he had helped her father pack up some of the personal items from the house, and how he had them stored in a trunk out in his shed? He shook his head silently as he walked down the stairs. No, he decided. He wouldn't tell her any of it, not today anyway.

By late afternoon, Julius, sitting upright in bed, was sharing some of Emma's molasses cookies with Mary while they sipped tea. He was getting a little sleepy after their long conversation, though he had let Mary do most of the talking, content just to listen to her voice as she told him all about Bay View. She sounded happy, and that was all that mattered to him. He forced his eyelids to stay open, not wanting to miss one minute of time with her. They talked of old times when Mary was a little girl. She was certainly not a little girl anymore, Julius had to admit to himself. As he looked into her eyes, he wondered where all the years had gone. It seemed only yesterday he and Jolene had fallen in love. He remembered all the plans they had made together, what a wonderful life they were going to have. And now, in the blink of an eye, it was over. Time had passed so swiftly. He cherished every memory—the day Jolene had agreed to be his wife, the day they had stood in front of the justice of the peace and said, 'I do,' the day each of his children was born, and all the wonderful years they spent together. And yet, somehow, it wasn't enough. There were so many more things he had planned to do, had wanted to accomplish, in his years on Earth. *Where did the years go?* he wondered. For just an instant, he contemplated the thought. If he had it to do over, what would he have changed? He smiled softly at Mary as he realized he would not have changed a thing, for if he had, he would perhaps have missed some of the sweet memories he now cherished.

Mary, smiling sweetly, sipped her tea. She was full of joy that Papa was seemingly better. Doc hadn't gone into great detail about her father's illness, only that he had known about it for a long time, and she should be prepared for the worst. She smiled at her father now as she watched his eyelids growing heavy. Perhaps, she thought to herself, Doc Gate had prepared her for the worst that could happen. *Doctors always told you the worst, just in case, didn't they?* It certainly seemed to her that her father was on the road to recovery. She was already making plans for when he was well. She would stay with him there at Doc's house until he was well enough to go home. She would send for her belongings at the Coltons' and would move back home and care for Papa. *Everything will be just fine,* she assured herself. As her father's eyes fluttered, she took the cup from his hand and placed it on the small table next to his bed. He smiled at her and fell off to sleep. She sat quietly there in the small room listening to her father's rhythmic breathing, and her thoughts turned to James. She wondered where he was and what he was doing and if he would be thinking of her. She hadn't even been able to speak to him before she left. After Doc phoned regarding her father's condition, Charles had telephoned the train station. The only train on that day to her destination had been scheduled to leave at six that evening. If she hadn't caught it, she would have had to wait until late the following day. James hadn't returned to the house before Charles had driven her to the station.

The sun was setting and cast soft rays of amber light into the room. Emma tiptoed in and told Mary she had a visitor. She smiled at Emma, rubbing her eyes and standing to smooth her dress.

"I'll be right down," she whispered, not wanting to disturb her father, who hadn't stirred. She reached out to touch his hand. It felt cold, so she tucked blankets around him and whispered softly, "I love you, Papa," before she left the room.

As she quietly descended the stairs, she wondered who could be there to see her. Perhaps, she thought, it could be her friend Betty Sue. Maybe, by chance, she had heard she was in town. It would be nice to see her. As she reached the bottom of the stairs and turned into the kitchen, there he stood, a bit disheveled from his journey but as handsome as ever. She could hardly believe her eyes. It was James, *her* James. Though he stood on the other side of the room, he was instantly by her side. He reached for her hands, and clasping them between his, he brought them to his lips and gently kissed them.

"Are you all right?" he asked.

She smiled and nodded her head in response.

"And your father?" he questioned hesitantly.

"He's doing much better." She shifted her eyes to Emma for reassurance. Emma simply smiled at her. "What are you doing here?" she asked, still quite shocked to see him.

"I was worried about you. I had to come to make sure you were all right. You're not upset I came, are you?"

Mary smiled. "You could have phoned."

James looked wounded.

"I'm very happy you came," she said, returning the smile to his face.

Just then, Doc came through the back door. Seemingly oblivious to them, he set his bag down on the small table that stood just inside the doorway—as he always did on his return from his daily house calls. He removed his eyeglasses, and pulling out a handkerchief from his coat pocket, gave them a good rubbing. Not looking up, he asked, "Well, who do we have here?"

Mary was silent, not exactly sure how she should introduce James.

Without hesitation, James quickly crossed the room and extended his hand. "Allow me to introduce myself. James Colton."

The old doctor shook the offered hand before replacing his glasses, then stood silently surveying the young man.

"I'm a friend of Mary's. I was concerned about her traveling this great distance."

Doc, still silent, appeared to be waiting for more of an explanation.

"Well, I was sure she would be upset by the news of her father." James, apparently feeling a bit awkward at the lack of response from the old man, seemed obligated to continue. "I thought it best if I came to be with her?" James stumbled over his own words, which had started as a statement, then ended as if he were asking permission for his actions. Doc finally smiled at him, releasing him from his obligation to explain himself any further.

Doc, a curious smile on his lips, shuffled through the kitchen toward his study. It warmed his old heart to see such a nice young man head over heels in love, and with a sweet young thing like Mary. He was sure Mary loved him just as much. It was written all over her face. He was happy for her. He knew the next few days would be very hard for her. At least now he knew she wouldn't be facing them alone.

CHAPTER 29

Tom Bellows sat in his small room staring out the only window at the snowflakes that fell heavily. He didn't like the snow or the cold—it made him feel alone. At least the holiday had been pleasant enough. He never thought much of the old spinster, Miss Bryer, but she was a good cook, and he had thoroughly enjoyed the Christmas cookies she had made, not to mention the baked pot roast and candied carrots she had prepared for their Christmas Eve dinner. Her niece, on the other hand, intrigued him immensely, though he was well aware Mary disliked him. He couldn't help but stare at her each time they had been together. Those green eyes sparkled the way his mother's had when he was a little boy.

He lay down and closed his eyes and tried to remember the warm summer days he had spent as a small child with his mother. Her face floated before him in the darkened room, but it was the face of an old woman with wrinkled skin and hollow cheeks, the way she had looked the very last time he saw her. He didn't want to remember that woman, though. He wanted to remember the way she looked before she had gotten sick. The green eyes that had sparkled just for him, the soft cheeks he would touch with his small hand, the way she would cover his fingers with her own gentle touch and then say to him, "I love you, Tommy."

No one had said that to him since she had left. He wanted to hear those words again—he needed to hear them. He tried to remember their life together in the big house with all the other pretty women Mother said were his aunts. How they all coddled him and looked after him when his mother was busy with one of the many gentlemen callers that were always at the big house. All his aunts—Aunt Polly and Aunt Lucy—they were all so very nice to him. Oh, he knew now what they really were, what his mother had really been. His father had made sure he knew. It didn't matter, though. He would always remember them as when he was a little boy.

He tried to stop the memories there, when he had been happy, but as they always did, the bad memories floated into his head, and he couldn't push them out. The bad memories started when his mother had gotten ill. It was the year he turned ten.

He hadn't noticed it at first, how tired she always was and how she had stopped seeing the gentlemen callers. He hadn't noticed until she hadn't wanted to play games anymore, and she started to not get out of bed in the morning. She had lain in her big bed, day after day, wasting away to nothing until her cheeks were hollow, her face was old and wrinkled, and her eyes became dull and lifeless. The doctor just shook his head each time he came to see her.

His aunts had looked after him, and even Madam Rochelle had tried to comfort him the way his mother had, but it just wasn't the same. Then came the worst memory of all, that awful day when his mother had dragged herself out of her bed and dressed in her very finest dress. His aunts had packed up all his belongings and put them in a small trunk. They had loaded the trunk, along with him and his weak mother, onto the back of a buckboard wagon, and a man from the livery took them on a long ride out of town. They had ridden for what seemed forever. He had tried to question his mother about where it was they were going, but she wouldn't answer him, so they rode in silence. No words had been spoken—there was just the steady creaking of the buckboard. He remembered the man helping him and his mother off the back of the wagon when they had reached their destination—a large house that stood alone out on the savanna. He had never seen such a big house before. It was at least twice the size of the big house he called home, and his house was far bigger than any in town. He wondered if a king, or the like, lived there. Then the man from the livery deposited the trunk next to where he and his mother stood on the front porch. He remembered wondering that if this was going to be their new home, why had his aunts only packed his things and not his mother's too? Then the man said he'd wait for her in the wagon. Not wait for them, but wait for *her*. He remembered it had worried him when the man had said it that way, but before he could question his mother about the man's statement, the door had opened, and a big Negro lady was questioning his mother. They had both been ushered into the house and stood quietly in the entryway. While the Negro lady disappeared down a long hallway, he stood close to his mother's side, clinging to her dress. Soon, an older gentleman with curly dark hair just like his had appeared and had ushered his mother into another room, shutting the door behind them. He had been left alone with the Negro lady, who had told him to sit and wait on a small bench in the entryway. Soon the voices of his mother and the man had become very loud, though he hadn't been able to understand what it was they said. Then suddenly the door to the room had burst open, and the man was shouting, "Maize! Maize!"

The Negro woman came running back down the hallway, her ample bosom bouncing up and down. Tom remembered how funny he had thought she looked. The older man who had been talking to his mother had looked at him then, as he sat there quietly on the bench. Tom smiled at the man, but the man hadn't smiled back. He had only glared at him before whispering something to the Negro lady. She had responded, "Yes, sir. Yes, sir, Mr. Bellows. Right away, sir."

Then she once again disappeared down the long hallway. In a very short time, another much younger man had come strolling down the hallway. He had a smiling face and wore small wire spectacles. Tom had watched him as he knocked softly on the door but entered the room without awaiting a response. The voices from behind the door had become very loud again. Tom could only hear some of the words the voices shouted, like 'ridiculous' and 'impossible.' There were other words he had never heard before—and he didn't learn their meaning until years later. It had gone on for what seemed to

Tom a very long time before the door finally opened, and his mother stepped out of the room. She had come and stood by his side and had stooped down next to him. He remembered how her eyes were glistening, and for an instant, he had thought perhaps she was getting better. The sparkle he remembered in her eyes had returned. He thought perhaps the men they had come to see were doctors. But then he realized it was only because she had been crying that her eyes sparkled, as they were still filled with tears. She had told him then she was going back to the big house with the man from the livery, and he would be staying there. Before he could comprehend what she was saying, let alone try to protest, her next statement had shocked him into silence. "You are going to be living here with your father."

She had said it plain and simple. Until that very moment, he hadn't even known he had a father, at least not a father that was alive. His father had died on a big ship out on the ocean. His mother had told him the story herself, many times.

He had wanted to shout at her. To ask why she was leaving him there, and who was this man that had suddenly come back from the dead to be his father? Why couldn't he go with her back to the big house? Why couldn't they be a family if he now had a father? In silent terror, he had watched her as she bent over him to kiss his cheek. Tears that fell from her eyes dropped silently on his forehead as she whispered softly, "I love you, Tommy."

She had pressed her gold and pearl brooch, the one she always wore, the one he thought was so pretty, into his little hand and told him to never forget her. Then, she left him. She had walked right out the front door, leaving him sitting on the small bench in the big hallway, too afraid to cry and too scared not to.

Tom wiped the tears from his cheeks with the back of his hand as he heard his father enter their apartment. He hoped he would assume he was asleep. He really didn't want to talk to him. He didn't even want to think of him, but he couldn't stop the memories.

He had only stayed in the new big house with his newfound father and grandfather a short while before his belongings were once again packed up, and he and his father had taken the train to Bay View. It was, his father had said, as far away as they could possibly get from Douglas County.

———————◦∘◦———————

Ezra Bellows stepped into his small two-bedroom apartment, still shaking the snow from his jacket. The day's receipts had been almost nonexistent, which only compounded the foul mood he'd been in for the last few days. He hated the thought of yet another year in this dismal town. Christmas sales had been down, not to mention the dozen handkerchiefs he had again specially ordered for Mr. Colton, which he had never come in to purchase. The weather had turned nasty, nothing but cold and snow. He hung his hat and coat in the closet and slammed the door shut. He supposed Tom was in his room asleep, but he didn't concern himself with being quiet for his sake. *After all*, he thought to himself, *what has the boy ever done for me but bring me grief?* In fact, Tom was the only reason he was living in this awful town, with its cold and snow, in the first place. Sitting down in his favorite chair, he pondered over the more comfortable weather he was sure was being enjoyed in Twin Bridges.

"Which is where I'd be right now if it wasn't for him," he complained aloud to no one but himself. "As far away from Douglas County as possible."

He huffed to himself the promise he had made to his father years earlier. He closed his eyes, and though he tried not to think about anything, those old memories seemed to nag at him, memories of that one day that changed his life so immensely. He had been a young man then, just twenty-six. How many years ago that seemed now. He still remembered Maize's exact words when she had found him reclining out on the back veranda on that awful day.

"Misser Izzy, your daddy wansa see you in the study. He don' seem too happy wif you, Misser Izzy. He say get you right away and I's should tells ya to hurry up." He remembered how he had chuckled at Maize's impatience with him as he had sauntered into the house and down the hallway. He remembered strolling down the corridor of his father's home toward the study. He saw the little boy. He had even smiled at him.

Ezra moaned as he recalled how he had also thought the little boy was cute, and how he had reminded him of himself at that age.

After he had entered the study, his father had told him the reason for the woman's visit. The woman was accusing Ezra of being the father of the little boy in the hallway.

"Ridiculous!" Ezra had bellowed. "Why, that boy has to be at least eight or nine," he had argued.

"He's ten," the woman said between coughs.

"Well, then it's impossible!" Ezra had shouted. "I would have been . . . Well, it just wasn't me," he had huffed.

"Had you been to the . . ." his father hesitated only momentarily, "brothel when you were that age, Ezra?"

"Well," Ezra answered more quietly, turning from the woman to his father, "yes, yes, I suppose I was there, but that doesn't mean anything."

"Have you ever been with this woman, Ezra?" his father had prodded.

Ezra had been silent, for indeed he remembered Carolina, remembered her well. Though she looked old and sickly, slumped there in the chair, he could never forget those emerald green eyes. Yes, he had been with her when he was fifteen. He had been with her several times that summer. That was the year he had become a man. But he hadn't seen her since that summer. He hadn't even been back to the big house since then. That next year, they had passed the Mann Act, and the law in Twin Bridges was constantly raiding Madam Rochelle's. They made it clear that human trafficking was no longer tolerated. Everyone knew it was just that they were trying to impose their moral standards on the town, but as the city's sheriff was very close to Ezra's father, Ezra knew if he continued to frequent the place, his father would soon get wind of it.

His father had started tapping his fingers against the ledger that lay open on his desk, his impatience apparent, waiting for Ezra to answer the question. As he started to ask it a second time, Ezra responded, "Honestly, Father, she's nothing but a strumpet. She can't prove anything. I'm sure any one of the hundreds—perhaps thousands—of men she's been with could be that boy's father. And why does she come here now, after ten years?" Ezra questioned his father rather than Carolina.

"As I explained to your father," Carolina spoke in a weak voice, "when I had Tommy—that's his name, Tommy—I had no intention of ever telling you about him, though I'm sure he's your son, Ezra."

Before Ezra could protest, she continued. "I'm not well. The doctor says I only have a short time left. If I . . ." She paused. "When I die, Tommy would be placed in an orphanage. I want a better life for him than that. I was hoping you would take him in."

With that said, Carolina had slumped more deeply into the chair, her energy spent.

"Look," Ezra said, showing a touch of compassion, "I'm sorry you're," he hesitated, "sick, but how can you be so sure that he's mine?"

His father interrupted. "Did you look at the boy, Ezra? I had to look twice at him when I saw him sitting there in the hallway. He looks just like you when you were his age, other than his hair, which looks just like mine. You will take responsibility for your actions!"

So Carolina had left, and the boy had stayed. And Ezra was expected to take responsibility for him, but not there, not in his father's house. No one, especially not his own son, was going to bring shame on the Bellows name. Oh, his father hadn't just thrown him out—he had given him a tidy sum of money but had placed conditions on its payment. Neither Ezra, nor the boy, was to ever contact him again, and they were to move as far away from Douglas County as possible. They had been living in Bay View for only about six months when Ezra had received a small newspaper clipping from a local Twin Bridges paper. It had stated that Carolina had died after a lingering illness. Scribbled at the bottom, it said, "Thought the boy would want to know." The return address had simply read, "Bellows, Douglas County." That was six years ago now, and the last time Ezra had heard from his father.

Six years, Ezra thought to himself. *Six long years.* Would he ever be rid of this burden? Hadn't he paid for his mistakes? He left his home and gave up any hope for a true family and any kind of happiness. He closed his eyes and listened to the howling wind outside the small apartment, an eerie hollow sound that made him shiver. He pushed himself up out of the chair and shut off the light. *Perhaps*, he thought, *if I crawled into my warm bed, my body would be rid of this chill that invades my bones.* Perhaps if he were more comfortable, his mind would offer him more enjoyable thoughts. Perhaps he would again dream about Mary, that lovely young girl he had been able to spend the holiday with. He remembered how her eyes had shined in the light from Miss Bryer's Christmas tree, which had glowed with candlelight. He wondered what his father's opinion of her would be? Surely, he could not find fault with the dear, sweet girl.

Miss Bryer had come down to his store, just today, to inform him the girl's father had passed away. He had voiced his worry of her traveling such a great distance by herself. Matilda had been quick to report that she had learned James Colton had gone as well. Ezra didn't like James Colton, and the fact that Mary lived in his house was not a comforting thought.

He wasn't at all sure if when it manifested itself, its presence was detectable. He supposed his physical appearance wasn't altered by its consumption, yet he knew he was no longer himself when it was in control. He could hear it moan, and he had heard it laugh. It was not his voice that escaped his lips, yet it was he who heard the cries of help—which only intensified the beast.

CHAPTER 30

James watched Mary as she stared out the window of the train. He didn't know what to do to comfort her. She had hardly spoken a word since her father's funeral that afternoon. The old doctor had given him some pills for her as they had boarded the train. He said they would help her sleep if she needed them. How could he convince her that her father would have died whether she had been with him or not? She somehow blamed herself for not staying with him that evening.

"I shouldn't have left him. I shouldn't have left him," she had cried over and over. Her face, distraught with pain, had etched itself into James's memory and made his heart ache for her.

They had just gone out for dinner—just to dinner—only a few blocks from the doctor's house. A small restaurant at the hotel the doctor himself had recommended. The doctor had suggested it would do Mary good to get out for a bit. Over dinner, they had talked of nothing but how well Mary thought her father was doing. She had told James how he had progressed just since she had arrived the day before. They had even discussed the need for her to stay on there until her father had fully recovered—an idea James hadn't wanted to think about, but nonetheless, he had agreed with her. They hadn't been gone long, an hour or so, yet by the time they returned, it had been too late. The old doctor had tears in his eyes as he tried to stop Mary from going into the room.

"He never woke, Mary. He passed in his sleep," the old man had said, trying to comfort her.

"I shouldn't have left him!" she had screamed. "I had prayed for him to get better, and he was getting better, but then I left him. I shouldn't have left him!"

She had slumped, weeping, into a little ball on the floor. James had to carry her to bed, and the doctor had given her something to help her sleep. The very next day, Mary had made the arrangements for the funeral. James was astonished at how well she handled every detail—what her father should be dressed in, which song she wanted Mrs. Burns to play on the organ at the church. She had arranged for a small luncheon to be served for the mourners. Doc Gate had graciously offered his house, after having to tell Mary of her father's financial condition and what had happened to his farm. She had asked James to purchase train tickets for their departure. She wanted to leave as soon as possible after the funeral.

"There is nothing left for me here," she had said coldly.

The night before the funeral, after Mary had retired, James had sat with the doctor in his study. He had commented on how well he thought Mary was handling the situation. The old man had smiled at him softly, then had rubbed his eyes before he spoke.

"I'm glad you brought it up. I wanted to speak to you before you left tomorrow. I don't think she is dealing with it at all, James. Oh, she pretends to be strong, and she's doing what needs to be done, but when it's over, when she has time to let it all catch up with her—and it will catch up with her—she's going to need you then."

James thought of the old man's words now as he studied Mary's blank expression while she continued to stare out the window of the train. He so wished he could take her hurt away.

The train pulled into the station at Springfield just before six in the evening. There would be a one-hour layover before re-boarding. Everything was running on schedule, and they could expect to be back in Bay View by the next afternoon, New Year's Eve.

Though she hadn't wanted to, he convinced her to get up and go out and at least stretch her legs a bit. She still hadn't spoken more than a few words. He contemplated whether returning to Bay View was the best thing to do. If the good doctor was right, James wanted to be with her, 'when it all caught up with her,' as the doctor had put it. At the house, he wasn't free to do that, not yet anyway. It would only be a few more months until he turned twenty-five, and then he would be free, free to make his intentions known to his mother, to everyone. The money his grandfather had left him would be his then and not tied up in a trust fund, requiring his mother's signature to obtain. Nor would his mother be able to have any control over it, as she did now. He and Mary could get married then, if she would have him, of course. They could live anywhere she wanted to. Should his mother decide to disown him because of his choice in a wife and cut off the fortune he thought would someday be bequeathed to him, it wouldn't really matter. He would at least have the trust money. Money enough to give Mary the kind of life she deserved, the kind of life he wanted for her. He wondered if he should tell Mary about the trust fund, but as he had on several occasions in the past, he decided not to. Mary had gone into the station to freshen up when the thought suddenly occurred to him. There was really no rush in getting back to Bay View. He doubted anyone at home even knew of Mary's father's passing yet, unless her Aunt Matilda had informed them, and all Mary's telegram to her said was that her father had died, that she was having the funeral, and then she'd be coming back to Bay View. She hadn't actually mentioned a date. As far as anyone knew, he had gone to spend a few days with an old friend. He had told his family not to expect him back, perhaps until after the New Year. Only Maggie knew of his true destination, and though he knew it was hard for her to keep secrets, he trusted her with this one.

While Mary was inside the station, James found the porter and had their bags removed from the train. He then inquired of the nearest hotel and arranged for a ride.

It was quite easy to convince Mary that his plan was best, though he doubted she even had the energy to argue with him. She didn't say a word on the short drive to the hotel, nor had she even acknowledged the boy as he placed her suitcase next to the bed in the small but cozy room. She just surveyed the simple furnishings. Two small but comfortable looking chairs and a small table were placed in front of a large window, which was covered by lace curtains. A small bureau of drawers, complemented by a large hanging mirror above, stood directly across from the bed. The boy pointed out the accommodations and explained the door next to the bureau would lead to James's connecting room, as he opened the door and deposited James's bag just inside. James tipped the boy handsomely, and after he left, silently walked through the small rooms while Mary removed her coat.

"Perhaps you would care to take a nice hot bath before dinner?" James suggested. "They do have full accommodations."

"It's a very nice hotel?" Mary remarked, more as a question than a statement, for she had never actually been in one before.

"It's quite nice, actually," James responded, as he, too, removed his coat and laid it across one of the small chairs. "Of course, it doesn't compare to the Waldorf in New York," he added, "but then nothing does."

He picked up Mary's suitcase and placed it on the wooden chest at the foot of her bed. "The dining room downstairs looked very inviting, don't you think?" he asked.

Mary sighed softly as she pulled the lace window coverings aside to look out the window. The sky was gray and dreary. Perfect weather for the way she felt. "I'm sorry, James. I really don't think I feel up to going down to dinner, but you go on ahead if you want."

"Well then," he suggested, "why don't I have them bring up something?"

"They'll do that?" James was delighted to see a small twinkle in her eye.

While she bathed, James ordered a nice dinner to be sent to her room. Roast chicken, potatoes, rolls, green beans, and apple pie for dessert. He would have added a nice bottle of chardonnay, would it have been available. Though he was sure he could acquire it for the right sum of money, he hadn't bothered.

Mary sat across from him at the small table that had been wheeled into the room for dinner. She was stabbing and re-stabbing her chicken, though she hadn't taken a bite.

"Don't you like the chicken?" James asked, thinking to himself that aside from Bea's, it was probably the best-tasting chicken he had ever eaten.

Mary sighed. "I'm sorry for being such poor company, James." Putting her fork down on her plate and lifting her napkin from her lap, she dabbed her mouth.

"You're anything but poor company, my dear, but I do wish you would at least try to eat something." For his sake, she picked up her fork and stabbed her chicken once again. He rose and circled around the table to stand behind her. Leaning over her, he placed a soft kiss on the top of her head and said, "You know, I never did get to wish you a Merry Christmas. Which reminds me . . ."

He dashed through the door to his connecting room, suddenly remembering the present he had hastily thrown into his bag after Charles had packed for him. He quickly returned with the small package, hidden behind his back.

"Merry Christmas," he said, handing her the package, which was covered in shiny gold wrapping and adorned with a little red bow.

"Oh," she replied, "my present for you is still hidden under my bed. Would you rather I wait to open this?"

"No," James smiled. "Please open it now."

Mary carefully untied the little bow so as not to ruin the pretty ribbon. She placed the wrappings neatly on the table before opening the little velvet-covered box.

The two identical heart-shaped pendants nestled in white satin twinkled in the light. She raised her hand and covered her mouth as she sighed, "Oh, James. They're beautiful."

"May I?" he asked. Taking the box from her hand, he removed the first locket and opened it to reveal the picture of himself that the jeweler had placed in it. Then, closing the cover, he turned the locket over so she could read the engraving.

"F.A.E." she read aloud. He then encircled her neck with the fine gold chain and clasped it for her. He then un-nestled the second locket and opened it to reveal the tiny picture of her, which brought a queried smile to her face. Then, he again turned it over to reveal the engraving before fastening it around his own neck and then tucking it under the collar of his shirt. "Now you will always be close to me," he said as he knelt in front of her. Taking her hand in his, he softly whispered, "I love you, Mary. F—forever, A—always, E—eternally."

"Oh, James." Her voice quivered. She bent closer to him, "I love you too." As her eyes closed, he put his arms around her and held her close.

She then laid her head against his chest. The tears begin to stream down her face. She wept softly in his arms. She cried for everyone she had lost—her father, her mother, Johnny. She cried for the very special someone she had found. She cried, for there was just nothing more she could do.

CHAPTER 31

The booming thud of things hitting the wall, and the resounding echo of shattering objects, rang through the entire west wing of the house. Miss Christina was throwing one of her legendary temper tantrums. The rest of the staff, long accustomed to Christina's proverbial fits, was going about their duties as if nothing was out of the ordinary. Mary, however, cringed at each reverberation, imagining all the beautiful things Miss Christina was surely destroying. With every crash of some inanimate object, Christina's voice bellowed a different indignant remark directed at her mother.

"You got sick just so we couldn't go! I hate you! You never really planned on taking me, did you?" she shouted at the top of her well-exercised lungs. Then, as suddenly as the ordeal had started, the house became quiet, and Mary found herself holding her breath, waiting, to be sure Christina had really ceased her tantrum. After a full minute of silence, Mary breathed a sigh of relief and resumed her dusting in the library as she had been instructed.

The whole silly cascade of her fit was because she had been promised for her fifteenth birthday, which was now only four days away, she would be able to accompany the rest of the family to New York. Mr. Colton and James apparently had business to attend to there, and Mrs. Colton and Christina were going to tag along and fill their days with shopping and their evenings with the theater. Christina had made her mother promise her the trip shortly after she, James, and Mary had gone to the moving picture show. James's accounts of the fabulous theaters in New York had Christina convinced she needed to see the big city for herself. The entire family had been scheduled to leave that very afternoon. However, Mrs. Colton had come down with a relentless ailment that had her bedridden for days now. The doctor had visited that very morning, and his diagnosis, though optimistic, only angered Christina, as he stated that Mrs. Colton would not be in any condition to travel for at least a week. Christina had commenced her verbal attack on her mother before the doctor had even left the house.

As Mary waved the feather duster over the many rows of books, she wondered what Mrs. Colton had done to subdue her fit-to-be-tied daughter.

Mary loved the Coltons' library. The thought of all those books right in the house fascinated her. The rugged smell of leather and the pungent aroma of expensive cigars filled the room. Along one wall stood an immense fireplace, the mantel ornately carved with lion heads and the Shell family crest. The heavy dark draperies, when closed, cloaked the room in total darkness. Mary could certainly understand why the Colton men often took refuge in this room of the house. It was a comfortable room with its overstuffed leather furniture and worn rugs. She couldn't help but think of the evening she and James had spent talking on the big leather couch, and the beautiful poem he had recited for her.

As she dusted along the shelves, she wondered if anyone ever took the time to read the volumes the library held. She knew Christina loved to read, but her selections were limited to steamy magazines like *Heart Throbs*, or *Love Story*, or *Telling Tales*, with articles like "Indolent Kisses" or "The Confessions of a Chorus Girl." Christina's favorite magazine, of course, was Bernarr Macfadden's *True Story*. When Mary had scoffed at her choice of reading material, Christina informed her that she also read the newspaper, but of course only the advice to the lovelorn column, *Dorothy Dix Talks*.

Christina had, on occasion, implored Mary to read to her as she relaxed in a hot bath, surrounded in bubbles to her chin. Mary now recalled the last excerpt she had read at Miss Christina's request, from one of the sultry magazines she'd bought.

> Carlotta was a woman of extreme discontent. No one
> man could make her happy. There was the lonely

butcher down the street who handled her body as he did a fine cut of meat. The man who came around every now and again selling his wares, who always seemed to come to her, for his last call of the day, with no wares to sell but other needed pleasures to offer. Yet her very favorite was the piano player down at the corner speakeasy. Duncan had long, supple fingers that could caress her skin as they did the keys of his piano, and the song she would moan for him sounded as melodic as any symphony he could ever play.

Mary had read as Christina had instructed, but she tried to detach herself from the words she spoke. Her mind's insistence, however, could not suppress her body's response to the passage she delivered, and it was soon responding of its own accord. As she felt her breath quickening with each lurid line, she had felt both the desire to read on and the principled response to throw the book into the hot water where Christina reclined.

She more earnestly fanned the feather duster over the volumes of leather bound books as she tried turning her thoughts back to Christina, who she was sure had somehow been pacified by Mrs. Colton. Finished with her dusting, she left the library and headed toward the kitchen to see what else Bea had for her to do. As she entered the main entryway, Christina came bounding down the grand staircase, clinging to the banister as she hurdled down the stairs.

"Mary, Mary!" she screamed in a shrill, childlike voice. "Mother needs you!" she shrieked as she came running across the marble floor, sliding to a stop just inches from Mary, grabbing the duster from her hand, and pushing her toward the staircase.

"Hurry!" she said. "She needs you right away!"

Mary, imagining everything but the unknown truth, raced up the stairs ahead of Christina, certain that Mrs. Colton was in dire need of help. Perhaps she had fallen. Perhaps Christina had made her the target, accidentally of course, of a flung object meant for the wall. Reaching the top of the stairs, she ran down the west wing toward Mrs. Colton's room, certain she would find her lying collapsed on the floor or bleeding from a gaping wound. By the time she reached the door, she was out of breath and holding her side. Not even thinking to knock, she burst into the room and shouted, "What's wrong, Mrs . . ."

The name Colton drifted faintly from her lips as she observed a very startled but perfectly coherent Cordella Colton sitting reclined against the several pillows in her bed. Raising a hand to her chest, Mrs. Colton huffed at Mary, "My word! What on earth do you think you're doing?"

Mary apologized profusely, trying to explain herself, but Mrs. Colton's waving hand had left her silent, while Christina, who had finally caught up, stood in the doorway beaming ear to ear.

"There's no time to explain. You're going to need to hurry and ready yourself. I've agreed to let you go to New York to accompany Christina. The train leaves at four o'clock this afternoon, and there are a number of things I must address before you leave."

Mary stood dumbfounded, staring blankly at Mrs. Colton, hundreds of thoughts coursing through her mind while Mrs. Colton spouted out a plethora of instructions. Mary's mind reeled with thoughts of New York, trains, four o'clock, chaperone Miss Christina, birthday, disappointment, pack, Charles to get a trunk, suitable attire, hurry, hurry, hurry.

All instructions given, Mrs. Colton dismissed Mary and Christina from her room and didn't bother to notice Mary's apparent dazed state. She laid her head gently down on the pillow, suddenly overcome by the whole ordeal. She clutched her stomach, thinking that perhaps she was going to be sick again. Before Mary had even shut the door, she started having second thoughts about her hasty decision, but what else could she have done? Christina was just so upset about the whole thing, and every alternative she offered, the child had instantly refused, along with an item from the shelf or dressing table being hurled against the wall. She was sure there was nothing, short of her decision to let Christina go to New York, that would have satisfied her daughter. She was now unsure her choice of Mary as a travel companion was the best, but who else could she send on such short notice? An insistent thought nagged at her mind as she reached to her nightstand and wrung out the cloth that had been soaking in a cool basin of water. She laid the cloth gently over her forehead and closed her eyes. The memory of the phone call she had received from Mary's Aunt Matilda while Mary had been away at her father's flooded her brain. It had been New Year's Day when Matilda Bryer had phoned the Coltons to inquire about Mary's return. Bea had taken the call and explained to Miss Bryer there had been no word from Mary since her departure on Christmas Day, but Matilda had insisted on speaking directly with Mrs. Colton, so Cordella had taken the call in the study.

"I'm sorry to bother you, Mrs. Colton, but I was just wondering if Mary had arrived yet?" She had spoken in such a nasally voice it had set Cordella's nerves on edge.

"Why no, Miss Bryer, we haven't heard from Mary since she left. Have you had word from her regarding her father's condition?" She had asked the question more out of obligation than concern.

Matilda Bryer had hesitated only slightly before she responded. "Mr. Watson passed away. The funeral was two days ago."

Before Mrs. Colton could respond, Matilda had continued. "I telephoned Dr. Gate after I received her telegram. I was very concerned that I couldn't be with her. However, Dr. Gate informed me she had already left to return to Bay View. It was a great comfort to learn James was accompanying her."

Cordella, though quite shocked by this information, never faltered. Instead, quickly calculating the assumptions Miss Bryer might make from any of her possible responses, and instantly choosing the best one, without a lapse in the conversation, said, "I'll be sure to have Mary contact you as soon as they arrive."

Mary had returned that same afternoon. She had phoned the house for Charles to pick her up at the train station. James had returned later that evening from his apparently fabricated visit with a friend. The next day, Cordella had taken ill and had been unable to question James or Mary regarding the whole matter. She would surely get to the bottom of it, but not now. Now she was going to clear her mind, close her eyes, and hopefully find comfort in her slumber. It would all have to simply wait until they returned from New York.

CHAPTER 32

There were no words in Mary's vocabulary to describe New York City. As she lay wide awake in the most comfortable bed she had ever been in, she kept telling herself she wasn't dreaming, that she really was in New York. The Statue of Liberty had truly been a sight to see. It was even bigger than Maggie had described it. She could only imagine what a welcoming sight it had been for Maggie when she had come to the United States. Everything was big in New York. The buildings stood so tall. James told her they were called skyscrapers, and Mary found it a proper name, for it almost appeared they did just that. Grand Central Station, where the train arrived, was enormous. The massive marble staircases and seventy-five-foot windows were almost indescribable. Sun streaked in through the enormous windows and fell in beams across the floor. They looked to Mary like huge stairways to heaven. Up above was a star-studded ceiling, and Mary found herself—more than once—almost bumping into people, as she could hardly take her eyes off the view above her. People bustled all over, and the many Mary had encountered were quick to offer their services to the Coltons. They carried bags, and opened doors, and doted on them.

By the time they reached the hotel, Mary had been overwhelmed with it all, but as they entered the Waldorf Astoria, her mouth once again fell open in wonderment, and her eyes bulged at the sight of it all—the ornate carpets, the heavy plush drapery, and the gleaming, polished wood. She knew James thought it entertaining that she was frightened to go into the little room they called the elevator, saying she would prefer to use the stairs. Only after he had explained to her that it would take them to their rooms on the seventeenth floor did she agree to join them. She could hardly fathom the concept when James had also informed her the hotel had one thousand guest rooms. Christina had been quick to point out, only after her father had informed her of the fact, that Mary's room, the servants' room, was through a small connecting door from her own lavish suite. Mary had unpacked Christina's wardrobe with glee, hanging each dress carefully in a tall wardrobe. She admired the velvet-covered furnishings and coordinated brocade draperies, the carpeted floors that muffled her steps, and the polished wood of the tables and bureaus in Christina's suite. Though her room was not as ornate, it was still very nice. She closed her eyes, as she knew it was well after midnight. Christina had planned an overwhelming schedule for the next few days, and Mary knew she would need her rest.

The next three days were filled with a whirlwind of excitement. Mary had tagged after Christina, through store after store of New York's finest. Macy's had been high on Christina's list, noted as the biggest store in the world. Christina had informed her they had a huge Thanksgiving Day Parade just the year before last, and now it was an annual event. Saks Fifth Avenue, a store that had opened in 1924, and Bloomingdale's were also on the list of stores they just had to see. Though Christina hadn't really purchased too much—by her account—she did have to see and try on every new fashion presented to her. While a chauffeur-driven auto had been provided by the hotel, Christina had to visit the New York subway. The driver had waited for them at the corner of Wall Street and Broadway while Christina and Mary surveyed the big black ironwork that covered the long stairway leading down to the subway. Though they did venture down the stairs and onto the platform, it was about as far as Miss Christina would go before she urged Mary back up to street level. Mary, however, found it all utterly fascinating and would have loved to take a ride on the funny-looking underground train.

Both girls had visited a boutique, where they were both fitted for gowns to attend the theater. Mrs. Colton had made the arrangements herself weeks earlier. Of course, when it had been planned, it had been for Christina and Mrs. Colton to be fitted for the new gowns. As the arrangements had already been made, however, James had insisted to his father that Mary should accompany them to the theater in his mother's absence. Of course, he had also recommended she would need an appropriate gown. So Mary had been measured and fitted for a new gown right along with Christina.

Though Christina was sure she could never tire of shopping, they had also visited many points of interest her father had outlined for her. They had gone to the Brooklyn Children's Museum and the American Museum of Natural History, as well as the newer Museum of the City of New York. They visited Times Square and had gone to the Metropolitan Opera Company, where they had seen the very moving *Aida*. Though Christina had not been so stirred, Mary had found it a thrilling event as they watched from the Coltons' private balcony. Days and evenings filled with excitement and unprecedented adventures—along with seven-course dinners at exclusive restaurants—had by the second to the last day of their trip left Mary in utter astonishment.

It was the first day they hadn't been up and out of the hotel by early morning. Christina lounged comfortably in the deep tub that graced her accommodations. She had insisted on a leisurely bubble bath before the woman arrived from the boutique with their dresses for the evening's excursion to the theater. Christina was moaning to Mary that she hadn't been feeling well all morning and Mary should read to her while she relaxed. Mary obediently sat next to the tub on a small padded stool reading, as Christina had implored, from a book she had picked up earlier in the week.

> Virginia was more or less a coquette. She used men then tossed them aside as she would the day's trash. As she strolled into the room, her eyes darkened with mascara cake, and her lips painted a deep red, she was ready for her next victim. She was, in no uncertain terms, a vamp.

Suddenly, Christina was yelling to be retrieved from the water, as she was going to be ill. After Mary saw to Christina's needs and tucked her into her bed, she had gone to find Mr. Colton. After speaking with the white-faced and moaning Christina, Mr. Colton and James had a lengthy discussion in which it was agreed that Mary and James would attend the theater. Mr. Colton procured the services of a nurse for his daughter and would stay behind with her for the evening.

By the time the woman from the boutique arrived with the gowns, Christina had fallen asleep, clutching her stomach with one hand and her head with the other.

The woman had been hired to deliver the gowns, help the girls dress, and aid them with their hair and makeup, and though Mary told her it was no longer necessary, as Miss Christina would not be able to attend, she had insisted on performing her services for Mary.

After the woman had left, Mary surveyed herself in the full-length mirror furnished in Christina's suite. The gown was truly breathtaking. The underskirting was a deep forest green, and the overlay, a light sheer material, was covered in faded flowers of muted raspberry and wine colors. The skirt offered graceful godet flare inserts of the deep green underskirting, which swayed elegantly as Mary turned back and forth in front of the mirror. The body of the dress was straight and sleek, revealing every curve of her figure. The dress was truly wonderful, but as she viewed her reflection in the mirror, she couldn't believe the image her own eyes offered. The woman from the boutique had slicked back her hair and pinned it tightly. She had then formed tight curls that cascaded down the back of her head. She had applied many different things to Mary's face, cheek and lip rouge and a concoction of coal dust and petroleum jelly to her eyelashes, making Mary imagine it was someone else in the mirror instead of her own reflection.

As the soft knock at the door interrupted her thoughts, she hoped she looked sophisticated and appropriate for the theater. As she crossed the room to the door, the image of Virginia from the book she had been reading to Christina suddenly popped into her head. She opened the door hesitantly, and James stared at her for what seemed to Mary an eternity before he spoke.

"You look exquisite," he said as his eyes moved slowly over her before resting back on her face.

Mary smiled, still fretting over her slicked-back hair and artificially darkened eyes. "Are you sure, James? I don't look like a . . ." she hesitated, "a vamp?"

James chuckled at her newfound verbiage. "Where did you ever hear that word?"

As he helped Mary on with her coat, he assured her she didn't look like a vamp. In thanking him, Mary turned her head slightly, and her chin brushed the fur of the trimmed coat collar, and she silently noted how wonderfully soft it felt against her skin. She had borrowed the coat from Christina, knowing that her cloth coat would appear much too shabby over her new gown. Christina had mumbled an affirmative answer to her request. At least Mary had thought it to be an affirmative answer. In Christina's state of incoherence, she wasn't exactly sure, but she hadn't bothered asking her to clarify her response.

As their chauffeured vehicle drove past 42nd Street, Mary marveled out the window at the city's indescribable grandeur. The lights of Broadway were astonishing. James explained that twenty-five million candle-power lit the million electric lamps. New York had both the highest and the largest lit signs in the world, the latter being on 42nd Street. It was two-hundred feet long and as tall as a five-story building and contained nineteen thousand lamps and twenty-one miles of electrical wiring.

Very soon, they were being ushered out of the motorcar in front of the Fulton Theater. Mary was very aware of James's hand, which he placed on her back just above her waist as they walked through the doors.

Once again, Mary was awestruck. She almost felt a pang of guilt that Christina was sick in bed and was missing out on this wonderful adventure. The theater was enormous. The grand stage was adorned with a canopy of cherubs and draped with large curtains. There were two balconies, in one of which she and James were seated. Once the curtain opened, Mary, absorbed by the actors and actresses, almost forgot it was simply make-believe.

After the theater, they dined at a wonderfully elaborate restaurant and discussed the play, which they both loved. James had been eager to see it since its opening in 1922, but he had just never had the time, on his previous trips to New York. *Abie's Irish Rose* was a whimsical play about a romance between a Jewish man and an Irish woman. Abie meets Rosemary Murphy in a hospital in France during the war. She is working in a field hospital as a nurse, where he is admitted with wounds. They fall in love and get married by a Baptist minister. Abie brings Rosemary home to meet his father, a traditional Jew. To please his father, Abie agrees to have a second wedding ceremony performed by a rabbi, but just as the ceremony is about to take place, Rosemary's father arrives with a Catholic priest. James thought the humor in it all quite delightful, and though Mary thought it quite humorous, she had felt ever so sorry for poor Rosemary's predicament.

Though it was already quite late by the time they finished dining, James suggested they go to the club before returning to the hotel. Mary quickly agreed with his request, knowing she was much too excited to have the evening end. James instructed the driver, and they headed to Washington Square in Greenwich Village. Mary read the marquee silently as they pulled to a stop. Club Gallant, it said. James offered the man at the door a card, which he produced from his wallet, and they were allowed entrance. The din of the crowd and the music met Mary as they entered the club's dimly lit and smoke-filled atmosphere. They took a table, and James ordered them both refreshments. The waiter asked, "Do you want a lollipop on the side with that?" to which James responded, "Of course."

Mary wasn't at all sure what they were talking about and busied herself by reading the table card.

"Do not get too friendly with the waiter. His name is neither Charlie nor George. Remember the old adage about familiarity breeding contempt. Do not ask to play the drums. The drum heads are not as tough as many another head. Besides, it has a tendency to disturb the rhythm. Make no requests of the leader of the orchestra for the songs of the vintage of 1890. Crooning "Sweet Adeline" was all right for your granddad, but times, alas, have changed."

As the band started to play their rendition of "Sweet Georgia Brown," Mary viewed the many couples dancing wildly on the dance floor. Women dressed in short beaded dresses were swinging their arms and legs to the beat of the music, accompanied by their male companions whose arms and legs twisted in the same fashion. Mary was sure she had now witnessed what Maggie referred to as cutting a rug. A waiter delivered to their table two cups of what Mary assumed was tea, and she took a long sip before James had been able to explain its true contents. She nearly choked on the brown liquid that stung her throat and brought tears to her eyes. James was quick to offer his assistance by patting her back and handing her his handkerchief which she used to dry her eyes without altering the makeup that had been applied.

The dance floor had cleared slightly as the band led into another less vigorous tune, and a tall, thin vocalist began to croon "Someone to Watch Over Me." James asked Mary if she cared to dance, and she followed him onto the floor. He floated her around the dance floor, and she was delighted by his grace. She could feel his hand placed on the small of her back, and it sent a tingly sensation up and down her spine. She closed her eyes and let the music fill her head as her body delighted in their closeness. All too soon, the melancholy tune was replaced with a roaring rendition of "Toot, Toot, Tootsie, Goodbye," and James coaxed her into remaining on the floor. She tried to imitate the other dancers by swinging her arms and legs in the latest fashion of dance but couldn't help but feel awkward at the display she was sure she was giving. As they reseated themselves at their table, James complimented her on her ability. She giggled. Quickly finishing his first drink, James ordered another, and Mary hesitantly tried another—smaller—sip of her own.

On the drive back to the hotel, Mary let her head rest against James's chest. She was sure she had sipped entirely too much of the many drinks James had ordered for her. They had danced several times, and by the time they had left, Mary was sure she had accomplished the Charleston. Once on the proper floor of the hotel, they walked arm in arm down the hallway toward their rooms. Mary covered her mouth as she hiccupped, and James laughed aloud at her insistent aliment, which had started just as they had gotten out of the auto.

"Shhh," she scolded him, "people are sleeping, including Miss Chrisssstina." She slurred the name, which caused her to giggle and hiccup at the same time.

"Why don't we go to my room for a while?" James asked. "So we don't wake Chrisssstina," he said in imitation of Mary's slurred speech. Mary accepted his invitation, though she knew it was against what should have been her better judgment.

James opened the door to his suite and ushered Mary inside. He helped her off with her coat, and she swirled around the room, dancing with an imaginary partner. He removed his own coat and laid them both over the arm of a chair. Swirling herself back to him, she threw her arms around his neck and pulled her body close to his. James, a little surprised by her boldness, invited her just the same by wrapping his own arms tightly around her waist.

He looked down at her eyes—which were closed—then to her lips, which were readying themselves in anticipation of his kiss. He couldn't help but chuckle at her. Her lips, poised in an exaggerated pucker, reminded him of a fish. With his chuckle, her eyes flew open, and she playfully snapped at him. "What's so funny?"

"You look like a fish!" he said honestly.

"Does a fish kiss like this?" she asked just before she kissed him. It was a long, passionate kiss, one he didn't want to end. When they hesitantly pulled apart, he smiled at her. She responded loudly with a hiccup.

"You're drunk," he whispered.

"I think you're right," she whispered back, just before she once again pressed her mouth to his. He slid one arm up her back and turned slightly to place his other behind her knees, scooping her up into his arms. He carried her to the bed and laid her on it gently. He removed his dinner jacket and flung it on a chair, then lay down beside her. She rolled from her back to her side, melding her body to his. James thought momentarily he might be taking advantage of her in her uninhibited and inebriated state, but the thought quickly dismissed itself as she wrapped her arm around his neck and pulled him to her. Again, they kissed.

He looked into the green emerald stars shining in her eyes that had somehow managed to capture his heart, and he whispered softly, "I do love you, Mary."

She responded with a hiccup then giggled. "I'm sorry, James."

"Perhaps I should get you a glass of water," he stated as he rose from the bed and shuffled off through his suite of rooms toward the facilities. Upon his return, he quickly noted that Mary, now lying on her side, had pulled the bedcover over herself. He neared the bed and looked down at her sweet face. Her eyes were closed, and though he softly spoke her name, he somehow knew she was fast asleep. He set the glass of water down on the small table next to the bed. He pulled the chair nearer the bed and sat down. It wouldn't be the first time he had watched her as she slept. The night of the costume ball came to his thoughts. He was surprised to realize it had only been two short months ago. *How can I have come to love someone so fully and so completely in two short months?*

He looked down at her beautiful face and smiled. It really didn't matter how or why he fell in love with her—just that he had.

CHAPTER 33

The boarding house was eerily quiet. I glanced at my watch. It was three o'clock in the morning. I checked my watch a second time just to be sure. Time always had a way of slipping past me when I was writing. I was pleased with the chapter about New York. John had thought I was crazy when I called him earlier that evening and made him go to my apartment and dig up the notes I had gathered years earlier about the lights on Broadway and the 1920s table card from the Club Gallant, but they seemed to fit so perfectly into the story. I wasn't sure why or exactly when I had even jotted those notes down, but I was glad I had.

I stood up from the desk and stretched my arms over my head. I would have liked to go out and take a walk through the house, but I supposed I really shouldn't–it was so late. *Early*, I scolded myself, a smile touching my lips. I loved walking through the old place. Though the ornate carpets and decor were now soiled and worn, I could almost imagine the elegance they undoubtedly once bestowed. The estate, I knew by the architecture, had been built in the mid-1800s, but the few furnishings that remained from the family home definitely dated to the 1920s. The manager, who I now referred to in my conversations with John as the pimply-faced kid, though after getting a better look at him, I was sure he was most likely in his mid-twenties, hadn't been able to lend too much information. He told me the original estate was owned by some rich guy who had given it to the city about fifteen years earlier, providing they turned it into a boarding house. I had been through most of the rooms on the first floor, except for his, which he had excitedly volunteered he got free, just for managing the place. Most of the tenants were older. The kid said they were easier to deal with than the young kids from the college who threw wild parties and were not concerned with destroying property. There had been some minor renovations throughout the mansion when it was turned into a boarding house, adding bathrooms and such, but quite a bit of the first floor had remained in its original state. He had offered me a tour after I inquired about the place. Of course, he could only show me the common rooms and the unoccupied tenant rooms, but it was enough for me to get a good sense of what the original home had been like. The library had been turned into a tenant room, but fortunately, it was not currently occupied. The bookshelves all remained intact, although they sat empty, as did the massive fireplace with the magnificently carved mantel. He had pointed out that it couldn't be used because of cracks in the chimney. I had used the name Shell for Cordella's maiden name, borrowed from the intricate family crest engraved in the beautiful wood. I wondered now if I should change the name, but G-Pat said I could worry about that later. The unique rounded corridor that led from one part of the house to the other and encased the circular stairway of the turret was truly a gem. The kid had unlocked the door and let me go inside. He said he kept the doors to the turret locked. "Don't want any of the old geezers fallin' down those stairs," he had joked. He had also told me an old town legend had it that someone had hung themselves in there a long, long time ago. The whole Genny Mueller idea had filled my thoughts as I had walked up and then down the spiral staircase in the turret.

The grand room, as I had come to refer to it, must have been magnificent in its day. Now it was used as a day room for the boarders to visit or to entertain guests. The bar that stood across the back wall was now filled with games and jigsaw puzzles, but I could visualize it with crystal drinking glasses and could almost hear the clinking bottles as I ran my fingertips across the worn wood. Most of the rooms on the second floor were occupied, but there was a definite distinction between the east and west wings of the house. In the west wing and the main part of the house, the hallways were much wider, and even the doors were larger and trimmed with very ornate wood frames. In contrast, the rooms in the east wing, where I was staying, were small and plain with no ornate woodwork or decorated light coverings, which led me to believe they had originally been servants' rooms.

It was strange, I thought, that somehow my ideas seemed to have some connection to the house. What was the saying? If walls could talk. Every room I was allowed to explore seemed to bring me thoughts and images as if they had something to tell me. I laughed at myself, or at least at the thought. I had tried to explain it to John on the phone earlier that evening, but he simply attributed it to my overactive imagination, which he concluded was a good thing considering my profession. I had shared with him a few lines of the story—in particular, the underlying story of the attacker. At first, he seemed a bit intrigued by the passages I had read, but he wondered, as did I, where it fit into the plot of the romance. I wasn't sure if it was just a question or if he, being my editor, was concerned about the content of the novel. I had tried to explain to him that it was a little eerie writing those passages, almost as if I really hadn't written them but they had just somehow appeared on the pages. He brushed it all off by saying I could always change it later.

I yawned. I really needed to get some sleep. I sat back down at the desk.

CHAPTER 34

The competition was no longer a game. The host was exhausted from the contest. No longer could the demon be pacified by the simple rewards the host could perform himself. The demon wanted for more. He was no longer content with winning insignificant battles. He wanted the power he deserved, the control he demanded.

It wasn't the fiend's fault they were all soiled. It certainly wasn't his doing that none of them was chaste. The host often wondered what he would do if the prey turned out to be innocent and pure. Yet he always knew they would not be. He could see it in their eyes, read it in their expression. Their fear was not a fear of the unknown. That knowledge intensified the beast's gratification. The demon was giving them all that he thought they deserved. After all, they had brought it all upon themselves by the choices they had made. "They had made their own bed"—so to speak. The host smiled to himself as he found the beast's cliché quite fitting.

The host had been watching the prey for days. She would be the next. He watched silently from the shadows of the night. Soon the beast would be appeased once again.

───◆───

Jud Egan glanced at the clock as it laboriously ticked by the minutes. The building was quiet. Only the duty lieutenant and the dispatch were left. The night patrol had already gone out to make their rounds. He thought of calling his wife but then decided she would have already gone to bed, leaving him a plate of food in the icebox that would go uneaten and have to be given to the dog. He took a long sip of cold coffee, lit another cigarette, then stood and once again paced his small office for what he supposed was the hundredth time that day. The latest piece of evidence lay on his desk, and the latest victim lay in the city morgue. He glanced at the newspaper that rested neatly on the file cabinet, the bold headline taunting him: "BEATEN AND LEFT TO DIE." The body had been found only late yesterday, but the early edition had managed to get it in print before the paper had hit the newsstands that morning. At least they had the decency not to print any of the pictures their photographer had managed to snap before he had to leave the scene to throw up in the alley. According to the medical examiner, the body had lain for nearly ten days before it had been found. Calculating as best he could, she had most likely been assaulted on New Year's Day or the day after. He was certain, however, she actually died a day or two later. She was so brutally beaten that he preferred to think she had never regained consciousness. The cold had kept the body from decaying too quickly, but rats in the old abandoned warehouse had begun to mutilate the corpse. Jud shuttered as he recalled the sight. They hadn't made a positive identification yet, but as no missing persons fitting her description had been reported in the area, he concluded when they did, identify her, they would find her to be a young runaway or the like. She was five foot five, one hundred and twenty pounds, had blond hair and blue eyes, and the medical examiner had recorded her age at approximately sixteen.

"Blue eyes!" Jud said it out loud. It just didn't fit. Nothing fit. All the other victims had been older, in their early twenties. Other than the last girl, whom the attacker had smacked across the cheek, none had been beaten. And up until now, they'd all had green eyes. And up until now, it wasn't called murder.

Finding that first handkerchief down on the riverfront was pure luck. The one left next to the dead girl's body was left there purposely, like a calling card. It was the same distinctive cloth as the first, but this one displayed a hand-stitched monogram, offering the initials J.C. Jud was sure it had been left there for them to find.

The MO just wasn't the same. Jud could smell it. He had a gut feeling the other girls had been chosen by the attacker. They had been culled out for their age, their size, even their eye color. Jud believed the other attacks had been planned. This one was different. It was *too* different. Yet his only suspect was James Colton. What gnawed at him the most was that now, with this new evidence, it seemed as if he was being led to his only suspect. Jud didn't like being led anywhere. He wasn't going to be used as a pawn in someone's sick game. He wasn't going to be left holding the bag, not this time.

He had been forced to carry on the investigation more vigorously. The mayor was all over him now, demanding he put an end to the madman that was raising havoc in his town, in an election year, nonetheless. Jud, of course, had to seek out any information regarding his only suspect. He was staying clear of the Coltons, though, and only questioning acquaintances of the family, hoping that word wouldn't make it back to them.

That morning, after he had left the warehouse, he had driven over to the Coltons'. He had chanced on an old man, the groundskeeper, who was chipping away at a buildup of ice under a clogged gutter on the old coach house, now used to house the family's collection of auto machines. Jud had started an innocent conversation and discussed everything from the weather to the construction of the old coach house before casually turning the conversation to James Colton. The old man had said James had returned from a visit with a friend late New Year's Day. The old man recalled that he, himself, had helped James with his bags, as he had been out working on the same ice problem that very day.

Further investigation of the Coltons' staff had turned up an aunt to one of the maids. She lived right here in Bay View. He had found her at her apartment around dinnertime that very evening. She had been a little skeptical of him at first, but after scrutinizing his badge, Matilda Bryer offered him entrance to her small apartment. She reminded Jud of his old Aunt Gerdy, a spinster, overly zealous for any kind of company, and quick to spread the latest gossip. She had been eager to offer all she knew of the Coltons, her niece's employer.

She had told Jud that James had accompanied Mary, her niece, back to her home for her father's funeral. They had returned together on the train on New Year's Day. Jud had silently noted to himself that the old caretaker hadn't mentioned James had been traveling with anyone. Moreover, he said he had been visiting a friend, never mentioning a funeral. Miss Bryer had confided in Jud that she found James Colton a little peculiar.

"In what way?" Jud had asked. She recounted for him James's visit to her right before the holidays and his request for a picture of her niece.

"He said it was for a present." The tone of her voice noted her skepticism.

"Is that all?" Jud had questioned.

"Well," she snipped, "he also said how disappointed he was that a photograph couldn't do justice to Mary's beautiful green eyes."

Jud rubbed his hands over his face and then through his hair. It was late. He was tired. He had just been informed by the lieutenant that they were bringing in a girl who had just been picked up downtown claiming she had been attacked that very evening. She worked at the new ice skating rink the city had opened on the edge of the park. She was just closing up for the evening when someone jumped her from behind and dragged her back into the shelter house, where he had his way with her. The attacks were becoming more frequent. Or were they? Jud wondered.

The lieutenant stuck his head back in the door.

"Hey, Chief, I thought you'd wanta know. This one's got green eyes."

CHAPTER 35

Even though he had repeatedly rehearsed the impending conversation he was about to have with Mrs. Colton, he was a bit nervous as he picked up the phone. He knew that no formal charges had been made as yet, and he hoped his impatience would not foul up his plans. But then, he had been informed the investigation was proceeding. He had to be careful when he spoke with Cordella Colton. He had to make sure she understood his offer completely. He knew it was too soon for her to accept his proposal. Indeed, she would most likely think him a kook and slam the phone in his ear. Yet he was anxious to proceed with his plan. Mrs. Colton would indeed accept his proposal, perhaps not now, but when the time came, he was sure, she would be more than willing to work with him. It was important that when the time arrived, things went as he'd planned. Once his plan was set into motion, he would have to work quickly. There would be no time for her to think about his proposal then. She would need to have things ready for him. She would need to have Mary ready for him.

Cordella Colton was engaged in conversation with Bea about the evening's festivities when Maggie informed her there was a call for her.

"Who is it?" she snapped.

"He wouldn't say," Maggie said.

Cordella turned quickly on her heel and left the kitchen, obviously annoyed with Maggie. She pushed the hinged door with such force it banged against the wall and proceeded toward the study. She hadn't the time for a phone conversation—the family was expected home soon. In fact, Charles had already left for the station to retrieve them. She was, of course, obligated to have a homecoming/birthday party for Christina, who would be expecting at least a family celebration with a myriad of presents. Cordella was just not up to planning such an event since up until just two days earlier, she had been forced to remain in her bed, still weak from whatever it was that even the doctor could not explain. Reaching the desk in the study, she picked up the phone, placed the receiver to her ear, and huffed into the mouthpiece, "This is Mrs. Colton."

The unfamiliar voice on the line responded, "Good day, Mrs. Colton. I wanted to call to make you aware of," the man hesitated only slightly before saying, "let's say, a business proposition."

"Who is this?" Cordella barked impatiently.

"Who I am isn't important. I only ask that you please hear me out. I can assure you, you'll be very interested in what I have to say."

"Get on with it then," she snarled more sternly.

"I'm sure, being the concerned citizen that you are, you're well aware of the attacks that have been plaguing our fair city?"

"Of course," Cordella snapped, her impatience still apparent.

"Well, it just so happens," the man paused and breathed heavily into the phone, "I've become privy to some information that might well concern you."

"Go on," she responded, her impatience now laced with disinterest at whatever it was the man had to say.

"I can assure you, as the investigation into this matter continues, you will undoubtedly accept my proposal. You see, Mrs. Colton, I have been made aware that the prime suspect happens to be someone very close to you."

Before Cordella could respond, the man continued. "Now, I understand you have in your employ a young girl by the name of Mary?"

"What does she have to do with any of this?"

"You see, Mrs. Colton, once the police finally press formal charges against their only suspect, and like I said before, it is someone very close to you whom you'll undoubtedly want to help, I can assure you, I, and only I, will be able to clear his name. But of course . . ." The man hesitated again as he silently scolded himself for perhaps talking too fast. He had planned on pausing before he continued with his offer. Already committed to speech, he continued. "I will require something in exchange. To put it simply, Mrs. Colton, I want the girl. I want you to turn Mary over to me."

He was, if nothing else, a good salesman. Even over the phone, he could hear the slight change in her breathing, which indicated her interest in the situation. He spoke quickly. "I'll be making all the necessary arrangements, Mrs. Colton. I'm sure we'll speak again."

The discomforting sound of silence lingered in her ear after the man closed the connection. She absentmindedly replaced the receiver on the hook. The man was clearly a lunatic, and yet the phone conversation plagued her throughout the remainder of the day. Not to mention that she had been hearing some rumors that Jud Egan had been inquiring with a select group of people throughout the city about James and his whereabouts around the New Year.

By that evening, she had tried to put the whole conversation behind her. After all, James—a suspect? It was simply ridiculous.

"You seem a little preoccupied this evening, Mother," James said across the dining room table. "Is there something wrong?"

"Nothing at all, dear," she responded graciously while she silently repeated the words, *Ridiculous, simply ridiculous.*

"So, James, how did you enjoy New York?" Cordella asked, though she was thinking, *How did you celebrate the New Year?*

"It was a most enjoyable trip, Mother." Without turning his head, he cast his eyes quickly to Mary, who was standing next to the sideboard, awaiting the need of her services.

"Most enjoyable," he repeated, turning his eyes quickly back to the conversation.

⸺◦⸺

Diane was sure she was the only one, other than Mary, to notice his shifted gaze, and she was now concerned with the faint smile that had momentarily touched his lips. In an earlier conversation that afternoon with Christina, she had learned that James and Mary had gone to the theater together in New York. Christina had been quick to point out that Mary hadn't returned to her room until quite early the next morning. Diane didn't care what Mrs. Colton put up with. She wasn't going to have any of it. Even if it meant having no servants at all. She certainly wasn't going to have a husband that fooled around with the hired help, or anyone else for that matter. Yes, she thought to herself, she definitely had to do something about Mary.

"So how was the theater, James? What play did you see?" Diane asked, trying to subtly note to James that she was well aware of what had gone on in New York.

"I didn't even get to go!" Christina boldly interrupted. "All I got to see was a stuffy old opera. All they did was scream out a bunch of stuff I couldn't even understand." She placed a formidable pout on her lips.

⸺◦⸺

"Well," Cordella said and cleared her throat. *Why had she not been told about this sooner? If Christina didn't go to the theater, just who did?* she wondered. She pacified her daughter by saying, "Perhaps we can do something to make it up to you."

Christina was quick to offer suitable compensation. "*Down to the Sea in Ships* is showing at the movie house this evening."

"Clara Bow stars in that film," Mr. Colton chimed in enthusiastically. Clara Bow was his second favorite actress, just behind Mary Pickford.

"Well," Mrs. Colton said, surveying the faces of all seated at the table, "that sounds like a lovely idea. Why don't we all go?" *Perhaps,* she thought to herself, *a moving picture will give me respite from thought.*

Everyone agreed, though James had hesitated slightly before he added, "Sounds like a wonderful plan."

After dinner, James, his father, and Diane lounged in the parlor as Mrs. Colton and Christina, in their respective rooms, readied themselves to go to the showhouse.

Diane looped her arm through James's as she pulled herself closer to him on the divan where they were seated. The elder Mr. Colton had poured them all snifters of brandy and was in the process of lighting his cigar. Suddenly, James pulled from Diane's grasp and stood.

"Well, I must go and inform Charles we will need the car brought around." He scrambled out of the room, ignoring Diane's suggestion to simply use the buzzer.

Diane sat stiff and expressionless on the small divan, listening to Mr. Colton ramble on about Clara Bow and the glorious Mary Pickford until Mrs. Colton and Christina finally made their entrance to the parlor. Just as Cordella was inquiring as to the whereabouts of James, there was a horrendous commotion in the front entryway. By the time they all hurried to the front entrance, both Bea and Charles were trying to help James to his feet. James winced in pain as he tried to stand and immediately sat back down on a step of the grand staircase.

"My word!" Cordella shouted. "What happened now?"

Diane rushed to James's side.

"I fell, Mother." James winced as he reached for his ankle.

"Did ya break it?" Christina asked a little too enthusiastically.

"No, no, I don't think so. Probably just a bad sprain." He grimaced again.

"Perhaps we should call the doctor," Diane offered.

"No, no," James was quick to object. "I'm sure it's not broken. Perhaps you should just help me to my room, Charles."

"We're going to miss the show," Christina whined, unconcerned about her brother.

Mrs. Colton insisted that William and Charles help James to his room, and then William should go on to the showhouse with Christina and Diane. She would stay behind with James. Diane insisted Cordella should go with the family, and she would stay behind with James. James, trying to hurry their decision, stood on one leg, and with Charles's assistance, began to hop up the steps one at a time as he shouted down to them, "Why don't you all go to the show? I'll be fine."

Then, with Bea's insistence that she would see to Mr. James, and after she retrieved their wraps, she readied them for their departure. Charles appeared almost too quickly to usher them out the door, and just before closing the large front door behind them, he assured Bea that Mr. James was resting comfortably and had asked not to be disturbed, then was quick to assure Diane that James had insisted that she not miss the moving picture.

James watched from the large window in the sitting area at the top of the grand staircase until the car had passed through the iron gates. Charles, once again, had been eager to help him with his scheme. He really thought it brought a bit of excitement and adventure to the man's otherwise mundane existence. A noticeable spring in his step, he cheerfully headed down the hallway to find Mary. He hoped Charles's instructions to Bea would be followed. He didn't want her coming up to check on him only to find his room empty.

The east wing was quiet. He knew Maggie was out with Joseph, and Jeanette would be busy helping Bea with the laundry after emptying the suitcases from the family's trip. He had at least two hours alone with Mary. As he neared the end of the wing, he could hear the sweetness of her voice, humming softly from behind the closed door of the smallest room in the house. He knocked softly on the door, while with his other hand he turned the knob to see if it was locked.

"Yes?" Mary had stopped her melody to answer, and James had heard the splashing of water, indicating that she was already in the tub.

The door was not locked, and he pushed it open slightly as he leaned himself against the doorframe and peeked around the corner.

"James!" Mary declared, instinctively covering herself.

He pulled the door closed as he chuckled at her scolding. "Perhaps I could offer my services. I am a very accomplished back scrubber."

Mary was silent for a moment as she toyed, if only for an instant, with the idea of taking him up on his offer. Scolding herself for even thinking such a thing, she pulled herself from the water, dried quickly, and slipped on her robe. Her hair was pinned haphazardly at the top of her head as she emerged into the hallway and smiled at James. Then she quickly scurried off to her room, knowing he was following closely behind her. She stood a few feet from her bed. And though her conscience was offering sensible alternatives to the situation at hand, she was silent as James entered her room, shut the door, and came to stand in front of her. She was quiet as he kissed her tenderly. When the kiss ended, she inquired about the other occupants of the house. James quickly silenced her. "They're all gone, off to the showhouse."

Her eyes closed as he kissed her once again. Her body responded instantly to his touch, and she drew herself closer to him as he wrapped his arms around her. Her head lay softly on his chest, and the steady rhythm of his heartbeat was comforting.

Pulling away gently, Mary tried to speak. "James . . ."

James attempted to silence her again, moving his lips back toward hers. She whimpered. He pulled slightly away from her to look into her eyes, those emerald green seas that captivated him. She again tried to speak. "James, I never . . ."

"I know," he whispered.

She wasn't sure what to say, or if she could even speak.

"We can't." She blurted the words out quickly. She had only spoken them because they had popped into her head.

From long conversations with Maggie, she had learned that sex, for the most part, was all men thought about, and she assumed James was no different.

"I love you, Mary, with all my heart. I will always love you—forever, always, eternally." He smiled. "And yes, I do want to, but only when it's right."

Mary seized the moment. She just had to know, though the words stumbled off her tongue. "Have you . . . have you ever . . ."

James was silent for a long time. The question he was sure she was about to ask had caught him off guard. He had certainly never been asked it before. Everyone assumed he had been with lots of women—his playboy reputation and all—and he had certainly never denied it when someone suggested it. Oh, he had dated a lot of women. Yet, the truth was—and perhaps, when it came right down to it, he was the only one who knew the truth—he was as much a virgin as she was. His mind rebuffed the thought. *Well, not completely innocent*, he told himself, *but still a virgin.*

Mary was watching him intently, waiting for an answer, and when one didn't come, she continued.

"Have you . . ." She hesitated, and James braced himself for her words, imagining the worst scenario, that if he had been with other women, she would never trust him or perhaps couldn't even love him.

"Have you ever loved someone before?" she finally blurted out.

James laughed, a little too loudly for Mary's comfort.

"Oh, my sweet Mary," he whispered, trying to stifle his laughter. He stared deeply into her eyes and knew there would be no one else on God's green earth, or beyond, that he could—or would—ever love again the way he loved her.

"No, Mary, not the way I love you."

CHAPTER 36

James spent two evenings cleaning away cobwebs and sweeping up the floor of the long-deserted groom's quarters above the old stables. He was quick to decide it would make the perfect hideaway for him and Mary.

He stood back and surveyed the table he had just set. The white linen tablecloth he had taken from the butler's closet had provided a simple remedy to covering the rough wooden table that stood at one end of the room. He had borrowed a few pieces from one of the many sets of china that were stored in the cabinets in the dining room. He had even grabbed a set of silver candlesticks while he was at it. The table, though still surrounded by rough bench seating, lent an aura of elegance to the rustic surroundings. Though the wind howled outside and found its way in through small cracks and crevices, James was surprised how warm the room could get once he fired up the old wood-burner. He had stacked an ample supply of wood in the woodbox, as he could only hope and wonder how many times he might be able to bring Mary to this newly found retreat.

He had already made arrangements with Maggie to prepare a dinner for Mary and him. Maggie would simply procure a few of Bea's leftovers that she would sneak out of the icebox and he could reheat on the cook stove in the groom's loft. Charles was to bring Mary in the auto, telling her that he was working under James's explicit instructions and being diligent to make sure no one else was aware of the goings-on. He should then drive her around the outside of the estate and enter through the small side entrance drive that led to the stables. After depositing her into James's waiting arms, he could then return the auto to the carriage house, and no one would be the wiser. No one ever came out to the old stable anymore, and with Charles in on the whole scheme, he would be trusted to quickly cover up any questions that should arise. James was sure Charles was being thoroughly entertained with all the recent shenanigans. The old man had been most willing, and almost giddy, about this latest ruse.

The next day passed much too slowly for James. The anticipation was tormenting. He had informed Mary that he had special plans for them that evening, instructing her only that she was not to eat dinner as she usually did with the rest of the servants in the kitchen and, if needed, she should offer an excuse that she would be dining with her aunt. He told her Charles would have further instructions for her.

When he finally arrived home at five thirty, he quickly changed his clothes and informed his mother he would not be dining with the family as he had made plans to go out for the evening. She had objected, saying she had really wanted to speak to him that evening. He assured her they would talk soon, but he simply had made unchangeable plans. He made a quick dash to the wine cellar and grabbed a bottle from the shelf, not concerning himself with the brand or vintage. He dashed into the kitchen, realizing he had forgotten to take any wine glasses to the loft. He supposed he could make do with the metal cups that still hung in the cupboards of the makeshift kitchen, but thought it might dull the ambiance of the fine china and good silver he had already set on the table. As he entered the empty kitchen, he instantly spied the apple pies Bea had left to cool on the cupboard near the side door. He noted they had most likely been made that very afternoon for the family's dinner. Apple pie, his father's favorite dessert, was served no less than once a week. Without giving it a second thought, he grabbed one of the three pies, knowing the two that were left would be more than enough for the family and servants' dinners. He quickly made his way back through the front entry hall and slipped quietly out the door. He noticed the light dusting of snow that had fallen as he climbed into the roadster, which he had left parked just outside the front entrance. He had to drive around to the side of the house, where Maggie assured him she would have waiting, on the side porch, a box full of food in small dishes and pots with which he could prepare the dinner. He chuckled remembering her warning that he should be sure to clean them all and get them back into Bea's cupboards before she noticed their absence.

The box was just where Maggie said it would be. James climbed the steps, grabbed the box, threw it onto the seat next to him, and backed the roadster back to the main entrance. He then sped down the long drive, through the gates, and then headed around the estate toward the stables. He would have approximately an hour to prepare dinner and ready the loft for Mary.

He parked the roadster just outside the large front doors of the stable, carefully placed the wine, goblets, and pie into the box Maggie had prepared, and got out of the car. Entering the stable, he made his way past the stalls and up the narrow steps that led to the loft. He lit two of the small oil lanterns and was whistling to himself as he started a fire in the woodstove.

Mary could only wonder what James had planned for the evening as she quickly helped Bea with the family's dinner dishes. Maggie, too, was in a hurry to be done with her duties so she could meet Joseph for the evening. Bea's head was in a spin as she watched the two young girls bustling through their chores. Charles, right on cue, was quick to offer that he would be driving Mary to her aunt's when Bea concerned herself with how Mary was going to get there, as it was surely too cold and dark for her to walk the distance to her aunt's apartment for dinner. He hadn't even hesitated when he assured her that Mrs. Colton had approved of the auto's use, though she, of course, knew nothing of it.

Most of the dishes done and food put away, Bea raised her hands in the air. "Shew, da boat of you. Go on and git out ov here, you're making my head spin da vay ya boat be running around. I vill finish up."

Mary and Maggie both thanked her and scurried up the stairs to their rooms to ready themselves for the evening, while Charles quietly snuck out of the house to retrieve the auto.

Bea went on with the business at hand and wiped the table and counters. As she wiped the crumbs from the cupboard, where she had earlier cut pieces of pie to serve to the Coltons, she shook her head. She couldn't imagine what had happened to the missing pie. It had been plaguing her thoughts since she had discovered its disappearance. She had also noted that there was other food missing from the icebox as well. She knew she had placed at least ten pieces of chicken into a bowl just the night before, planning to make soup, and now only five pieces remained. And that wasn't all that was missing, she fretted, like the silver candlesticks that sometimes adorned the dining table, which she had recently polished and put away in the cabinet. She had noticed their disappearance as she was setting the table for dinner. She threw the dishrag back into the sink and wrung her hands on her apron as she headed toward the dining room. As she quietly crossed the darkened room, she glanced out the window, which faced the back of the house. Something catching her eye, she took a second look. Was that a light she saw from the far end of the estate? She moved closer to the large window and peered out into the darkness. *Ya, ya, it is a light coming from the upper level of the stables.* Instantly, her mind reeled with a thought that might explain everything. She quickly went back into the kitchen and crossed to the side door. She pushed her face up against the glass and peered out, then lifted her hand to the glass. She shielded the glare from the kitchen light, allowing her to survey the small porch and steps. There were indeed fresh footprints in the soft dusting of snow. It was enough to convince her that a bum or some derelict had taken up lodging in the stables. Even more appalling, he must have snuck into the kitchen through the side door that was never locked and stolen food right out of the icebox, along with one of the apple pies. She headed back to the dining room, on her way to find Charles.

Mary came down the stairway and walked through the kitchen then into the long hall that led to the front entryway. She was, without being seen, supposed to meet Charles at the front entrance.

She entered the large entry hall at the same moment as Bea entered from the opposite end. They both set their eyes on Charles, who was standing near the front door.

"Charles!" Bea cried and, noticeably troubled, quickened her steps across the marble floor. "I tink we have intruders," she declared in a loud voice as she ambled across the large room. Mary stood silently, clad in her coat and hat, watching Bea making her advance toward them.

"Da pie, and utter stuff!" She was, in haste, trying to make Charles understand.

"Whatever are you talking about?" Charles was questioning, while his expression was warning Mary to duck back down the hallway and out of sight.

As he was trying to quiet Bea's overzealous account of the missing items and the light she had noticed in the stables, Mrs. Colton's footsteps clicked into the entryway.

"What's going on out here?" she demanded from the furthest side of the entryway.

A smile touched Mary's lips as Charles, in one fluid motion, turned his head nearer to Bea, whispered a quick explanation to satisfy her, then continued to turn until he faced Mrs. Colton and said, "Everything's under control, mum."

"What is all this yelling about intruders?" she insisted.

Without pause, Charles said, "Bea just saw a mouse in the kitchen, 'tis all, mum. Nasty intruders, you know."

"A great big von!" Bea added, and Mary noticed that Charles's eyes smiled, though his demeanor stayed ever somber.

Charles assured Mrs. Colton that he would immediately set a trap for the varmint, which satisfied her, and she retreated back to the parlor. Mary wasn't sure what Charles had told Bea, but she was well on her way back to the dining room before Charles motioned to Mary to hurry and quickly ushered her out the front door and into the waiting auto.

She was a little bewildered by the short drive around the estate, but as she climbed out of the auto and crossed the short distance to the stables, as Charles instructed her to do, James greeted her at the door and ushered her inside.

They passed by the stall, where James had first spoken the words I love you. She shivered and wasn't sure if it was from the cold or the remembrance. Hand in hand, they made their way to the small, narrow steps and climbed into the loft. The dimly lit room was warm, and the shadows from the oil lamps danced on the rough wood of the walls and ceiling. James seated her at the table he had prepared for them, and they enjoyed the dinner he had heated up. He offered her a glass of wine, but remembering how she had felt in New York the morning after the theater, she politely refused. He apologized for not having anything else to offer her.

The apple pie was delicious, as Bea's pies always were, and they each had a generous piece. When they finished, James tidied up by putting everything back in the box. Mary watched him, silently having second thoughts about the wine he had offered. Perhaps, she thought to herself, she wouldn't be so nervous if she had accepted it. She couldn't help herself. It was hard to explain, and she wasn't sure she even understood it. She was very comfortable with James. She loved him, but yet somehow he still managed to make her nervous. When he was close, there was an energy between them, and although it was very exciting, and yet somehow comforting, it was also frightening. Not scary frightening, but unsure of herself frightening.

When James had finished, he came around the table and extended his hand. She gently placed hers into his. He kissed it tenderly. "Would you care to dance?"

Mary looked at him curiously as she stood.

"What shall we dance to?" she asked.

James circled his arm around her waist, and in his best Henry Burr voice began to croon.

> I care not for the stars that shine
> Dare not hope to e'er be thine
> Only know I love you
> Love me, and the world is mine.

CHAPTER 37

Though spring had not yet arrived in Bay View, the house held the aroma of freshly cut flowers. Mrs. Colton had ordered in dozens of red and white roses for the Saint Valentine's Day Dance. Even the most trivial of holidays gave Mrs. Colton the need to throw some sort of party, cotillion, or gala. She had the servants busy for days cutting out red paper hearts and images of birds of every shape and color. Mary had obediently cut heart after heart but had to question the reason for all the birds. Maggie had explained to her, just as Charles had explained to Maggie years earlier, it was an old English notion that the fourteenth of February was the day of the year that birds first choose their mates. Thus, the birds of many shapes, sizes, and color would hang from thin strings from the ceiling of the grand room, appearing to be flying around, delivering the hearts that would also hang there. Although Maggie thought it to be all a lot of hooey, Mary thought it quite romantic.

Maggie had also explained that to further make the event a memorable evening, Mrs. Colton had also adopted the English tradition that on Valentine's Day, each young bachelor and maiden received, by lot, one of the opposite sex as "valentine" for the year. It was a kind of mock betrothal. However, in Mrs. Colton's version, the participants were neither bachelors nor maidens, and the mock betrothal was only for as long as the evening lasted. Each female guest's name was printed on a small piece of paper and then placed into a large crystal bowl. As the guests arrived, the men would each, in turn, pick a name from the bowl, and the name they picked would be their valentine for the evening. The older male guests, who would by chance choose the name of one of the much younger female guests, usually enjoyed the little game most thoroughly. Certainly, to what extent the guests participated in the little game was left entirely up to each individual, or more correctly stated, each man's wife. For the most part, the idea was thought to be entertaining and performed in differing degrees by most of the guests.

That evening, as Mary walked through the grand room, offering small heart-shaped pastries, which she had helped Bea prepare earlier that afternoon, she scrutinized the many oddly coupled partners Mrs. Colton's little game had produced. Mr. Colton had been partnered with Judge Murdoch's wife. At eighty-two, she kept falling asleep in the middle of their conversations. Mary couldn't help but wonder if Mrs. Colton hadn't somehow managed to have something to do with that particular arrangement. Most of the guests had already arrived by the time James had returned to the house with Diane. Mary watched them as they entered the grand room. Diane was, of course, clinging to James's arm. James reached into the crystal bowl, which, by now, held only three small slips of paper. As he pulled one out, Diane was quick to grab it from him. "Mrs. Hammerstead," she announced gleefully. Mary, who knew the mayor's wife was well into her sixties and immensely overweight, was pleased with the pairing. She stifled a chuckle after James and Diane crossed the room to the Hammerstead's table, only to discover that Mr. Hammerstead had chosen Diane's name. Mary was sure Diane would have to sit through a lengthy conversation about the Scopes Trial, as it was all that Myron Hammerstead spoke of since the trial had ended that last July. "It's just ludicrous," he would say. "They think we all came from monkeys, you know."

Mary had smiled at James just as he was taking his seat next to Esther Hammerstead, then gleefully went about her duties.

James had shared with her the fact that Diane felt he was spending too much time down at the factory or with his buddies, when in reality, most of it had been spent with Mary. In an attempt to appease Diane, James had assured her they would attend the

Valentine's dance together. He said that Diane had only been satisfied for a short time before she remembered that because of Mrs. Colton's little party game, she and James would still not actually be together. Mary was more than pleased.

<hr>

James let his mind wander while he listened to Mrs. Hammerstead complain about Mr. Hammerstead's obsession with the Scopes Trial. He wondered if he should bother to explain to them both that the Scopes "monkey" trial was less about the debate between a supreme being and the theory of evolution than it was about money. Truth was, the local businessmen of Dayton, Tennessee thought they might drum up a little income for the city by challenging the law over such a controversial subject as evolution. The whole travesty was nothing more than a publicity scheme, but the papers hadn't reported on that. John Scopes hadn't even taught the lesson in class as he had been accused. It was all about money. It was always about money.

"What do you think, James?" Esther asked.

"What do I think? I'll tell you, Mrs. Hammerstead, I'm a pretty open-minded person, especially when it comes to innovation and new ways of thinking, but honestly, I think it takes a bigger leap of faith to believe in evolution than the Bible."

Esther Hammerstead immediately turned her conversation to her husband. "James agrees, Myron . . ."

James fell back into thought. He had more pressing things to think about, including the stupid mistake he had made. He had been concerned lately about keeping Diane content for a few weeks longer, so in an effort to remain in her good graces, he had written her a poem for Valentine's Day. He had worked for hours writing Mary a poem, his gift to her for February fourteenth. He had then scribbled Diane a short limerick that referenced roses and violets. Though it did rhyme, it could in no way be described as poetic, but he hoped it would at least pacify her for a while longer. He had tucked both letters into identical envelopes, which he had procured from the desk in the study. Days after their writing, he had retrieved Diane's and addressed it for mailing, assuming it would reach her home on the day of the Valentine's dance. He had kept Mary's poem tucked away in his bureau. He would present it to her on Sunday the fourteenth, the day after the dance, when they would once again secretly meet in the loft. The loft had proved to be the ideal place for them to meet, and he had planned yet another leisurely Sunday afternoon for them. It was convenient that the family spent most Sunday afternoons visiting outside the home.

He had only discovered his error earlier that evening as he had dressed for the dance. He had opened the bureau drawer to retrieve a fresh handkerchief and had noted the envelope he had tucked there. He had picked it up, wanting to read, one last time, the sonnet he had written. He was shocked as he opened the folded paper. Scribbled there were the corny verses he had written for Diane. He had been dumbfounded until he realized that he must have inadvertently mailed Mary's love sonnet to Diane. He had beseeched his memory to recall word for word the lines he had written for Mary. Though the passages confessed his undying love, he was sure Diane could in no way guess it had been written for anyone other than its recipient. He was relieved that he had changed the salutation in the final copy from My Dearest Mary to My One True Love. Luckily, he hadn't referenced the color of her eyes, only how they danced and sparkled.

He smiled at Diane now as he silently noted her brown eyes. She had only thanked him for the letter—no more, no less.

Diane smiled back at him. She knew he hadn't a clue of what she had in store for him. She had already arranged with Mrs. Colton that she would stay in one of the guest rooms that evening. She had not told James. When the house was quiet, she would sneak down the west wing to his room. She had been arguing with her conscience for days over her decision. Though she and James had certainly engaged in harmless petting, they had never let it go beyond that point. To her dismay, over the last few months, he had seemed almost oblivious to her advances. She was certain now it was because he assumed that his advances would end as they always had in the past, with her telling him they had to stop before they went too far. She knew from the tales of most of her friends that she was clearly one of the last holdouts who had not actually gone past the limit, or as James and his friends referred to it—Rock and Roll. It had been their term for nookie for years now since Trixie Smith had sung in that dreadful song, *"My baby rocks me with one steady roll."* Diane found the term quite vulgar.

It had been James's valentine that had made the decision for her. His words of love had melted her heart, and she was now sure of his intentions. She would show him that she felt the same.

Late that night, as James crawled into his bed, he breathed a sigh of relief. He was glad the evening had finally come to an end. The only problem from his stupid mistake in mixing up the letters was that he had nothing to give Mary. He was sure he could rewrite the sonnet for her, but knowing Diane had read it and thought it had been written for her had somehow, in his mind, tarnished the words. He closed his eyes and found comfort in the fact that the next day was Sunday, and he would once again be with Mary. He wondered what Diane was up to. For his sake, she had appeared to leave the party, supposedly catching a ride with a friend, but James knew she was just down the hall in one of the guest rooms. His mother had actually let the cat out of the bag when she inquired of Diane's whereabouts around 11:30. When James informed her she had already left, his mother noted it was odd, as she had asked if she could stay the night. James had had Charles check it out for him, and he had verified her presence in the house. James wasn't sure what she was up to, but he was soon to find out.

The house was quiet as Diane slipped out the door of her room. She tiptoed down the hallway of the main house toward the west wing. Quietly, she turned the handle of James's door and slipped into his room. It was dark, and she could hear his steady breathing. She assumed he might very well be asleep. She knew he drank quite heavily that evening and hoped he was not too blotto, so as to prevent him from accepting her advances. She spoke his name softly as she lifted the covers and slipped under the quilt beside him. She whispered his name again as she wrapped her arm around his chest and began to massage him. He rolled onto his back but only moaned at her as she breathed his name a third time. She gripped his arm and shook him, at first softly, and then with a bit of urgency. His only response was a dreadful sound as he gulped at the air through his open mouth. Diane threw the quilt back from around her, got out of his bed, and left the room. She stormed back through the west wing, and entering her room, she slammed the door behind her, unconcerned if it should wake anyone.

James lay awake, chuckling, but when he heard the slamming of her door, he laughed out loud. Settling himself into a comfortable position, his thoughts soon turned back to Mary as he silently calculated in his head the days until March sixth. *Just twenty-one more days*, he thought to himself. On March sixth, he would turn twenty-five. He would then inherit the trust his grandfather had left him, and his mother would have no control over his actions. He would be free to marry anyone. March sixth would be the day he asked Mary to be his wife. With the sizable amount of money he would acquire, they could do anything they wanted. They could move as far away from Bay View as she wished and start their new life together as husband and wife.

Just yesterday, he had picked up the ring from the jeweler. He had it hidden in the drawer of his nightstand. It was a beautiful gold band with green emeralds that sparkled like her eyes. He was sure that Mary didn't suspect a thing. In fact, as far as she knew, he wasn't even going to be in town on his birthday. She, of course, knew nothing about the trust fund. James knew it wouldn't matter to her—money didn't matter to Mary. He would surprise everyone, including Mary, with his proposal.

He believed the family suspected this trip, which he had just informed them of that very morning, was a getaway planned for him and Diane, though he had not offered any explanation for his departure on the sixth. Diane thought it was a vacation with one of his friends, for that is what he had told her.

Of course, it was with the same fabricated friend with whom he had spent the New Year holiday. Diane wasn't thrilled with the idea, and James knew she seemed suspicious of the whole thing. *Perhaps,* he thought to himself, *I should just tell Diane about Maggie's secret wedding.* After all, it would appease her, and what could it hurt? She wouldn't tell anyone if he asked her not to. She didn't know about Maggie's contract, so there would be nothing to gain in her telling his mother. She had been suspicious of him ever since his return from New York, after Christina had informed her that he had gone to the theater with Mary. Then shortly after that, she had caught him and Mary in an embrace in the servants' hallway. And although he had explained he was just comforting her as she was still upset over her father's passing, he didn't think Diane bought the explanation.

In his original plan, he had imagined that when the sixth of March finally arrived, he would immediately ask Mary to be his bride. She would accept, of course, and they could both march themselves to wherever his mother was at that moment and inform her of the news. Maggie had, however, changed his original plans. She had confronted him just days ago, pleading for his help. She and Joseph were making plans of their own to be married. Joseph had the opportunity to purchase a nice plot of land, in Montana of all places. James chuckled now at the thought of Maggie living on a farm in Montana. Maggie had told him that Joseph had been saving every penny he could and had determined that with the wages he would receive on the fifth of March, they would have the money needed to leave. The problem was, of course, Maggie's contract with the Coltons didn't expire for another five years.

"That 'tis where you come in," Maggie had informed him. She needed to secretly remove her belongings from the house without anyone noticing.

"You mean you're running away from home?" he had questioned her teasingly. She had only raised her eyebrows at his comment. He had then, more sincerely, told her he would always consider her to be part of his family. She had hugged him for his kindness and told him that was why she also wanted him at her wedding.

"Aside from Mary and Bea, ya be the closest thing to a family I be havin', James."

Though it would be a quick ceremony in front of the justice of the peace, just half an hour before their scheduled train departure, she wanted him to be there as their witness. Her plan was to simply leave with word to no one except, of course, James.

"Let her just try ta find me!" she had taunted him with regards to his mother. James had questioned her as to whether or not she had shared her plans with Mary. Maggie had assured him no one else knew. She longed to tell Mary, but Joseph forbade her to tell anyone besides him, and only after she explained that she needed a way to get her things out of the house. James had, of course, agreed to help her, even though it meant changing his own plans. The plan then, as Maggie had outlined it for him, was that James was to make it known to everyone that on Saturday, the sixth of March, he would be leaving on a trip. He would advise Charles to pack his bags as he usually did, but after Charles had done so, Maggie would secretly remove his things and repack his baggage with her belongings.

"Ya has to be sayin' you will be stayin' away long enough to require two bags," she had instructed him. "I need to be fittin' all my belongings in."

Then he was to pretend he was leaving the house with his luggage to catch the train, when in reality he would bring the luggage with him and meet Maggie at the justice of the peace. After Maggie and Joseph were wed and safely on the train headed to Montana, James could return to the house and complete his own plan. Of course, Maggie had no knowledge of what James himself was planning. He could tell no one. It would just be safer that way.

He reminded himself he would have to be very careful when speaking with Mary. He didn't like keeping secrets from her, but he had no choice. He already knew she suspected something was going on with Maggie–she had just told him yesterday that she thought Maggie was acting peculiar of late. Mary's concern was that perhaps Maggie knew how serious she and James's relationship was becoming. James absentmindedly dismissed her concerns and blamed Maggie's peculiarities on her own impending wedding vows. He had caught himself, but only after the word wedding had slipped from his lips. He then quickly covered over his words with nonsensical ramblings about the fact that Maggie had told him she wished Joseph would propose.

Twenty-one more days! He smiled as he closed his eyes and drifted off to sleep.

CHAPTER 38

The unmistakable sound of someone throwing up echoed up and down the east wing. Mary, white-faced, small droplets of sweat clinging to her brow, retched over the basin for the second time that morning. It was the third time that week she had been ill. She knelt to the floor and leaned against the clawfoot tub, laying her head against its cool surface. The words from her conversation earlier that week with Maggie rang in her head.

"Ya not be with child, 'tis ya?" Maggie had questioned. Mary had accepted the cold cloth Maggie had handed her, and though she had immediately denied Maggie's question, she couldn't lie to herself. She knew she hadn't had her monthly since just before Christmas.

Sitting there on the floor of the tiny room, tears began to fall silently to her cheeks. She so wanted her mother. She so wanted to be back home. Very quickly, her sorrow turned to anger as she scolded herself silently. *How could I have let this happen?*

Diane Beaumont pulled through the front gates of the Colton estate. She had been out early, shopping for James's birthday present. She hadn't been able to speak with him when she had phoned the plant earlier. His secretary said he would be tied up in meetings the entire morning. She thought about phoning the Coltons, but she really couldn't leave her message for James with anyone in the house without raising suspicion. She wanted to make sure he understood that she wanted him to pick her up on his way to the justice of the peace to meet Maggie and Joseph. She wanted to make sure all he was telling her was indeed the truth. Besides, she thought to herself, they'd be going out to celebrate his birthday afterward anyway. That's what he had agreed to. So what difference would it make if he picked her up before or after Maggie's wedding?

She thought it totally uncalled for that James was bothering to help Maggie with her covert departure. When he confided in her about his involvement in Maggie's plan, she had insisted he was entirely too chummy with the servants. She hadn't protested too much, of course, being that he had at least told her the truth about his fictitious trip. Of course, he had only told her the truth after her insistent pestering about why he was leaving for a trip on his birthday in the first place.

It was his twenty-fifth birthday. after all, and he would be inheriting that trust fund his grandfather had left him. Diane was sure he would finally be popping the question. At least she kept trying to convince herself she was sure of it. She had her doubts, though, especially about that little chit Mary. She had caught James in just too many lies about her. As she pulled her auto up to the front entrance, she was pleased with her decision to come to the house. Perhaps she'd do a little investigating while she was here. If James was being truthful with her about the whole charade, then his bags would be packed in his room with Maggie's belongings. It was Friday, and Diane knew Mrs. Colton would be out of the house at her weekly mah-jongg game, so she wouldn't have to make small talk before she could make her way to James's room to leave him a note and, of course, inspect his baggage. Charles greeted her at the door with his ever somber expression. After telling him her purpose in being there, he offered to give any message she had for Mr. James to him upon his arrival.

"It's . . ." she hesitated, "a personal message. I would really rather just leave a note in his room."

"Very good, Miss Beaumont. Would you like me to show you to his room?" he offered.

She haughtily refused by saying, "I certainly know where it is, thank you."

Holding her chin unnaturally high, she crossed the large entryway and ascended the grand staircase. Once out of Charles's sight, she raced up the remaining stairs, gave a quick glance around the upper landing to make sure no one was in sight, and then scurried down to the west wing and quickly slipped into James's room. She immediately spied his luggage, packed and waiting for him as he had said it would be. She crossed the distance to his bed, not taking her eyes off the brown leather bags. She inattentively opened the small drawer of his nightstand and began to fumble for a piece of paper and a pencil so she could scribble him a note. Then, preoccupied with the luggage, she retrieved one of the bags and flung it to the bed. Quickly unfastening the latches, she opened it apprehensively. At first, not believing what she saw yet somehow knowing all along it would not hold Maggie's belongings, she stared at James's neatly folded shirts and trousers. She tried to convince herself that perhaps Maggie had not been able to make the switch yet, but the small voice inside her head was screaming, trying to convince her there was never a switch to be made. Had James lied to her yet again? she wondered. She stood back from the bed and sat heavily onto the chair that sat in the alcove. What was she to do? What was she to believe?

She stood and reached into the nightstand to find the paper and pencil she had been searching for earlier. She was going to write James a note, an awful note. As she opened the drawer wider, she spied the small velvet-covered box that lay nestled in the corner. She picked it up and rubbed it with her shaking fingertips. Her hands were trembling as she slowly opened the cover. The green emerald stone sparkled brilliantly. Instantly, the thought popped into her head— James was going to pop the question. But just as her mind registered the thought, it instantly offered her a barrage of convincing alternatives. Popping the question, but to whom? Was the whole story about Maggie's impending matrimony a charade? Why couldn't Maggie just openly leave the Coltons' employ? Montana, how absurd! Were James's bags packed with his own things because he was indeed leaving on a trip, a honeymoon perhaps? Was what Christina had suggested after the New York trip indeed true? Had Mary spent the night with James in his hotel room? Hadn't she herself seen the smiles both he and Mary frequently exchanged when they thought no one was looking? Hadn't he been letting Mary's name slip into their conversations of late? Hadn't she caught them in an embrace shortly after their return from New York? Just where had he been all those past Sunday afternoons when he said he was doing paperwork down at the office? It didn't take long for her mind to convince her that the most plausible conclusion was that James and Mary were going to run off and get married. What was she to do? She couldn't just simply let it happen without a fight. She had given James two years of her life. She wasn't about to have to start over because some silly little wench had managed to distract him. She sat for a long time in the little alcove, calculating her plan. Once formulated in her head, she stood from the chair, a look of determination on her face. She quickly closed the suitcase and returned it to its original place. She tucked the velvet box back into its hiding place but purposely left the drawer open. She found the paper and pencil she had been searching for and scribbled a quick note, which she left on the nightstand. She left the room. She knew what she had to do.

"I don't know what she be doin' up there," Maggie was telling Bea as the two of them stood near the stove where Bea was stirring a large kettle of soup.

"You saw her go into Mr. James's vroom?"

"She come running up the stairs, she did, and then right into his room," Maggie confirmed.

Both women fell silent as Diane burst into the room from the entryway door.

Where's Mary?" she demanded boldly.

Maggie was silent, and her eyes burned into Diane's. She had been on her way to James's room with a laundry bag filled with her clothes and personal belongings when Diane had come up the stairs. She had hidden herself out of sight behind the tall linen chest but couldn't have imagined what she would have done had she already been in James's room switching out his clothes for hers in the luggage she knew Charles had so meticulously prepared earlier that morning.

"She's not feeling vell," Bea answered Diane's question. "She in her vroom."

Without further word, Diane crossed the kitchen and climbed the small stairway, which she knew led to the servants' rooms. Standing in the narrow hallway, she could hear the girl's sobs. The sound intensified her fury, and she found strength in it. She silently rehearsed her speech once again before she soundly knocked on the door.

Mary simply uttered, "Come in," while she quickly dabbed at her eyes with her handkerchief.

Diane entered the room boldly and crossed the short distance to stand in front of her as she sat on the edge of her bed. Diane set herself squarely and stared down into Mary's eyes as she spoke firmly.

"I know that you and James have ..." she hesitated slightly, suddenly unsure if her conclusions were correct, "a relationship." She quickly scanned Mary's face. The girl certainly wasn't shocked by the accusation, the knowledge of which refueled Diane's fury.

"Do you honestly think you and he could ever really be together? I don't know what kind of nonsense he's been telling you, but believe me, it's just to get you into his bed. The truth is he and I are going to be married. Tomorrow in fact!"

She suddenly realized that in her rage she was not delivering the speech as she had silently rehearsed it, but she continued just the same.

"We are to be married by the justice of the peace, and then we are immediately leaving on our honeymoon. His bags are already packed, and the ring is in his nightstand. I just wanted you to know that once we're married, I will not tolerate his liaisons, even if his mother thinks I should simply overlook them." She realized she was again wavering from the speech she had rehearsed. "I really think it best, no, I insist, that you look for other employment and be gone by the time we return." She turned on her heels and left the room. Then, without haste, she left the house through the front entrance.

Cordella Colton returned home early from her mah-jongg game. She had too much on her mind to simply sit and make small talk with the other ladies. Many thoughts ran through her head as Charles helped her off with her wrap and she proceeded to the parlor. Taking a seat on the divan, she tried to sort her thoughts. She hadn't been able to talk to James yet. The police were apparently continuing to question people regarding his whereabouts. One of the ladies had mentioned that Mr. Egan had inquired about him. It simply had to be some mistake, she assured herself. James certainly couldn't be the one committing those awful crimes, she was certain of that, but why then were the police continuing their questioning of his acquaintances? And that strange phone call she had gotten—could that man have been referring to James when he said that the person going to be charged with those crimes was someone close to her? It all had to be a dreadful mix-up. Certainly, the wrong conclusions had been jumped to before. Genny Mueller's name sprang into her head, which led her directly to her other concerns. Mary had been sick again that morning. She was convinced that the girl was pregnant. She most unpleasantly recalled her own bouts of morning sickness with both James and Christina. The same signs that Genny had displayed, so many years ago, though at the time they had gone unnoticed. She knew Mary had been sick several times in the last week, according to Bea's accounts. She believed she knew for sure, this time, who the father was. She herself had seen Mary sneaking down the west wing after leaving James's room late one night. She wasn't about to make the same mistake. She would get the girl to leave willingly. She certainly couldn't allow her to stay. James might be smitten enough to want to marry the little flap, and she certainly couldn't allow that.

"You have a phone call, mum," Charles announced, startling her. As he disappeared, she crossed the room, picked up the phone, and placed the mouthpiece to her lips. "This is Cordella Colton."

"Hello, Mrs. Colton," the vaguely familiar voice responded.

Cordella was silent, at first trying to place the voice. Then it suddenly dawned on her—it was the man who had contacted her before—and the perfect solution popped into her head. She contemplated her response, not wanting to seem too enthusiastic about his call.

"I'm sure you remember our last conversation. As I previously informed you, the police are going to be charging someone close to you for those attacks in the city, and it will be soon."

"Yes, yes," Cordella responded, immediately wishing she hadn't sounded so eager. "When we last spoke," she continued in a calmer voice, "you said you wanted my maid, Mary?"

"Indeed."

"If I were to deliver her to you, how can I be sure you will be able to clear up this matter with my son and the police?" Her voice had changed to the calculated tone she was well-accustomed to using.

The man was silent, trying to hide his delight at his impeccable timing in making the call. She apparently already knew that the suspect would be James.

"When and where is it that you want me to deliver Mary?"

At the thought of Mary, the man drooled into the phone. "This evening, four o'clock, the train station."

Cordella checked the time on her watch.

"How can I be assured you will clear up this matter with my son?" she asked, but before the man had time to respond, she continued. "I want three thousand dollars delivered to my home, no later than three o'clock this afternoon. Mary, in turn, will be delivered as promised, and once my son's name is cleared, the money will be returned to you."

The man instantly agreed to Cordella's terms, but before he could say a hasty goodbye, Cordella added, "And I expect to never hear from you or her again."

———————

Within the hour, a small package was delivered to Cordella by courier. She verified its contents and tucked it away for safekeeping.

She didn't know who the man was, nor did she care. She couldn't fathom what he wanted with Mary, but that mattered even less.

She knocked only once on Mary's door, and not waiting for an acknowledgment, abruptly entered the room. Mary was bent over her bed, folding clothes, neatly stacking them into a pile. She straightened herself and silently stared into Mrs. Colton's cold blue eyes.

"First of all," Mrs. Colton started her speech, as she fixed her face with no expression and silently told herself that this was simply a duty she needed to perform, "I know of your condition."

Mary said nothing as Mrs. Colton continued. "I don't know what you plan to do about it, but I can assure you it will in no way involve this family. I have arranged for a car to be outside the side entrance in a half hour. It will take you to the train station. There will be a man at the station to meet you. You will leave my home with word to no one. You will never return." As Cordella turned and left the room, she assured herself she was doing the right thing.

Mary supposed she should have been outraged, but she was too numb to feel anything. Besides, after Diane's earlier visit, she had already made her decision to leave the Coltons. After Diane had left, Mary had gone to James's room. The room was filled with the essence of him and the memories of them. She had hoped to find comfort, and at first she did, remembering the soft words of love he had spoken to her there, but then she spied the suitcases that stood ominously in the center of the room. *He's going to visit a friend*, her subconscious offered. Stepping further into the room, she noticed the nightstand drawer that stood open. She grabbed the little piece of paper and read the words that Diane had scribbled there.

See you tomorrow. Pick me up at one-thirty.

Don't want to keep the justice of the peace waiting!

Love, Diane

The paper had fallen from her hand and floated to the bed as she recalled James's reference earlier that week. She had been telling him her concerns about Maggie. What was it he said? Something about a wedding? He had covered over his words quickly. Perhaps Maggie even knew of his true intentions? Hadn't she and James been involved before Mary's arrival there? Maybe that's what he did, jumped from one servant's bed to another, while all the time planning on marrying Diane. Maybe that was why Maggie was acting strangely too? When she noticed the small velvet box, she was quick to open it and view its contents. She hadn't bothered returning it to the drawer. She had let it lay on his bed, where it had fallen from her fingertips. With tears streaming down her face, she had run blindly from his room, down the corridor of the west wing, through the seating area at the top of the grand staircase, and down the narrow hallway of the east wing. She had thrown herself onto her small bed. How could she have believed him? He wasn't any different than the family he came from. It hadn't taken long for her mind to convince her that Diane had spoken the truth, and when she had settled with the reality of the situation, she dried her eyes and began to gather her things. She had decided quickly, and long before Mrs. Colton had come into her room, that she would leave the Coltons, leave James. She and her baby, James's baby, would simply disappear. She hadn't yet decided where she would go, but it didn't really matter. She would slip out of the house with her satchel, taking only a few of her belongings, and get herself to the train station and as far away from Bay View as the money she had saved would allow. She had planned on walking to the station, but as she tucked the last of her belongings into her satchel, she contemplated taking the ride that Mrs. Colton said would be waiting for her.

She could faintly hear the chimes of the large clock that stood in the entry hall as she reached the bottom of the stairs. The kitchen was unusually quiet, though she could hear voices filtering in from the dining room and knew it was most likely Bea and Maggie. She wished she could go in and hug them both goodbye. As she slipped out the side door, the car was waiting there, just as Mrs. Colton had said it would be. As the auto drove down the drive and through the wrought iron gates, she didn't look back. The driver had not spoken a word to her, nor she to him. She didn't know who he was, but he apparently had been instructed on where to take her.

She entered the train station, clutching her satchel with one hand, and with the other, the money she had tucked into her pocket. She had never felt so alone. She still hadn't made a decision on where she would go. She had thought about going home, but she really had no home. She knew she had friends there, and they would be kind enough to take her in, but she wouldn't be able to face them in her condition. She had thought briefly about going to her aunt's but instantly decided against it. Once inside, she took a seat on a bench that stood against the wall. Tears filled her eyes, and though she tried to fight them back, they began to stream steadily down her cheeks.

A white handkerchief suddenly appeared in front of her lowered head. She accepted it, wiped her eyes, and then looked up to see who had offered it.

"Hello, Mary," Ezra Bellows said, his demeanor more subdued than usual.

Mary sniffed a hello before she blew her nose.

"May I be of some assistance?" he asked as he took a seat next to her on the wooden bench.

"No," she sniffled. "Thank you anyway."

"Well, there's certainly something wrong. I can't just leave you here like this."

Mary was silent.

"Are you going somewhere?" he prodded.

"Yes," she sniffled.

"Where to?" he persisted.

Mary bit her quivering bottom lip, but it didn't still the emotion building inside her, and she began to weep uncontrollably.

"I don't know," she sobbed.

As Ezra wrapped an arm around her, her head lay on his shoulder, and she collapsed into his waiting arms.

CHAPTER 39

Matilda Bryer had never been inside a jail as she'd never known anyone locked up behind the iron bars. The paper said that by the end of the week, Tom was going to be moved to a bigger facility out of town to await trial. She thought someone should see him one last time.

The jail was housed in the basement of the Westside Precinct, the largest building on Water Street, not too far from the library where she worked. After a lengthy debate with the detective on duty, she convinced him to allow her a short visit. She could be rather persuasive when she asserted herself. An officer led her down the cold gray stone steps into the basement of the building where the prisoners were held. The first room he led her into was an office. He told her to wait by the door while he approached one of the desks and talked quietly with a guard. The officer nodded at her and said, "Good day, ma'am" as he left the room, while the guard eyed her from head to toe before standing to greet her.

"So you want to see Bellows," he said, more of a statement than a question, but Matilda nodded her head silently.

He opened his desk drawer and produced a small ring of large keys and hesitated for a moment before slamming the drawer shut and motioning for her to follow him. He opened another door and ushered her into a long hall then through another door which led into yet another small room. There, another guard sat at a wooden table drinking coffee and reading the paper. At the opposite side of the room, another heavy iron-barred door led to the next room.

The guard turned the key in the heavy lock, swung it open, and motioned her through. Matilda straightened herself, set her head high, and taking a deep breath, stepped over the threshold, expecting to see Tom on the other side. She quickly surveyed the area. The iron-barred door had not opened to a jail cell but yet another room. The room was large, poorly lit, damp, and smelled of urine. A large jail cell filled most of the room but left an aisleway to walk past the inhabitants behind the iron bars, which she quickly concluded did not include Tom Bellows. One of the ragged-looking men it did hold jumped to his feet, moving swiftly toward her. She hugged closer to the dirty brick wall to keep her distance from the cell.

"Hey, honey!" he called, reaching through the iron bars in her direction. Without hesitation, the guard pulled a nightstick from his side and batted at the man's arm before he could pull it back through the bars. The man howled in pain and then scurried over to the toilet that stood unsheltered in the corner of the cell. They had reached the other side of the room by then, and the guard quickly unlocked the iron gate that led to the next room and ushered Matilda through, and though she stepped quickly forward, she could hear the sound of the man as he began to urinate into the toilet. She blinked her eyes and curled her nose, regretting that she had come.

Finally, after another short hallway, they came to a larger iron-barred door. The guard sitting there rose.

"She's here to see Bellows. I'll be back in fifteen to get her."

The new guard unlocked the barred door and guided her through. Unlike the other cell that held only benches and a toilet, Tom's housed a cot, topped with a lumpy and stained mattress, a small table, a chair, a toilet, and a sink. Matilda, being as observant as ever, noticed there was nothing else—no sheets, no blankets, not even a towel to dry his hands. There were four such cells all in a row, and all were empty but Tom's. To her surprise, the guard opened the cell door and let her in, locking it behind her.

"I'll be right over there, ma'am," he said and pointed to a chair just inside of the heavy gate. Matilda nodded.

Tom sat up on the edge of his cot and looked up at her. "What are you doing here?" he asked, his voice no more than a whisper.

Matilda, though shaking inside and wondering why on earth she had come, pulled the wooden chair out from the table and sat down across from him.

"Well," she said, straightening her back and folding her hands in her lap. "I thought someone should come to see you before they moved you to that other jail." She took a deep breath before she continued. "Being as your father has left the city."

Matilda hesitated. Should she tell him that Ezra was waiting for her in a small city just outside of Chicago? That she had to stay in Bay View and report to him by sending him newspaper clippings of any importance, and then once all the commotion was over, she could leave her job at the library and join him. That was the plan, their plan, but Ezra had told her to tell no one.

Tom looked at her with distant eyes. He suddenly seemed much younger to her. She had always thought of him as a simple-minded young man, but here in this place, he appeared to be just a boy. He mumbled something in her direction as he shot a quick glance at the guard, who had taken a seat on the wooden chair and pulled his hat over his eyes to take a snooze. Matilda shifted in her chair. "What did you say, Tom?"

Tom turned to look at her. "Do you think I killed that girl?"

Matilda shivered at his words. She wasn't quite sure what she thought. Before today, she might have believed that to be the case, but looking at him now, he appeared to be a scared child incapable of committing such a crime.

"I loved her, you know." Tom's voice was soft as he kept watch on the guard from the corner of his eye.

"The girl?" Matilda's words struggled from her throat.

Tom lifted his head but lowered his eyes. "No, my mother. I loved my mother."

That single statement seemed to open the floodgates of Tom's emotions. Matilda sat in disbelief as Tom told her about his mother—the soiled woman who lived in the big house was how he described her. He told her how he was a happy little boy who lived with all the pretty women and how his mother loved him in return.

"But she was a bad woman. My father told me what she really was. He hated her, you know? He told me I should hate her too." By this point, Tom was sobbing, his head and shoulders convulsing uncontrollably. Matilda didn't know what to do. Deep down, some instinct told her to comfort the boy, to hug and soothe this confused child, but her mind was reeling with every word that seemed to spew from his lips.

"I bet you didn't know he beat me."

Matilda wanted to run. To just get up and scream for the guard, who must have actually fallen asleep as he had not so much as stirred while Tom poured out his unbelievable twisted life to her.

Tom laughed then, but it was a quiet, guttural, hideous sound—a beastly noise.

"I got stronger, though," he spat. "I showed him! He was afraid of me, you know? Not always, but at least the last couple years. Before that, though, he just hated me." Tom's voice changed again, and the little boy was back. Matilda sat stunned. "But I didn't kill that lady." Tom hung his head, not looking at Matilda. "I hurt the others. I know I did. They had green eyes just like my mother. The evil seed had to teach them a lesson. That's what it is, you know?" He lifted his head again and looked straight at Matilda. "What I am. The evil seed. The beast, it lives inside of me. But I didn't kill that lady—even the beast couldn't have done that."

"You know what I think, though?" Tom's voice had changed yet again. To Matilda, he sounded like an adolescent as he gleefully offered his explanation.

As he recited his suspicions, that's when the numbness had entered her body. He explained to her that he thought it was Ezra's way of getting rid of him. He said he was almost certain Ezra knew he was the one who had been molesting young girls in the city and had devised a plan to put him away for a long, long time by killing that lady and then leading the police to him.

Matilda listened in horror until she just couldn't take anymore. She hollered for the guard three times before he finally jumped from his chair to let her out. She hadn't waited for the guard that was supposed to escort her but instead ran blindly through the maze back to the barred doors, screaming at each to be set free. And the whole time, she could hear Tom's voice yelling after her. "It was Ezra! I know it was Ezra!"

She wasn't exactly sure how, but somehow she had managed to make it back to her apartment. She sat at the small wooden table in her tidy little kitchen, her forehead propped by her hand as she was sure her neck could not support her head on its own. She had used all the strength she had to just make it home and up the long flight of steps.

She started the burner on the small electric stove and heated water for tea. She cradled the cup of tea she held in her hand and hesitantly took a sip, welcoming the steaming liquid though it scorched her tongue and tingled down her throat for it brought feeling to the state of numbness her body had slipped into. She closed her eyes and shook her head as she remembered Tom in that cold, hard jail cell.

After a bit, the tea calmed her nerves, and she was able to think straight. She knew she had to somehow get in touch with Ezra, but all she had was a PO Box, no other way to reach him.

By late that afternoon, she had convinced herself the only option she had was to pack a bag and head for the small town near Chicago. Her bag packed, she was taking one last look around her apartment when there was a knock at the door. Opening it, she found a very distraught James Colton in search of Mary, who seemed to have disappeared.

The host had been horrified when they accused him of being a murderer. He knew that the beast was in control, but he was completely aware of its actions. The beast had made him hit one of them, but he had to silence her screams. He knew he had not killed anyone. Even the beast would not have done that. Though, he supposed, he would have to be punished for what IT had done—for what IT had made his body do. He had, after all, pleasured in its actions. He knew if it were allowed to be free, it would stalk again and again, and its need would never diminish, its hunger never be satisfied for long. There was really no other way to extinguish its flame, squash its desire. He removed the belt from his trousers. It was a fine leather strap. He slipped it around his neck. The beast was silent. It knew, this time, the host was in control.

Later that evening, Matilda sat on the divan in her apartment. She appeared desolate, void of any emotion at all. Her nerves were entirely frayed and, shaken by Tom's accounts, she feared for her missing niece. She was desperately trying to convince herself that Ezra was a good, decent man who was waiting for her. The radio played softly. She was hoping for word on her niece. They normally broadcast the police reports in the evening. Then, from its stand in the corner, the special news bulletin on the radio shattered her thoughts. Tom Bellows, being held at the Westside Precinct, had hung himself in his jail cell.

CHAPTER 40

Mary sat down carefully on one of the wooden chairs that stood around the table in her small kitchen. She took a sip of the tea she had just made for herself. She had decided to take a short rest before continuing with her cleaning. Surveying the small room, she admired how every inch of it sparkled. She had spent the better part of the day scrubbing every corner, every nook and cranny. It was the second day of the unexplained need she had to make sure everything in the small apartment was cleaned to perfection. She had done the same in the sitting room the day before, polishing the wooden tables and dragging the rug down the stairs and into the yard to beat out the dust. The bedroom was the only room left, and she planned on tackling it after her cup of tea. There were four hours before she would need to start Ezra's dinner, and she was sure there would be plenty of time to give the room a good going-over. Placing her hands on her large belly, she rubbed it softly. The doctor had told her everything looked fine. It was hard for her to believe six months had passed since the day she had left the Coltons'. On that day, she never would have believed she would end up where she was now, but as she assessed the last six months, she supposed her decision had been for the best. Ezra had been so comforting to her that evening at the train station. He seemed so different to her. He smiled kindly and seemed so concerned about her welfare. He had persuaded her to travel with him, convincing her she shouldn't be traveling alone in the state she was in. On the train, she had broken down and confided in him her whole sordid predicament. She remembered how surprised he had been of her condition, yet he had been quick to offer her a solution and convinced her it was her only alternative. He told her he had been toying with the idea of selling his shop and moving out of Bay View anyway. When she questioned him about Tom, Ezra had simply said that he was going to be moving on. She wasn't sure what that meant exactly, but she hadn't questioned him further. Ezra said they could start a life together. They would appear to be a married couple, awaiting the birth of their first child. He said it would be simpler if she just agreed to marry him, something he would be honored to have her do. He was very understanding, though she thought he appeared a bit concerned she should refuse that part of his offer. Ezra was aware she didn't love him, but it didn't seem to matter to him. He assured her he would take care of her and only hoped that someday she might care for him and agree to be his wife. She somehow knew the only true love of her life was James. She still wore the locket he had given her, which pledged his undying love, and even though she now knew it had all been a lie, she still loved him, though it made her sad when she thought about him. And though she tried not to, she thought of him often, daily, constantly.

She and Ezra had settled into a small town just outside of Chicago, and Ezra had immediately found employment. Everything just seemed to fall into place. Even the small furnished apartment they rented had almost seemed to be waiting for them when they arrived. Mary assured herself it was a sign that she had made the right decision, and though they only appeared to be a married couple, Ezra pledged he would raise the child as his own. He had even found Mary a doctor, wanting to be certain of proper medical attention for her. Ezra was a good provider and would probably make a good husband. He did everything for her. He did the shopping and had even said he would purchase the things she said she would need for the baby. She, in turn, cooked and cleaned their small apartment. He was never too eager for her to leave their home, but he left her wanting for nothing. Mary doubted she could ever love him, though she was indebted to him. She thought she might perhaps feel at least a fondness toward him someday.

Sipping the last of her tea, she rose from the chair awkwardly. She placed the cup and saucer carefully into the freshly scrubbed sink and made her way to Ezra's bedroom. He had, of course, offered her the only bed, but she had declined. He was, after all, being most generous to her. She didn't mind sleeping on the divan in the sitting room. As she surveyed the task at hand, she quickly decided the place to start was to strip the bedding and attempt to flip the mattress. She pulled the quilt from the bed then stripped the linens from the mattress. Mustering all her strength, she pulled and then pushed at the mattress, trying to stand it upright on the bedsprings. Something caught her eye. She let the mattress fall back onto the springs. Kneeling on the floor, she pushed at the mattress until the heavy brown folder was revealed. It was a large folder, and its contents made it quite bulky. Mary flipped it over and undid the strings that tied it shut. Her conscience tugged at her slightly, cautioning her that they were Ezra's papers and she had no right to look at them. Curiosity got the best of her, and she pulled the contents out of the folder. The first of the many neatly folded papers was a rental agreement for the apartment. It was dated February 15. She thought it odd, as they had not rented the apartment until the eighth of March. She remembered the date exactly—it was just two days after James's birthday. The next few papers she opened appeared to be stock holdings. As she surveyed the papers, she was surprised by the large figures. Apparently, Ezra was wealthier than she had suspected. After viewing each document, she folded them precisely so she could place the papers back in the file in exactly the same fashion she had found them. As she carefully unfolded the next group of papers, she recognized her signature at the bottom of the first page. She remembered Ezra having her sign the document several months ago. It was, as Ezra had explained, adoption papers. He had convinced her that the Coltons, especially Cordella Colton, was not a woman to be trusted. He had assured her it would be in the best interest of the child for him to legally adopt the baby, just in case something should happen to her. Mary hadn't really seen the need for anything so formal, but Ezra had convinced her it was the best thing to do. She began to read the lengthy contract. Ezra had assured her it was just a lot of legal terms she probably wouldn't understand. He said his attorney had prepared it, and he completely trusted his attorney. It was headed 'Legal Adoption.'

"The undersigned, known to be the natural mother of," she whispered, reading to herself. Suddenly, her face turned ashen white, and her hand began to shake uncontrollably as she realized that what she was reading, what she had signed, was not a paper giving permission for Ezra to adopt her baby but instead stated she was giving her baby up for adoption. She read over the words again and again. She didn't understand all the legal terms, but she understood the words "giving up all rights." She understood enough. She threw the papers aside and began to tear through the remaining contents of the folder. She opened the first of many newspaper clippings. Instantly, she noticed that they were all from the Bay View paper, and then was shocked as she read the first headline:

March 6, 1926

JAMES COLTON CHARGED AS BAY VIEW ATTACKER!

She grabbed the next clipping:

March 10, 1926

ANONYMOUS LETTER CLEARS COLTON

She briefly scanned the article, which stated the police had received a letter from an unknown source that cleared the name of James Colton. The letter had led police to evidence leading to the arrest of Tom Bellows.

The next was a small clipping, which held no date:

HEATH AND BEAUMONT TO WED

Daniel Heath and Diane Beaumont announce their engagement. They are to be wed this fall, though a date has not yet been set.

May 1, 1926

COLTON OFFERS TEN THOUSAND

James Colton today offered a $10,000 reward to anyone having information leading to the whereabouts of a Miss Mary Watson. Mr. Colton has been searching for the Colton maid since her disappearance in March.

Mary was shocked!

"James," she cried his name. He hadn't married Diane! He was looking for her! *Does he still love me? Has he always loved me? What does Ezra want with me and my baby?* "My baby," she gasped out loud as she wrapped her arms around her rounded belly, suddenly remembering the adoption papers. She no longer knew what was truth and what was not. She forced herself to try and sort out her thoughts while her head filled with a barrage of possibilities. Perhaps it was all a plot by Diane or Mrs. Colton, or maybe both of them? Ezra . . . perhaps he was in on it too? Why does he have all these newspaper clippings? Why had she simply believed what Diane had told her? Why hadn't she confided in Bea or Maggie? Why hadn't she waited and talked to James? Does James even know about the baby? Surely, Mrs. Colton wouldn't have told him. She picked herself up off the floor. She had to get to James. She picked up the papers and slid them back into the folder, which she replaced under the mattress. She bent down to grab the soiled bedding, and the pain overwhelmed her. She grabbed her belly and doubled over. It was too soon—the baby wasn't due for three weeks. She sat down on the side of the bed, holding her belly, until the pain subsided. Just when she thought she could get up again, the pain, once again, overtook her.

CHAPTER 41

Mary looked into the face of her new baby daughter. As she cradled her in her arms, tears filled her eyes. She was so beautiful. She had James's eyes, beautiful blue eyes. She'd had had no choice but to call Ezra at work. He had rushed to their small apartment and had gotten her to the hospital—just in time, the doctor had said. The baby was small but perfectly healthy.

———◦———

Ezra sat soberly on a wooden chair, which he had pulled close to Mary's hospital bed. He smiled when she looked at him, though a sinister gleam shone in his eyes. He was pleased with how well his whole scheme had fallen into place. He had been taken aback a bit when he had found out she was with child. Though it changed his plans slightly, he would soon have what he wanted. It hadn't taken him long to find a doctor willing to help him. Of course, his fee had been steep, but Mrs. Colton had actually returned his three thousand dollars once he had sent the letter clearing James's name. To his surprise, she had sent it to the post office box, just as he had instructed. Just a few more days, he reminded himself. Mary would be ready to go home then. The doctor would administer a drug that would put her under, and Ezra could take her home. She would awake there, and Ezra would have to give her the news that the baby had died suddenly. He would tell her she had been so distraught the doctor had had to give her something to help her rest. They would do it at night when there were fewer people around to ask questions. Mary would be his then, and they could get on with the life he had planned for them. The doctor had already lined up a nice couple for the adoption. It would be all legal of course. Mary had signed the papers herself.

Yes, he thought to himself, his plan had worked out quite nicely. Even that sniveling Miss Bryer was keeping her end of the bargain. She had been sending him newspaper clippings over the past six months, just as she had promised she would. A simple request, really, for the man she loved, the man she thought loved her as well. It took a little persuasion to convince Mary that she shouldn't contact her aunt once they had settled in. Luckily, the girl agreed that Mrs. Colton was ruthless and could easily drag the information out of Matilda. He had convinced her that it was best that no one knew of her whereabouts. He chuckled slightly to himself as he wondered what Matilda would do if she knew he'd had Mary here with him all these months. All he had given her was an address for a post office box. She had no real way of finding him. It hadn't been hard to win her trust, not hard at all. He had managed not only to gain her confidence but, he was sure, her undying love as well. How long would she wait for him, he wondered? How long would it take her to realize he was never coming back for her, never going to be sending for her?

He had gone to see her at the library after he had arranged for the three thousand to be delivered to Mrs. Colton. He had appeared quite distraught, with nowhere else to turn. She had been quick to offer him comfort. He led her right into his snare, had made it almost seem to be her idea that he should leave town. How could he stay, knowing his son was the one who had been attacking young women and who had now apparently committed murder?

"How can you be sure it's him?" she had questioned in her nasally voice. He had injected a sorrowful whimper as he had told her he had found evidence and how he had learned, by Jud Egan's investigation, that the attacker was apparently using a special handkerchief, just like the ones he sold in his store. He had found some of them in Tom's closet.

"He must have stolen them from the store!" he had exclaimed. They were very expensive, and the only customer that ever purchased them was Mr. Colton for his son James, and he just knew the police would be suspicious of James Colton. He certainly couldn't let them just accuse an innocent man. Not for too long anyway, he had gleefully thought to himself.

"I have to tell them the truth, even if it means Tom must go to jail. I can't just cover up this kind of evidence." He had appeared to hold back tears for Matilda's benefit as he stated it was all sure to bring shame on the Bellows name.

"I'll have to sell my business," he had literally sobbed, knowing all along that the sale was already complete, and the money transferred to his new account in Chicago. There had been tears in her eyes as she comforted him. She even wrote the letter for him as she sat at the small desk in the storage room of the library, as he had convinced her his frayed nerves had left his hands too shaky to write the needed letter. She addressed the letter to Jud Egan himself and wrote everything he had instructed her to. And all the while, he smiled as he stood behind her, watching her write about the handkerchiefs and how they could be found in Tom Bellows' bedroom closet. It was a stroke of genius. He complimented himself on how he had placed the handkerchiefs in the box where Tom kept his mother's brooch. If the police were at all competent, they would surely question Tom about the brooch. What better motive could there be for attacking those young women than a young boy who hated his mother for leaving him?

He smiled now. Everything was going just as he had planned. He had known from Jud Egan's inquiry about the handkerchiefs that James Colton had been Jud's initial suspect. What better way to get him out of the picture for a while, just long enough to get Mary out of the city? Mrs. Colton had eagerly accepted his arrangement. Getting rid of Tom for an indefinite length of time had worked out equally as well. A little jail time wouldn't hurt the kid, and it was little price to pay for all the years he himself had felt like a prisoner. The whole idea had come to him after he happened to run across that dark jacket and cap in the empty crates under the back steps of the store. The jacket was about the right size to fit Tom. Maybe, for all Ezra knew, Tom was the attacker. Tom wasn't a murderer, though, but what else was he to do? He had to do away with that young girl he found wandering down around the riverfront. He needed the police to get a move on. The murder had certainly pushed them along a little. Yes, everything was going just as he had planned. He was out of Bay View. Miss Bryer was keeping him well informed, while secretly waiting for him. He was at last out from under that tedious job of selling men's clothing. Tom was out of his life and probably wouldn't spend too long in jail once he could convince them that he wasn't the attacker—unless he was, and then, of course, he'd be there a long, long time. It didn't matter to Ezra either way. Most importantly, he had Mary. She would eventually agree to be his wife. Then he could perhaps make a trip to Douglas County. He could take Mary to meet his father. Surely, he could find no fault with the lovely young girl, once the baby was out of the way. He would have a lot to show his father. Show him he was able to get rid of his past mistakes. Show him all the money he had made with his substantial investments in the stock market, and how he had won the love of a respectable young woman. He could show his father he was worthy of his love and respect.

He smiled at Mary when he noticed how intently she was watching him. It wouldn't be long now. Just a few more days.

———◦———

As soon as Ezra left the hospital, Mary formulated her plan. It wasn't much of a plan, she admitted. She just knew somehow she needed to get back to James and away from Ezra Bellows. She had managed to get the bedding replaced before Ezra had gotten to the apartment. She certainly didn't want him to suspect that she had discovered his secret. She would wait until nightfall. She was sure she could sneak by the nurses on duty with little problem. It had been two days since she had given birth—she was strong enough now.

CHAPTER 42

The dark of night cloaked Mary's figure as she walked as swiftly as she could through the streets of the city. It hadn't been difficult to sneak out of the hospital after the nurse had come in and thought she was asleep. She had just finished nursing the baby and was sure the nurse wouldn't come back to her room for a couple hours. The train station was only seven or eight blocks from the hospital. Her plan was to check the board for the next day's train schedule and hope she would be able to hide herself and the baby away until morning. She had no money to purchase a ticket and silently scolded herself now for handing over the money she had saved from her wages working for the Coltons to Ezra for the kindness he had shown her. She hoped it wouldn't be too difficult to elude the porter when he made his way through the cars, punching the tickets.

By the time she reached the darkened and deserted station, the wind was howling. It was an unseasonably chilly, dark night, and though she hugged her baby close to her, she feared that even though she had snuggled the baby into her own sweater, it was not shelter enough from the buffeting gusts. She checked the train schedule which hung on the big board on the outside wall of the station. The first train that made a stop in Bay View, the number 319, was scheduled to leave at six o' clock the next morning. Suddenly, she wasn't feeling well, and she sat down on the long bench that stood against the outside wall. Her tears stung her cheeks as the cold wind blew, and dreadful thoughts began to fill her head. What if she were to become ill? How could she keep her baby safe? What if the baby got too cold out in the damp air? She was so little. Though she might be able to hide from the porter, might a young woman with a small baby be too conspicuous? What if they threw her and the baby off the train in the middle of nowhere? She clutched her daughter tightly against her breast, stood up, and left the station. Though she felt weak, and tears now flowed freely down her cheeks, she braced herself against the howling wind and walked north. She knew Saint Patrick's Orphanage was just a few blocks away. She and Ezra had driven by it on the way to the hospital. She remembered it because she had thought of Genny Mueller as they had passed it.

Crouching just outside the steps that led to the front entrance, she cradled her daughter in her lap as she pulled a piece of paper and pencil from her satchel and penned a note.

> Please take care of my baby. Her father and I will be
> back for her as soon as we can. Her name is . . .

Mary's hand was still. She had not yet given her daughter a name. She had thought of many possibilities over the last several weeks but hadn't decided on what name she would give to a daughter. She had thought, perhaps, Jolene. She had considered both Maggie and Bea. Then, there in the dark and cold, as her own tears fell silently on the paper, she wrote, "Her name is FAE." She then unclasped the heart pendant necklace from around her neck, and reading the inscription one last time, she said to her daughter, "F. Forever, A. Always, E. Eternally" She then folded the locket into the piece of paper. She put the note inside her daughter's blanket and wrapped her coat around her tightly. As she left her there on the steps of the orphanage, she whispered, "I love you, Fae." She rang the bell and then quickly crossed the street and concealed herself among a tall row of bushes. She watched until the door opened and a woman dressed in a long black robe scooped Fae into her arms and closed the door.

A cold rain began to fall as she walked back toward the train station. She shivered. She was weak, and her head was pounding. She would find somewhere to hide for the night—out of the rain and cold—until morning.

CHAPTER 43

James glanced at the round wooden clock that hung on the wall of his office as it methodically ticked away the minutes. It was after nine o'clock—another late night at the plant. He'd been staying later and later day after day, week after agonizing week, month after unbearable month. Ten months had passed since Mary had disappeared. He waited each day with new hope that there would be word, something, *anything*, but again today, just as the countless days before, he was no closer than the day she vanished.

In the beginning, there were leads. The private investigator he had hired would get a bit of information from someone and build up his hopes, but each new clue proved to be a dead end and led them no closer to finding Mary. He had hired four different investigators in the last nine months, none of whom had come up with anything new. Most of them never got as far as the first. Not even the ten thousand dollar reward he had offered made a difference. His father had been nagging at him for the last three months to stop throwing away money on a lost cause.

"They didn't find Maggie either. Maybe they both ran off together!" his father had shouted at him that very afternoon. James had simply shaken his head.

He rubbed his palm across his face then cradled his forehead in his hand, his elbow propped on the edge of the desk. He closed his eyes. He played the days over and over in his head, as he had done countless times since Mary's disappearance. He tried to remember each detail in hopes there was something he had not thought of before, something he missed. There had to be more, something more, anything more.

Wanting to finish up some loose ends at the plant, he had gotten home late that night,. At the time, he wasn't sure if he'd be back or not. He just wasn't sure what his mother's reaction would be when he told her he and Mary were in love and he planned to marry her. On the way home from the plant, he arranged the events of the next day in his head. He was going to go over to Diane's and break the news to her that he was in love with Mary and planned on asking her to marry him. He hadn't at all been looking forward to it, but he thought he owed her that much. He was then going to go back to the house, pick up his luggage, which would be filled with Maggie's belongings, and meet her and Joseph at the justice of the peace. Once she and Joseph were married and safely deposited at the train station, he would go back to the house, find Mary, and ask her to be his wife.

Things hadn't worked out that way, though. He shook his head, not wanting to relive that evening.

He had gotten home a little past eight. Maggie had met him at the door and informed him that Mary was gone and no one seemed to know where she was. Charles had searched the entire house, but she was nowhere to be found. Maggie had searched Mary's room herself and noted that some of her things were missing, including the picture of her mother and father that always sat on the little table next to her bed. Both Maggie and Charles had told him about Diane's visit earlier in the day. A quick inspection of his room turned up Diane's little note and the ring box tossed casually on his bed. Without explanation to anyone, James ran from the house, jumped in the roadster, and raced to Diane's.

Diane, of course, went off the deep end and accused him of having an affair, and when he blatantly told her he was in love with Mary, she went over the edge. She had slapped him across the face before telling him she had talked to Mary that afternoon and told her to find employment elsewhere.

When he left Diane's, he rushed over to Mary's Aunt Matilda, hoping Mary would be there, but she was not. After that, he went straight to the police, insisting they search the city.

When he finally returned to the house, Maggie informed him she would call off her plans of leaving with Joseph. James convinced her to go through with her departure. That next day, it had been hard for her to leave with Joseph on the train after the ceremony, but James had given her a big hug and assured her he would find Mary safe and sound, and when he did he would send her word.

When he hired the first PI, his mother suggested they instead try to find her "worthless maid." James assured her numerous times there was no sign of Maggie either, even though he knew full well of Maggie's whereabouts. He opened his desk drawer and pulled out her latest letter. He knew exactly where Maggie was, safe and sound with Joseph in Montana.

After several weeks with no luck in finding Mary, and although he had no intention of locating Maggie on his mother's behalf, he gave the PI all the information on Maggie and Joseph in hopes Maggie knew something he didn't. It only took the man two days to locate them. Maggie had written the first letter to him immediately after the PI's visit, sending it to the plant, where she knew it would get to him without first being steamed open by Mrs. Colton. She and James had been corresponding on a monthly basis ever since.

"Maggie, a mother," he said aloud, and the very sound of it managed to bring a soft smile to his face. He opened the pages of Maggie's letter and reread the lines in which she described her beautiful newborn red-headed little boy. Then, disinterested, he skimmed over the many paragraphs about how proud Joseph was, how the farm was coming along, and how happy they both were. When he reached the last paragraph, he straightened in his chair and rubbed his hands across his tired eyes before reading it for the hundredth time since it had arrived in the morning's mail.

> 'Tis with shame that I don't be tellin' you this till now. 'Tis only I not be wantin' to tell you somethin' I was not sure of.

Now, that I be holdin' this wee little one, I know I must tell you if what I was spectin' might be true.

In the few weeks before I left your mother's house, Mary was not feelin' well.

After I got in the family way, it started to remind me of how Mary was those last few weeks. Tired, and sick in the mornin's. When I first wrote to you, I don't be tellin' you as I not know. Now, after I hold my little baby , I know I needs to be tellin' ya just in case it be so. I hope you not be mad with me.

With Love, Maggie

James carefully folded the pages of Maggie's letter, tucked it back in the envelope, and then back into his desk drawer with the others. He had contacted the latest PI immediately after reading it, but the man would hardly even listen to him. Just like the others before him, the PI told him it was no use, Mary was just not to be found, and whether or not she was knocked up made no difference. James hated that term and had fired the man immediately.

In the first few days after Mary's disappearance, he had badgered everyone—in fact, *anyone*—who had ever had any contact with her. He had, of course, started with Mary's aunt, Matilda, on that very first night. The odd thing was she already seemed distraught by the time he had gotten to her apartment. James hadn't noticed it then, but weeks and even months later, the memory of their encounter dogged him. So much so, he had gone to see her a number of times at her apartment and the library. Initially, Matilda led him to believe she would be moving away, and he suspiciously wondered if she perhaps knew where Mary was and was going to join her, but she hinted that it was a man she would be meeting up with. James hadn't meant to pry, or maybe he had, but he needed to find Mary. The strange thing was Matilda never left town.

Bea was beside herself assuming the worst, that Mary had been killed by the madman who was assaulting young women and had even murdered his last victim. Then, the next day, when James himself was charged as being the Bay View attacker, it felt as though the entire thing was just a bad nightmare. It was to everyone's relief when they put Tom Bellows behind bars the very next day. It was certainly no surprise that Tom's father had sold the clothing store and left town.

However, making the street safe once again for the residents of Bay View halted the police from continuing their search for Mary. They told James that people who disappear usually mean to. That was when he hired the first private investigator, Louie Kimball. He had gotten his name from Jud Egan, and he had come highly recommended. Jud had worked with him in his early days in Chicago, before Jud transferred to Bay View on his way to retirement. Lou, as he preferred to be called, was a short, stocky man with a military haircut. He had retired a few years earlier and took up private investigations. He was a no-nonsense kind of guy who got straight to the point. He liked digging around in other people's business, and he was good at it.

When James first contacted him, he was reluctant to travel the distance to Bay View from his home further south for "nothing but a missing person," but James convinced him quickly with the sizable fee he had offered. Along with all Lou's travel expenses, James paid out a small fortune over the six months that Lou searched for Mary.

He remembered how harsh Lou could be when he was sniffing out information. Both Bea and Charles took his questioning as offensive accusations. He was ruthless when he got to Diane, knowing she had probably been the last person to see Mary before she disappeared. James hadn't felt sorry for her, though, not a bit. By the time Lou got to his mother, he was brutal, and even James had almost felt sorry for her. Lou had really done his homework, and although the whole Genny Mueller thing hadn't been spoken about in years, Lou had managed to dig up all the sordid details, and he threw it all back in Cordella Colton's face. His father had finally stepped in and put a stop to the interrogation. His mother had recovered quickly after his father had stepped in, though she never spoke Mary's name again and changed the subject whenever James spoke of her.

But poor Matilda Bryer, James couldn't help but feel sorry for the old spinster. It had been a little over six months after Mary's disappearance, and Lou was running out of leads when James, almost as an afterthought, had mentioned he had noticed that Matilda had a bag packed the night he went to tell her of Mary's disappearance. Immediately, Lou started nosing around, like a hound on a trail. After learning of Matilda's visit to the jail to see Ezra's son Tom the day the boy committed suicide, he had suspected there was something between Ezra Bellows and Matilda Bryer. He didn't know if it had anything at all to do with Mary's disappearance, but with this new information, Lou found a renewed sense of enthusiasm. Matilda, as eager to find Ezra as Lou was, shared with him their secret, or at least what she thought of as their secret—how Ezra had left Bay View and had gotten an apartment for the two of them. When things settled down, Ezra was going to send for her. Matilda shared with Lou the post office box number and city she'd been using to send Ezra letters. She told him Ezra had wanted her to send him news regarding his son. Lou left town the next day, headed to the little village of Forest View, just outside of Chicago.

Lou was gone over a week, and he found Ezra, but not in Forest View as Matilda had indicated, though he had been there. Lou still knew a number of the Chicago cops, and they were quick to fill him in on the goings-on in Forest View, or as it had been dubbed by the locals, Caponeville. It seemed Ezra had rented a small upper apartment in Forest View almost a full month before he had left Bay View. Lou was convinced Tom Bellows being arrested wasn't the reason—or at least not the entire reason—Ezra had left town. It was hard to pick up information from anyone in Forest View. The Feds were constantly questioning people about Capone and his thugs, who were apparently purchasing buildings in Forest View and putting up little antique shops and laundromats as fronts for their money laundering endeavors. No one wanted to talk to Lou about much of anything, and definitely not about strangers who drifted in or out of town. He finally caught a break when the man at the meat market told him Ezra had settled his bill there before moving to Bedford Park. Bedford Park was just a hop, skip, and a jump from Forest View, and a little further away from Chicago.

Lou found a lead on Ezra within a half hour or so after breezing into Bedford Park. It was a small community built up in the last ten years mainly by a corn refining plant that built most of the homes in town for their foreman. There were smaller dwellings the plant owned, usually rented by the men who worked there. To Lou's surprise, Ezra didn't work at the plant but rather in Chicago for a stock brokerage.

Lou's first stop in Bedford Park was the meat market. Through years of experience, he had come to know that the local butcher possessed a wealth of information—everything from the daily gossip the women shared while picking out the perfect roast to the local constable that just came in to chew the fat, so to speak. After asking just a few questions, the man knew who Lou was speaking of right away. He had heard Mrs. Willard mention the name Bellows. Ezra, her new neighbor, had just moved in within the last week or so.

Luckily, Mrs. Willard was Lou's favorite kind of person to question, the kind that unwittingly rambled on and on without a clue or a care as to who was asking the questions, who the questions were about, or why they were being asked in the first place. She was, to Lou's surprise, no face stretcher either. He noticed immediately her nice set of gams, as she wore a flowery printed dress a little shorter than what was the socially acceptable length for a woman her age. She told Lou everything he wanted to know. Ezra rented the house next to her, though he worked in Chicago. Lucy Willard said Chicago with utter exasperation, so upset that anyone would drive sixteen miles to get to work. You would have thought she had done the driving herself. According to Lucy, he was a "nice enough fellow." He had moved there from Bay View. Lou didn't find it odd that Ezra apparently hadn't mentioned his brief stay in Forest View to the very inquisitive Lucy Willard. According to Lucy, because Ezra worked for a very busy brokerage firm in Chicago, he found it relaxing to return home to the quiet streets of Bedford Park. She said she was concerned with the heavy margins he was dealing with on the stock market. Lou thought it a little odd at first that Bellows was sharing so much information with his newfound friend Mrs. Willard, but then he suspected it was the reason Miss Bryer hadn't gotten the word from Ezra to come and join him in Forest View. Lou was quick to discover that Mrs. Willard was a widow. Her husband had been killed in a freak accident at the plant. The plant let her stay on in the home she and her husband had rented, now free of charge. Lou was pretty sure Bellows would be looking to comfort the little bearcat, Mrs. Willard, in any way he possibly could. Mrs. Lucy Willard was a far cry from Matilda Bryer, the bug-eyed Betty. After a delightful afternoon with Lucy, Lou was ready to close the books on Mr. Ezra Bellows.

James thought it a bit slapdash of Lou that he didn't go into Chicago to question Ezra, but Lou assured him it was a dead end. Lou told him the way he had it figured was Ezra wanted out from under his kid Tom, and he and Matilda had made plans to move away, but then the whole mess with the kid molesting the women and the police investigation forced Ezra to change his plans. Ezra left Matilda behind to keep an eye on things and keep him informed. Lou's guess was Ezra had every intention of sending for Matilda until he met Lucy Willard. Lou convinced him had he gone to question Bellows, he would have found that Ezra had to leave Bay View when he did to start his new job at the brokerage firm. Had the whole mess with Tom not happened, he and Matilda would have probably left together a month earlier, which totally explained why Ezra had rented the apartment in Forest View a month before he actually left Bay View. Lou had added that moving from Forest View to Bedford Park was explained by all that was going on in Caponeville.

The news came as a great shock to poor Matilda Bryer, and James wished Lou had been a little more gentle in his telling of Ezra's new life, especially in his description of the doll, Lucy Willard. Though she tried to cover her anguish, even she could not hold back the tears, and

James felt sorry for her as she wept openly in front of them before excusing herself to the back room of the library. From then on, he made it a point to stop in and see her now and again.

The last time he had seen Matilda was just a few short weeks ago. She had aged considerably in the last ten months. She had never been much to look at, but the last time he had gone to the library, her appearance was that of a tired old woman who looked years older than he knew she was. She was almost lifeless as she stood there at the counter scouring over her card catalogs.

It was shortly after Lou's trip to Chicago that he told James he was simply out of leads.

"There's nothing more to go on, kid." He said it had gotten to the point that he was taking James's money for nothing. He had checked out every shred of evidence he had found, but Mary had just vanished, and there was nothing more he could do. After that, James had hired others, but none of them found anything new. He was at a dead end. He wouldn't give up, though. He knew Mary was out there somewhere. He would find her if it took the rest of his life. He *had* to find her.

He stood from his desk, picked up his hat and coat from the hook on the wall, and opened the door of his office. He hesitated a moment as the thought entered his mind once again. *Mary, with child?* No, he shook his head as he pushed the button to shut off the light, *I would have known.*

CHAPTER 44

Late August 1997

I picked up the last of my belongings, which lay scattered around the tiny room, and put them into my suitcase. My PC and printer were packed in the trunk of my car. The desk the manager had brought in to accommodate my computer had been taken out, and the small chair and table already brought back up from the basement where they had been stored. My suitcase lay open on the small bed, already been stripped of its linens and awaiting the next tenant. I picked up the final draft of *Forever, Always, Eternally* and placed it carefully on top of my neatly folded blouses. I had written the book in just a few weeks. The only problem was the book wasn't finished, and I wondered now if it ever would be.

I knew my readers would not be happy with the open ending. A few years back, I tried leaving an open ending in the book *Rapture at Sunset*, and I had gotten more than a few letters from unhappy readers through my publisher. The readers always wanted the ultimate happy ending, the complete circle of events—boy meets girl, boy loses girl, boy and girl reunite and live happily ever after. *Oh, who am I kidding?* I wanted the happy ending too. I glanced at the happy ending, which still lay crumpled in the green metal trashcan. I had written the final chapter with the anticipated conclusion. Mary made it back to Bay View and to James's waiting arms. The two of them reclaimed Fae from the orphanage, and they all lived happily ever after. I had struggled with that final chapter for two days, and when finally finished, it just didn't seem to fit. I couldn't help it if the book ended the way it did, that's where the story ended. Whatever, or whoever, had been filling my head with the story of Mary and James had simply stopped. It was almost as if when James pushed the button to shut out the light in his office, the connection between the story and me was gone. It was the strangest thing. I had always felt I wasn't so much writing the story, but rather it was being told to me, and now I knew it to be true. I had nothing, not even a clue of what happened after that or how this story ended—because it just wasn't my story.

I looked around the tiny room. It had been Mary's room, or so I had imagined it as her room while I wrote there the past few weeks.

"Just what happened to you, dear sweet Mary?" I asked the walls.

I leaned over the suitcase to pull the cover over its contents and felt the chain as it slipped across my neck. My locket fell into the suitcase and rested on the title page of the book. I picked it up carefully and examined it to see if the chain had broken, but found it to be intact. It was the third time that week the necklace had slipped off. I fumbled with the clasp for a short time and then decided I didn't want to chance having it come loose again. I tucked it safely into the pocket of the tweed jacket I was wearing, making a mental note to remember to take it to the jewelers to have them take a look at it.

I flapped the cover of the suitcase closed and zipped it shut. Suitcase in hand, I took one last look around the tiny room before I closed the door behind me.

Walking toward the sitting area at the top of the stairs, I glanced down the west wing, almost waiting for James Colton to step out of his room. Of course, he didn't. I started down the grand staircase. Halfway down, I found myself chuckling remembering the time James had dragged Christina down the stairs so fast she had stumbled trying to put on her shoe. No, this was not like any novel I had ever written. I didn't so much have a feeling of satisfaction in my work but rather a sense of having been entertained. The story had been told to me. I reached the grand entryway and looked back up the staircase, remembering Mary's first day at the Coltons' and the figure of Cordella Colton descending the stairs, and I shuddered.

The manager was nowhere in sight as I wandered down the short hallway toward the library. I pushed the pocket door open and imagined the empty room filled with overstuffed leather furniture, a roaring fire in the hearth, and James and Mary snuggled on the couch sipping wine. I sighed heavily and pulled the door closed. I made my way back through the entry hall and headed toward the kitchen. The door to the manager's room was just to the left of the servants' stairway. Bea's room, I silently noted. I knocked twice, but there was no answer. I noticed the buzzer system high on the wall. It probably hadn't worked in decades, just hung there, silent—not blinking, not buzzing. I waited for a short time, thinking that perhaps a light might come on, but of course, none did. Retracing my steps to the entry hall, I stood just inside the front entrance, my eyes scanning the room—the grand staircase, the massive chandelier, the once polished marble floor. I recalled fondly the night Charles had stood there, and Mary had kissed his cheek. I sighed again. It felt as though I was leaving a home I knew I would never come back to, and it made me sad. I turned, opened the door, and left the house.

I found the kid-manager just outside the front entrance, hacking away at the overgrown ivy that was engulfing the bricks. I walked over to him, still carrying my suitcase, key in hand. "Thank you," I said, handing him the key "I enjoyed the stay." The key slipped from my fingers and fell to the ground. As I bent to pick it up, I noticed the small brass plaque attached to the wall that he had just uncovered from its hiding place behind the ivy. *Donated in 1982 to the City of Bay View by James Colton.*

"That can't be," I whispered in disbelief. "Who's James Colton?" I demanded of the pimply-faced kid.

He stared at me. His words were slow and exaggerated. "That's the old rich guy. I told you, he donated the building to the city."

"But who is he? Where is he?"

"I dunno, probably dead," the kid said and shrugged his shoulders.

I sat in my car for nearly fifteen minutes trying to decide what to do next. G-Pat and B-Pat were beside themselves. I had almost convinced myself the whole thing was just a coincidence. I must have seen the name James Colton somewhere. Perhaps I had passed a park on my way into town that had been named after him, a library, a school. The kid said he was a rich guy, so certainly in a small town like Bay View, something had been named after him. I must have just subconsciously picked up the name. There was no other explanation.

A short while later, I sat on the most uncomfortable wooden-backed chair in the small conference room at the city clerk's office. I was flipping through pages of a large volume of city tax records. I had almost convinced myself that I was being silly. I was sure it was just a strange coincidence. Out of the corner of my eye, I could see the middle-aged, heavyset clerk who seemed perplexed at my request to see the records of ownership of the boarding house. It had taken her more than ten minutes to locate the correct volume. She had hefted it to the counter and pushed it toward me, saying, "It's in here somewhere. You'll have to look it up yourself. Just what is it you're looking for?"

"James Colton," I replied as I picked up the heavy book and went into the small conference room she had pointed out to me.

As I flipped through the yellowing pages, I again peered at the lady through the open door. She was now on the phone. I thought to myself it was little wonder why the information wasn't on a computer disc, or at least microfiche. The name in bold black print in the middle of the page leaped from the paper to my eyes. I sat perfectly still, even my breathing momentarily suspended, as I looked in disbelief at the name—Cordella Colton.

"That's impossible," I silently mouthed the words. Then, catching my breath, I read the entry.

> James Colton acquired the property in 1948 through
> the estate of his mother, Cordella Colton. He donated it

to the city of Bay View in 1982 with the provision it be used as a boarding house.

I sat dumbfounded. I closed my eyes and tried to steady my breathing. My mind was reeling. The whole idea was becoming totally unsettling.

"Excuse me."

I flinched, and my eyes popped open as the deep male voice intruded my thoughts.

"I'm sorry," the man apologized. "I didn't mean to startle you." He stepped into the room and closed the door behind him. Setting his briefcase down on the table, he extended his hand. I instinctively stood and shook it as I quickly sized him up. He was very attractive, late thirties, early forties perhaps. He wore a well-cut khaki-colored suit that complemented his sandy hair and tanned complexion. He had chiseled features and fascinating hazel eyes.

"Allow me to introduce myself. Lewis, Greg Lewis." Letting go of my hand, he waved toward my chair. "Please, sit down." As I did as he asked, I glanced quickly out the window of the small conference room, noting that I had only been there a short time, but the splashes of sunlight that had before lit the room had disappeared, and the skies had turned dark. Mr. Lewis, apparently noting my concern, walked back toward the door and flipped on the light as he said, "Appears to be a storm brewing out there."

I watched him curiously as he took a seat directly across from me. Immediately noticing my apprehension, he said, "I'm sorry. I should explain myself."

I raised my eyebrows and nodded my head in agreement, but was silent.

"You see," he said and hesitated, and I could tell he wasn't sure what he wanted to say, as he appeared to be searching for words. He stood from the table and turned from me, looking through the door's window at the lady at the counter, who was now staring at us. Though confused by Greg Lewis's presence, I wondered why I also seemed intrigued by him, as once again I noted he was quite handsome. I was not ready for his next question, which took me completely by surprise. "Did you know James Colton?"

I was silent for a long time. Long enough for him to again pull out the chair and sit down at the large wooden table.

I finally echoed, "Did you know James Colton?"

"Well, yes, as a matter of fact, I did," he replied, and I noticed a twinkle in his eyes.

"I understand he once owned the boardinghouse on the other end of town?" I asked, still trying to fathom the direction and purpose of our conversation.

"Oh, yes, he owned several properties and businesses in town, years ago anyway. He was once a very influential man in this city, and very wealthy." Greg put his hands on the table and folded them as he leaned his shoulders in. I did the same, though I wasn't quite sure why.

"I was Mr. Colton's attorney," he said, then clarified. "Well, for the past ten years, that is." Mr. Lewis rubbed his forehead, and again I assumed he was trying to decide how to continue. He shifted slightly in his chair and took a deep breath. "You see, when you came here asking about James Colton, Mrs. Fletchman, the clerk, called me." He turned slightly to point at the woman at the counter, who was still staring at us. "My office is just across the street."

He hesitated, once more lifting his hand and shaking his finger in the air. "Let me go back. My great-grandfather, Winston Lewis, was James Colton's attorney." He paused. "Years and years ago, the Coltons were a very prominent family in this town. In fact," he emphasized, "they pretty much owned the town, from what I've heard over the years." Greg Lewis was scratching his head, and I realized I found his distractions not so much annoying, but charming. I listened attentively as he continued. "Anyway, from what I know, a lot of controversy surrounded the family. But then, you have to remember this was back in the 1920s, and life was different back then."

I sat in silence as Greg Lewis presented me a sketchy synopsis to the story I had spent the last number of weeks writing. He offered just a few names, and no elaborate details, but there was indeed a man named James Colton who had a romantic relationship with a maid. There was a man named Bellows who had a son and owed a clothier. There was definitely a police detective by the name of Jud Eagan, but most perplexing was the fact that the maid had disappeared. And though James Colton spent his whole life and a huge amount of money trying to find her, he never had.

A sudden streak of lightning, followed by a loud clap of thunder, caused me to practically jump out of my chair.

"Boy, looks like it's getting a little nasty out there," Greg said in a steady voice which calmed my nerves.

I rubbed the back of my neck then flexed my shoulders. "So are you telling me that James Colton is still alive?"

"No, no." Greg shook his head and smiled softly. "If he was, I probably wouldn't be here. You see," Greg continued as I stared at him intently, "when I said I was James Colton's attorney, I was, but he really didn't need legal services, not since he became my client anyway. Like I said, my great-grandfather was his attorney, then my grandfather, then my uncle. My father was a doctor," he said, raising his eyebrows and shrugging his shoulders as he answered my unasked question. "James was just passed down to me as a client of the firm. I hadn't really done any work for him. He really didn't have any need for an attorney. The story, as it was passed down to me through the years, is that he spent a fortune trying to find the woman he loved. The maid who had disappeared."

"Mary." The name escaped my lips unthinkingly. Greg looked at me curiously but continued.

"From what I was told, he became a very bitter man, and pretty much penniless. The last thing he owned of any value was the boardinghouse you asked me about. He ended up giving that away to the city when he moved into the nursing home."

I sat quietly, staring at Greg Lewis, not even noticing the raindrops that were now beating against the window of the small conference room. The whole thing was just too mind-boggling to comprehend.

Greg tilted his head slightly and gave me an inquisitive look. "Could I ask your name?"

"I'm sorry . . . Pat Walker."

"Well, Pat Walker, I think I may be just as bewildered as you look. I'm not really sure what's going on here either. I certainly have a lot of questions for you."

I just blank-stared poor Mr. Lewis. None of this made any sense. He cleared his throat slightly to get my attention before he continued.

"About five weeks—a month and a half ago—the nursing home called me. James Colton wanted to see me. He didn't even know who I was—I had never actually met him before that."

"Are you telling me that he was alive just last month?"

Greg Lewis shook his head. "As I said, the nursing home called me and wanted me to come over. When I got there, the nurse who usually cared for James—apparently one of the few he got along with—explained to me that it had all started the day before. James was watching TV in the lounge. It was apparently something he rarely did, but for some reason, that evening, he wanted to. The nurse had found it strange, but it only got stranger. She said he was watching a documentary that had just happened to come on about some scientist. Then, all of a sudden, he starts yelling something. Just shouting the same word over and over. She said she didn't even know what it was he was shouting—sounded like gibberish. Finally, she got him to calm down a bit, and he told her he didn't make the right choice. He said, *She told me to make the right choice, but I didn't listen. I shouldn't have waited for the money.* He was quite upset.

"So anyway, I guess whatever it was it worked him up so much he ended up having a heart attack right then and there. By the time the paramedics got there, they thought he was gone, but somehow they managed to revive him. The nurse said the next day he was a changed man." Greg chuckled. "Well, according to those I talked to, in the fifteen years James Colton lived at the home, he was a crotchety old buzzard. Their words, not mine," he clarified. "But the day after his heart attack, he was different. Immediately upon waking up that morning, he had insisted they call me. He seemed deliriously happy to me. Certainly not the crotchety old man the nurse had described, nor the bitter man my uncle had spoken of. The nurse said he had completely changed into a different person. He told me he was living on borrowed time. Well, I thought his statement understandable, considering the experience he'd had. And after all, the man *was* ninety-six years old." Greg stopped, raised his eyebrows slightly, and looked me straight in the eye before he continued.

"He made me promise him something that day. It was the strangest request, really. As I said, he told me he was living on borrowed time, but he said it was *literally* borrowed time. He assured me he had died the day before. Said he'd gone to Heaven. He said he could not have imagined—no one could. He said that once he knew the truth, he had to do something about it. He just couldn't leave her here all alone. He said dying wasn't the end—it was just the beginning."

Where had I heard that before?

I stared at Greg in disbelief, and not even the lightning strike and loud clap of thunder that followed caught my attention.

"I know, I know, believe me, his words have inspired a great deal of thought."

"Who's this 'her' he spoke of?"

"I don't know." Greg cocked his head a bit and gave me a skeptical look. "You, maybe?"

By this time, both G-Pat and B-Pat were shaking. This was getting just plain weird.

"Anyway," Greg continued, "who was I not to honor his last request, strange as it might be?"

I stared at Greg a while. I could tell he was eager to get on with the story.

"What was his last request?"

"Well," Greg said raising his eyebrows, "he had me digging around in old newspaper archives for over a week. Said he had to find the proof. I joked with him about why he needed proof, but he said the proof wasn't for him, but for her. He told me that when he died—again—a young woman was going to be coming around asking about him. He couldn't tell me who it was, only that it was inevitable. He couldn't tell me when. He just said that eventually she would be asking about him, he'd see to it, and when she did, I was instructed to give her these clippings. You know, I asked him why he didn't just find this person and give her the papers himself. You know what his answer was?"

"No," I said, shaking my head.

"He said he was already doing more than what was usually allowed. Then he said, I am attempting to survive my time so I may live into hers. Make sure to tell her that."

Now, that line really sounded familiar to me, but before I had time to think about it, Greg reached for his briefcase and flipped open the cover. He pulled out a manila folder, opened it, and handed me a copy of a newspaper clipping. Apprehensively, I took it from him.

Park City News, 1929

DEATH BLAMED ON BLACK TUESDAY

Thursday, November 7, Ezra Bellows, vice president of the Park City Trust Company, took a pistol from the teller's cage and shot himself. The news was suppressed until after the bank closed at noon Saturday, to avoid causing a run on the bank.

I stared skeptically at the paper, wondering what else Mr. Lewis had in the folder. Greg broke the silence, "Good thing I didn't have to look back any further. The paper had only gone back to 1925 when they archived onto microfiche."

Greg handed me the next sheet, also from the Highland Park News, dated September 8, 1927. I stared at the date for a moment, linking it with the story of James and Mary—the fictitious story, I silently noted to myself before I began to read the clipping.

FIVE KILLED IN TRAIN COLLISION

Five people died and several were injured in a suburb near Chicago. One train derailed as another train plowed into the tail end of the other. Additional cars had been added to accommodate the Labor Day holiday crowds. The conductor of the oncoming train incorrectly calculated the length of the train because of the added cars and timed their crossing at the intersection incorrectly.

Now I was shaking, too, as I dropped the paper onto the table, stood up from my chair, and crossed the room to the window. The rain was letting up. I found it odd that I had even noticed, but it was the only thing my mind allowed me to focus on. All my other thoughts were jumbled as I tried to make sense of it all. I turned to look at Greg, but before I could speak, he said, "One last thing I was supposed to tell you." He hesitated slightly. "Not sure what this means either." He reached for the folder he had the clippings in. There was something written on the outside. "I wrote it down," he said. "I didn't want to get it wrong. He said to tell you, *Murmurs of Earth are whispers in Heaven.*"

He looked up at me, and for a moment there was a look of hope on his face, Then he simply shook his head. "Doesn't mean anything to you, huh?"

"No, not especially, and what makes you think it's meant for me anyway?"

Greg lifted his eyebrows. "I don't know." He shrugged. "You're the only one that's asked about him. Oh wait, just one more thing, and this is the last of it, I promise." He reached back into his briefcase and produced a small manila envelope. "I was supposed to give you this, too."

I stared at the small envelope for a moment before taking it from him. When I did, I apprehensively tugged open the flap, then holding out my palm, emptied its contents. I stared in shock at the heart-shaped locket. My fingers shaking, I unlatched the cover to reveal a small picture of a very attractive young girl. Except for the large bow in her hair, it could have been a picture of myself when I was a teenager.

"Mary," I said aloud, and my whole body shivered from the thought. Instantly, my fictitious plot collided with my own life. *Grandma Fae was . . . James and Mary were my great-grandparents.*

Greg watched inquisitively as the envelope fell to the floor and I reached into my pocket, producing my locket.

"Oh my!" he gasped as I placed the lockets side by side in my palm. I closed the cover over the young girl's picture and flipped the locket over to reveal the very familiar three letters: F.A.E. "Forever, Always, Eternally," I whispered. "I always thought it stood for Grandma Fae."

Greg was quiet then. I think he was waiting for me to say something. I could tell by the look on his face that he knew the newspaper clippings had upset me, but the locket had overwhelmed me, and I'm sure he wondered what it all meant.

"When did James Colton die?" I finally asked.

"Shortly after I found the clippings, beginning of August."

Just before I came to town, I thought to myself. "I assume he's buried in the Bay View Cemetery?"

Greg nodded. I knew I would pass the cemetery on my way out of town, as I vaguely recalled seeing it on my way in. I hadn't paid attention at the time but now recalled the stone entryway and a sign that had read Bay View Cemetery. Greg was quick to offer me a ride, concerned that I was in no condition to drive myself, and not to mention he was still looking for some answers.

His car was parked just outside in front of his office. It was a short drive to the cemetery, and neither of us spoke a word on the way there. The rain had ended, and the sky was clearing as he parked the car in the correct vicinity. He said he was one of the few people at James Colton's funeral, and he vaguely remembered where the plot was. I got out of the car before he could get around to open my door. He followed me as I headed across the wet grass, reading the names on the headstones as I passed. Then suddenly, there it was, the freshly sodded plot with the large granite stone bearing the name of James Colton, 1901-1997.

At that very moment, the sun peeked through the clouds to cast a single ray of sunlight onto the headstone. It shone there, as if a spotlight, for me to see the small, linked heart shapes engraved on the top corner of the stone. Underneath was inscribed *John 20:29 "Blessed are those who have not seen and yet have believed."*

As I lifted my eyes to look at Greg, I couldn't help but notice the gloriously beautiful double rainbow in the sky. Instantly, I remembered Grandma Fae's explanation of rainbows. When something here on Earth made angels happy, they would shine, and when they did, all their magnificence would fall down to Earth in the beautiful colors of a rainbow. I was instantly sure James and Mary were those angels, together forever at last.

I knew the drive back home would be a long one, but I would welcome the time to think. No one would believe me of course. Greg Lewis probably wouldn't even believe it, and he himself had found the newspaper articles for James Colton. By then, Greg's eyes were practically pleading with me for an explanation. I smiled at him, and he smiled back.

"Say," he said, and hesitated, cocking his eyebrows, which broadened my smile, "would you perhaps like to have lunch with me?"

I nodded my head.

Yes, I thought, it would be a long drive home. I would need that time to find the words to explain to John why I couldn't accept his proposal, but first I would have lunch with the very charming Mr. Greg Lewis.

B-Pat and G-Pat, for the first time ever, were both in agreement.

On the long drive back to New York, my mind was awhirl with thoughts of James and Mary, and John, and of course, Greg Lewis.

How would I explain it all to John? I had accepted Greg's invitation to lunch, which had run into dinner. I had felt so comfortable with him right from the start.

It had taken me two days to drive back to New York, and on the way, I did a lot of thinking. I wasn't sure about much of anything, and yet I felt more assured of myself than I ever had before. I wasn't sure how or why it had all happened, but I had gotten the message—James's message. There was such a thing as true love, and it would last into eternity.

By the time I finally saw John, I was so excited about the manuscript that I'd almost forgotten I also had to break off our engagement.

He, of course, thought the whole thing to be just another story. He had no explanation for the second locket Greg had produced, nor the newspaper clippings, but he was sure there was a logical one. After pleading with him, he had finally agreed to publish the book—at least a short run—though it was against his better judgment as he was sure it just wouldn't sell. Then, after I told him I couldn't accept his marriage proposal, he childishly refused to publish it at all.

I had hung around Manhattan for a couple more weeks, clearing out my apartment and putting it on the market with a realtor. John said I was being ridiculous, but I just didn't want any part of it anymore. I escaped back to RUNY and tried to sort out what I really wanted. I tried other publishers, and though they were delighted with the opportunity to get me on board, they weren't thrilled with the manuscript and would prefer my usual genre. I tried to get back to writing, but I simply couldn't write that made-up romance drivel anymore.

It was about a month after I left Bay View when I got Greg's call. And the rest, as they say, is history. He was coming to New York for a business meeting, and two months later he had taken a position at an up-and-coming firm, we were looking for a nice place to live, close yet out of the city, and we were getting married.

CHAPTER 45

August 2017 (Twenty Years Later)

Cold Spring was a quiet little village on the bank of the Hudson. It was a friendly town where Greg and I built our house and raised our two boys, Greg Jr. and James. Greg Jr. was now in his second year at Columbia, and James his first year at Cornell. The town reminded us both of Bay View. The one thing Greg missed? The quiet little town where he grew up. As a first-month anniversary gift, I had gotten him a subscription to the *Bay View Compass*. It came every month without fail, though I don't think Greg has read it in years. He just sets it on the credenza in the foyer where it stays until I toss it into the recycle bin.

I pretty much gave up romance writing, but I really didn't miss it. I joined the PTA and the village council, wrote a small column for the local paper, did gardening, and planned summer vacations and everything else that went into the wonderfully remarkable last twenty years.

I thought about James and Mary often. Our son James resembled his great-great-grandfather, a very handsome young man. I hadn't really thought about the manuscript, though, in a very long time—until today, when I picked up the *Bay View Compass* that lay in its usual place on the credenza and, on my way to the recycle bin, happened to glance at the front page.

The picture of the old boardinghouse didn't do it justice. They were tearing the old place down. The city said it was unsafe and in too much disrepair to renovate or restore.

That night at dinner, I was trying to share the information with Greg, but James just couldn't be still. He was so excited about starting his first semester at Cornell.

"So are we all set for next weekend?" he was asking while almost inhaling his dinner.

"James," I scolded, "don't talk with your mouth full."

"Sorry, Mom," he said after swallowing.

Greg chimed into the conversation, wiping his mouth with his napkin. "Yes, James, we're all set for the weekend. I'll pick up the rental trailer near the end of the week. Believe me, your mother and I are just as anxious as you to get you moved into Cornell and out of the house."

"Greg!" I scolded, though I knew he was joking.

"Oh, by the way, Pops," James said, knowing that Greg hated being called Pops, "I downloaded a book today I need for one of my classes. I put it on your charge."

Greg nodded with raised eyebrows. I could tell he was mulling over a response, which he left unsaid. I quickly jumped in before he could change his mind. "What book, James?"

"I don't remember the name offhand. It's some philosopher, or no, a physicist who taught at Cornell back in the sixties wrote it. Anyway, he made some kind of record or something that they sent into outer space, like back in the day. I don't know . . . somethin' like that."

"Are you talking about the Golden Record on the Voyagers?"

"Yeah, yeah, I guess so. You know about that?"

"Well, yes, I do. I was a senior in high school the year those were launched. I'd forgotten all about them. I wonder if they're still up there."

"Yeah, I guess they are. The fortieth anniversary of the launching is like in a few days."

I thought about that for a moment. *Forty years! Wow!* "Has it been that long?" I tried to sound completely oblivious that it could have been forty years since I was in high school. It went right over James's head, but Greg smirked as he shook his head back and forth.

"So this guy," I beseeched my memory for his name, "Sagan . . . Carl. Carl Sagan, is he still alive?"

"No, I think the *Cornell Chronicle* said he was buried in a cemetery not far from campus."

"Oh, so this is an older book they have you reading?" My curiosity was piqued now, wondering what had happened between him and his wife, the story I'd thought so romantic 'back in the day,' as James would say.

"Yeah, it's a book he published in 1978, the year after the Voyagers were launched. I guess it's about those records. What did you call them? The Golden Record?"

Greg had already distanced himself from our conversation by checking something on his phone.

"What's the name of the book?" I asked.

"Um . . . voices . . . no, sounds . . . no, wait . . . murmurs. *Murmurs of Earth.*"

Greg looked up instantly. He and I locked eyes. We were frozen— frozen in time back to that day in that tiny office. In unison, we echoed, "Murmurs of Earth."

I finished the line that we both knew so well. "Are whispers in Heaven."

"Wait, what?" James asked, a strange look on his face.

"Nothing," I said as I wiped my mouth and laid my napkin on the table. "If you'll excuse me, I have some research to do." Greg was calling after me as I hurried off to the library. *What had I missed?* There must have been something more James wanted me to know. I mean, not that him being my great-grandfather and making me believe in true love wasn't enough, but I hadn't understood what he had told Greg—the message he wanted to get to me. Murmurs of Earth are whispers in Heaven. *What does that mean?* Why hadn't I tried harder to figure it out? What on earth did James have to do with Carl Sagan? *Or, maybe, that's not even it!*

I sat down at the computer and opened the browser. I wasn't sure what or who to look up first. Google came up, and I typed in 'murmurs of Earth.' Just as I had suspected, Carl Sagan popped up. 1934-1996. *Interesting*, I thought. He died only about eight months before James. *Could they have known each other?* I read a little more. Born and raised in New York, wrote several books, hosted *Cosmos*. Hmm, that was interesting he wrote the book *Contact*. I loved that movie. Just then, Greg came into the room and hovered over my shoulder.

"Find anything?"

"No, not really. Did you know he wrote *Contact*?

"You mean that movie with Jodie Foster? Wasn't he an atheist?"

"No, he said he didn't believe in God, but he didn't *not* believe either. I don't know . . . he said something like there wasn't enough proof either way."

"Hmm," Greg huffed, knowing I would then ask what he was thinking. We had become so patterned over the years.

"What are you thinking?"

"Well, I don't know, just seems like the movie *Contact* was like a battle between faith and science, and if I recall, the faith side was pretty well-represented in that move."

"Yes," I said and raised my eyes over the top of the readers I always wore when working on the computer, or pretty much to do anything these days. *Gosh, when did I get old?*

"Well, don't you think it's odd if the guy wasn't a believer that he'd write a whole book arguing about whether there was or wasn't a supreme being, and then in the end not prove it either way?" I looked at Greg a little sideways, thinking, *Exactly how was he going to prove it one way or another*? I didn't even have to speak the words—my expression explained what I was thinking.

"Well, you know what I mean," Greg said, instantly defending his statement.

I was skipping in and out of other books Sagan had written. "Hmm," I said as it was my turn to be predictable. In perfect form, Greg asked, "What are you thinking?"

"Well, it's just in this book," I pointed to the screen, "he uses a quote from the Bible. Job 30:29." I flipped to another tab I had opened. "And here, look at the cover of this book he wrote. I don't know if the book has anything to do with religion, but what does the picture remind you of?"

Greg looked at the screen. The book's cover was of a baby in a basket in front of an open door. I didn't know exactly why, but it reminded me of the story of baby Moses being put in a basket to float down the river.

"Moses," Greg replied.

"Here's another one." I clicked over to another tab. "'We wait for light but behold darkness.' Isaiah 59:9. He used this in another book. So," I pondered aloud, "if he really didn't believe in God, why does it appear that he was a bit obsessed with religion?"

"Come on, Pat," Greg chided. "Obsessed? You know, maybe this doesn't have anything to do with Sagan. I mean, maybe it's more about the phrase. You know, whispers in Heaven. Where does Google say Heaven is?"

Just to humor him, I queried up "Where is Heaven?" I picked one out of the page full of choices and read it aloud. "The Bible speaks of three Heavens. The first is the one we see when we look up and see in the sky where the big fluffy clouds float almost aimlessly on a lazy afternoon, where the birds soar and the planes go by. The second is beyond that. It's where the stars hang in the night-filled sky, where the moon and the sun reside. It encompasses the Milky Way and our galaxy, which is just one of billions of galaxies within our universe.

Our universe is contained within the second heaven. The third, which is beyond the second, is where God resides."

"There ya go!" Greg said.

"There I go what?"

"The Voyagers—they've been running through space for what, forty years now? Don't you remember a couple of years ago there was all that news that one of the Voyagers passed beyond our solar system?" I just stared at him. I had no recollection. "Yes, yes," he said, "and then a few months later, they were like, no, no, guess we were wrong. Don't you see?" He could tell by the look on my face I had no clue where he was going with this. He relaxed his shoulders, his signal that he'd calm down and start over. He spoke slowly, which usually irritated me, but I never said anything.

"If those things have been going for forty years now and haven't even left our solar system and Heaven, the third Heaven, the one where God is, out past our universe . . ." He was staring at me like I should be making some connection.

I lowered my chin, furrowed my brow, and turned my palms up—the 'I give up' stance. "What?" I asked.

"Murmurs of Earth are whispers in Heaven. After forty years, those things aren't even close! That's how far away Heaven is. Those things are only a whisper."

"Oh, that's stupid," I said, waving my hand at him.

He shrugged his shoulders. "What? You believe in Heaven."

"You know I do, but that doesn't make any sense."

"Okay, what do you got then?"

"Nothing," I sighed.

"I'll go start the dishes," he said, kissing me on the top of my head. He turned back toward me just before he left the room. "Maybe it was just something he thought you could relate to because you studied about it in school."

Maybe that was it, I thought, but it still didn't make much sense.

I looked through the open tabs, reading the screens over and over. After an hour or so, I closed them one by one. I had no answers. I let out a heavy sigh. Maybe, I thought, maybe Greg was right. Maybe it was like those psychics I'd seen on TV who said people communicated with them from beyond the grave. They all said that the 'passed' didn't actually talk to them but would *show* them something they could relate to in order to get their message across.

But what was James trying to tell me now?

I heard the phone ring as I shut the light off in the library, and I headed to the kitchen. Greg's face was almost ashen as he listened to whoever was on the other end. My mind went into panic mode. Greg Jr.? What was wrong? Greg was shaking his head but not saying anything. Finally, he uttered, "Okay, okay, yes, yes, I'll tell her. Okay, Martha. Yes, I'm glad she forgot too."

Martha was a good friend. She and her husband Jack were a few years older than Greg and I. We had met them years ago. They lived on the other side of town. Oh, no, I thought, had something happened to Jack? Greg hung up the phone.

"What? What happened?"

"There was a gunman at the mall tonight. A few people were killed and a number injured."

"Oh, my gosh! Was Jack there?"

"No, but you almost were. Martha said you were supposed to pick her up over an hour ago."

"I completely forgot! We were supposed to go dress shopping tonight."

"Yeah," Greg said and nodded. "That's what she said."

I sighed as Greg hugged me close. "Bashert," I whispered.

"Bashert," he repeated.

We had both used the word many times over the last twenty years when something was eerily unexplainable. I'm sure this instance was the eeriest. *Maybe that's it!* My mind started to wander. "Maybe, that's how *bashert* works," I said, pulling away from Greg. "Maybe it was murmured on Earth that a gunman was going to the mall, which was then a whisper in Heaven, and James intervened by preoccupying my mind so I would forget to go pick up Martha to go to the mall."

Greg looked at me, his eyebrows raised and a little smirk on his lips. It was a look that said, "You've got to be kidding me." He rubbed his hand over his face and spoke slowly. "Pat, that makes less sense than my Voyager theory. At least my idea had a connection between James and Sagan. Which, by the way," he was sounding a little condescending now, "the murmurs of Earth, part of James's saying, is the same as the book Carl Sagan wrote, and the whole reason the topic came up, which made you forget about going to the mall in the first place, makes a lot more sense."

I took a deep breath and hugged Greg close again. "You're right. There would have to be a connection between James Colton and Carl Sagan for it to make any sense at all."

"I guess only He knows," I sighed as I pointed a finger to Heaven.

That night, after Greg had gone to bed, I went back to the study. I just couldn't let it go. I guess it was the writer in me. I needed closure. I needed a conclusion. I hated those stories that left things up to your imagination. I sat down at the computer and clicked the mouse to open the browser, and I typed in *Carl Sagan* then hit videos, thinking there might be something interesting there. *A Cosmic Celebrity* popped up, one of those A&E biographies. I turned up the volume, started the video, and leaned back in my chair.

Three and a half minutes into the forty-five-minute video, a name jolted me to attention. I sat upright and grabbed the mouse, backed the video up a bit, then replayed. I was skeptical. Could it really be? ". . . Rachel and Samuel Sagan had found each other."

Could Carl's mother be James's Rachel? I rolled the thought around in my head for a bit. I watched a bit more of the video, hoping to find something else, some fact, something a bit more solid. Biographer Keay Davidson suggested that Carl Sagan's "inner war" (between religion and science) resulted from a close relationship with both his mother and father. Both instilled in him a drive to get ahead. His father, not a religious man, was a Russian immigrant, a factory manager in the garment industry. Sam gave Carl his sense of wonder. His questioning side came from his mother.

I looked more closely at the documentary itself. It originally aired on July 11, 1997. The dates weaved themselves through my mind. Greg would know the date better than me, but in short order, I convinced myself that this had to be the TV program James watched at the nursing home. *That's what got him so upset.* There was a picture of Rachel. That's what he meant when he said, "*She told me to make the right choice, but I didn't listen. I shouldn't have waited for the money.*" It was Rachel he was talking about.

I opened another tab and typed in Rachel Sagan. I still wasn't sure what it all meant, and perhaps I would never understand until I reached the place where they all were. I still needed something, though. Something a bit more concrete than just a name. I had to somehow prove that Sagan's mother was the girl James met at Coney Island. I had to prove it to Greg, and I needed to prove it to myself.

After just a bit of surfing, I found what I was looking for—a short excerpt about Rachel, Carl Sagan's mother. She was Jewish and believed in God. Rachel was a bold, feisty woman with a sense of fashion. She took chances. In her younger days, she was removed from the boardwalk at Coney Island for wearing an indecent bathing suit.

We live on a blue planet
that circles around a ball of fire
next to a moon that moves the sea,
and you don't believe in miracles?

— Anonymous

CPSIA information can be obtained
at www.ICGtesting.com
Printed in the USA
LVHW02s0504240118
563402LV00004B/26/P